OUTSIDERS

OUTSIDERS

22 All New Stories from the Edge

Edited by

Nancy Holder and Nancy Kilpatrick

A ROC BOOK

ROC
Published by New American Library, a division of
Penguin Group (USA) Inc., 375 Hudson Street,
New York, New York 10014, USA
Penguin Group (Canada), 90 Eglinton Avenue East, Suite 700, Toronto,
Ontario, Canada M4P 2Y3
(a division of Pearson Penguin Canada Inc.)
Penguin Books Ltd., 80 Strand, London WC2R 0RL, England
Penguin Ireland, 25 St. Stephen's Green, Dublin 2,
Ireland (a division of Penguin Books Ltd.)
Penguin Group (Australia), 250 Camberwell Road, Camberwell, Victoria 3124,
Australia (a division of Pearson Australia Group Pty. Ltd.)
Penguin Books India Pvt. Ltd., 11 Community Centre, Panchsheel Park,
New Delhi - 110 017, India
Penguin Group (NZ), cnr Airborne and Rosedale Roads, Albany,
Auckland 1310, New Zealand (a division of Pearson New Zealand Ltd.)
Penguin Books (South Africa) (Pty.) Ltd., 24 Sturdee Avenue,
Rosebank, Johannesburg 2196, South Africa

Penguin Books Ltd., Registered Offices:
80 Strand, London WC2R 0RL, England

First published by Roc, an imprint of New American Library,
a division of Penguin Group (USA) Inc.

First Printing, October 2005
10 9 8 7 6 5 4 3 2 1

 REGISTERED TRADEMARK—MARCA REGISTRADA

LIBRARY OF CONGRESS CATALOGING-IN-PUBLICATION DATA:

Outsiders : 22 all-new stories from the edge / edited by Nancy Holder and Nancy Kilpatrick.
p. cm.
ISBN 0-451-46044-8
1. Science fiction, American. 2. Alienation (Social psychology)—Fiction. 3. Social isolation—Fiction.
I. Holder, Nancy. II. Kilpatrick, Nancy. III. Title.

PS648.S30944 2005
813'.0876208—dc22   2005020479

Set in Fairfield Light
Designed by Ginger Legato

Printed in the United States of America

PUBLISHER'S NOTE

These are works of fiction. Names, characters, places, and incidents either are the product of the authors' imaginations or are used fictitiously, and any resemblance to actual persons, living or dead, business establishments, events, or locales is entirely coincidental.

The publisher does not have any control over and does not assume any responsibility for author or third-party Web sites or their content.

To Stephen Jones,
editor par excellence!

— ACKNOWLEDGMENTS

Nancy Holder and Nancy Kilpatrick owe a debt of gratitude to many people who were instrumental in helping with this project. They include literary agent Howard Morhaim and his assistant, Allison Keiley, of the Howard Morhaim Literary Agency; Dave Hinchberger of the Overlook Connection; Maryelizabeth Hart of Mysterious Galaxy Books; Douglas E. Winter; our succession of editors at Roc/NAL for their insights and their patience: Laura Ann Gilman, Jennifer Heddle, Liz Scheier; Jo Fletcher; and most especially, Mandy Slater and Stephen Jones. There were many others—friends and family—who performed kindnesses great and small, and we are grateful to all of you. We also want to acknowledge each other. Without the Other Nancy, this anthology would have been the poorer.

CONTENTS

Outlaw, goth, skinhead, fetishist, bag lady, pit boy, necrophile. Outsiders are misfits, alienated from the larger society, scarred human beings, wounded mentally or physically; spiritually twisted. On a good day, the edgy few are funky, innovative, outré, hip, avant-garde. On a bad day, they'd just as soon gouge out your heart.

Today's three hundred cable channels and gated communities do their best to keep society's misfits apart from the mainstream. But are the cast out so different from you and me? In the darkness of night, we also find ourselves squirming inside our skin, wondering who we are, how we got here, and why we feel so damned frightened so much of the time. We are terrified to listen to the voice of our nightmare thoughts, the dark side shrieking to be heard. And we listen at our peril—if we let the voices in, we might have to stop all the pretending and cop to the truth: We are spirits drowning in a *Truman Show–Pleasantville–*prefab bliss pot that is not cutting it as a lifestyle.

Still, through the drone of the elevator music, some of us manage to hear the voices.

Come with us and explore strange new worlds through stories that investigate the darkest of fantasies: a New Weird bathed in classic Gothic eeriness, and touched by metaphors of human darkness that reflect what Franz Kafka believed: "I think we ought to read only the kind of books that wound and stab us. . . . A book must be the axe for the frozen sea inside us."

Start chopping.

—Nancy Holder and Nancy Kilpatrick
November 2004
San Diego and Montréal

OUTSIDERS

Neil Gaiman first came to fame as the writer of the *Sandman* series of graphic novels; since then he's written such award-winning novels as *American Gods* and *Neverwhere*, and for children, such books as *Coraline*. He sometimes writes screenplays and picture books and poems. He's in his early forties and owns two black leather jackets, and occasionally he grows a beard.

THE EMPTY CHAMBERS

by Neil Gaiman

Do not fear the ghosts in this house; they are the
least of your worries.
Personally I find the noises they make reassuring,
The creaks and footsteps in the night,
Their little tricks of hiding things, or moving them, I find
Endearing, not upsetting. It makes the place feel
so much more like home.
Inhabited.
Apart from ghosts nothing lives here for long. No cats
No mice, no flies, no dreams, no bats. Two days ago
I saw a butterfly,
a monarch I believe, which danced from room to room
and perched on walls and waited near to me.
There are no flowers in this empty place,
and, scared the butterfly would starve, I forced a
window wide,
cupped my two hands around her fluttering self,
feeling her wings kiss my palms so gentle,
and put her out, and watched her fly away.

I've little patience with the seasons here, but
your arrival's eased this winter's chill.

Please, wander round. Explore it all you wish.
I've broken with tradition on some points. If there is
one locked room here, you'll never know. You'll not find
in the cellar's fireplace old bones or hair. You'll find no
blood.
Regard:
just tools, a washing machine, a drier, a water heater, and a
chain of keys.
Nothing that can alarm you. Nothing dark.

I may be grim, perhaps, but only just as grim
as any man who suffered such affairs. Misfortune,
carelessness or pain, what matters is the loss. You'll see
the heartbreak linger in my eyes, and dream
of making me forget what came before
you walked into the hallway of this house. Bringing
a little summer in your glance, and with your smile.

While you are here, of course, you will hear the ghosts,
always a room away,
and you may wake beside me in the night,
knowing that there's a space without a door
knowing that there's a place that's locked but isn't there.
Hearing them scuffle, echo, thump and pound.

If you are wise you'll run into the night, fluttering away
into the cold wearing perhaps the laciest of shifts. The
lane's hard flints will cut your feet all bloody as you
run, so, if I wish, I'll simply follow you,
tasting the blood and oceans of your tears. But I'll just
wait, here in my private place, and soon I'll put
a candle
in the window, love, to light your way back home.

The world flutters like insects. I think this is how I
shall remember you,
my head between the white swell of your breasts,
listening to the chambers of your heart.

Steve Rasnic Tem's latest books are *The Book of Days* (novel, Subterranean Press); *The Hydrocephalic Ward* (poetry collection, Dark Regions Press), and *The World Recalled* (chapbook, Wormhole Books). He is a past recipient of the World Fantasy, Bram Stoker, International Horror Guild, and British Fantasy awards.

THE COMPANY YOU KEEP

by Steve Rasnic Tem

Richard lived alone in an apartment above a decrepit carriage house off an alley in the oldest part of the city. He believed that once upon a time rich people had occupied the neighborhood—that's why there were so many large houses (now divided and redivided) and oversize utility buildings, like his carriage house. These had been people whose faces and reputations were known, even written about. People who might sneak out in disguise from time to time for a brief vacation in anonymity, that place where he—and most people he knew—lived all their lives.

Of course, the rich all picked up and drifted away at the first smell of shabbiness, not even waiting until that shabbiness made its actual appearance. Now he survived as best he could, the end recipient of a progression of hand-me-downs.

He'd been in the carriage house at least twenty years. When he attempted to recollect his move-in day more precisely, he became irretrievably lost in the lies and self-deceptions of memory. Surely, it couldn't have been that long ago. Surely, it had. Surrounded as it was by taller buildings with thicker walls, and a shadowing backdrop of huge trees preserved through some rich woman's personal campaign, it was quieter here than a room so close to the heart of the city's commerce had any right to be.

"People will judge you by your companions," Richard's father once said, responding to one of the countless confessions Richard had made concerning some trouble he and various friends had gotten themselves into. "You become known by the company you keep."

Good advice, he thought now. *Very perceptive.* But unbeknown to his father, somewhat off the point, as all of Richard's confessions had been lies. There had been no trouble. No legal entanglements due to bad influences, no youthful misadventures with peers less conscientious than he, despite dozens of such tales told and retold.

Richard would much rather have his father think he chose his companions poorly than know that Richard had no companions at all.

Not that he lied out of shame. He simply didn't want to have to explain himself to his father. Although he'd always desired friends, he wasn't sure what friendship might mean for him. He'd imagined the state of friendship as one in which your friend understood you, supporting your dreams, empathizing with your failures and imperfections. Someone always on your side. But he'd seldom seen such friendship in the relationships of others. And over the years his idea of a friend seemed increasingly improbable, a creature more at home among unicorns and banshees. Loneliness, on the other hand, was something he could always bank on, a predictable destination at the end of every workday when solitude became total, but more than that, an attitude he might carry with him into the office, out to restaurants, even into one of the increasingly rare social gatherings he might feel duty-bound to attend. He had come to carry that loneliness around with him much the way a monk carried bliss.

It would be difficult to say precisely when he discovered that his particular brand of solitude might not be as simple as all that. But certainly it solidified the day he met the pale man on the corner by the library.

Richard had been returning some long-overdue travel guides. He'd been in a hurry—he didn't like to linger in or near the library. Something about the enforced quiet, and all that wealth of information at your disposal if you knew the right questions to ask. But of course Richard *never* knew the right questions to ask.

Although there'd been no particular reason to isolate this one man among the many who gathered there that day, there had been something about the posture—something vaguely anticipatory about the man's stance—that filled Richard with a sudden, peculiarly overwhelming, and inexplicable empathy for this lone figure awash in the torrents of flesh, bone, leather, and cloth that flooded the sidewalks of this inhospitable concrete sprawl.

For a brief moment the man had turned to face him, and Richard had been struck immediately by the paleness of the face; then a look as of recognition vaguely distorted the sheet-white features, and the man turned away with a kind of desperate speed, stumbled, and almost fell.

Richard might have forgotten all about the incident, despite the strong impression of the man's seemingly bloodless complexion, when several other people in that vicinity made the same stumbling move.

Nothing remarkable or similar about these individuals in any way, both men and women, a variety of races, dress, and facial types—and yet for some reason they had stumbled almost identically.

But stranger still had been Richard's reaction. He felt as if he knew them, although surely he'd never seen them before. They were like him. They were meant for greater things they did not understand. They possessed capacities unrecognized, even to themselves. They had lived their lives as solitary warriors, and now at last their army had begun to form.

He had no idea why he should think such things. His life had not altered appreciably in years. He had seen no signs of change, had heard no call. No one approached him in the street, and at work he was still known by his last name and the relative coordinates of his cubicle walls.

When he was a boy he'd imagined himself imbued with superpowers. The drawback had always been that he didn't know what those powers might entail. But he had faith that they would reveal themselves at the appropriate time: A child would fall from a window and he would suddenly find himself flying up to catch her. Some disaster would occur—a factory explosion, a collapsed parking garage, a hospital on fire—requiring his unusual strength and courage. Everyone would be surprised by his transformation, but no one more so than he.

Richard was due for a two-o'clock appointment up on the sixth floor. He found himself at the elevator in the lobby at a quarter till. He'd developed this habit of referring to himself in the third person. *Found himself* was a deliberate choice of words—often lately he would catch himself that way, find himself in some location or situation with no clear memory of what came immediately before.

It was a small group gathered before the elevator, staring at the downward progress of numbers over the doors as if in suspense over the outcome. Normally he would fix his own eyes on that fascinating numeric display, but in recent weeks his habit had become to examine the members of any group he might find himself in, looking for some vague confirmation of questions he had no language for, seeking some signal or sign, some indication that he had at last landed in the right place and time.

There was nothing remarkable about any of these people: four men and three women dressed in gray, black, and brown business attire. The one Hispanic woman who'd attempted to add color with an orange scarf looked uncomfortable in it, as if the attempt might strangle her. One of the men was taller than the others by a few inches. He appeared to stoop further the longer they waited, as if attempting to reduce himself before anyone noticed.

They barely left room for the exiting passengers as they rushed into the opening doors, but those they jostled betrayed no discomfort at this, nor did Richard's group appear aware that they might have created some discomfort.

Once inside, they fit closely together. The elevator seemed to ascend slowly, as if hauling weight well beyond its posted limits. Richard watched as the man in front of him placed a hand on his right hip, sending a narrow elbow against the Hispanic woman, who in return leaned away and placed her own right hand on her own right hip.

The man beside her did the same. And the man beside him, all around to Richard, who, so embarrassed he found it difficult to breathe, did the same.

The man ahead of him put one foot forward and the others, including Richard, did the same.

A very slight shuffle to the right and a step back. Richard struggled to maintain his composure, did the step just the same, feeling as if he'd been kidnapped. By the time they reached the sixth floor, he felt barely capable of exiting. He turned quickly to see what might be in their faces, but they'd fallen back into their still, stuffed positions. He entered the offices of the insurance company sweaty and disheveled. And sorry to have left the elevator behind.

He was told he was ten minutes late and would have to wait an hour for the next appointment. The clock above the receptionist's desk pointed to two o'clock exactly, but he did not object. The reception area was full. He found a solitary chair against the wall, mostly hidden by a large potted plant. He had to remove a large pile of magazines from the seat in order to sit down. Not seeing anyplace to put these, he pulled them into his lap, hugging them and hunching over to keep them from falling.

A few feet away a fat man raised his right hand slowly and placed it on the front part of his head, immediately above the hairline, pressing down with obvious strain, as if trying to keep one particular train of thought from jumping track.

On the other side of the reception area, almost behind the desk, Richard saw another man—well-groomed, hair slicked back—do the same.

A younger man with his face buried in a financial magazine raised his hand slowly, palm up and wavering like a snake's head, then brought it over in a stretchlike motion, finally settling it somewhat surreptitiously onto the same region of his head.

Richard's vision filled with the nervous flapping of shadows like dozens of birds exhausted from their long journey. He closed his eyes, looking for his place of quiet solitude, and, unable to find it, opened them again. The men still held their heads in the same way, as if waiting.

Richard searched a last time for a place to put down the magazines, and, failing that, raised his hand high and slapped it over the same region of his head. The magazines crashed to the floor and spread in a wave over the shoes of the people sitting nearest him. Everyone in the room glanced his way except for the three men with hands on their heads, who now lowered their hands without a glance in his direction. He felt his face burning, got up, and left the office.

Out on the sidewalk and everyone appeared to be walking his way. As he pushed through them they raised arms and elbows, overlapping one against the other as if to prevent his flight. On the next street corner a small group stood off to themselves, wrists raised at exactly the same angle as they stared at watches that were missing, pale bands of skin left as evidence.

* * *

He felt only a whisper of guilt about stealing a car. Richard maneuvered the stolen car through streets full of chatting, focused people, people with important appointments to go to, places to see, definite things to do, conversations to have, parties to attend, shadows to scatter, loneliness to bury in a cascade of forced laughter. He at last felt the growing anxiety of someone with a destination. And he would not permit a crowd of other people, *those* people, the people whose full lives had always put the lie to the so-called life he had cobbled together on his own, to delay him in any way, make him late for the meeting he had waited for all his life.

It saddened him that the truth of it had never been clear to him before, that people like him, people who had endured a solitary desperation all their lives, required no words for their secret communications, that their private handshakes demanded no actual exchange of touch, that their meeting places were spontaneous and secret even unto themselves, that, like the early Christian churches in a world of persecution, they met wherever and whenever more than one of them came together in one place.

Richard looked out the driver's-side window into another car that had pulled alongside. He wagged his head to the left, veered the stolen car to the left, and that other driver did the same. And another car beside that one, as a result driving up onto the sidewalk, plowing over the crowds there, striking the front wall of a department store, exploding into flame.

Richard grimly focused again on the road to his destination, hoping that none of the people he had recently recognized were out on the sidewalk just then, and sparing a good thought for the brave and devoted driver who had no doubt lost his life in service to the cause.

But of course we are legion, he thought. *When one of us dies there is always another to take his or her place. We always thought we were alone, and our gratitude at discovering our belonging knows no bounds.*

The building ahead of him looked little different from the rest, which was appropriate. No crowds pushed inside as if this were some concert hall or sporting event, and that, too, was appropriate. Because no matter how many of them there might be they would never be a crowd, not in the way these successful and fulfilled unenlightened ones made a crowd.

Richard was pleased to see that no one lingered around the entrance to the building. No one paid it any particular attention, and that was as expected, and wonderfully, joyfully, appropriate.

He stopped the car a few feet from the entrance and abandoned it there. Going in he glanced at the sky, the way the roofline pierced it so nicely, demanding respect.

A few gathered before the elevators, joining him as he made his way through the doors, repeating his gesture of rubbing at his left eye (*let it not offend*), scratching at his neckline (*let it bare itself before thee*), pulling at his trousers (*my legs belong to you*).

They were on the rooftop, waiting, although they did not appear to be waiting. They did not appear even to be aware that others were up on this rooftop with them. They stared at the sky. They stared at the streets below and at the horizon of stone and steel containers stretching in all directions. His company. His associates. They did not look at each other.

But they were here together. Richard understood that the way of silence, the way of solitude, was their way. There was no plan or determination. None was needed.

Well after it began, Richard realized there were fewer of them. Then fewer still. Then he saw a few slip over the edges, like birds sucked one by one into a rising tide of wind.

He was proud that when his own urge arrived he did not hesitate, but floated across the border between gravity and release without a second thought.

They descended like huge, mad fowl, their mouths open in anger or weeping. There were a few hundred or more, and it was said that the way they twisted as they fell to their deaths, the way they swept their arms and legs out viciously in their final few feet of air, they seemed to be trying to kill as many in the crowds below them as they could.

Léa Silhol, nicknamed "the weaver" by her readers, is, at thirty-seven, one of the leading voices in French fantasy. With fifteen edited anthologies and more than sixty short stories and three short-story collections published, she seems to possess—or so believe her publishers—a machine that creates time. Her first novel *Of Sap & Frost* was published in 2002 and won the Merlin Award 2003 for best fantasy novel of the year. "Under the Needle" is her first story selected for an English publication.

UNDER THE NEEDLE

by Léa Silhol

(translation by Estelle Valls de Gomis)

There are shadows in the street that were not there yesterday, or to which my eyes were blind. I see them now, tearing themselves away from the walls to walk behind me. The crumpled piece of paper in my right hand tells me where I am going. My heart knows what for. My clenched teeth do the rest, like a decision too ancient to be averted. More stubborn than hate, or love. Or nothing. Me.

Descending under the road, on the left, there is a vault, a gaping mouth into which I sink, pulling back some strands of my hair which pretend to be guardian angels, clinging to my face. There, a window, a door framed in steel, without a name, smooth. It is here.

As I enter the shop, at the tunnel's end, Jazz stares at me from the sofa where he is lying. I have heard of him, and he does not know my name. Only the name I gave him on the phone. An assumed name, a cliché. Nemesis. He must have been offered this name some three thousand times, or almost. He remains stretched out there, with head thrown backward. I do not know what he has been taking and I do not care. I have been assured that his hands never shake.

"I am Nemesis."

He slides off the couch like a waterway. Tall, lithe, his hair the colour of smoke, his eyes indefinable. He wears a black cotton T-shirt and leather trousers. He has exactly five rings on his left ear, and his fingers are barer than steel. He smiles. If wild animals could smile, this is how it would look. His eyes amused and fierce, his teeth sharp. He is beautiful. A shrine statue, a primitive dancer, a shaman. If death were to have a face, I have always known it would be as beautiful as that of an angel, or of the devil. I look hard at him without blinking, until my eyes burn.

"Do you have what is needed, Nemesis?"

I nod and I hand him a picture of you, and two or three strands of hair taken from the brush. Snakeskin, molting, pieces of the day before yesterday. He takes these fragments of you, narrowing his eyes, his nostrils throbbing. The backs of his hands are marked with brandings of utter thinness. He does not ask if I am sure. All the better. I am, but in an obscure way I do not think I would be able to put up with being asked the question.

He precedes me into the back room, where the leather couchette glows under a blinding lamp. All around us, the rest is hemmed in by shadows. With the tips of his fingers, he grabs a silver dish, and puts the hair into it. I have told him your name already.

"Where?"

"On the back. Seems appropriate."

He nods and points to the couchette with a shake of his chin.

"You settle down there, little sister."

I drop my bag onto the floor. My blouse comes over and off my head, giving out its silky cry in the hollow of my ear. I slip onto the smooth and crackled surface, facedown. I smell the fragrance of leather beneath my face. And further, where some rites are undoubtedly coming together, the smell of burning. Organic matter, incense. Glazed paper, just like your heart.

Jazz sits down by my side and inspects my skin with his nimble fingers.

"Mmmm. You know what must be done."

I bend my arm and present my left hand. He takes it in his own and I see his palms are branded too; branded with fire, but lacking those lines that make a man's life. He sees my stare and smiles slightly, his eyes narrowed. His skin is smooth, dry, burning; he is not wearing gloves. He bends my wrist, quiet as a priest. The blade of the razor slides on my skin. The cut shines, distant and deep. He puts the dish on the ground and my blood drops onto the ashes it contains. My arm is left dangling. I turn my head to look at him while he takes his instruments.

"Relax."

A slight laugh slips out. Relax? I am more tensed than a piano string and nothing will change that, save completing what I have come to do. I hear the white noise of the spray gun starting. The needle bites me deep and I clench my teeth. Over me, over you, over my seeping blood, and over the decaying of the world.

I feel it, yes, the first blow, I *hear* you receiving it. Where are you right now? In a bar? In your office above the city, consulting files by the dozen? What are you thinking of? The pain drills through your temple and you search for it with your fingers, as if you could drive it in, dissolve it, soothe it. Three slaps on the head, a stroke, as if to a good dog. No way, my love.

I smile while the needle traces its line of fire on me, lulled by the voice of Jazz humming, and the haunting buzz of the conniving machine. In the great bowl, my blood flows out drop by drop, stroke by stoke. There, in the distance, pain takes you in her vise. You have undone the first buttons of your shirt and opened the window (your office, then). The burning is on me, but the fire rages in you. Fever, slowly, like the rising of a wave.

"Jazz?"

"Hmm?"

"How long will it take?"

I feel his smile as if I could see it.

"How long do you wish it to take, little sister? I can do it quick, or I can make her last all day long. It depends on how long you want to punish her. And of the blood you are intent on pouring."

"Blood I have. And time, she owes me. Go slowly."

He nods, and one long strand of his hair brushes my spine.

"It is as you like, Lady Nemesis. Just as you like."

I close my eyes, feeling the pressure of the needle getting lighter, its course slowing down to casualness. I close my eyes, and I see you. I see you as you were, standing up, looking detached, when you told me that it was over. That life between us had become too difficult, that my rhythm did not suit you. You told me all this, yes, but like that, from a distance, already gone. You did not tell me you had met someone else. Not that. No easy solace. In your eyes, at that point, it is not even any of my business. Hollow pretexts, ready to use, lures. Lures and lies, as always. You told me then, coldly shifting to the practical aspect of things, what you intended me to take. Almost nothing, since you paid for everything. And you keep the apartment. It is hard to find, a loft in this area. You packed me up like a crate, and gave me "three days to get back on your feet" while you were going to a seminar in Deauville with your staff. I unhooked my velvet corsets and looked at the Zoot suits in the wardrobe. I saw the distance between us. Side by side, but oceans apart. I left the keys with the caretaker.

It has been a month. And you know nothing of that month. Of the silence, the burning eyes, of the wide-open gape right where you used to stand. You know nothing of it. And you do not care. I have willed to kill you, you know. Buy a gun and shoot you in the head. But I have no gun, and it is too fast. I went to Kashka's. One of those too-dark buddies you wanted me to stop seeing, those "stupid little gothies." Those eternal losers lost in their childish games, as you put it. I cried, perhaps, slept on her sofa. Kashka talked me out of buying a gun. She told me about Jazz. About his hands that never shake.

There, I feel you starting to grow weaker. Your breathing becomes sibilant, oppressed. The girl from the next office told you as she went by that you were pale, that you should go home, maybe even go to a doctor. You smiled and said it would be all right. Brave little soldier! You really are too dumb. Your damned arrogance will kill you. Yes.

I laugh and Jazz laughs with me, as if we are sharing some cruel private joke. Like wolves, like birds, like driftwood. Jazz, and I, and the needle plowing me. More painful, more burning than usual. Acid and sorrow mixed. I feel the oppression on your heart, its mad rhythm, and the growing endless suffering. Oh, yes, Jazz knows how to make it go slowly. . . .

"Beware, she is going to resist, now. Are you ready?"

"Yes." (*Oh, yes . . .*)

"Then here we go."

You are drifting toward the door clinging to the furniture, and my hands are on you. Evanescent, eager; sharp claws, fingers of steel. On your hips, on your shoulders, on the precious fabric of your executive woman's suit. You pant and proceed against the current. You burn. Irrepressible laughter swells in me. You have always had the power, always. But no longer. Your hand slips over the chrome-plated handle and you slide down to the ground, breathing hoarsely. I am listening to you dying on the tiled floor. For hours, but not enough.

"Now!" The tips of my fingers of smoke glide into your throat, here, between tongue and palate. I pay no attention to the colleagues surrounding you, touching you, taking you away. No one sees me, not even you. Too bad. You are shaking, trying to get back your breath, your eyes rolled upward. A blond strand of hair has slipped down your cheek. I am going deeper, closing my fingers on this white nucleus, incandescent, which is trying to glide out of my reach, to find refuge in the back of your smooth skull. The core of you, and all that makes you what you are. Your salvation, perhaps . . . Perspiration runs in my eyes under the effort and I feel, from very far, a rough piece of rag wiping my back. The hand of Jazz and the smoke curtain of his hair are crossing my sight as he bends to pick up the dish and replace it with a new one. I hear him drone out a few chanted words, like a song, before the hypnotic noise of the spray gun starts again.

"It is almost done," he says in a voice both tensed and languid. "Bring her back."

"Yes."

I close my fingers on you and the nails bite. You scream. Pain and despair, flat electrocardiogram.

The heat of a blaze explodes inside my skull, irradiating the whole of my skin. And the spray gun stops. I almost feel, in slow motion, the needle rooting itself out of my flesh. And where it has been, the burning, and more. The flapping of a butterfly's wings, an inarticulate cry. I am standing upright on the couchette, torn wrist squeezed in my fingers. I stare at Jazz, standing up before me, grave and beautiful like a killer. He hands me some cotton wool and an adhesive plaster.

"Did it work?" I ask.

"It always works with girls like you. But you know that very well. Do you not feel her inside you?"

I smile faintly while patching up my wrist. My head spins.

"Her life . . ."

He shakes his hair back. His stare is serious. "More than that. Is it not what you asked of me, Nemesis?"

I shiver, but it is not unpleasant.

"You did not tell me what your price would be."

He smiles and slips a firm hand on the back of my neck. He

draws my face to his. His kiss tastes of blood, but I do not know whether it is yours or mine. I yield to it as if it is the last kiss I am ever to receive, and I do not care at all about the rest.

"I have been paid already," he says, smiling. "Maybe you want to see it?"

He vaguely points at the great mirror standing upright in a corner. And goes back to the table where his instruments are laid. I move toward the mirror and turn around on my heels to have a look at my shoulder blade. Your face shines there, black on the red of my opened skin, encircled by runes, cabalistic signs, and long thorns. Unrecognizable, and impossible to mistake for another.

I put my shirt back on and retrieve my bag, feeling dizzy, as if drunk.

"You know the rule," Jazz tells me.

"Only once we find the way."

He nods and smiles. "It has been a pleasure, Lady Nemesis."

When I get out of the shop under the tunnel, night has fallen over the city. The shadows glide across the tarmac to avoid me, and I hear, far in the distance, an endless cry. Like an echo, or the insistent call of a tattooist's spray gun. But we are together anew, my love, and for a long time. And I do fear, this time, your heart was not enough for me. I glide over the pavement, a smile at the corners of my eyes, and the song of Jazz on my lips.

Tanith Lee was born in 1947, in England. Unable to read until she was almost eight, she began to write at the age of nine. She worked as a library assistant, waitress, clerk and shop assistant, and spent a year at art college before becoming a full-time writer in 1976. She has published almost seventy novels, nine short-story collections, and well over two hundred short stories. Lee has also written for BBC Radio and TV. Her work has won numerous awards, and has been translated into over sixteen languages.

SCARABESQUE:
THE GIRL WHO BROKE DRACULA
(A chapter from the as-yet-uncompleted fourth novel of
The Scarabae Blood Opera)

by Tanith Lee

Friday is the Day of Freya (the Nordic Venus): the Day of Love.

The girl in the night:

It was summer, the sun just gone, the sky Lycra blue. So far not a streetlamp lit, not a star. But the girl carried midnight with her. It made up her long hair, her long dress, the long boots she wore. It filled and surrounded her eyes, and sprinkled from her ears in tiny shiny drops. At one shoulder only was a silken scarlet slash, left by some descending sun much older than the orb recently fallen behind the high street. That ancient sunset had also splashed her lips and nails. And a bone-white moonlight her skin.

She moved in her own darkness, personal to her as all fantasy, yet externalized into armour and a mask.

Some of the late shoppers up by Sainsbury's certainly stared at her, in disapproval and contempt, envy . . . lust. Not only at and of her body, but of her insulting ability to be *alive*. She was slender and young. She looked beautiful, and strange.

"Fucking goth," said someone.

She heard the voice, the girl, but she was in her armour, sealed in safe as any knight—or night.

She walked through the tree-hung alley to the station, and met only a cat, also coal-black and white of face. They exchanged a momentary greeting, and like sentries on some castle wall, passed on.

No one was in the booking hall, the ticket office shut. But the night-girl had her ticket.

She stood on the platform and waited for the train.

Already she could smell, over the treey scent of the suburbs, the hot-cinder pheromones of London.

Her name was Ruby Sin.

Behind her, in a one-room flat of the dilapidated house across Woolworth's car park, she had left lying the body of her schizophrenic other half. This was a girl of the day and the working week, with short, mouse-brown hair and nervous pale eyes. *She* was called Sue Wyatt.

Ruby Sin had to kill Sue Wyatt every Friday evening. First in a bath with salts of cedar, frankincense and myrrh. Then with black clothing and red and black costume jewels, and a long black wig. Next smothering her in black and white and red makeup and nail polish. All through the murder, poor Sue Wyatt stared in horror and fear—but at the end her eyes were shut behind jet-black contacts. Dead, dead, left behind on the floor like a shed toenail clipping.

A man on the train reminded Ruby Sin of Sue Wyatt's father. She had seen him before once or twice, traveling up to town behind his newspaper. He wore an expensive middle-aged suit and strongly smelled of cologne and aftershave. But of course, it could never have been Sue's father—*he* would, at this hour or earlier, have been traveling the other way, out to Guildford.

Nevertheless, she never liked to see him there.

He got out at Waterloo, as always.

It was dark by now, after ten, and London opened like the well-lit basement area of a huge department store, whose upper floors were coloured neons and an unreal, darkly milky sky.

Ruby Sin walked obliquely westward, toward the pub known as the Vixen, on Carder Street.

Here in the metropolis, very few turned to gaze at her—a herd of hoodies once, and later a guy who sailed by on a skateboard, and flicked her sleeve in apparent approval of her looks.

The pub was packed, standing room only by now. Music throbbed and tangled, while yellow light slid over the pub's skeletons in metal, and posters strafed with painted blood.

Big young men, bare-shouldered in black leather, allowed Ruby Sin to squeeze her way up to the bar. She gestured for her drink, the usual sour red wine, in sign language. Then she pressed her way into a corner. She slotted herself between the heat-palpitating tables and the shouting patrons. She lifted her head into the smoke and music. The band being played was Lash. She knew the words, so she did not need to hear them.

The first sips of wine, the percussion's thud, these enabled Ruby Sin to continue inward and upward on her journey of self-release.

She appeared cool and static, but her brain was growing by the moment lighter. It was beginning to fill with the dream that every night pathetic Sue Wyatt also indulged, lying on the flat mattress opposite Woolworth's.

This was, nearly, a Cinderella dream, of going out into the night disguised as Ruby Sin. In excited terror, almost nauseous with it, heart pounding and missing beats, Sue Wyatt then saw behind her closed eyes and all over the inside of her body a dark male Being who walked between the crowds, as a full-fed black leopard sometimes walks between the restless passivity of feeding deer.

But to Sue Wyatt in the dream, "Who are you?" said the leopard, and she must answer. So she, (who anyway, in these fantasies under the sheet, was already re-possessed by Ruby Sin and so dead again) appropriately said, "Ruby Sin." "And I," he said, "am Darkness."

There was never sex in these fantasies. There was only a fearful prolonged hiatus, and dialogue like a slow, fencing duel, during which she was always about to fall and he about to catch and seize her. She knew he would then obliterate her. But it would be an orgasm of the spirit, not the genitals.

Besides, it can never happen. Never does.

Finally every night she (or Sue) collapsed asleep from exhaustion. And sometimes then really she dreamed of him, though still she never saw his face.

Standing in the Vixen on Friday, waiting, also like Cinderella—but in reverse—for midnight, Ruby Sin burned slowly up like a black candle. For she believed, if only on Fridays, that one night he *would* come out of the lacy, metallic, leathery, rubber crowd, out of the reds and blacks and silvers, the knives and spikes of steel and hair.

One night. In the end.

She was only twenty-four, after all. She had been waiting ten years. Which of course had lasted forever. But any Friday, the first forever might finish. And then the next wonderful Forever would begin.

"Hi, babe," said a young man. His jet-black mane was streaked with blue. She had never seen him before, or she had and he had been different. But she had seen others who might have been his clones. "Want to get us both a drink?" he asked her, crisping the note temptingly before her eyes.

Sue Wyatt, who had to serve customers by daylight, when her vampire other-self slept in a shadow-coffin of the psyche, would have been polite. Oh, no, thanks, Sue Wyatt would apologetically have replied.

But Ruby Sin coldly turned her head away.

"Fuck yourself then," said the blue-streaked goth. He spoke mildly. More a formality. Fifty years ago he would have said substantially the same: *Please* yourself then, he would have said.

Ruby Sin however did please only, did fuck only, herself.

She sipped her second wine, which had to last. Soon it would be midnight, and the club would open.

As always, it had occurred to her that the night-stalking leopard might be there, not here.

Ten years of waiting. Since she was fourteen.

Her family, the Wyatt family, had lived—perhaps still did—in a nice cul-de-sac near the river. Lots of greenery, trees and lawns, a semi with white walls and pseudo Tudor accoutrements.

Oliver Wyatt worked in the city, at one of those mysterious male jobs that were quite lucrative. And Sue's mother, Jane, was the manageress of a small smart dress shop. The income was good. They wanted for nothing—three bathrooms, a well-stocked fridge and freezer, closets of clothes, cabinets of videos and even a few shelves of books. There were also two cars, his a silver Merc, and Jane's a blue Vauxhall Nova: her "little runaround." There were holidays in Italy or the Lake District.

Sue went to a good school as well. She was supposedly quite "bright," if only she would "concentrate."

An only child, Sue wandered through her childhood fairly happily, admiring her parents, accepting them as the alpha male and female. Because she was amiable, impressed and reasonably obedient, they were adequately satisfied with her, though a little disappointed by her lack of looks.

Once she was past eleven, Sue saw less darkly through the optic glass.

The view of both her parents and herself altered. She knew she was plain, skinny, unpromising, and that her mother was a bit over-made-up and a bit shrill, her father stuffy and quite prim.

It was the day after her fourteenth birthday that Sue looked into her mirror. Something in the amber setting of sunlight caught her face. It showed—not exactly beauty—but a *possibility*. She stood marveling, until the light moved on and left her there, marooned and ugly again.

Two weeks later she found out about *Dracula*.

Somehow, like much else, he and his kind had passed her by. She had if anything been scared of the idea of vampires—afraid of an enduring image, fostered in her by a male cousin when she was six, of the insectile undead crawling up the brickwork of the wall toward her, in the hardly tomb-black luminescence of the Guildford night.

Now everything had changed. Insidiously at first. Next by advancing wild leaps. She had begun to menstruate the year before. Perhaps it was hormones, mostly. She never thought of this, and never would, because the clever little informative books Jane had given her child to read seemed to have nothing whatever to do with the physical, let alone the mental, life of Sue Wyatt.

At midnight the club across from Carder Street opened its doors.

The club's name, written in purplish-blue light, was The Family Axe.

Two girls, about twenty, were in front of Ruby Sin in the queue that waited to get in. One was all in shimmering white, with a necklace of glass blood drops. The other wore black male clothing from the Victorian era, sequined, and with a boned external corset. Sometimes they glanced back at Ruby Sin with their long eyes.

The darker one said to her at last, as the line trod forward again, "I've seen you here before."

Ruby Sin said nothing.

The girl in white commented, "She don't talk."

"Don't you?" asked the girl dressed like a combination Liberace-Byron–Frank N. Furter.

Ruby Sin barely heard them. Her own black eyes had skimmed the slowly moving crowd. Although *He* was nowhere in view, as once or twice before she *sensed* Him. He was here, somewhere here, in the essence of the loud daylit night, the polluted overcast of swarthy milk. This did not mean, of course, that she would *see* Him.

The black- and white-clothed girls leaned their heads together and murmured.

Up by the doors, the bouncers, Chick and Zara, were checking customers before admitting them. To enter here you must be properly attired in one of the many goth fashions, reasonably sober, and not in any way off your skull.

Even at this instant, Chick was shaking his cropped head at two guys in yuppie gear, plainly high on some powder. Chick was built like a human ox, his arms trying to burst the sleeves of his parachute-silk-effect jacket, his thighs straining the seams of his black jeans. But the yuppies were just too far gone to give up; one even playfully wagged a finger at Chick. "What yer gonna do, pussy-pie?"

Chick moved, but before he could take hold of them, Zara had both guys by the arms. She swiftly manhandled them out of the line and down the street, turning them as she did so to face away from the club. She must have said something too. One of the yuppies stared at her, greenishly. Then they both scuttled off.

Zara came back flipping the tail of her severely tied-back hair. She was half South American, thin as whipcord and about as strong.

Ruby Sin had no trouble in gaining admittance. Nor did the two girls in front of her.

Inside the dark-bright foyer, another female bouncer, blonde Chloe, felt the girls over, investigated any pockets and purses. From Ruby Sin's little beaded bag came a stick of mascara; two crayons, for lips and eyes; a Kleenex; some money; and a door key to the flat by the car park.

The second male bouncer, Barry, had found some pills on the tall goth male with blue-streamered hair. "They're fuckin' Nurofen!"

"Expecting a bad headache, are you?"

Beyond the foyer the music was beginning in fractaled shards of sound: the Damned. A huge dark space rose and rose, splintered with light that pinpointed or swirled or blinked.

Ruby Sin moved into the space, and the sound and the light undid the lid of her brain, so her spirit could fly right up, and look about, clear-sighted as a hawk, from the tower-top of her body. The beating heart of the song remade her flesh. She was all part of it now, the night. Safely locked in, yet her soul flying free, connected to her only by a hair-fine silver chain.

Even as Ruby Sin stood at the ground-floor bar, pulsing in the music pulse, under the hanging festoons of swords, axes, scimitars, ordering one double vodka with Cherry-Red, her soul was fluttering up to the gallery that overhung the dance floor.

Her soul perched there on the rail, and that was when Ruby Sin, at the bar, felt *something*—*someone*—touch her . . .

The most intimate of touches.

Not to breast or groin, but stroking over the fiber of her psychic life.

Her head jerked up, the crimsoned glass in her grip.

And before she could turn to see, the girl in black from the queue set her hand (physical, only that) lightly on Ruby Sin's shoulder.

"Hey, don't be startled. Or do you like to be startled, little no-talk bunny, eh?"

Chloe looked down her blunt nose at the dance area beyond the inner doors.

"That guy," she said, "is up on the gallery."

"What guy?" Barry was still busy disposing of the "Nurofen" abstracted from the blue-haired goth. "Don't he know," mused Barry, "that he can get all this in *there*—and *only* in there?"

"E, you mean? Is that what they are?"

"I don't even *know* what these tabs are—Christ, maybe they *are* painkillers. . . ."

"He's just up there," said Chloe.

"What are you on about?"

"The guy what came in earlier—the one who came in before we opened. Hank let him in before he went off—said this guy knows Frank Collins."

Barry patted his pocket, where the initials of the security firm were emblazoned. FRC, for Frank Roland Collins. "Well, if Collins said okay, it's okay."

"Don't like him," said Chloe. "Don't like the guy. Something. Trouble."

Barry too squinted through the doors. In the fractured lights he took a moment to locate the man Chloe was bothered about.

Tall, all in black, as most of them were. Long black hair, a flood of it, like a woman's . . . pale face leaded in by probably mascared black eyes and eyebrows.

Chloe, squat as a tank with muscles, still maintained an active imagination, apparently. But even so, Barry went out of the front doors to check with Zara and Chick. Just in case.

Sue read the book first. She found it dense and almost difficult, to begin with. Then the vampiric sequences of Stoker's rogue masterpiece of transmogrified sex, began to quicken her. Why had she *wanted* to read it in the first place? Someone must have said something. Ten years after, recalling everything else, neither Sue nor Ruby Sin could remember.

Almost a month later she realized—or heard—about the film. Not the earlier versions of *Dracula*, but something more contemporary.

"Dad, there's this video I want to see."

Oliver Wyatt had peered at her with impatient indulgence over some report he was studying. "What did you say?"

"There's a movie—a film I'd like to watch, Dad."

"Well, tell your mother."

"I did. She won't let me."

"Why not?" Absently now.

"She said it's too old for me. But it isn't. I've read the book."

"A schoolbook, is it?"

Sue had not, then, learned properly to lie to her parents. Had never thought she had to.

"No."

"What's it called?"

Sue told him.

His look. A look initially of surprise, then scornful amusement. And then of somber disapproval.

"No, Sue. That's not one for you."

She had tried to argue.

Oliver lost his temper, threw down his papers and got up, looming there in his study like a big tanned pig in a suit. "You will not argue with me. I've told you, it's inappropriate. Besides being utter rubbish. I suggest you go and get on with your homework, Sue. *That's* where you need to concentrate your energies, believe me, or you're going to amount to nothing. Is that what you want?"

Cowed, distressed—for even by then, she still bowed to

parental authority perforce, and to the unknown ambiguous future, during which she must become "adult" and "responsible"—Sue Wyatt lowered her head and slunk away.

In her room, with its Jane-chosen floral prints and curtains, and frilled-over bed, among the ancient toys that could no longer help her, she got out her maths homework. The questions might have been written in French—another subject she never managed, either, to grasp. She cried. Then she went and looked in her mirror.

She saw a young, ugly girl, with tear-reddened eyes.

She was (feebly?) angry with herself, and with all the rest of them.

That night she woke up at some vague hour of morning with one of the sharp cramps her periods caused when starting. Fumbling to the bathroom, and then for aspirin in the bedside drawer, Sue rehearsed other means to acquire a forbidden film.

"I told you. This one don't talk."

"Course she will. With me. Won't you, bunny?"

Ruby Sin looked at the girl in white, the girl in masculine black.

Through her transcendental Friday-night equilibrium, a worm of panic began to ooze. (The unknown touch on her soul—muddled now, fading away . . .)

What did they want, these girls?

At school . . . Sue had been bullied. Oh, rarely a physical assault—or, if one occurred, no more than a pinch, a slap, someone spitting into her eye: That's for *this*. . . . This is for *that*. . . . They could frighten her so easily with threats and name-calling, insults and subtle promises, blows were largely redundant.

She had always been bullied. At the infants' school, eight years old, Sue, crying with horror at the thought of more terror in the morning, had reduced Jane to running her to school in the bright blue car. Then marching into the head's office—Jane marched, Sue, like a convict, marched.

"This can't go on, Mr. Mayberry."

"But it's nothing, Mrs. Wyatt. She has to toughen up a bit. Has the child any marks on her? No? Well, then."

And presently thereafter, in the so-called *play*ground: "You went to see Fartberries, didn't you?" Slap, pinch, etc.

Sue had only, briefly, ever had one friend, a colorless studious bore called Clare, that nobody ever bothered to bully because she was too limp.

This now, however *this*, under the fractal lights and the beat of drums, of all things reminded Ruby Sin of Sue Wyatt's child-hood coercion. She realized the two girls had cornered her, in just that same way, and were now driving her back along a wall, people obligingly making room for them to pass.

Ruby Sin turned abruptly, and walked off across the dance floor.

The white and black girls, one frowning, one smiling, went after her.

"Look, she don't dance neither."

"Yes, she will."

Black Sequins seized Ruby Sin's wrist and forced her arm awkwardly upward in a dancer's movement.

"You need to loosen up."

Arm dropped again, Ruby Sin watched her tormentors as they circled round her like two young wolves.

She was suddenly truly afraid. As if, despite everything, she were Sue standing here.

Real life, always less lovely, less wanted, more terrible than fantasy, had hunted for and found her. Unforgivably *here*.

Why should she have thought herself exempt? It had hap-pened before. Happened most definitely on that night ten years ago—that first Dracula night.

Now they were leading her, despite her resistance, off the

dance floor, between the bolts of synthetic lighting, the writhing and swaying figures, the blade-edged shadows of things that did not look possible, and were not.

Ruby Sin gripped her glass. They were in an alcove, just off the floor, out of the lights.

Sequins was leaning forward, kissing Ruby Sin's neck, while the girl in white held Ruby Sin's arms, casually, ready to be firm.

"Want to be a donor tonight, little vampire bunny?"

Even in the half dark, Ruby Sin saw the glint of metal and glass. It was a syringe ejecting from a plastic wrap.

"In my bootstrap—clever, yes? But see, still quite clean."

Too fast for the girl in white, who had thought the victim quiescent, even complacent, Ruby Sin's right hand sprang forward. Vodka and Cherry-Red splashed into Sequins' face and eyes. The syringe fell. Someone trod on it with a splintering crunch. The girl in white screamed, like an actress in a horror movie of the 1960s. Perhaps she was practiced.

The scream was violent enough that it reached the nearest dancers seen over the music and the beat. Heads turned, eager or disdainful.

Ruby Sin and the girl in white struggled, and Ruby Sin's enamel nails opened three long clawings across the screamer's cheek, so now she *shrieked*.

Up on his rostrum the deejay swayed, lethargic, noting nothing, lost in ear-protected sound. But the bar staff had glimpsed the fracas, and a button was pressed.

Out in the foyer a fiery light erupted like freshest blood.

"Here we go," said Barry, and shouldered through the doors.

There had been a large ceramic bowl on the Wyatt hall table, both bowl and table carefully dusted by the cleaning woman. In the bowl lay most of the family plastic, aside, naturally, from credit cards.

Sue flipped through the cards for library and various memberships, until she found the one for Epic Videos.

Wearing her Saturday nonschool clothes and shoes, her face powdered as her parents now permitted, she entered the store one evening when she was supposedly meeting the long-discarded Clare for a walk.

At first Sue failed to find the movie. Then she did find it on a special display. The pictures on the box alone filled her with an incoherent, nearly panicky excitement.

But she kept her (fake) cool quite well. The rude younger man, who never bothered with anyone, was at the till, as Sue had hoped. He didn't bat an eyelid at her choice, nor her mother's card. Though when she paid cash, he shortchanged her, which Sue discovered only later.

It scarcely mattered. She had the film, hidden in her bag. It was hers for three whole nights.

The best thing of all had happened, too.

Jane and Oliver were going up to town tomorrow. It was a Friday, and they were intending to shop, as Jane insisted, for Christmas presents. But really it was only October, and they would be visiting some gallery they had been invited to, perhaps having lunch, and later decidedly having dinner somewhere expensive.

"We won't be back until after one A.M., I shouldn't think," Jane had said. "We're taking your father's car, so he can't drink, but never mind," spangled Jane, who—not allowed to drive Oliver's Merc—could drink herself silly and no doubt would.

(There had been other giggly nights like that. Sue had overheard them; she would have had to have been deaf not to. Oliver staying a while downstairs to catch up via the whiskey decanter. Then noises in the bedroom along the corridor. Sue knew what they were doing. All those bizarre little educative books had informed her—without understanding, of course. It wasn't that the sounds of the Wyatts in full rut scared Sue. They simply appalled her, that was all.)

But she had no thought of any of that. She smiled and wished her mother and father a lovely day and evening, quite warmly promised she would spend at least two and a half hours on her homework, and would be in bed by ten P.M.

She was, better late than never, learning how to lie.

Ruby Sin found she had been taken prisoner again. These arms felt inhumanly hard and irresistible. The breasted chest her spine was pressed to was almost as hard.

Chloe said, with icy menace, "Relax. Good. That's it."

But not letting go.

Then they were out in the foyer.

Zara had the black sequins girl by one arm only, and Barry stood over the assemblage glowering, while the girl in white-no-longer dripped incarnadine on him.

Barry proclaimed, "You're all going out. Okay? And you're all barred. *No* trouble. It'll hurt you more than us."

"That bitch started it—" (Sequins.)

"Too bad."

The inner doors behind them moved. "Stop," someone said. It was a command.

Barry looked sidelong.

Everyone had turned. Even Ruby Sin (hung on the cross of Chloe), her slender muscles splitting at the tug of Chloe's tank-top torso.

Ruby Sin . . . she *saw*. . . .

Her eyes dropped shut like those of a doll. For a second she sagged, and only Chloe's rottweiler frame held her.

But then Ruby Sin's eyes flew wider than wide. A blind woman given sight, she stared. For He was there. *He* had come here.

He spoke again, in a tonelessly musical voice. "Let her go."

Barry lunged.

Barry was good, but somehow *not* so good, not tonight. The tall, black-haired man was neither floored nor in custody, and somehow Barry was down on one knee.

Only for a second. But it counted.

"No," said the young man with long black hair, to Barry, to all of them. "Don't. None of you would like it."

Chloe said, "It's him, off the gallery. Says he knows Frank Collins. I told you."

"I do," said the young man. "Why don't you call him? Say, *Anduin*."

"What?"

"A-N-D-U-I-N. Me. I think you'd better. You might not want to make Frank angry."

Chick was there. "I'll do it. Andwin, you say."

"Yes." He stood by the doors, and behind him the light went on exploding, and the dark hemorrhaging over all.

"It's all right," he said softly, looking into her eyes.

Ruby Sin found she was shaking. Chloe had lessened her hold.

The sequined and shimmer-white girls quarreled. Tears and blood rolled down the scratched face.

Sue would have been distressed by what she had done in self-defense—for, once or twice, in self-defense, she *had* done things. Ruby Sin, however, was sinless.

Chick had gone out on the pavement, away from some of the noise. He was talking on his mobile. Then listening. Then: "What? He's who? Okay, Mr. Collins. Sure, Mr. Collins. Right."

Chick reentered and looked at Zara. Nodded.

Zara took hold of both the girl in black and the girl in white and seemed to lift both of them off their feet. They were slung out of the front doors of the club. They huddled like orphans under the blue glare of The Family Axe, hissing and calling: It was *her* . . . was *her* . . .

But the club doors shut again, and Chick and Barry stood in front of the man who had named himself Anduin, and Chloe still kept her grip on Ruby Sin.

Until through the blaze of music there was the abrupt undercurrent of a car screeching around a corner and drawing up outside.

"Jesus, 's him," said Chick.

The night parted, then with a rush the doors. A big man, in heavy and gym-honed middle age, pushed through, two others at his back.

His head was covered with short thick hair and his eyes by an a-physical lens like vitreous.

He glanced at the bouncers, then directly at the young man in black.

Frank Roland Collins said something in another language, which could have been Russian. This took his crew by surprise, but not the young man, who answered in two or three unknown, alien words.

Frank turned to Chick.

"Didn't know I had any foreign, did ya?"

"No, Mr. Collins."

"One word I want ya ter learn."

"Yes, Mr. Collins?"

"All of yer. *Scarabae. He,* this gentlemen, is one of the Scarabae. Right?"

They nodded. He made each of them, bemusedly, repeat the name. Then Frank walked over to the young man, who, Frank alone was aware, might well be much, much older than Frank himself. "My apologies, Anduin."

"Accepted. But tell your woman to let go of mine."

"Clo," said Frank, "do as the gentleman says."

Chloe let Ruby Sin go.

Ruby Sin put out her hand on the air, to catch something to steady herself. But the air was empty. Then she discovered that the black-clad shape, the black *eyes* of Anduin, now held her up.

"Did you both want to go back inside, Anduin?" asked Frank Roland Collins politely.

"No."

"I hope you'll forgive my people. Forgive 'em, eh, they know not what they fuckin' do."

"We're leaving," said Anduin.

He walked across to Ruby Sin, and Chick hurried to open a door.

"Come back anytime," said Frank. "Free admission. Drinks on the house."

"Thank you," said Anduin.

When the doors had closed behind him and the girl with long black hair, Frank drew the pewter brandy flask out of his jacket.

Normally he never did that, not during a night when he was patrolling his clubs.

"Jesus Christ," he said to Chick. "One more go like that, I'll need me fuckin' heart pills."

"Who was he?"

"You don't wanna know. Just remember that name."

"Scarab-bye."

"Scarab-*bee*. Scarabae. Just fuckin' remember."

She had scratched one of the bullies in the playground. About a quarter inch above the eyes—there had been quite a scene, Jane summoned to the school, and so on. It was all apparently Sue's fault. Somehow, if she had felt she must, she should have defended herself in some more honorable, even more feminine way.

"She may have to be suspended, Mrs. Wyatt. We can't have this sort of thing. The other girl could have lost an eye."

Sue had felt fear and awful remorse (which Jane's subsequent lecture fueled). But also a weird, secret delight. It was that year she was fourteen.

And the bully failed to attack Sue again. It was the last time any of them bullied her, although she still had no friends.

Later, of course, there had been greater crimes, the last one of which (and the one which ten years after, still continued) was when Sue Wyatt started to blackmail her father.

"My family is an old one."

They were walking through the London streets. It was late, after two A.M. Ruby Sin could not be sure how long they had walked, nor which direction they had taken, took.

The sky stayed milky, and the neons painted rainbow colors on the upper stories of the city. Here, there were few people on the streets. But they had come into a district where the street lamps were pale gold, rather than Martian orange, and the shadows lay violet on dry paving. All the night was vampiric now.

They walked side by side, not particularly fast, and now and then he spoke to her in his low, extraordinary voice.

Not once had he asked her what she wanted, or told her what he might want. Only at one point, there was an off-license, curiously still open, lit yet deserted, and going in he took a bottle of wine from one of the shelves and left a twenty-pound note lying on the counter. No one came to remonstrate, or to accept the money. No alarm sounded either as he entered or as he left with the bottle.

He undid the foil cap and drew out the cork, somehow, with his white teeth. How strong they must be. But naturally they would be.

"My father," Anduin said, once he had passed her the wine and she had drunk some, "rides with a gang of bikers. He looks younger than he did. Or perhaps he's older again, or he's doing something else. He has always refused to credit that I exist, as if that could unmake me. My mother was Spanish-Hungarian. Where she is I've no idea either. But I'm hardly alone. There is the Family. My Family," he added, "is very old."

"Yes," whispered Ruby Sin. She held out the bottle to him and he drank.

His family was old as history. Older.

"What do you think?" he asked her gently, as they turned down a long and winding alley under high blank walls. She said nothing. He said, "I mean, what do you think I am?"

Ruby Sin stopped. She had to. Her heart was leaping and choking her. She could not anyway have said his name—not even that other name, which must be a modern lie, a camouflage. *Scarabae.*

But he turned to her now and, for the first time, touched her, putting his hands on her upper arms. It was like warm electricity. And it burnt straight through her sleeves, her skin and flesh and bones, and touched her soul, just as it somehow had on the gallery at the club.

"You don't know me, but you think you do, don't you? And you're not afraid," he said.

He was not like any other ever imagined, let alone seen. His face was perfect, like a carving, and the eyes were made of real jewels, black as obsidian.

As in all her fantasies, Ruby Sin should now play with him the verbal fencing game of her dreams.

But nor would these words come.

She said, "This isn't my hair. It's a wig. My hair is brown. Short. And . . . it's contacts, the color of my eyes."

"Ah, darling," said Anduin. He drew her to him and held her close, folding her in against the contoured strength of his alien, supernatural and astonishing, *real* body. "Don't you think I can guess all that? You only look like my kind. Your kind is different."

"Then—"

"It's you," he said, his mouth against her temple. "I am interested in *you*. Tell me what you're called."

She shuddered. "Sue."

He laughed, and she felt the laugh move through his chest, and through her breasts, as he held her.

"No," he said. "Your true name."

Ruby Sin thought. She knew he did not mean her invented name. Then she remembered what was written on her birth certificate, which she had stolen, even if it were hers, from her mother's box file, nine years ago.

"Susanna."

"Beautiful," said Anduin. "That's a Hebrew name. Do you know what it means?" She shook her head against him. Something like the warm, delicious sleep of snow-death was stealing over her. "It means *the lily*. Susanna the Lily. Come on," he softly said. "It isn't far now."

Sue's parents had left for their jaunt to town just after eight o'clock that Friday morning. They would have been off a little earlier, but Oliver's car had acted up, and there was a small row. They left in a flurry, Oliver scowling and Jane huffy. "Do that homework!" was the parting shot, as the Merc slid away like a shark up the cul-de-sac, and out into the land of adult pleasures.

But Sue went into the house. As she had a free period this morning, and it was not a day for the cleaning woman, Sue was supposed to do the washing up before she left for school.

Instead she ran upstairs and drew the video of *Dracula* out from under her bed. Going down again to the spacious cream and maroon sitting room, she set up the TV and pulled the heavy drapes.

Before she sat down to watch her fantasy world brought to life, she poured herself a stiff Fino sherry. She had got into the habit of sometimes sneaking one before school in any case. Now it wasn't fear that drove her to it, only an extreme excitement that made her mouth arid, her palms damp.

Sherry swallowed; she started the film.

What unrolled before her was a magic carpet. Lush, erotic, full of terrors, lamped by beauty and desire, spiritually *appetizing*, and so intense that this alone might have persuaded her forever to some elevated and unusual form of yearning. It woke her fully from the dismal torpor of a pallid existence. It tore her open to show her the passion and cruelty, the creation and artistry that might just be there in her own self.

She was at an age of turnings. Beginnings.

The influence could well have been wonderfully good.

After she had played the movie through, some (well-trained) part of her thought she must now behave rationally. Sue wandered out, dazed, into the kitchen. She saw the stacks of last night's fouled plates and glasses. And stared at them, unrecognizing, like a being from another world.

Anyway, it was now too late to clear up any of this mess; she would have to do it this evening, before her homework, when she got back from school.

So then she thought of school. A couple of hours of dull geography, badly taught, and lunch in the noisy friendless dining room. Then a double period of math—incomprehensible horror, presided over by sarcastic Mr. Brenn.

This, her world. Not flame, peacock eyes, perverse delirium, tragic galvanic love. Solely this . . . crap.

She moved to the phone like a robot. When someone answered, she spoke into it like a robot, too, preprogrammed and clever, and with a London accent.

"Hallo, this is Mrs. Wyatt's cleaning lady. I'm afraid Sue's been ever so sick. She won't be in, very sorry. Mrs. Wyatt? No, dear,

I'm afraid she's off to town. Doctor? Oh, he's been. Says it's a bit of tummy trouble, that's all. You know what they're like at that age."

It was a fair impersonation, even if Sue's voice was a little too high for Jane's cleaning woman. The accent was exact. (Sue had heard Jane scornfully mimic the cleaner very often.)

After she put the phone down, still in a sort of trance, Sue made herself a piece of toast. Then she had another sherry and put the film on again.

She watched it through altogether five times. The intervals between the shows were brief—enough to allow her to pee, to eat more toast, to pour two more sherries. Somehow the sherry combined with the movie, in a way Sue did not analyze.

The more she watched the film, the more she felt herself changing. She knew that she was *becoming* part of it. She knew also that, by the sorceress process of reiteration, she was making *it* come to life.

She wanted nothing else. Even if—yes, even if it meant her death.

But then it did not mean death. The vampiric kiss meant, evidently, immortality. Yet really, she could not think beyond that embrace of fire, that thrashing whirlpool of scarlet—

It was after nine P.M., the film once more just ended, when the other idea came to her, swimmingly.

Again then like a robot, Sue got up and left the sitting room, and unstumblingly glided her newly coordinated way up the cold (she had forgotten to revive the central heating), dark house. Not a light burned, only the blue postvideo screen of the TV downstairs.

There was suddenly something tremendous about being alone here, in this masonry tower that no longer had anything fake, let alone fake Tudor, about it.

There was nothing worthwhile, nothing Art Nouveau or Victorian, available to her here. But nevertheless, there were adult things—things to do with erotic mysteries. Intuitively, infallibly, she sought them.

In her parents' vast bedroom, Sue opened her mother's forbidden drawers. Here lay the black silk kimono, the black silk uplift bras and narrow black lace panties with their red ribbons, the expensive perfumes and costly makeup. And, on a perch inside the wardrobe, the long black wig that Jane sometimes put on, either for a party, or to entertain Oliver in bed. It had clips, the wig, to fasten it securely into Jane's short-cut hair.

The fourteen-year-old Sue had no compunction now. She drew the curtain, put on the lights about the mirror.

A miracle had happened, as she had known it must.

Sue Wyatt was already mostly gone.

Her name now must be Mina, or Lucy.

Her clear white skin, large eyes that were full of the shadows . . .

She had watched her mother makeup several times, though never being allowed herself to use more than powder. As for the lingerie, Sue knew how to put on underclothes. And if these were generally a little too big for her, there were also some that had been deliberately purchased that were too *small* for her mother.

Sipping the last of her fourth sherry, Sue-Mina-Lucy stripped. She ignored her body in the harsh light until she had reclad it in black lace, red ribbon and balconied wire, and draped over it the short black kimono, which on her almost reached to her ankles. Then she dressed her face—the first time ever—in the fruits of the tree of carnal knowledge.

These were the accoutrements of Jane's excursions and rutting nights. Sue did not even consider that her mother might well be putting them on *herself*, much later, when she and Oliver came home.

Sue managed her face quite well. In fact, very well. Her eyes were shaded with dark grey and the lashes inches thick in black, her face white, lips carmine. She did her nails, too, perhaps not quite so skillfully, but the effect was, in the mirror, not bad. Lastly she drew on and pinned the black wig, over and into her own mousy hair.

There then she stood. A contemporary Mina-Lucy. Truly. Finally.

Gorgeous, and sexual, ripe as the moon for one searing scarlet cloud . . .

Mina-Lucy turned out the lights again and went along to her own bedroom, by the flicking gleam of two of her mother's aromatherapy candles.

Mina-Lucy shut her bedroom door, set the candles at the bedside, and, going to the window, flung it open on the still, frosty, garden-darkened night.

Despite any streetlights, once she lay back on her bed, Guildford became Transylvania.

Her head spun a little. She smelled, over the perfume, the cold and the freshness of chilled autumn trees and the river-dark forest, freezing falls. She shivered and did not mind it. Her ears roared, as if the cataract poured there—it did; her waiting blood.

She anticipated Him.

She knew He must come to her.

Her own intensity would lure Him to her.

Up the wall, up the brickwork, an insect, a bat, graceful and crawling, young again in hopes of the feast she would be for Him . . .

Up and up—scaling the wall of her body . . . His hands on her . . . His mouth closing, savage and ecstatic, on her throat . . .

Of all that she anticipated, what came was not any element of it.

What came was sleep.

Drained by excitement and desire, drunk on Fino sherry, the candles, and her mother's lavishly sprayed scent, Sueminalucy fell miles down into a sleep of undeath.

She woke again just before eleven thirty to scalding light and her father's furious voice shouting in the doorway: "What in God's name do you think you're doing?"

The building was condemned. Like all the others in the street.

Briars and nettles stood up like ornamental iron railings.

Anduin pushed wide a piece of boarding that had looked immovable, and courteously held it for her, like an open door.

He must live in a squat of some kind—as she had once tried to do, in her case rather unsuccessfully.

But even a squat . . . surely there would by now be some lights visible? None showed anywhere, except for a pair of street lamps, one at either end of the row of tall, dead houses.

"Appearances," he said, "deceptive."

She nodded mutely. Did not care.

As they crossed the garden, summer smells of garbage, sweating grass, the fragrance of night trees. Something rustled, and two tiny pins of eyes flashed garnet.

"It's only rats," he said.

There was a boarded door that was also opened. Then, in blackness, an uncarpeted staircase in surprisingly good repair.

They climbed, up and up.

He undid the last door, not with keys, but by pushing a button in the frame. Another eye flashed, not a rat's: technology.

"It knows my fingerprint," said Anduin.

And they walked through into a suite of rooms at the top of the derelict house.

Hanging lamps bloomed on, soft honey colors and rose, through white and indigo glass. The ceilings lifted high, and their 1800s plasterwork of cherubs and fruit had been renewed and gilded. A huge fireplace, marble, was empty but for a terra-cotta pitcher that looked like something from an epic Roman film.

There was a long window—full of daylight. Of course not. It must be illuminated from behind. The opaque glass had no picture, but a complex pattern, the red of blood, the blue of moons that make wishes come true.

He was moving toward her with two goblets of grayish crystal in his hands, full of the wine he had taken or bought on their journey here.

"What a lovely face you have," he said. "Lovely Susanna who is a lily."

Something broke inside her. It was like eggshell porcelain breaking at a single quiet sigh.

"Please don't," she said. She started to cry. She felt the tears like burning cotton pulled from her eyes, loosening the waterproof mascara. "Don't fuck me," she pleaded, weeping.

He removed her wineglass and put down his own. He drew her, lightly, without threat, onto a couch with a high carved back. He held her hands. "Why not?"

"Please—no. Just . . . please . . . just drink my blood. I know you will, you can—I want it so much. But not . . . not to have sex." And incredibly, unknowingly, in the words of some clichéd Victorian herione, now given frightful veracity: "Anything but that."

He had filled the doorway, as stabbing light filled her bedroom and all the house—it had been set on fire.

He bellowed.

"The place is a tip—you haven't done a stroke, have you, haven't done the washing up—you are a parasite, Sue. Worthless. Your poor mother breaking her ankle like that—I've had to leave her in the bloody hospital—and then the ruddy traffic—and now this, this *shambles*. You know you've destroyed that video, don't you, which anyway you shouldn't have been watching? It's an eighteen, Sue, for adults only. You've broken the law. And something's happened, the damn thing's got itself all wound round itself—snapped when I pulled it out—and all that washing up, just left there, stinking. Do you expect your mother to do it? Christ almighty, she'll be on crutches for six bloody weeks. You need to buck your ideas up, girl. And look at you. What in Christ are you up to—is that your mother's bra you've got on?"

Made moronic by shock and terror, Sue sat up to face this ranting being, supposedly her father.

She felt as sick now as she had lied she was to the school.

"Sluts dress like that," said Oliver Wyatt. His voice, however, had become less strident. He looked at her, long and hard. "Prostitutes," he added.

Then he came over to the bed and slapped her, once, across the face.

This stunned her. She cried, but far away. He pushed her backward, and when she felt the bra, like tape and ankles, break across her breasts, she thought it was only one more part of the punishment.

As indeed it was.

"Filthy little cunt," he panted, his sweat and spit dribbling down her face and neck, "this is what filthy little cunt bitches get—"

The pain was like thunder. He split her. Like an evil lightning.

When he left the room, still thickly raging, muttering, her bed was seeped in the blood of her ripped virginity. But there had been little menstrual accidents in the past. Even when she now threw up all over the carpet, vomit reeking of sherry and shame. Even that could be blamed on one more bad period.

Downstairs she heard far off the furious resentful crashing as he washed up the plates.

"I thought it could only happen once," she said, in the elegant rooms above the derelict house. "But after a week, he did it to me again. First of all he said it served me right; it was to teach me a lesson. But then he came into the bedroom when Mum was asleep from the painkillers for her ankle. He said, I didn't tell her you broke the tape or left the washing up. So don't you tell her about this. Don't tell your mother; she'll be angry with you."

"Fathers often have a bad record among the Scarabae. How long did this go on?"

"Another year. Then I heard . . . a girl at school told a teacher her father was abusing her. The whole school got to hear about it. And I saw it wasn't meant to happen. And her father had said just what Dad had said, *Don't tell.* So when he came in again, I said to him, You'd better stop now, or I'll tell Mum, and you'll go to prison. He said, She won't believe you. They'll put you in a madhouse. I said, You have a big purple birthmark on your willy. How could I know unless I've seen it? He said—incredibly, as if he forgot, and pompously, the way he always spoke—I'd never let any daughter of mine see me unclothed. And I said, Yes, exactly."

"Clever Susanna the Lily," said Anduin.

She said, "I ran away soon after. By then he'd had to pay me to keep quiet. He was scared of scandal, and the police. And Mum." Ruby Sin breathed in and breathed out. She said, on no breath at all, "He had to pay for the video, too. Coppola's *Dracula*. The one I broke."

"Lie back," Anduin said. "I'm not my father. Or yours. My kind—you know us. Yes, we're vampires. And I think this was agreed between us, you and I, many centuries ago. Do you trust me?"

"Only you."

Sueminalucy lies deep on cushions. Through the dim gold of the lamps, He bends above her. He is shadow and He is light. A solar midnight, the dark of the sun.

Scaling the impossible wall . . .

He strokes her breasts, kisses them, sweetly. He makes love to her, which no one has ever done, or been allowed to do. At last, he cups her center strongly in one hand and lowers his mouth to her throat.

The bite is agonizing. Marvelous. What she has dreamed of.

As he draws her blood into his mouth, she comes in long, full, pouring waves of joy, crying aloud, and does not recall any other such cries ever, nor realizes that anyone else has ever known this paroxysm, since the beginning of the world.

"Sleep now," he says.

She is tired . . . or perhaps he has put something into her wine.

But this time she can slumber fulfilled. What she has always longed for has occurred. The real virginity is taken at last. Now her immortality can commence, her life as Ruby Sin. Or Susanna.

She woke up in the prepaid taxi with strangely obscured number plates, which was carrying her "home" to the flat facing Woolworth's (and quite near the bank, where, once every month, she could access fifty pounds, courtesy of Oliver Wyatt).

She was drowsy and disorientated, but not unhappy or ill. Someone had put a clean dressing on her neck. And wound over it a priceless piece of black-and-red Chinese silk, dating from around 1760.

In the flat, though, she sobbed till hours after sunrise, keeping the noise down to avoid other tenants coming to complain.

At about nine A.M., memory of the past, she called in sick.

"Well, Miss Wyatt, this really is most awkward. It *is Saturday*, you know. Our busiest day."

But Susanna did not bother with that, and a few weeks later anyway, she sacked herself, and moved farther into London, telling Oliver, by e-mail straight to his laptop via a booth, that she would now need one hundred and fifty a month.

Oliver apparently thought he had no sure way to reach her, only she could reach him—or Jane. He could have bluffed it out by now. But he paid up.

How then does she spend her Friday nights? Susanna, in garments of darkness and blood, still prepares herself, and travels to the heart of the metropolis. She walks, walks the byways of the city, up and down, round and about. She has no time now to visit clubs or pubs. Only once did she visit The Family Axe, but the bouncers were different ones, and besides would not say anything about a man called Anduin, let alone Scarabae, or Dracula.

She is looking for the street of derelict houses she was at first too entranced, later too sleepy, too satiated, to identify. She should have asked the taxi driver that night. Yet he had seemed rather unusual, rather silent. It might have been no use.

So far (two years now), neither Susanna nor even Ruby Sin has found a clue.

Anduin has therefore returned into her dreams and fantasies, where, like before, his face is fading from her inner eye. But then, he was a demon lover, and he and his mansion have vanished from the earth. As they normally do.

David J. Schow's short stories have been regularly selected for over twenty-five volumes of "Year's Best" anthologies across two decades and have won the World Fantasy Award, the Dimension Award from *Twilight Zone* magazine, and a 2002 International Horror Guild Award. His novels include *The Kill Riff, The Shaft, Rock Breaks Scissors Cut,* and *Bullets of Rain.* His short stories are collected in *Seeing Red, Lost Angels, Black Leather Required, Crypt Orchids, Eye, Zombie Jam* (2004), and *Havoc Swims Jaded* (2005). He is the author of the exhaustively detailed *Outer Limits Companion* and has written extensively for films (*Leatherface: Texas Chainsaw Massacre III, The Crow*) and television (*Perversions of Science, The Hunger*).

His bibliography and many other fascinating details are available online at his official site, Black Leather Required: www.davidjschow.com.

EXPANDING YOUR CAPABILITIES USING FRAME/SHIFT™ MODE

by David J. Schow

Half the buttons on the fucking remote? Dorian could not tell you what they were for . . . unless they were dead tabs for some higher-end version of the DVD player he had scored for seventy bucks, at some bargain barn specializing in floor models and discontinued stock. Manufacturers did that; gave you the same remote, no matter what, with special functions reserved for the costlier units. It was a cruel tease that reminded you of what you *didn't* have, a wiggle-worm of bait to goad you to consume even more.

He, however, counted himself among a more elite group—the ones dedicated enough to surf around the constraints of any system, particularly when it came to all phyla of media. It was an unseen fraternity, this underground scene of video adepts. Its skills were wily pirate skills—how to nuke copyguard, how to outfox foreign formats, how to play and copy damned near anything. One could gain friends through such utility.

Dorian had hacked the player using a download from the Internet. He had burned a disk of the hack, installed it into the DVD tray, and crossed his fingers. The machine had taken twenty nerve-racking seconds to reprogram itself, per a better device, different brand, allowing Dorian to wave bye-bye to all forms of copy protection and region coding. Now at last, he had achieved video transcendence. *What, you can't play that? Give it to me.*

Now he could play anything out of a single box—a concept that was sometimes more important than eating, not that he could ever explain that usefully to Gelina. She could not appreciate that he could fire up new gear without ever cracking the damned manual. That was a skill, a talent, wasn't it?

After checking to ensure the kitchen cabinet held an adequate stock of packaged ramen, Dorian blew about a hundred bucks on assorted priced-to-clear disks of Italian gore movies. If Gelina complained, he'd cook, see? DVDs really were worse than crack. None of the furniture in their downscale, one-bedroom apartment (half a duplex) was worth a shit, but they could now by-god *watch* any damned thing, including pirate copies and bootleg downloads of movies still playing in theaters. This way, Dorian reasoned, they were actually *saving* money.

Besides, Gelina was a waitress at Alphy's. She always managed to pick up bonus shifts at the coffee shop, and wasn't there some rule that said management had to feed the staff? Right?

Consolation was a fluid, shifting thing.

The remainder of the afternoon was gobbled up by a double bill of *Chainsaw Cheerleaders II* (the Special Director's Cut), and a dubbed, full-screen version of *Shriek for Mercy* ("with restored

disembowelment scene!"). For Dorian, this all classified as research. Every eighteen months or so, he was able to nail a gig as
production assistant or gofer on some microbudget, straight-to-
video epic—sporadic sideswipes he could honestly call "work in
the film industry," thus rationalizing his obsessive input of
movies in all forms. Whenever his cinematic skill ran to fumes,
Dorian had tried (in no particular order) freelance Web design
for porn sites, driving a taxi, graveyard shift at some twenty-four-
hour xerography shop, slinging espresso, and tootling all over hell
and gone as a messenger. He had tried to bipack the cabbie and
messenger jobs according to a complicated but workable sched-
ule, and gotten shit-canned. The espresso boutique was overrun
with trendy losers, pecking away on laptops and trying to sound
important during endless cellular calls. They tipped for shit. The
downside of free caffeination was getting so wired that all Dorian
wanted to do was rip out poseur throats aplenty. With his teeth.
The copymat job, like the coffee job, reminded him that he was
no farther along as Hollywood's Next Big Thang (though the former *did* provide a lot of free office supplies). The porn Web work
had dried up when San Francisco, to the north, had gotten its
smugness quaked by the dot-com crash.

Dorian was the longest-running temp worker that Dorian
knew, and he saw no irony in this. At least Gelina's job was
steady. Her tips paid their rent, leaving him free to court the cutting edge of the tech that would one day set him free.

Most crazy-making was the third row of buttons on the new
remote. Dorian saw cryptic designations such as INT/ALT+,
FR/SHFT, and SELECT EXIT. He pressed them at random, and
nothing happened. On-screen, an Italian starlet got her brain
crowbarred from her open skull, to be devoured by cannibal
zombies. Dorian flipped the remote for clues and read the
sticker there: ASSEMBLED IN TAIWAN. Below that was a bar code
and an inventory control number.

A true terrorist of video would already *know* what those buttons meant, he reasoned. He refused to retreat to the coward's option of checking the manual.

At his computer, he recalled the data on the hack he had employed. He compared strings of digits representing the model he had purchased, versus specs from the unattainable model to which he had sneakily upgraded. It, too, had been discontinued, superceded by an even more unattainable version . . . but he located another inventory number, and based on that, he sniffed up the button sequence for accessing the "service menu."

CD and DVD players were all little computers. Even though they were designed to be discarded and replaced—not repaired—they all came with some sort of back door for simple adjustments. Invisible to the buying public, this information was almost never provided in the already incomprehensible manual, just another example of the contempt in which sellers held buyers. For example, each numeric key was also assigned a letter value. Punching these in a certain sequence, after, say, hitting the MENU button three times in a row, could get you in. Dorian found precious little on the upgrade model, but did discover the service menu code for a *similar* model, courtesy of one of the links on the hacker's chat board. On some machines, this elementary access allowed you to cancel copyguarding functions in a simple on/off way. Other machines needed a specially configured chip to be manually placed on the motherboard (there was a guy in Australia who would burn the chip you needed for twenty bucks, postage paid).

As the now-brainless Italian ingenue was being raped by a possessed demon tree, Dorian entered 1197-MENU-SELECT-MENU-69 on his remote. The movie was covered by a click-down menu in a square of translucent blue. The fifth item down read FRAME/SHIFT MODE. Its status read as DISABLED. Dorian arrowed over to ENABLED, then clicked EXIT MENU. *Shriek for Mercy's* victim filled up the screen again, in her final death throes prior to her resurrection as a lurching ghoul, freshly impregnated with a baby tree demon. The scene cut to a pair of guys arguing on a minimal office set, the voices of their English surrogates hollow and booming, due to inadequate miking. Their early seventies wardrobe was a riot of flared trousers and plaid suits with aerodynamic lapels.

Dorian pointed the remote at the player and clicked FR/SHFT.

Now the same two guys were still standing there, same goofily dubbed argument as before . . . except they were decked out in crumpled boxers, wife-beater T-shirts, and socks with garters. Their shoes had vanished, but their heels were still canted four inches off the floor.

STOP!

Dorian cued to the beginning of the scene. Two guys, loud garb, arguing tough. He hit FRAME/SHIFT. Same deal, only now they were in their underwear again. The switch was *not* part of the movie. Dorian blinked and rubbed his eyes (he had seen people react this way in films, when confronted with an anomaly). Purist that he was, he ran the scene in its entirety, just to make sure the men remained the same. As soon as he hit FRAME/SHIFT, their outer garments ceased to exist, and they carried on as though nothing within their movie reality had changed. Or shifted.

He hit the button again. Now the men were naked, still floating surreally above the floor on platform soles no longer visible. Their pubic hair was mashed, and penises crooked, by now-invisible underwear. The guy on the left had a long, skinny dick that was actually pointed upward, inside clothing that no longer impeded Dorian's view.

Dorian was now inspired to backtrack to the debut scene of the future tree casualty, which, thanks to low-budget coincidence, had been staged on the same indifferent office set, where she was a secretary or something. It was a medium shot, up angle of her sauntering to her post, wearing an abbreviated suede skirt. Miles of leg plummeted into designer boots. She wore a loose, saucy silk blouse, and owned at least a yard of elaborately coiffed hair in burnished brown. Bracelets, bangles. Eyes hidden by couture shades intended to mimic those costing at least four hundred dollars.

No longer did Dorian have to look at the remote; his fingers had learned the sequence. Reverse. Track slow. Play normal. Then, FRAME/SHIFT.

Same angle, same actress, same movements . . . but a brand-new point of view. Now Dorian could see the marvelous length of pale thigh that led from black garters to breathtakingly brief lace panties. The arc of the garter belt framed her navel. She had a treasure trail. No tan lines. Her formidable breasts moved in a furtive, repetitive pattern as she walked, engirded in the grasp of a brassiere that was mostly a wisp of spiderweb fabric. Her eyes, sans glasses, were revealed as a blazing, killer green.

Dorian was getting an erection.

FRAME/SHIFT.

Now she was nude, walking, apparently, on air. Her pubic hair was lush and rudely full. Her areolae were large to the point of being slightly grotesque, her thumb-sized nipples flattened by the nonvisible bra.

Dorian paused to cohere an opinion: *Like, this is like sooo totally the ultimate peeping tom deal.* Just as film theory held, the screen *could* be a window to exciting otherworlds. You just had to know the code; which buttons to push. You had to have the savvy and know-how of the video adepts. He decided to let his cock catch some air while he, you know, massaged it.

FRAME/SHIFT.

Dorian's nonremote hand froze on the upstroke. The actress's flesh had transposed to dermis, threadbare with vasculature. In front of her chest hovered two opaque teardrops, which Dorian realized were breast implants—still wiggling around in midair. She looked as though her outermost layer of skin had been sandblasted off, to reveal glistening wetness, mostly crimson. She was wearing a tampon.

Dorian's little best buddy began to wilt in his grasp, a candle in a hot room. There was no GO BACK button. In order to see the woman naked, not *skinned,* he had to start the sequence all over. He scanned until he found a substantially longer take of her.

Gelina walked in late, while he was still jerking off.

They had their usual fight about money. Then they ate some takeout Gelina had brown-bagged home. Then they had their usual fight about how gross it was for him to masturbate to what Gelina assumed was simple porn. Then they had the usual, terrific make-up sex.

Tonight, Gelina seemed amplified. Turned up, supersensitive, multiorgasmic, practically voracious. Instead of waiting for her to drift to sleep so he could race back to the TV, Dorian dozed, played-out and sweaty. The air cooled him, and when he startled awake in the dark, his pelvis was sore and his balls hung like bruised fruit. Gravity hurt. The pit of his stomach howled for relief, so he meandered out and boiled some ramen, throwing in a chopped green onion at the last minute.

The DVD player waited patiently for him through all this procrastinating nonsense. Knowing he would come back; knowing he would not resist clicking it on again, like a lover who wields your desire as a weapon against you.

He felt sorry for all the people incapable of wiring a stereo, of programming the timer on a simple VCR. They didn't care about bit rates for dual-layer DVDs. They would be bushwhacked when high-def Blu-Ray discs came along next year to render their ordinary DVDs into antiques. They would buy what they were told. And he, Dorian, would be light-years ahead of *that* game.

Padding around in sweatpants, minding the creak of floor-boards beneath his bare feet, Dorian roughed up his video shelves until he fished up a dusty VHS tape, no sleeve, labeled *Tasha's Wedding*.

It was time for Phase Two—to see if FRAME/SHIFT worked on videotapes, too.

His interest was strictly academic. This trick, this hidden truth, this secret key, might be parlayed into a cure-all boon, and Dorian wanted to be ready. After all, the asshole who invented the AirBong had reaped a gazillion dollars, and he hadn't even *designed* the fucking thing. (Thanks to his recognition of opportunity's knock, said asshole had made it possible for smokers to smoke anything they wanted, practically anywhere they wanted, without the discharge of hazardous pollutants into the lungs of bystanders.) Blammo—wealth, pools, exotic drugs, and blow jobs on call. Dorian felt like a mad scientist on the brink of a similar revelation. This gimmick, properly unleashed on the unsuspecting world at large, might become, like, *Celebrity Skin* on demand, for anybody, anywhere, right?

Plus, there was suspense, too—he had to unlock the secret before some other loser in some other apartment figured out FRAME/SHIFT to his or her advantage.

Naturally, his selection of test material had nothing to do with the prospect of seeing many women (and some girls) after whom he had once lusted (some, to this day) in the altogether, without the knowledge he was step-framing them, and zoom-boxing their privates. There was more at stake here.

The eponymous Tasha had once been Gelina's best bud, prior to some falling-out—one of those deals where nobody picks up the phone, and, a decade and a half later, nobody can remember what the original conflict had been. Tasha looked hot in her bridal whites, and Dorian recalled an intermittent fantasy about smothering himself between her substantial and absolutely real tits. He stopped hitting FRAME/SHIFT when he saw the fetus, gestating inside her.

Yeah, now he remembered: Tasha had spewed a kid with her matrimonial manburger, about five months into their legal union. Pregnancy had left her resembling a street waif, beaten by thugs, and much devalued on Dorian's personal sexometer.

Some of his own pals looked pretty stupid naked. *Don't even go there.*

Now he could see his old flame, Belinda, clearly enough to distinguish the razor burn on her shaved pubes, and a tattoo she had acquired after breaking up with him (HOT STUFF, right there on her inner thigh). One of the bridesmaids, Sally Something-or-other, had soaked her panties with lubrication during the vows. Cheryl Lindemann had stuffed her bra, after simulating cleavage by duct-taping her boobs together.

Dorian's penis, loose and nasty inside his sweats, still smelled like Gelina. It rose, then drooped, like a cranky guy hitting the snooze button over and over, as Dorian cycled through the ladies on the old wedding video, undressed them with FRAME/SHIFT, and found each of his idealized liaisons lacking.

Then Dorian had a new idea, and his dick roused to parade attention.

Technically, Dorian's video camera was "vintage"—outmoded, too cumbersome, brand-new when you could still buy LPs in record shops. It took full-sized VHS tapes, and required no interpretive cabling or little-brother adapter to play through his TV. The recording cassette was your nondigital, original, first-generation image. The low-light and filtering features (now rendered obsolete by two decades of consumer progress) would impart a warm, analog feeling to whatever was shot. Dorian had kept the thing in the closet so long that its power cells were cold, beyond repair, deader than beef jerky. To make it function tonight, he'd need an extension cord for the AC input, and that meant he'd have to find something else in the apartment to disconnect.

His mind was snowed in by a blizzard of concepts. He could direct a whole series of porns, like that Buttman guy. He could film pedestrians on the street, and interpret them in such a way as to compel flesh-starved jerkoffs to plunk down twenty bucks for an hour of tape. Nobody wanted to see the usual junkie sluts, spread out like leftover lunch meat or sniper victims. Everybody wanted to see the Girl Next Door, naked. He could do commissions for anyone who had ever nurtured a randy thought about a coworker. Maybe even private-eye side jobs.

Emission: Possible.

He was counting on Gelina's love of wake-up sex. That gentle stir of nipples, prior to more focused groping, amidst the gentle smells of sleep. Once Dorian coaxed the camera back to life, he stuck electrical tape over the red running light and concealed the unit near his dresser (where he could still find the outlet in the dark). There was plenty of laundry in which to hide the unit—garments in the twilight realm between one more wearing and the hamper. Gelina would beeline for the shower before dressing, and in that moment—later—Dorian could stash the whole setup, so she would never ask the wrong questions.

Very possible.

He imagined an interview: With this power, why in hell would you want to see your own girlfriend naked? You see her naked all the time. The sort of moronic question that would be asked by some backer with a homely wife and stupid kids and no idea of what was erotic. The kind of guy with zero prospects and even less imagination; one of those zombies that ogled men's mags and just . . . plain . . . didn't . . . get it.

The Italian starlet, implants and all, was a fantasy; Dorian already knew he could control what wasn't real. Gelina was the real-world end of the seesaw, and besides, Dorian had to admit (with more than a sting of apprehension) that he had never actually seen himself in the process of coitus. FRAME/SHIFT could reveal harsh truths, and allow hard conclusions. He was doing this for the greater good of all his future customers.

Sleep was impossible, so he explored a bit more, in those hours before dawn. The nudie-cutie stuff got tired fast. Dorian did take note that only organic objects within a picture seemed to be affected by FRAME/SHIFT—animals, plants, food. They became translucent, exposing their hidden networks and schema. If there were organic components in inert objects, such as a toothpaste tube, say, or leather chairs, the shift was too subtle to pinpoint, or was a mere redistribution of color patterns. Intriguing, but not distracting. His main objective, his master plan, guaranteed that his boner never completely subsided.

He was deeply fond of banging Gelina, absolutely. But it had been more than a bit of a while since the *thought* of her had horned him up this much. He knew how to flip her switch, and rev her motor, and sometimes her responses cranked him up when he had begun indifferently. She probably mistook his attentiveness for actual affection; chicks were weird that way. He slid into their secondhand bed next to her and began to infiltrate her nightshirt with his hands.

After he had cued the camera, of course.

Gelina's bloodline was principally Mediterranean *robusto* (similar enough to the femme lead in *Shriek for Mercy*), and soon she was breathing as though half-awake, scooting around to permit him better access. Dorian's finger came up thickly moist, and she practically dragged him on top of her, tangling their legs in the warm cocoon of sheets. Dorian was pretty wet, himself; an abundance of preseminal fluid streaked his leg. He flew blind, balls rasping down the curt bristle of her cropped public hair, but she collected him into herself as though she had a laser sight down there.

Making Gelina a surrogate for the hottie from *Shriek for Mercy* was a turn-on; Dorian's thoughts of playing to his own camera, ditto. Gelina waxed and bucked through a preliminary climax, then started to ram him as though trying to bash him inside-out with her pelvis. They even climaxed at the same time, just like in the movies. Then (as Dorian knew she would), she immediately looked at the bedside clock, muttered, "oh, shit, oh, shit, shit!" and dashed to the bathroom.

Dorian hurriedly stashed his surveillance setup. A gleaming ice pick of potential discovery separated his lungs and made it difficult to breathe. His pubic bone felt worked over with a rubber mallet; he was walking funny. It hurt in a good way.

It always aroused him to watch Gelina pulling on panty hose prior to donning her ridiculous Alphy's uniform, which had obviously been designed by some pig anxious to showcase a lot of leg in his food-service staff. It was sort of an abbreviated, Bavarian beer-wench getup, and although bonus stretches of thigh and cleavage were *not* on the menu, they did account for a fair degree of overtipping. The panty hose looked just as scrumptious coming off, too, at the end of the workday. Dorian had successfully cornered Gelina, several times, into fucking while her uniform was still half-on, with the added lewd kick of no underwear and unrestricted access. Just flip up the skirt and do it. Maybe he had a thing for women in uniform; maybe it was just the tang of enacting the good old Waitress Fantasy for real.

Gelina wrestled into her gear, while spieling off her usual diatribe against . . . well, everything. It was virtually the same speech, every day, as regular as TV news. She hated her hours, despised her boss, and held most of her lecherous regulars in total contempt. She complained about her clunky work shoes, and bemoaned a few faintly evident varicose veins. She railed at pinning up her hair for the job. She loathed the commute. For employees, the parking sucked. She really had to discover some new adjectives.

Dorian lay in as good a mock of innocence as he could muster, the sheet blotting his crotch. He let the tirade wash over him. He was still half-hard.

Just leave, *already, will you!?*

Gelina grabbed bag, keys, and blazed out the door in a tempest of protest, forgoing the juiceless good-bye smooch. Dorian nap-zoned for a while, his fatigue exceeding his conniving excitement.

You had to give Gelina credit for trying to tilt their lopsided relationship toward normal. Her social genetics were biased toward family meals, taken together at something called "dinnertime," carbon-copying the sitcom parameters the mass-market world had adopted as gospel, therefore, average. If people hung out and fucked long enough, they were expected to procreate. It was what people did. Occasionally, Dorian wondered how their relationship would end. He accepted that it had a clear ceiling, and knew that one day, critical mass would be achieved, but he did not want the responsibility of initiating any sort of messy breakup. Entropy would destroy them. Their gentle, Tinkertoy latticework of mundane disappointments and bided time would ultimately collapse. But probably not today . . .

. . . unless Dorian's experiment provided the kind of breakthrough he craved. With money, with notoriety, with resources, he might evolve into a different person—one who might even be capable of loving Gelina, perhaps, despite all her delusional architecture about what people did and did not do.

His predawn assault had climaxed with Gelina on top, her favorite horsey position, giddyap. Dorian would hold his fists in the air, locking his elbows, and Gelina would grab them as she teetered on the brink of orgasm, and begin chugging him (hence the bruised pubic bone). From his supine vantage, this made Gelina look like a character in fractured-flicker fast motion, trying to kick-start an invisible motorcycle. You had to give extra points to the people with whom you fell in love, or, at least, in lust—after all, they consented to get into totally ridiculous positions with no clothes on, all in the name of getting off, or getting closer to whatever you hid inside yourself.

Therefore, Dorian made an effort not to judge what he saw on the videotape. How stupid they looked, fucking. This was never supposed to be observed, and he had no desire to judge the merits of his own bobbing white ass. What was the rule of thumb for porn? Watch it for five minutes, and you want to have sex immediately. Watch it for *ten* minutes, and you never want to have sex again.

He started clicking FRAME/SHIFT.

Dorian and Gelina, fucking. *Click.* Two twine-wrapped musclebags, fucking. *Click.* Two floating arrays of internal organs, seeming to fuse into one pulsating membrane of wormy-colored tissue, fucking.

He had proven his point. Right now, he could saunter out into the world with his proof, and begin recording his future fortune.

Click. Two skeletons, fucking. Dorian muted the embarrassing sound track; the inadvertently recorded noises they had made.

If he clicked again, would he see braids of bone marrow in a humanoid schematic, humping away?

Click. Click. Click. Click. Further than he had gone before. Always test the operational limits of the phenomenon.

Their bedroom looked the same, the colors and shapes slightly out of phase due to the distortive nature of FRAME/SHIFT on inorganic objects. He had to remind himself that physical bodies were still present in the frame, but they had been rendered virtually nonvisible. That hump of sheet, for example, was made by one of his feet. For disorientation, he had been prepared.

Logic, he thought. Any of the other people out there, people like him, maybe trying to deconstruct FRAME/SHIFT *at this very moment,* would stop where he began, with the hoodoo of making clothing vanish. He had to press further, faster; to take it two levels beyond the *next* level, in order to be worthy of a revelation.

He kept clicking the button until his attention was arrested by what he saw on screen—the stuff that was there *instead* of their physical bodies.

He thought: *hairs in the gate.* But this was not projected film.

He saw a kind of gossamer lace, hanging in midair, twisting and twining and recombining. Its hue was beyond the capacity of the camera or television to interpret correctly; it came out as black and green and a dirty silver. Threads, spiderwebs, smoke, maybe. Swirls like ink in water, a negativity in the picture, similar to a matte hole into which a special effect was yet to be inserted. Nothing really there, except for the eyes. At least, the things that Dorian's shocked view classified as "eyes."

Two sets of them, approximately where their heads had been, which made the uppermost set Gelina's. Nasty, sawed-off pinpoints of solarization, so bright that they left video lag trails in pale yellow when they moved.

They were grotesque, yet mesmerizing, these undulating filaments of self, with the pupilless, sodium-colored eyes. Their psyches? Their souls? What they really boiled down to, deep inside? Dorian blinked hard. Nothing changed, because this was really happening.

The only difference now was that the eyes had shifted, both pairs, to look toward him. Toward Dorian, the watcher, the guy with the remote in his hand. They seemed to regard him specifically, as though they had caught him spying. Dorian's flesh prickled. No way he had *imagined* the wave of hatred that washed across him; the flood of disapproval emitting from his own TV set.

He wanted that feeling to go away. He clicked FRAME/SHIFT. The cobwebby things became dissipate, lighter brown. The eyes stayed the same. Their hatred of Dorian stayed the same, too.

He wondered if this might be some sort of karmic lesson. Payback, maybe, for having marginalized Gelina. In his memory of last night and this morning, he had not given her a single line of dialogue. Even her name had been truncated, from Angelina. There was no plot, no plan. It had just happened that way. It was what people did.

Experiment concluded. He needed to bring this to a screeching halt, like right goddamn now. When he hit STOP, the remote illuminated its own key buttons. It was obviously suffering an interior meltdown. So he got up to punch the onboard controls and eject the tape manually. Turn the TV off, already.

When he put down the remote (as carefully as he would radioactive material), he noticed the musculature of his own hand, sinews aglisten.

As he stood up, he saw his own skeletal feet. *Click*. The previously dead INT/ALT+ button was glowing a nervous green.

His trip to the TV set was stalled by the vision of his own lungs and liver, becoming transparent. *Click*. The INT/ALT+ button on the remote was still fluttering. It occurred to Dorian to press the dark SELECT EXIT button. Wasn't that what he needed to do? Choose to get out?

He dropped the remote when the flesh slid off his hand and piled up around his now-invisible feet. The nerve pain was astonishing.

Just as film theory had proposed, Dorian's TV screen really was a window to an exciting otherworld. And on the far side of that window, someone holding a remote had just figured out how to enable the *other* buttons, the more important ones. Not like Dorian, who had started with FRAME/SHIFT.

Whoever it was, they made sure Dorian never reached his TV.

> FRAME/SHIFT™ mode permits instant and comprehensive editorial access to alternate points of view within an already established continuity. In plain speech, it can be a useful and entertaining tool for the personalization of any piece of recorded material. Parents, for example, can modify or eliminate any perspective of objectionable character, leaving intact only the footage acceptable for family viewing. Foul language can be globally deleted, and the resultant "blank spots" tightened (or "looped") with less caustic alternatives (see DIALOGUE WIZARD™ function, p. 52). Film students may employ FRAME/SHIFT to examine how the components of a program can be tonally attenuated by the enhancement or negation of items within a story line. FRAME/SHIFT™ "makes your screen a window." It can be a fun and educational tool to broaden the experience of watching all media. It permits not only a wide menu of choice, but personal participation in what was formerly a "one-way" process. Now the viewer can become writer, editor, or director with the simple touch of a button. Remake your own version of a Hollywood hit! With FRAME/SHIFT™, good taste can replace bad, and every story can have a happy ending.
>
> For even more radical alterations of prerecorded material—or to eliminate it altogether—please see SELECT EXIT on p. 52.
>
> —from manual, pp. 47–48.

Freda Warrington is the author of seventeen novels, including the acclaimed vampire novel *A Taste of Blood Wine* (Meisha Merlin). Her latest book, *The Court of the Midnight King* (Pocket Books), is an alternative magical slant on the enigmatic King Richard III—partly inspired by events local to her home in the English Midlands. She's now working on a project involving some of the characters introduced in the story in this anthology, provisionally entitled *All About Elfland.*

CAT AND THE COLD PRINCE
by Freda Warrington

The all-night café was squeezed between two factories that soared up and up into the night. Grids of windows hung along the endless breadth and height of their walls, shining bleakly into the dark rain. The metallic chug of machinery never ceased. Crushed yet indomitable, the small café seemed to be bracing itself between the walls of an abyss. Its windows spilled oily yellow light onto the wet street.

Aurus stood alone, observing. His arms were folded over his pale full-length raincoat, his long hair tucked up beneath the crown of a wide-brimmed hat. He watched the comings and goings at the little oasis of light, and all the time the rhythm of industry shook the very ground under his feet.

This was as good a place as any.

All night, every night, Cat served fried food and coffee to factory workers going on or off shift, to administrators seeking sanctuary from their desks. Always the same bleary faces, same bland clothes of denim or neutral acrylics. No visible expressions of difference. Soaked in the perfume of chips, burgers and kebabs, marinated in fluorescent light and deadened by the drone of manufacture, Cat slaved and watched, like a goddess turning on a spit.

She'd rarely seen the world in daytime but from the glimpses she'd caught, she had missed nothing. Under the heavy, oily skies of New Encomium, day no longer came.

Her childhood in a home for surplus infants was a half-forgotten blur. The café owner, Dika, had plucked her from there when she was thirteen or so, but as a pseudoparent he did not even come close; barely came close to being an employer. He owned her; that was all. Surly and volatile, he stopped short of actual abuse; kept his distance enough that she feared him only a little and, thankfully, hardly knew him at all.

Cat drifted through the hours. She cooked, served and cleaned with the energy of youth. When exhaustion felled her, she slept in the pantry. If this was life, she found no reason to engage with it. She had dreams in which she was running and running, but these terrified her. Beyond the café lay one soaring abyss of factories after another, to the end of the world. To her there was no concept of escape, only of being lost in a dreadful labyrinth.

Casual staff came and went, but Cat stayed. All she feared was losing what little she had.

Dika was bearable. He even made her laugh sometimes, lording it over his little empire. One day a new customer came in from the rain. He was tall, and had a commanding presence that his beige raincoat failed to disguise. His face was long and hawkish with strong bones, his eyes a chilly gray. As he leaned over the counter to pay for his coffee, a silver symbol on a chain spilled out over his collar and caught the light. Cat glimpsed a stylized human shape with a lion's head.

Dika went mad, swearing at the man in a savage whisper and threatening to report him for breach of the Visible Expression of Difference laws. Customers stared. Cat edged away. The man only smiled, tucked the offending jewelery out of sight, and slipped two crisp red notes of high value into Dika's hand.

The effect on Dika was gloriously predictable: an instant switch from indignation to smooth, greedy excitement.

Cat suppressed a smile, but the stranger caught her eye. "That seems to have made a visible difference," he said. Holding Dika's eyes like a stage hypnotist, he added softly, "Tell me, do you have an unused room of any description?"

Aurus hardly registered her at first. The café owner, with his black mustache, olive skin and grease-stained apron, was a bundle of energy and business sense. The girl was always in the background, nondescript and virtually silent.

After a few visits, though, Aurus began to think her silence interesting. Usually she wore the face of a mannequin, but sometimes he saw her smirk at some private joke. Except for utterances such as, "Onion salad?" or, "Three-forty, please," she never spoke. What did that mean?

Perhaps nothing. Just another vacuous being in a vacuous world. All the same, Aurus began to watch her.

Her name was Cat and she had a fine, slim figure beneath the white banality of her uniform. She was about seventeen, he guessed, or even a gauche twenty. Sleek blond hair curved around a slender, pale, elfin face. Her long green eyes were shiny and watchful. The café lights and the oily heat seemed to baste her in a golden sheen of her own sweat.

Aurus stood shivering in the heat, hating this place. Hating the city. Hating everything.

On Friday evenings, Cat observed the trickle of strangers who slipped past the counter and vanished into the rear corridor. To an indifferent eye it looked as if they were heading for the washrooms. In ones and twos they came, drably dressed and making eye contact with no one. She counted thirty-three in all.

Dika had hired out the café basement to them, and she assumed it was as good a place as any for clandestine activities. Renting out the room meant good money, and a big risk.

Naturally it was forbidden to ask who they were or what they were doing. Forbidden even to think it. As each Friday night wore on, Cat went about her duties and tried to pretend they weren't there; but all the time she was acutely aware of their presence. She could feel them, like grit on her skin. She sensed their presence in the spaces between the metallic, throbbing chorus of the factories. Sometimes, if she lingered in the corridor that led to the kitchen, she thought she heard faint voices, snatches of song or chanting. Then she would hurry past, averting her eyes from the closed door.

She had heard rumors that such things went on: underground religious or political groups, hiding away in basements. They might be arranging fake flowers, for all she knew, since—for the sake of fairness—even the most innocuous group meetings were frowned upon. Every year for many decades the law had been extended. The discouragement of religious festivals had eventually become a ban, along with the proscription of any form of religious symbol or clothing. Affiliation to political parties had followed, and at last the sweeping harvests of all self-expression. No more shirts bearing the names of pop stars or football teams, no individual clothing of any kind. Clubs of all kinds were banned, since, however innocent their activities, they were by their nature exclusive and divisive. All to avoid even the slightest risk of causing offense to those of a different persuasion, there were now, officially, no persuasions at all.

There was only industry.

Cat had never tasted those far-off days of Difference. There couldn't be many still alive who had. She couldn't even visualize what it was that might have offended her or others. A brightly colored scarf? The wrong kind of silver pendant? Why?

Sometimes she had a vision of men and women in a factory yard, dancing naked around a bonfire with ivy in their hair, but that only made her smile. The reality couldn't even be guessed at. It was deep, dark and sinister, a mystery that whispered and rustled with terrifying energy.

The closed door drew her. It was narrow and nondescript, tucked in behind mops, brooms and coat hooks. As the weeks rolled on, she passed closer and closer to the door on her trips to the kitchen. She began accidentally to brush against it, trailing her fingertips across the off-white paintwork. Once or twice, it swung ajar.

The first time, she fled in guilt. The second, she looked quickly around to make sure no one was watching. Then she edged toward the gap.

She saw the stairs leading down, a light glowing from below. She heard the low, mysterious murmur of voices. She forgot herself, forgot her duties; tasted a wild excitement that spiked her heart and her loins with heat.

The next moment, Dika caught her arm and threw her back against the wall.

"You don't ever go near that door again," he breathed into her face. "You don't even think about it. You know what happens if the authorities find out?"

"Y-yes," she gasped, choking on his ripe breath. "No."

"They close us down. They throw us in prison. All of us." He shook her for emphasis, glaring into her eyes. "*All* of us."

"I would never say a word!"

"But if *they* catch you"—he pointed at the door—"it will be worse."

"Worse than this?" she whispered. She looked up, feeling her body vibrate with the grinding heartbeat of machinery. She meant the café, New Encomium, their existence.

Dika gave her a last shove and stepped back, looking her up and down with exasperation. "You don't know how lucky we are." He tapped his two middle fingers on her temple. "You're a good worker, but there's something missing up here." His voice became gentle, even sincere. "It's for your own good I tell you, Cat, to keep away from that door. Perhaps they collect stamps. Perhaps they beat each other with spiky whips. It's not our business. I'm trying to protect you. You understand?"

"Yes."

"You will tell no one, because there's nothing to tell. Ain't nobody here but us chickens."

When she came to take his empty coffee cup away, she always watched him with those glistening green, impassive eyes. Aurus held her gaze. He felt he knew her now, well enough to play with her. She was innocent and special.

"What do you dream about, Cat?" he asked.

That stopped her in her tracks. She showed only the barest trace of surprise. "I don't dream," she said.

"You must. Everyone does. Do you dream about silence? Green fields and forests? Birds in flight?"

"I don't know what those things are," she said.

He touched her wrist. She jumped at the iciness of his fingers. "Do you dream about me?"

Cat stood at the top of the basement stairs, like a high diver poised on the brink of a cliff. Behind her lay the banal glow of the café and kitchen. Below her, dark, fathomless waters.

She saw figures moving in slow formation—dancing?—all in black; tight leather shining softly, sooty lace frothing at wrists, pale skin shining though black chiffon. Some sinuous, pale creature she couldn't identify wove among them. A fiery light from below painted them with orange and crimson. She saw them all pause and rotate, in perfect formation, to look up at her. In their center towered Aurus. She saw thirty-two upturned faces shining in the hellish light, shining with hunger.

Behind her, the door closed. The metallic factory throb became muffled. Someone seized her arms from behind and she found a wild-eyed, red-haired woman grinning over her shoulder.

"No remarks about cats and curiosity, but we wondered how long it would take you," said the woman. "We took bets."

Cat caught her breath, said nothing. Below, she saw Aurus's harshly carved face tilt upward a little as he regarded her. He wore black leather trousers and waistcoat, and over them a black, loose-sleeved open robe. His hair was long, spilling down his back like raven wings.

"Medea, be careful with her," he said.

The woman released her, whispering, "Show respect to the Cold Prince."

"Come down, Cat," Aurus called gently. "Come and join us."

Cat moved among them as if in a trance as they passed her from one to another around the circle. She felt their long fingers and hard, painted fingernails on her skin, breathed the heavy incense of their perfume. They looked human but were not; she sensed it, tasted it. Arriving, they had looked ordinary, but here they were transformed; their faces sharp and pale, with elongated eyes, their hair wildly styled and rich with ebony, scarlet and purple. The faces were not all beautiful, but they were all exotic. The shimmer of luscious velvety fabrics was delicious and strangely exciting. Around each pale throat hung the same symbol, the shapely female figure with the head of a wildcat.

She no longer recognized the basement, with its concrete

floor and stacks of crates and boxes. The group had changed it with lamps and incense, with their presence. It was a glowing space without boundaries. Circles with intersecting lines and strange symbols shimmered beneath her feet.

Cat was acutely conscious of her own plainness, her dull white uniform, the frying smell impregnated into her skin and clothes. Her mouth was dry.

Someone gave her a drink from a purple glass goblet. The liquid was syrupy and strong, burning her throat. Defiant, she drank it all. Soon the room began to swim and everything she looked at floated in a thick golden light and was edged with flaring rainbows. She groaned. She was drowning.

She came face-to-face with Aurus and he loomed over her, a god hewn out of marble with eyes of silver ice. His fingers moved over her face, leaving prints of coldness where they'd rested.

"You smell of meat," he stated. "We'll cleanse you."

The group closed in upon her. Cat stood helpless as intrusive hands unzipped and took away her clothing: apron, tunic and trousers, shoes and socks, vest and panties. She stood naked among them, aware of what was happening yet detached from it. Drugged, dreamy, watching herself in amazement. Male and female hands brushed gently over her; tongues touched glossy, painted lips. She expected to feel teeth in her flesh.

Deep within her a tide of fear began to rise, only to break into harmless foam on the seawall of drugged acceptance.

A slender woman in black satin came through the crowd and on a golden chain she was leading a leopard. If not a leopard, then some similar creature, a big, sleek, fierce-looking feline. Cat had seen such things—in old, old films sometimes shown on the TV that Dika kept in the kitchen—but she had never imagined that such a being in reality would be so solid, so beautiful and terrifying.

Its fur was snow-white and marked with spots of cream and

pale gold. Its eyes, too, were golden, and as cold as Aurus's gray ones.

The woman had a finely carved, hard yet tragic face, and wings of black hair. Over her perfect satin-sheathed body she wore a cape of fur, like the pelt of the creature she handled. She bent and unclipped the chain from its collar.

Waves of fear washed inside Cat, but failed to move her. She stood and waited as the leopard came to her, began to sniff at her. She smelled of beef and lamb and bacon, and they laid her like bait for its hunger. . . .

The beast reared lightly and put its front paws on her shoulders. Magnified, she saw the gleam of its fangs, the redness of its lips and a blue-black, gleaming tongue. Its breath had a soft, sweet scent, like clean skin.

The creature began to lick. First her forehead, cheeks and neck. She winced, laughing with the peculiar tortured mirth of being tickled. The dark souls around her gasped, perhaps with wonder that she simply stood there, passive and fearless. The tongue lapped lower, scratching deliciously at her skin; hollow of her throat, both arms, all around and over her breasts, working down over her abdomen and into the cleft between her thighs.

The intense pleasure of its muscular delving shocked her. Her arms stiffened and her head fell back. She gasped and cried out. The audience sighed with her.

The leopard dropped to all fours and completed its careful washing, over thighs and knees and calves, down to the tips of her toes, then moving over her buttocks to finish with her back. The tongue worked patiently until it had lapped up every drop of juice and sweat.

Cat stood shivering from the moisture drying on her body. There was a spattering of applause from the watchers. Medea and a skinny young man brought a black gown, slipped it over her shoulders, wrapped it around her and tied it with a cord.

Through a glaze of unreality she saw the fur-clad woman clipping the chain onto the leopard's collar, then standing proud at Aurus's side. They could have been brother and sister.

The Cold Prince, Aurus, came forward, moving slowly through a haze of rainbows. "Do you know who we are?" he asked.

"No," said Cat.

"I think you do."

"I really don't."

His eyes pierced hers. His presence was intimidating, but she faced him squarely, refusing to be controlled.

"Perhaps now you know how it feels to enter the otherworld for a time?" he said. "The grind of industry and this bleak, hateful world turn to paper and are torn away—just through simple ecstasy."

"So you come here to playact," she said, aware she was slurring her words. "To dress up, take drugs and have sex. I've heard about things like this. Dika thinks I'm an idiot, but I listen and I hear more than he knows."

"Do you disapprove?" His eyes turned colder.

"No. What you do is nothing to me."

"Nothing? Playacting?" He paused. "Are you afraid of us?"

"Yes."

"You don't look it. Your mouth proclaims innocence, yet your eyes tell a different story." The Cold Prince was trying to stare her down. She didn't know how to answer, but she wouldn't look away. She saw fine lines of pain around his eyes. Eventually he said, "If the ecstasy were intense enough, we could make it real."

"Make what real?" she asked, but he turned away.

The souls began to sing, some of them clapping and humming a rhythm beneath the insistent melody. Cat had the weirdest feeling that this had all happened before. An image pressed just on the edge of her memory, impelling her instincts. As they began to dance, she danced with them, hips swaying, arms weaving over her head, ever more wildly until she turned dizzy and fell.

Aurus caught her and set her upright again.

"You do appreciate," he said thinly, "that now that you have seen us, we cannot let you go?"

Cat awoke in darkness. Her head ached; she felt ghastly, hungover. There was cold concrete beneath her. When she tried to sit up, her head hit metal and she swore with pain.

Lamp glow appeared and she saw a jumble of shapes that quickly resolved themselves. A woman was coming toward her, bearing a lamp. Cat saw the basement with its piled boxes; and then she saw that there were bars enclosing her in a six-foot-square space.

They had meant it. They had put her in a cage.

Cat rose to her knees, squinting against the light. The woman, Aurus's sister, squatted down on long, balletic legs and looked her in the eye.

"I'm Ginia," she said. "I am sorry, but we really do have to keep you here. You're part of us now."

"Is there any water?"

"Of course."

A bottle from the café came through the cage bars. She drank.

"You can't keep me. Dika will miss me. He'll come and let me out."

Ginia only smiled. "I'm sorry," she said again, and rose to move away.

"Who is Aurus?" said Cat, desperate to keep her there. "Why do they call him the Cold Prince?"

"There is always a Cold Prince," said the woman. "And I am the Ice Queen."

Cat knelt up, holding the bars of her cage. "You're his sister?"

Ginia smiled. "His wife."

The words were a slap. Cat must have made some visible re-action, for the woman's smile grew thinner. "You're jealous. Did you think he wanted you? Did you think you could thaw him?"

"No," Cat whispered. "All I want is for you to let me go."

"That's what we all want. Escape." The Ice Queen moved away. "I'll leave the lamp. Try to sleep where you're supposed to sleep."

Cat glanced round and saw that there was a low, flat couch in the cage, padded and upholstered in red fabric. A blanket was heaped on it. She must have fallen out.

Ginia said, "I'll come again with breakfast—yours and his."

"His?" Then Cat realized there was another cage joined to hers, and in it, the leopard. His curved back was pressed against the bars, and she'd been sleeping so close to him that he could easily have reached through and swiped her with a paw.

She couldn't bring herself to lie on the couch again; it looked like a butcher's slab. Instead she crouched in the far corner of the cage, shivering and miserable. She glanced at the ceiling, at the stairs where she could sense her guard, Ginia, waiting in the darkness.

"Dika will come for me," she mouthed to herself, but she must already have been missing for hours, and he must know where she was, and yet he had not come. Finally she realized.

"He's sold me," she said out loud.

Cat put her head on her knees and came close to tears. Close, but couldn't actually cry. There was an empty pit inside her at knowing that even if she escaped, there was nothing to escape to.

Who has sold you?

The voice spoke inside her head, making her jump. She looked up and saw the leopard sitting up, gazing at her with in-tense, frosted-gold eyes.

"My—my boss," she said hesitantly.

The head tilted and the eyes narrowed a little in reaction. The voice was definitely the leopard's. *You must feel betrayed. Do you?*

"Not really. Dika would take money for anything. It's only what I would have expected."

Now we're both prisoners. Are you cold? You look cold and sad.

"I am." She gave a faint brittle laugh. "You?"

Just sad. My fur is warm. Come here, and I'll warm you.

"Eat me, more like. You look hungry. I'll bet I tasted nice earlier."

She heard a rumbling purr of amusement. *You did.*

"Eat me, then." She uncurled and moved to the side of the cage where the leopard sat. "I don't care."

He came to the bars and pressed close. She put her hands through and buried them in the soft fur of his flank. His scent was softly musky and comforting. "I'm Cat," she said.

I'm not.

"No, it's my name."

I know. It was a joke, a very bad one. They call me Leonid. But I'm not an animal.

"You look like one. You feel like one."

But I'm not. This isn't my true shape. Can't you tell?

Leonid turned his beautiful head and looked straight at her. Behind his eyes was an intelligent soul. Her mind reeled. Again she felt the press of memories that would not quite enter consciousness.

After a time she said, "So these people aren't human, and you're not a cat."

Any more than you are. You're one of us.

"Who is 'us'?"

You don't yet remember?

"There's nothing to remember!" Frustration made her angry. "I don't know what any of you are talking about!"

His whiskers shivered with a sigh. *We look human but we are ancient. We have been called elves, demons, faerie folk, gods, many other names. We're old beyond the earliest reach of history, princes of the unseen realms. There is no division between us and nature, and our energy is elemental; some of us can still change shape. . . . Cat, you are frowning. I am telling the truth.*

"But I can't believe it," she said. "Or part of me can't; the other part feels as if I already know everything you're saying."

Leonid's tail flicked, and his thoughts poured in faster. *Yes, that's how it was for me. Some of them—the most ancient—have always known what they are. Others, like us, lost our way and our memory, and we thought we were born fully human, surface dwellers . . . but when they come and touch us and remind us, the light goes on inside and then you can never turn it off.*

Intense, suppressed fear radiated from him. He felt more trapped than she did. "What happened to you, Leonid?" She spoke gently, caressing his warm neck.

I don't know. They swept me up, and in the heat of the moment, I changed shape; to please them, to please myself, to prove I could: and now I cannot change back. It happened a long time ago. Now I'm part of the rituals and I play the role.

"Rituals? Is that what they do here? What does it mean?"

If you will let me finish the story: once, the ancient ones lived alongside the surface dwellers and we passed freely in and out of the otherworlds as we desired. Over the centuries, as surface dwellers grew powerful, our freedom dwindled and somehow . . . It must have taken us unawares, as if the world spun a thick cage and closed around us, sealing us like pearls in an oyster. The world changed. New Encomium is our tomb. We must escape or die.

Strange feelings and images were budding inside her. That she felt paradoxically terrified and tranquil at the same time was not due to any drug. It was her nature, her gift. "They can't escape," she said sadly. "No amount of dressing up and chanting will change that."

They're not playacting. They believe they can escape to another world through ritual.

"Magic?"

It would seem so, to surface dwellers.

"Do you believe it?"

The glittering eyes dulled. *I don't know. We must do what's required. Forgive me.*

"What are we?" She clung closer to him, caring only for his life, not her own. The knowledge came from a deep well inside her; not from anything she'd learned on Dika's TV. "We're sacrifices, aren't we? Sacrifices."

On the seventh day, Aurus visited the captive goddess. He found her in calm spirits, sitting cross-legged on her couch, bathed in lamplight that turned her luminous. Each night, a different member of the order had watched over her, and all reported that she'd been docile, calm and watchful throughout her imprisonment. She and Leonid had slept on the floor, hugging each other as best they could through the bars of the cage, the girl whispering into his fur.

"That is as it should be," said Aurus.

He moved to the cage and called, "Cat?"

Her eyes flew open and fixed him, glistening pale green, gathering all available lamplight and beaming it back at him.

"It will be tonight," he said. "I don't ask your forgiveness. You must understand that you are an essential part of this and therefore there can be no way out. But there's no need to be afraid."

She only stared back, unblinking. "I'm not afraid, Cold Prince."

When Cat woke again, the door of her cage stood open. Her couch had been moved and Leonid's cage was empty. The whole basement was bathed in a red-gold glow, and she could not resist the lure of freedom.

As she stepped out, black-clad figures came out of nowhere to claim her. Her robe was taken; Medea and Ginia washed her with scented waters and left her standing there, naked. Chanting swelled, carrying her along, sweeping her into its rhythm. She saw swirls of magical symbols spiraling on the floor, and at the center stood the couch, on fire with the light of lamps and candles.

She felt as she had when they had first drugged her; but this time she was clearheaded, in a trance of her own making. A strong and serpentine power moved within her.

Murmuring as they appeared out of the darkness, the ancient ones came to take her. Female hands held her firmly, turning and easing her backward over the padded couch until she was lying on her back, a sacrifice on a satin altar.

Ginia led the leopard on a chain and he padded forward softly, eyes intent, whiskers scenting her. She did not realize what was meant to happen until the last moment, when he began to rub his silken cheeks along the insides of her thighs, to ply her with his tongue. She felt the briefest pang of shock and protest, gone in an instant. There was nothing to fear; the ritual must take place; and because of that they were more than beasts, more than human.

As he mounted her he looked into her eyes. She saw the trapped soul within the beast, and loved him. *I'm sorry. Trust me.*

She thrust her hands into his fur and let the pleasure and the energy pour through her. They were transported in a fierce golden sphere of energy, god and goddess in union.

Through the fire she was dimly away of the thundering of feet on the floor above them. Faint shouts of, "Police! This is a Difference raid." Visions of terror-frozen customers, of Dika pale and distraught, helpless as the Difference squad searched, kicking down doors until they found their way into the basement, uncovered the juicy red-handed evidence of illegal assembly . . .

But it was all swirling, distant. Cat could hear only her own heartbeat, feel the slight weight of Leonid on her and the waves of pleasure building, piercing her. Her skin burned. In her mind she felt Leonid's climax as well as her own and the ecstasy was intense, unbearable. Inside her, tension broke and she knew who she was; became herself. Fiery lights seared the air. They convulsed together and the world broke open. Green light spilled through a sparkling rent in the air.

The basement door shook. Police dogs bayed.

Aurus and the others were running, crowding through the portal. Leonid and Cat fell off the couch together, scrambled up and followed them.

Silence.

There was a flood of emerald light: the saturated green of trees, misty rain turning the forest to one green veil after another. They stood in a new world; an ancient world. The dew-soaked wildwood around them gleamed with blue light.

"We're home," said Aurus.

Cat looked about for Leonid, couldn't find him. Then she saw something pale unfolding from the ground. A white leopard pelt lay discarded on the ground and a young man stood in front of her, naked and glistening as if newborn.

"Cat," he said, smiling.

"This way," said Aurus. No smile touched his face, but an intense look of triumph sat on the haughty bones. Even Ginia's face had lost its hardness. He strode off and his followers ran after him, dancing and singing, hair flying like banners. Cat and Leonid walked after them.

Where the trees ended there was a steep hillside, a green

landscape beyond, and in the far distance, a silver-blue city glittering. "There is our destination, our home, the ancient towers of—"

"Are you mad?" said Cat.

Aurus turned to stare at her. "Say on."

"You escape one city, only to plunge straight back into another? You can do what you like, but I'm not going there."

"You must." He spoke kindly and sternly, expecting his will to be obeyed as always.

"Why must I?"

"You're part of us now, Cat. You've become our goddess, our muse. We can't let you go."

"You have no choice," she said.

The gray eyes shifted, thoughtful and implacable. "Your ingratitude is amazing, considering that I have just rescued you."

"We rescued *you*!" Cat exclaimed. "You used us! And now you expect gratitude, subservience? Is your name Dika? I've lived all I need of that life. You've got no power over me, Aurus, any of you. I can shed you all like a skin and simply run away."

The Cold Prince continued to glare down upon her, but the look was impotent. "Where to?"

"The wildwood looks inviting. I shall never set foot in a city again."

Aurus had tears in his eyes. One fell, catching the light.

She stepped away, almost dancing as she went. The wet grass trailed over her feet, thrilling. The ancient ones watched, but no one tried to hold her. When Leonid began to follow her, she put a hand to his bare chest and stopped him.

"No," she said sadly, "I can only love you as you were. I don't know you in this shape."

"I'm still the same."

"No. Not without that. She pointed to the glorious white-and-cream bundle of the pelt. "It's up to you."

She felt her own skin turning to silk, her teeth lengthening, every sense sharp and sensuous. The power of her true self surged, sun-bright. Cat plunged into the virgin forest and ran, for the sheer pleasure of running, into the heart of the mystery.

Caitlín R. Kiernan (www.caitlinrkiernan.com) has published four novels: *Silk, Threshold, Low Red Moon,* and, most recently, *Murder of Angels.* Her short fiction has been collected in *Tales of Pain and Wonder, From Weird and Distant Shores, Wrong Things* (with Poppy Z. Brite), and the forthcoming *To Charles Fort, with Love.* Born in Ireland, she now lives in Atlanta, Georgia, where she often dreams of genetic augmentation.

FACES IN REVOLVING SOULS

by Caitlín R. Kiernan

The woman named Sylvia, who might as well still be a child, is waiting for the elevator that will carry her from the twenty-third floor of the hotel—down, down, down like a sinking stone—to the lobby and convention registration area. She isn't alone in the hallway, though she wishes that she were. There are several others waiting to sink with her—a murmuring, laughing handful of stitches and meat dolls busy showing off the fact that they're not new at this, that they belong here, busy making sure that Sylvia knows they can see just exactly how birthblank she is. Not quite a virgin, no, but the next worst thing, and all that pink skin to give her away, the pink skin and the silverblue silk dress with its sparkling Mandarin collar, the black espadrilles on her feet. The others are all naked, for the most part, and Sylvia keeps her head down, her eyes trained on the toes of her shoes, because the sight of them reflected in the polished elevator doors makes her heart race and her mouth go dry.

No one knows I'm here, she thinks again, relishing the simple nervous delight she feels whenever she imagines her mother or sisters or someone at work discovering that she lied to them all about going to Mexico, and where she's gone instead. She knows that if they knew, if they ever found out, they'd want explanations. And that if she ever tried to explain, they'd do their best to have her locked away, or worse. There's still a multitude of psychiatrists who consider polymorphy a sickness, and politicians who consider it a crime, and priests who consider it blasphemy.

A bell hidden somewhere in the wall rings and the elevator doors slide silently open. Sylvia steps quickly into the empty elevator, and the others follow her—the woman who is mostly a leopard, the fat man with thick brown fur and eyes like a raven, the pretty teenage girl with stubby antlers and skin the color of ripe cranberries—all of them filing in one by one, like the passengers of some lunatic Noah's ark. Sylvia stands all the way at the rear, her back turned to them, and stares out through the transparent wall as the elevator falls and the first floor of the hotel swiftly rises up to meet her. It stops only once on the way down, at the fourth floor, and she doesn't turn to see who or what gets on. It's much too warm inside the elevator, and the air smells like sweat and musk and someone's lavender-scented perfume.

"Yes, of course," the leopard says to the antlered girl with cranberry skin. "But this will be the first time I've ever seen her in person." The leopard lisps and slurs when she speaks, human vocal cords struggling with a rough feline tongue, with a mouth that has been rebuilt for purposes other than talking.

"First time, I saw her at Berkeley," the antlered girl replies. "And then again at Chimera last year."

"You were at Chimera last year?" someone asks, sounding surprised and maybe even skeptical; Sylvia thinks it must be whoever got on at the fourth floor, because she hasn't heard this sexless voice before. "I made it down for the last two days. You were there?"

"Yeah, I was there," the girl says. "But you probably wouldn't remember me. That was back before my dermals started to show."

"And *all* the girls are growing antlers these days," the leopard lisps, and everyone laughs, all of them except Sylvia. None of them sound precisely human anymore, and their strange, bestial laughter is almost enough to make Sylvia wish that she'd stayed home, almost enough to convince her that she's in over her head, drowning, and maybe she isn't ready for this, after all.

Another secret bell rings and the doors slide open again, releasing them into the brightly lit lobby. First in, so last out, and Sylvia has to squeeze through the press of incoming bodies, the people who'd been waiting for the elevator. She says "Excuse me," and "Pardon me," and tries not to look anyone in the eye or notice the particulars of their chosen metamorphoses.

Fera is waiting for her, standing apart from the rest, standing with her long arms crossed; she smiles when she sees Sylvia, showing off her broad canines. There's so little left of Fera that anyone would bother calling human, and the sight of her—the mismatched, improbable beauty of her—always leaves Sylvia lost and fumbling for words. Fera is one of the old-timers, an elder-changeling, one of the twenty-five signatories on the original Provisional Proposition for Posthuman Secession.

"I was afraid you might have missed your flight," she says, and Sylvia knows that what she really means is, *I was afraid you'd chickened out*. Fera's voice is not so slurred or difficult to understand as the leopard's. She's had almost a decade to learn the mechanics of her new mandibular and lingual musculature, years to adapt to her altered tongue and palate.

"I just needed to unpack," Sylvia tells her. "I can't stand leaving my suitcases packed."

"I have some friends in the bar who would like to meet you," Fera purrs. "I've been telling them about your work."

"Oh," Sylvia whispers, because she hadn't expected that and doesn't know what else to say.

"Don't worry, Syl. They know you're still a neophyte. They're not expecting a sphinx."

Sylvia nods her head and glances back toward the elevator. The doors have closed again, and there's only her reflection staring back at her. *I look terrified,* she thinks. *I look like someone who wants to run.*

"Did you forget something?" Fera asks, and takes a step toward Sylvia. The thick pads of her paws are silent on the carpet, but the hundreds of long quills that sprout from her shoulders and back, from her arms and the sides of her face, rustle like dry autumn leaves.

"No," Sylvia says, not at all sure whether or not she's telling the truth.

"I know you're nervous. It's only natural."

"But I feel like such a fool," Sylvia replies, and then she laughs a laugh that has no humor in it at all, a sound almost as dry as the noise of Fera's quills.

"Hey, you should have seen me, back in the day. I was a goddamn basket case," and Fera takes both her hands, as Sylvia turns to face her again. "It's a long road, and sometimes the first steps are the most difficult."

Sylvia looks down at Fera's hands, her nails grown to sharp, retractable claws, her skin showing black as an oil spill where it isn't covered in short auburn fur. Though she still has thumbs, there are long dewclaws sprouting from her wrists. Sylvia knows how much those hands would scare most people, how they would horrify all the blanks still clinging to their illusions of inviolable, immutable humanity. But they make her feel safe, and she holds them tight and forces a smile for Fera.

"Well, we don't want to keep your friends waiting," Sylvia says.

"It's bad enough, me showing up wearing all these damned clothes. I don't want them to think I'm rude in the bargain."

Fera laughs, a sound that's really more like barking, and she kisses Sylvia lightly on her left cheek. "You just try to relax, *m'enfante trouvée*. And trust me. They're absolutely gonna love—" But then someone interrupts her, another leopard, a pudgy boy cat clutching a tattered copy of *The Children of Artemis*, which Fera signs for him. And she listens patiently to the questions he asks, all of which could have been answered with a quick Internet search. Sylvia pretends not to eavesdrop on an argument between one of the hotel staff and a woman with crocodile skin, and when the leopard boy finally stops talking, Fera leads Sylvia away from the crowded elevators toward one of the hotel's bars.

And this is before—before the flight from Detroit to LAX, before the taxi ride to the hotel in Burbank. This is before the bad dreams she had on the plane, before the girl with cranberry skin, before the elevator's controlled fall from the twenty-third floor of the Marriott. This is a night and an hour and a moment from a whole year before Fera Delacroix takes her hand and leads her out of the lobby to the bar where there are people waiting to meet her.

"What's *this*?" her mother asks in the same sour, accusatory tone she's wielded all of Sylvia's life. And Sylvia, who's just come home from work and has a migraine, stares at the scatter of magazines and pamphlets lying on the dining table in front of her, trying to make sense of the question and all the glossy, colorful paper. Trying to think through the pain and the sudden, sick fear coiled cold and tight in her gut.

"I asked you a question, Sylvia," her mother says. "What are you doing with this crap?"

And Sylvia opens her mouth to reply, but her tongue doesn't

want to cooperate. Down on the street, she can hear the traffic, and the distant rumble of a skipjet somewhere far overhead, and the sleepy drone of the refrigerator from the next room.

"I want an answer," her mother says and taps the cover of an issue of *Genshift* with her right index finger.

"Where did you get those?" Sylvia asks finally, but her voice seems farther away than the skipjet's turbines. "You've been in my room again, haven't you?"

"This is my house, young lady, and I'm asking you the questions," her mother growls, growling like a pit bull, like something mean and hungry straining at its fraying leash. "What are you doing with all this sick shit?"

And the part of Sylvia's mind that knows how to lie, the part that keeps her secrets safe and has no problem saying whatever needs to be said, takes over, and, "It's one of my stories," she says, trying hard to sound indignant, instead of frightened. "It's all just research. I brought it home last week—"

"Bullshit. Since when does the agency waste time with this kind of deviant crap?" her mother demands, and she taps the magazine again. On the cover, there's a nude woman with firm brown nipples and the gently curved, corkscrew horns of an impala.

"Just because you don't happen to approve of the changelings doesn't mean they aren't news," Sylvia tells her, and hastily begins gathering up all the pamphlets and magazines. "Do you have any idea how many people have had some sort of interspecific genetic modification over the last five years?"

"Are you a goddamn lesbian?" her mother asks, and Sylvia catches the smell of gin on her breath.

"What?"

"They're all a bunch of queers and perverts," her mother mumbles, and then snatches one of the Fellowship of Posthuman Evolutionists pamphlets from Sylvia's hands. "If this is supposed to be work for the agency, why'd you have to go and hide it all under your bed?"

"I wasn't *hiding* anything, Mother, and this isn't any of your business." And Sylvia yanks the pamphlet back from her mother. "How many times have I asked you to stay out of my room?"

"It's *my* house, and—"

"That, means I have no privacy?"

"No ma'am. Not if it means you bringing this smut into my house."

"Jesus, it's for *work*. You want to call Mr. Padgett right now and have him tell you the same damned thing?" And there, it's out before she thinks better of pushing the lie that far, pushing it as far as it'll go, and there's no taking it back again.

"I ought to do that, young lady. You bet. That's *exactly* what I ought to do."

"So do it and leave me alone. You know the number."

"Don't you think I won't."

"I have work to do before dinner," Sylvia says as calmly as she can manage, turning away from her mother, beginning to wonder if she'll make it upstairs before she throws up. "I have a headache, and I really don't need you yelling at me right now."

"Don't think that I *won't* call. I'm a Christian woman and I don't want that filth under my roof, you understand me, Sylvia?"

She doesn't reply, because there's nothing left to be said, and the cold knot in her belly has started looking for a way out, the inevitable path of least resistance. She takes her briefcase and the magazines and heads for the hallway and the stairs leading away from her mother. *Just keep walking,* she thinks. *Whatever else she says, don't even turn around. Don't say anything else to her. Not another word. Don't give her the satisfaction—*

"I know all about those people," her mother mumbles. "They're *filth,* you understand? *All* of them. Every single, god-damned one."

And then she's on the stairs, and her footsteps on the varnished wood are louder than her mother's voice. She takes them two at a time, almost running to the top, and locks her bedroom door behind her. Sylvia hurls the stack of changeling literature to the floor in a violent flutter of pages, and the antelope girl's large, dark eyes gaze blamelessly back up at her. She sits down with her back against the door, not wanting to cry but crying anyway, crying because at least it's better than vomiting. And later—after her first three treatments at the Lycaon Clinic in Chicago, after the flight to L.A., after Fera Delacroix takes her hand and leads her into the murmur and half-light of the hotel bar—she'll understand that *this* afternoon, this moment, was her turning point. She'll look back and see clearly that this is the day she knew what she would do, no matter how much it terrified her, and no matter what it would mean, in the end.

They sit in a corner of the crowded, noisy bar, two tables pulled together to make room for everyone, this perfect, unreal menagerie. Sylvia sits to the left of Fera, sipping at a watery Coke. Fera's already introduced her to them all, a heady mix of changeling minor royalty and fellow travelers, and Sylvia has been sitting quietly for the last fifteen minutes, listening to them talk, trying to memorize their names, trying not to stare.

"It's a damned dangerous precedent," the man sitting directly across from her says. He has the night-seeing eyes of a python, and he drums his long claws nervously against the top of the table. His name is Maxwell White and he's a geneticist at Johns-Hopkins. Her last year in college, Sylvia read his book, *Looking for Moreau: A Posthumanist Manifesto*. It's made the American Library Association's list of most frequently banned books seven years straight.

"What the hell," Fera says. "I figure, it's just fucking Nebraska."

Maxwell White stops drumming his fingers and sighs, his long ears going flat against the sides of his skull. "Sure, this year it's just fucking Nebraska. But, the way things are headed, next year it's going to be Nebraska and Alabama and Utah and—"

"We can't afford to be elitists," says a woman with iridescent scales that shimmer faintly in the dim light. As she talks, the tip of her blue forked tongue flicks across her lips; Sylvia can't recall her name, only that she was recently fired from Duke University. "Not anymore. That asshole De Vries and his army of zealots is getting more press than the war."

"Oh, come on. It's not *that* bad," Fera says, and frowns.

"How bad does it have to be?" Maxwell White asks, and starts drumming his claws again. "Where do you think this is going to stop? After these anticrossbreeding laws are in place and people get used to the idea that it's acceptable to restrict who we can and can't marry, who we can fuck, how long do you think it's going to take before we start seeing laws preventing us from voting or owning property or—"

"Maybe that's what we get for signing a declaration of secession from the human race," Fera replies, and Maxwell White makes an angry snorting sound.

"Jesus Christ, Fera, sometimes I wonder which side you're on."

"All I'm saying is, I'm not so sure we can realistically expect to have it both ways. We tell them we're not the same as them anymore, that, by choice, each of us will exist as our own separate species, and then we act surprised when they want to treat us like animals."

"De Vries has already started talking about concentration camps," a woman named Alex Singleton says; she glances apprehensively at Fera and then quickly back down at the napkin she's been folding and unfolding for the past ten minutes. Alex Singleton has the striped, blond fur of a tiger-lion hybrid, and six perfectly formed breasts. "Are you still going to be talking like this when they start rounding us up and locking us in cages?" she asks, and unfolds the napkin again.

"That's never going to happen," Fera replies, and scowls at Alex Singleton. "I'm not saying there aren't a lot of scary people out there. Of course there are. We've just given the bigots and xenophobes something new to hate, that's all. We knew there'd be a difficult adjustment period, didn't we?"

"You have the most sublime knack for understatement." Maxwell White laughs.

And then Fera turns to Sylvia and smiles, that smile so beautiful that it's enough to make her dizzy, to make her blush, and, "You're awfully quiet over here, Syl. What do you think of all this? You think we're all about to be rounded up and herded off to a zoo?"

"I'm afraid I've never been much for politics," Sylvia says, not meaning to whisper, but her voice is almost lost in the din of the bar. "I mean, I don't guess I've thought much about it."

"Of course she hasn't," Alex Singleton mutters. "Look at her. She still wears clothes. She's pink as—"

"I think maybe what Alex is trying to say, in her own indelicate way," the woman with iridescent scales interrupts, "is that you're probably going to find the political ramifications of our little revolution will suddenly seem a lot more important to you, once you start showing."

"That's not at all what I was trying to say."

"Some of us forget they were ever blank," Fera says, glaring at Alex Singleton, and she stirs at her martini with an olive skewered on a tiny plastic cutlass.

The thin man sitting next to Maxwell White clears his throat and waves at Sylvia with a hand that's really more of a paw. "Fera tells us you're one of Collier's patients," he says, speaking very slowly, his lupine jaws and tongue struggling with the words. "He's a good man."

"I'm very happy with him," Sylvia replies, and takes another sip of her Coke.

"He did my second stage," the wolf man confides, and his black lips draw back in a snarl, exposing sharp yellow canines and incisors. It takes Sylvia a moment to realize that the man's smiling.

"So," Maxwell White says, leaning toward her, "what's *your* story, Sylvia?"

"Like Fera said, I'm a journalist, and I'm preparing to write a book on the history—"

"No, that's not what I'm asking you."

"I'm sorry. I guess I didn't understand the question."

"Apparently."

"Max here is one-third complete bastard," Fera says, and jabs an ebony thumb at Maxwell White. "It was a tricky bit of bio-engineering, but the results are a wonder to behold." Half the people at the two tables laugh out loud, and Sylvia is beginning to wish that she'd stayed in her room, that she'd never let Fera Delacroix talk her into coming to Burbank in the first place.

"Is it some sort of secret, what you're hiding under that dress?" Maxwell White asks, and Sylvia shakes her head.

"No," she says. "It's not a secret. I mean—"

"Then what's the problem?"

"Back off just a little, Max," Fera says, and the man with python eyes nods his head and shrugs.

"He does this to everyone, almost," Alex Singleton says, and begins to shred her napkin. "He did it to me."

"It's not a secret," Sylvia says again. "I just—"

"You don't have to tell anyone here anything you're not ready to tell them, Syl," Fera assures her, and kisses her cheek. Fera Delacroix's breath smells like vodka and olives. "You *know* that."

"It's just that none of *us* are wearing masks," Maxwell White says. "You might have noticed that."

"Excuse me, please," Sylvia says, suddenly close to tears and her heart beating like the wings of a small and terrified bird trapped deep inside her chest. She stands up too fast, bumps the table hard with her right knee, and almost spills her drink.

"You're a son of a bitch," Fera growls at Maxwell White, and she bares her teeth. "I hope you know that."

"No, really, it's okay," Sylvia says, forcing an unconvincing smile. "I'm fine. I understand, and I'm fine. I just need some fresh air, that's all."

And then she leaves them all sitting there in the shadows, murmuring and laughing among themselves. Sylvia doesn't look back, concentrates instead on the sound of her espadrilles against the wide stone tiles, and she makes it almost all the way to the elevators before Fera catches up with her.

On the plane, somewhere high above the Rockies and streaking toward Los Angeles through clearing, nightbound skies, Sylvia drifts between the velvet and gravel folds of dream sleep. She dozed off with the volume setting on her tunejack pushed far enough toward max that the noise of the flight attendants and the other passengers and the skipjet's turbines wouldn't wake her. So there's only Beethoven's Sixth Symphony getting in from the outside, and the voices inside her head. She's always hated flying, and took two of the taxicab-yellow placidmil capsules her therapist prescribed after her first treatment gave her insomnia.

In the nightmare, she stands alone on the crumbling bank of a sluggish, muddy river washed red as blood by the setting sun. She doesn't know the name of the city rising up around her, and suspects that it has no name. Only dark and empty windows, skyscrapers like broken teeth, the ruins of bridges that long ago carried the city's vanished inhabitants from one side of the wide red river to the other.

The river is within us, the sea is all about us, and isn't that what

Matthew Arnold wrote, or T. S. Eliot, or Maharshi Ramakrishna, or some other long-dead man? Sylvia takes a step nearer the river, and a handful of earth tumbles into the water. The ripples spread out from the shore, until the current pulls them apart.

Behind her, something has begun to growl—a low and threatful sound, the sound of something that might tear her apart in an instant. She glances over her shoulder, but there's only the buckled, abandoned street behind her and then the entrance to an alleyway. It's already midnight in the alley, and she knows that the growling thing is waiting for her there, where it has always waited for her. She turns back to the river, because the thing in the alley is patient and the swollen crimson sun is still clinging stubbornly to the western horizon.

And now she sees that it's not the sunset painting the river red, but the blood of the dead and dying creatures drowning in the rising waters. The river devours their integrity, wedding one to the other, flesh to flesh, bone to bone. In another moment, there's only a single strangling organism, though a thousand pairs of eyes stare back at her in agony and horror, and two thousand hearts bleed themselves dry through a million ruptured veins.

And the way up is the way down; the way forward is the way back.

Countless talons and fingers, flippers and fins tear futilely at the mud and soft earth along the river's edge, but all are swept away. And when the sun has gone, Sylvia turns to face the alley, and the growling thing that is her life, and wakes to the full moon outside the skipjet's window.

"You can't expect more of them," Fera says. "Not more than you expect of the straights, not just because they're going through the same thing you are."

"None of us are going through the same thing," Sylvia replies, not caring whether or not Fera hears the bitterness in her voice.

"We're all going through this alone. Every one of us is alone, just like White said in his book. Every one of us is a species of one."

"I think you expect too much," Fera says, and then the elevator has reached the twenty-third floor, and the hidden bell rings, and the doors slide silently open. Sylvia steps out into the hall.

"Please promise me you won't spend the whole weekend locked in your room," Fera says. "At least come back down for Circe Seventeen's panel at eight, and—"

"Yeah," Sylvia says as the doors slide shut again. "Sure. I'll see you there," and she follows the hallway back to her room.

Sylvia is standing in front of the long bathroom mirror, her skin tinted a pale and sickly green by the buzzing fluorescent light. She's naked, except for the gauze bandages and flesh-tone dermapad patches on her belly and thighs. The hot water is running, and the steam has begun to fog the mirror. She leans forward and wipes away some of the condensation.

"There's always a risk of rejection," Dr. Collier said, and that was more than three weeks ago now, her third trip to the Lycaon Clinic. "You understood that before we began. There's always the risk of a violate retrovirus, especially when the transcription in question involves nonamniote DNA."

And of course she'd understood. He'd told her everything, all the risks and qualifying factors explained in detail long before her first treatment. Everyone always understands until they're the one unlucky fuck in a thousand.

No one ever lied to me, she thinks, but there's no consolation whatsoever in the thought.

In places, the bandages are stained and stiff with the discharge of her infections. Sylvia dries her hands on a clean white washcloth, then begins to slowly remove the dermapad just below her navel. The adhesive strips around the edges come away with bits of dead skin and dried blood still attached.

"I'm not going to lie to you," Dr. Collier said, the first time they met. "Even now, with all we know and everything that we've been able to accomplish in the last fifty years, what you want is very, very dangerous. And if something does go wrong, there's very little hope of turning back." And then she'd signed all the documents stating that he'd told her these things, and that she understood the perils and uncertainty, and that she was submitting to the procedures of her own free will.

She takes a deep breath and stares back at herself from the mirror, the sweat on her face to match the steam on the glass, and drops the dermapad into the sink. It stains the water a dark reddish brown. And her mother, and all the faces from the bar—Maxwell White and Alex Singleton and all the rest—seem to hover somewhere just behind her. They smirk and shake their heads, just in case she's forgotten that the rest of the world always knew she was weak and that, in the end, she'd get exactly what she's always had coming to her.

I know all about those people. They're filth, you understand? All of them. Every single, goddamned one.

The rubbery violet flesh beneath her navel is swollen and marbled with pustules and open sores. The tip of a stillborn tentacle, no longer than her index finger, hangs lifeless from her belly. Dr. Collier wanted to amputate it, but she wouldn't let him.

"I hate like hell to say it, but he's right," Fera Delacroix told her, after the scene in the hotel bar, while they were waiting for an elevator. "You *can't* keep it a secret forever, Syl. What you're doing, what everyone here this weekend is doing, it's about finally being honest about ourselves. I know that doesn't necessarily make it easy, but it's the truth."

"No," Sylvia says, gently touching the dead tentacle. "*This* is the truth." She presses her finger into one of the tiny, stalked suckers, teasing the sharp hook at the center. "I think this is all the truth I need."

She cleans the cancerous flesh and covers it with a fresh dermapad, then peels off one of the patches on her left thigh and repeats the process. It takes her more than an hour to wash and dress all the lesions, and when she's done, when all those dying parts of her that are no longer precisely human have been hidden behind their sterile masks, she shuts off the water and gets dressed. She still has time for a light dinner before Circe Seventeen's talk on the link between shamanism and the origins of posthumanism, and Sylvia knows that if she isn't there, Fera Delacroix will come looking for her.

Jack Ketchum is the author of *Off Season, Hide and Seek, Cover, The Girl Next Door, She Wakes, Offspring, Joyride* (aka *Road Kill*), *Stranglehold* (aka *Only Child*), *Red, Ladies' Night, Right to Life, The Lost* and *The Crossings*. His short fiction has twice won the Bram Stoker Award and is collected in *The Exit at Toledo Blade Boulevard, Broken on the Wheel of Sex,* and *Peaceable Kingdom.* His cats are Zoey, Cujo, George, and Gracie. Say good night, Gracie.

LIGHTEN UP

by Jack Ketchum

It was about eleven thirty and Adoni was messing with the lighting again.

The lighting was track lighting, and he was forever adjusting it slightly downward. Up a little here, down a little there, but mostly down. By ten or so it was nearly impossible to read the menu. The consensus among us was that that was the idea. He wasn't making the place any more romantic. He was making it cavernous. You couldn't read, you couldn't order. Time to go home.

Joe, Michael, Robert, Amy and I were all a little drunk, so we didn't mind the gloom. Gert was already so far gone she could barely talk, and when she did talk you had no reason to listen to her. Behind the bar Stella kept pouring. The music was so familiar we could probably have sung along without knowing a single word of Greek.

Night at the Santorini.

The conversation had descended into rarely known facts. Or maybe *barely known facts* was more appropriate, because you could bet that some of this was bullshit. Sure, an ostrich's eye is bigger than its brain, and butterflies taste with their feet. But is it *really* impossible to sneeze with your eyes open?

I needed proof on that one. Unfortunately none of us had allergies.

"Okay, did you know that 'stewardesses' is the longest word you can type using only your left hand and 'lollipop' the longest using your right?"

Michael was a writer, so we had to believe him there.

"And that the average person's *left* hand does most of the typing?"

"Nah, why would that be?" said Joe.

Joe worked with computers all day, setting up online systems for hotels and motels, so he'd logged in plenty of time at the keyboard himself.

"Dunno. Just is."

"Even if you're right-handed?"

"Yep."

"Doesn't make sense."

"Palindromes," said Robert. He sipped his beer. It was probably his seventh.

"What?"

"Palindromes. Racecar. Kayak. Level."

"What the hell's he talking about?" said Amy.

Robert tended to be strange and mysterious now and then, so you never knew.

"They're the same whether you write them right to left, or left to right," said Michael. "That's what he means."

"Thassright," said Robert. "Palindromes."

"What's that got to do with your left hand doing most of the typing?" said Joe.

"Absolutely nothing."

" 'The quick brown fox jumped over the lazy dog,' uses every letter in the alphabet," said Amy. "We learned that back in typing class. And you know what else? There's no Betty Rubble in Flintstones chewable vitamins."

"Jesus wept," said Joe.

He looked at me. "I need a smoke," he said. "You ready?"

"I'm gonna wait awhile. Finish my scotch. It's fuckin' cold out there."

"I know it's fuckin' cold out there." He was already putting on his coat.

"Fuckin' *cold* out there," said Gert.

We ignored her.

"Amy?" said Joe.

"I'll wait."

"Michael?"

"Same here."

"Fuckin' Bloomberg," said Joe.

"You got that right," I said.

"Fuckin' Bloomberg!" said Gert.

It was practically a mantra by now. *Fuckin' Bloomberg.* Since the smoking ban in New York City bars, we citizens who favored our tar and nicotine had to step outside evenings for a smoke, and now the weather had turned cold on us. Bloomberg was going to freeze our little subculture to death if had his way.

Even those of us regulars who didn't smoke hated the son of a bitch, if only for interrupting our conversation.

I watched him drift out the door. Behind him a couple from the tables was leaving too. The tables were empty now, in fact, except for one other couple by the far right window. The only patrons of Santorini were the two of them, us down at the far end of the bar, two young Spanish guys at the front end hitting on a lovely young brunette who seemed to like their attention and a pair of yuppie types—a man and a woman, probably in their mid-thirties—talking earnestly about something or other in between. I saw Joe's match flare and die behind the plate glass.

"Babies are born without kneecaps," said Robert.

"Really?"

"Really. You don't develop them until you're about two or something."

"So if you want to get in trouble with the mob," I said, "the thing to do is to do it *early*."

"Exactly."

"No word in the English language rhymes with 'month,' " said Michael.

"*Dunth,*" lisped Robert.

"Or 'orange.' "

"Porridge," said Robert.

"Doesn't count," I said. "No *ng* sound."

"Or 'silver.' "

"Hi-ho to that!"

"Or 'purple.' "

"*Sphurpable*. Like Amy."

"You really are a *dunth*," said Amy.

We listened to the music for a while.

The door opened and it wasn't Joe but some other guy, heavy-set, in a woolen coat much too thin for the weather. He sat down between us and the yuppies. He looked half-frozen and rubbed his bare hands together vigorously, smiled and ordered a Heineken. Stella set the bottle down in front of him along with the frozen mug the guy obviously didn't much need. He poured anyway, took a sip and set it down. Then he fished in his pocket and came out with a pack of Winstons and a clear plastic lighter. He lit up.

"Check this out," I said.

And then it was *eyes left* for all of us.

It took the yuppies a couple of puffs to get a whiff of it. Concerned glances were exchanged. Looks of disgust. It was the woman—not the guy she was with—who finally stepped up to the plate.

"Excuse me? Sir? You can't smoke in here," she said. "It's against the law."

"Uh-huh."

"Sir?"

The Spanish guys had noticed too. "She's right, man," said the taller of the two, "I could care less, you know? But you get busted, man. You get *fined*. All that bullshit."

"Please put that out," she said. "It's against the law."

"You already said that." He took another drag. *Slowly*.

Adoni stepped in from the kitchen. Like most Greeks he was a smoker too, but he had no choice. He was manager. He did his job.

"I'm sorry, but you will have to put that out, my friend," he said. "It's the law."

"Okay," said the guy.

He dropped the butt and stepped on it.

Good choice, I thought. Adoni didn't have a mean bone in his body but he'd been Greek army in Afghanistan. He was big. He had a grip that could bruise mahogany, and though he didn't use it often you wouldn't want to cross him.

"You are from out of town?" he said.

"Nope. Lower East Side. Just wanted to see what you folks'd do." He drank his beer and smiled. "I'm with CLASH. We're doing this all over town."

"Clash?"

"Citizens Lobbying Against Smoking Harassment."

"Ah, yes, I see. You lobby for smoking. I wish you a very good night, sir. But on this?—you must wait. Enjoy yourself."

"Thank you."

"CLASH, huh?" I said. "I've heard of it."

"Lawsuits," said Robert. "That's the ticket."

"We're filing them. Plus a little guerrilla theater now and then, if you know what I mean."

He winked at us and smiled.

"We wish you all the luck in the world, sir."

Robert raised his glass to the guy. We all did—with the exception of Gert, who was wearing a puzzled expression. As though we'd all turned to Steuben glass figures suddenly and she couldn't for the life of her understand how or why.

Joe came back in, and the yuppie made a face as he passed her. I guess she noticed he'd been smoking. ". . . bet his mouth smells like an ashtray . . ." I heard her mutter. I guess I was the only one who did. It got a smile out of her partner.

But she was beginning to piss me off.

"I'm Jerzy," I said, and offered my hand to the CLASH guy. "This is Joe, Robert, Amy and Michael."

I didn't bother with Gert. Gert was puzzled.

"I'm Art," he said. We shook hands all around.

I saw that the table was paying Stella. She moved off to get them change. The Spanish guys had already settled up with Stella and they were smiling, herding the pretty young brunette out the door. I judged her slightly sloshed. One of them just might get lucky tonight if they didn't both blow it with too much eager competition.

I ordered another scotch. So did Joe and Michael. Amy finished her red wine and ordered another. Robert was still sipping his beer. He licked the foam off his mustache. The CLASH guy, Art, asked for another Heineken. The couple beside us ordered too—theirs was the house white. Of course it was.

Stella poured, quickly and efficiently. You had to love the woman.

"I got one for you," said Joe. "Thought of it outside. Did you know that Al Capone's business card said he was a used-furniture dealer?"

"I did not," said Robert.

"Did you know that our eyes stay exactly the same size from birth," said Amy, "but our noses and ears never stop growing?"

"I did not," said Robert.

Maybe that was why Gert was looking at us so strangely. Maybe she was watching our ears grow.

"Did you know that Adoni has just locked the front door?" said Michael.

It was true. The couple from the table had just stepped out the door and Adoni'd locked it behind them. He was walking toward us, smiling, digging in his shirt pocket.

"If you got them, light them," he said.

He put a cigarette in his mouth, walked by us and disappeared in the back.

I lit up. Michael and Amy lit up. Art lit up. Joe lit up even though he'd only just had one. Robert didn't smoke. Gert fumbled around in her pocketbook for a while and then even she managed it.

The couple beside us looked aghast—like they'd maybe seen a ghost. The ghost of barrooms past.

"I don't believe this," said the guy.

"You realize this is against the law?" said the woman.

There it was—the law again. The woman was obsessed.

"A man's bar is his castle," said Robert.

"This is a public space," the man said. "There are staff here. Waitresses, cooks, busboys. Not to mention how rude this is to us."

"He's gonna mention secondhand smoke any minute," said Joe to me sotto voce.

"Secondhand smoke has been proven to—"

"I told ya," said Joe.

"Secondhand smoke!" said Gert. "That's right." There was lipstick on her Virginia Slim.

"We have every right to demand you put them out right away," said the woman.

"That's right," said Art. "You do."

"Then in that case would you please put them out right away?"

"Sorry, but no," Michael said.

Adoni walked in. You could hear his pockets jingling. There was a Marlboro fired up in the corner of his mouth.

"There is a problem?" he said.

"We've asked these people to put their cigarettes out and I'll ask you to do the same. This is outrageous! Does the owner know about this?"

"The owner is Greek." He shrugged. "A smoker, sorry to say."

"We have just ordered drinks. We have every right to be able to drink our drinks in peace without having to deal with smoke being blown in our faces."

"Face away from the smoke, then. This is the solution."

"Don't you get it?" said the man. "We could have you *closed down* for this!"

"I don't think so. For first offense, they fine you."

"*Fined*, then."

"I don't think so."

He took the handcuffs out of his pocket, snapped one on the guy's right wrist and the other to the shiny brass bar rail. The guy barely knew what hit him. His lady friend slid off the bar stool, purse in hand, with the clear intent of heading for the door away from all these lunatics, but Amy was there in front of her and so was I, and Adoni made short work of cuffing her to the rail too. He seated them both back down.

We knew the drill pretty well by then, so Amy went through the woman's purse for her wallet while I dug his out of his inside jacket pocket. I handed it to Michael, more for show of solidarity than anything else. He read off the driver's license.

"James Wade Holt," he said. "Hey, you're a neighbor! One seventy-five West Sixty-ninth Street."

Amy was reading the woman's. She shook her head.

"They don't live together," she said. "This one's Thirty-three West Forty-eighth Street—Hell's Kitchen. Joanna Bowen."

"Why do we have a tendency not to give women middle names in this country?" said Robert. "I've always wondered about that. This one's James Wade Holt and this one's just plain Joanna. Doesn't seem fair."

"No, it doesn't," Joe said.

"What . . . what are you doing? What are you going to do to us?" said James Wade Holt.

The woman said nothing, only looked around anxiously from face to face.

"Did you know a dragonfly has a life span of only twenty-four hours?" said Michael.

"I did not," said Robert.

"Stella? Give me a check pad, please," said Adoni.

She handed him the pad. We handed him the wallets. He took a pen out of his shirt pocket and opened them and started writing. The place was totally silent. Somebody—probably Stella—had turned off the bouzouki music. When he was finished he closed the wallets up again and put them on the bar.

"First of all," he said. "You will not report this. You see, I have your names and addresses. I will make copies for all my friends here so that they will have them too. You do not have *their* names or addresses, however. So if anything should happen to me or to the restaurant Santorini, they will know where to find you. In a moment I will release you and you will finish your glasses of wine and you will each have another, on me, on the house. We will smoke because that is what smokers do and you will not complain. You will be our guests."

"A crocodile," said Robert, "cannot stick out its tongue."

"What if we simply want to leave?" said just plain Joanna. "I mean, what if James and I—"

"You will not leave until we say so. We have done this many times, you see. Do not think you are the first to act as you have acted and be inconvenienced for it. If you had simply said nothing and walked away thinking, *Live and let live*, then fine. But you did not. You will not be harmed but you will endure what we have had to endure and feel like a second-class citizen in your own city. It may make you angry. It makes *us* angry. But that is life, no? And when you leave here you can forget all about this. A goldfish, after all, has a memory span of approximately three seconds."

He unlocked the cuffs.

"Enjoy yourselves," he said. "I will go and Xerox the copies."

"You guys are amazing," said Art. He laughed. "I'm putting this little tactic up on the Web site."

"No names, no places," I said.

"Goes without saying."

"Not a single study, by the way, has validated the claim that secondhand smoke can be dangerous to humans," said Robert. "What *is* certain is that your clothes are going to stink a little. Mine always do. But hell, what are friends for?"

The couple said nothing. They sipped their drinks. I saw that the woman's hands were still shaking. I didn't mind.

"Did you know that cats have over a hundred vocal sounds, and dogs only around ten?" he said.

"Ten!" said Gert. "Ten dogs!"

Our personal captivity wore on.

Elizabeth Massie is a two-time Stoker Award–winning author. Her books include *Sineater, Welcome Back to the Night, Wire Mesh Mothers, Dark Shadows: Dreams of the Dark, Shadow Dreams, The Fear Report*, and more. Her story "Fence Line" will appear in the upcoming *Joe Lansdale's Lords of the Razor*. Her tale "Pisspot Bay" will be included in *The Last Pentacle of the Sun: Writings in Support of the West Memphis Three*. Massie has also authored numerous historical novels for young adults, and she is the creator of the *Skeeryvilletown* series of cartoon monsters. She lives in Virginia with illustrator Cortney Skinner.

PIT BOY

by Elizabeth Massie

Erik grunted in the shadows to my right, cussed, and then grunted again. I couldn't see his face, only the rough outline of his hunched-up body. I didn't care that I couldn't really see him. He was an asshole, and ugly, too, with fucked-up buckteeth and a nose that looked like an old potato gone bad. Erik didn't like to shoot the shit like the rest of us did, and most of the time just grunted or cussed or talked to hisself. Occasionally he spit big old wet loogies in my direction. He blamed me for everything wrong in his life, but fuck it, it wasn't my fault. It was his mom's fault for being who she was, not that getting pissed was going to make any difference. My mom was pretty much the same, but you didn't hear me complaining. Erik was a damned baby.

"Rob," Chuck called from my left. I glanced over as he was lighting a cigarette. The match flame revealed his sharp chin, the stubble on his lip, the droopy eyelids over brown eyes. Then he shook the match and the sight was gone, leaving only the meteor trail of the cig as he drew in on it, took it from his mouth, and then swung it back and forth to watch the glow. Over Chuck's shoulder was a faint rectangle—a window in the wall near the ceiling. Most of the time at night there was only navy blue in the rectangle, but when Ricky hosted a party, there would be flashes of headlights through the window as guests arrived, stroking the floor like spotlights at some old-fashioned movie premiere. I fucking loved party nights.

"What, Charlie?" I asked.

"You got them weights? Gimme 'em."

I picked up the silvered fifteen-pound hand weights from the floor next to my bed and passed them over. They glinted dully as Charlie began to pump them up and down, up and down, the cig tip swelling bright, dim, bright, dim as he sucked on it.

"Hey, Chuck-man, you got a extra cigarette? I'm clean out." This was Alfred. I couldn't see him at all. He was directly across from me by the cellar steps, where no light reached. Alfred wasn't really a smoker—he liked chewing better—but I could tell he was bored. "Toss that pack over here."

"Fuck you, you never give me nothin', why should I give you a smoke?" Chuck chided.

"Fuck you, too, then," said Alfred. "Thought we shared everything with each other."

"Everything?" I laughed. "You wanna do the down-low?"

"You ain't purty enough, Hogie," said Alfred. "I like a bigger ass, tighter cheeks. You got that skinny butt looks like it got caught in a slammin' door."

Chuck chuckled, and then I saw him fling something in Alfred's direction. Then Alfred said, "Where the matches at, dude?" Another something was tossed. Alfred lit up. His face glowed red, then disappeared in the darkness once more.

I was out of smokes, too, but didn't really want one. I wanted a drink, and bad. All I had was a plastic bottle of Pepsi, Coke, some cola shit Ricky'd given me earlier in the day along with what was actually a damn good pizza covered in onions and sausage. The soda was opened, flat, half-drunk. That's what I wanted to be, half-drunk. Half-drunk was always good, though all drunk was better. I never knew exactly when Ricky would throw a party—he thought the surprise was as much fun as the gatherings—but when he did I liked to be drunk and ahead of the game. I'm better when I'm drunk. I'm stronger and louder and have a lot more fun when I'm drunk. But Ricky could be a real tight fist with his cash. Sometimes he bought booze for parties; sometimes he expected the guests to bring it. He hadn't dragged any beer-filled coolers down here to the cellar yet.

And tonight there was gonna be a party.

I'd heard Ricky on the phone upstairs early in the afternoon. He talks damn loud for a little dude hardly five feet tall. He was callin' up all his buddies and sayin' it was time to get together. I wasn't sure when it was gonna happen. Sometimes Ricky liked to have parties early; other times he was busy with his other stuff and called for a party eleven o'clock or midnight. I didn't care one way or the other. Sometimes late parties were more fun, because the guests seemed to be happier later at night. The shit of the daytime was meltin' down off them; they'd be on some high and would be less angry in general. Sometimes when a party was late at night, guys would bring their whores over and they'd let us boys all have a go. I knew whores. I knew what to say to them and how to look at them and how to touch them. They'd go for me first every time, over Alfred, Chuck, and even the new boy, Erik.

I sat on the edge of my bed, opened my pants, and touched myself, pretending my hand was a hooker's. I was quiet, and knew the other boys couldn't really see what I was doing.

A light strobed across the wall, pouring in through the rectangle window. I heard the rumble and cough of a car's modified engine. In that moment I could see the other three boys, their heads cocked toward the light, their eyes narrowed yet bright. Then the light vanished. The car engine shut off. I zipped up.

"Sounded like Jeek's car," said Chuck.

"Wonder who Jeek's bringing with him tonight?" said Albert.

"I hope nobody," whined Erik.

"Shut up, Erik," said Chuck.

"Goddamn it, you cuss me for not saying anything and then when I do to—"

"Shut up, Erik."

"I hope Jeek brings some of that pussy like last time," said Albert. Even without being able to see his face, I could imagine it drawn up in expectation, his ragged eyebrows dancing up and down like kids bouncing on their toes. Then, "Fuck, I dropped my cig on my pants! Ow. Burned through."

The car door opened, and then slammed shut. I heard low voices of men, and a high, whistling giggle of their whore.

"That's Lily," I said. I'd recognize that giggle anywhere. Lily grew up with me. When she was twelve she was sold to a pimp named Pinkie over on Stone Street. I'd seen her a few times back when I was keeping lookout for some of the dealers on my block. She was mighty fine in her green halter and slit leather skirt. But she always looked like she was ready to bolt, to run off somewhere if Pinkie lost focus for a couple hours. Now, I knew she'd accepted that it was her job to hook and didn't fight it no more. Either that, or they kept her drugged.

I knew lots of whores. My mother was one. A big fat, ass-jiggin' ho. I don't know where she went after giving me up for good, but my guess was that she was dead and rotting somewhere, buried in a trash pile on Staten Island or down in Virginia where the barges go. No matter how good they are, street pussy don't live forever. She raised me as best she could. We lived in her pimp's house. It was a dump, with bloodstained walls and semen-stained floors. I didn't care. I liked it there. I was born on a mattress in one of the back rooms, and according to the whores I was smart. I was strong.

Mama's pimp's name was Duffy, and he was thin and he was mean. To the women, though, not to the kids. He treated us like we was his kids, though I think only some of us was. We played inside most of the time when we was toddling; then when we got four or five we got to play 'round the backyard inside the chain-link fence. Duffy took time with us kids, teaching us how to hide when the Man came down the alley in his car or came walking along with his stick and gun. When we turned seven, Duffy taught us how to steal our cigarettes and candy out the convenience stores and how to lie without looking guilty. At ten we boys were taught how to fight and the girls learned how to flirt. At twelve the girls were turned out and the boys took jobs looking out for the dealers that was Duffy's friends, running packs 'round the neighborhood, hiding and trading guns. At fourteen my Mama sold me up to do parties. I knew it was coming. I was ready for it. I was now fifteen and a half. I'd been traded twice, from Windsor Jones to the Upman and then to Ricky. Ricky was okay. Windsor was better; Upman was worse. It came with the territory.

Erik didn't like Ricky at all. Course, he didn't have nobody to compare with, and didn't believe my stories about Upman. Erik'd been with us only a month. His mom wasn't a regular ho like mine, doin' it since she was a kid. Erik's mom had been a nurse or a cook or something respectable. She lost her job and then her husband when Erik was thirteen. She didn't have any other way to make money. She was pissed she had to trick to feed herself and her kid. She got beat up by her pimp a lot. She got hooked on heroin and sold Erik to Duffy. Duffy worked with Erik a little, then gave him over to Ricky. At first I was glad there was a new boy with us, somebody new to talk to, but when I heard him grumble and cuss night after night after night I wanted to punch the shit out of him to shut his flapping jaws.

Another car came into Ricky's yard, throwing more brief spears of light through the room. I could see Erik tensing up. He hated parties. He spat hard in my direction. It fell short, into the pool of darkness between us. I heard the tiny wet patter as it hit the floor.

I took a sip of the flat soda, and then dug in my bag of chips for a couple good, salty handfuls. I liked chips, especially the ones called crab chips that had some kind of seafood seasoning on them. Alfred liked barbecue; Chuck liked salt and vinegar. We didn't know what Erik thought were the best chips. He never said and so Ricky never got him any. I could tell Ricky had started to think Erik was nothing but a pussy. That wasn't such a good thing. I'd tried telling Erik.

I'd said to him, "Erik, you ever see that ad on television with those army guys? Ad says, 'Be all that you can be'? Well, you got to do that, you got to be all you can be and stop your pissing about what your mama did and what she didn't do, what food you get to eat and what you don't get to eat, that you think Ricky stinks or you think I stink. You hear me fussin'? No, and you won't, either. I'm good. You could be good, too, you'd stop groanin' and bitchin'."

Erik said, "I hate you."

I quit trying after that. Screw him, he wanted to be miserable.

More cars parked in Ricky's yard; more people came into the house. I couldn't quite tell how many from the heavy footfalls above us, but I speculated around about twenty. Men, their whores. Their boys. There was laughter, shouts, a glass breaking, cabinet doors slamming shut, loud thumping music from a boom box somebody had brought along.

Then the door at the top of the cellar steps opened, and the lights overhead were turned on.

They always made me blink, the lights. They sputtered and hummed and came to full life. I stood from my bed and rubbed my eyes while they adjusted to the bright. I could see the other boys now, each in his own cage. Three cages were side by side on the wall opposite the stairs—me, Chuck, and Erik. The fourth cage was across the concrete floor and up against the steps. That held Alfred. Each boy stood up and faced his cage door as was required, dressed in only denim shorts and shoes. The long, red, jagged scars on the other boys' bodies were clear in the overhead light, as were my own. Chuck was missing both ears, ripped from his head last week and just now starting to heal. Alfred's lower jaw was crushed in like an old aluminum can, and he had a white, blind eye. Two of the fingers on his left hand were nipped off, leaving uneven stubs. Didn't matter, never slowed him down. Erik, though, was still fresh. He'd never really partied before, had just practiced with Alfred under Ricky's supervision, a couple times with Chuck. He bore only a few long marks from his chest to his gut, and his right nipple'd been torn off.

My own body was slashed and damaged. There was some meat missing from both palms of my hands, but it didn't bother me. I was the best of the four; I knew it, they knew it, though they didn't hate me for it. They admired me.

Ricky thundered down the steps, followed by the party guests. Their eyes were bright with expectation, and money was already changing hands. The bookie, Darrell, scribbled the bets into his little notebook. Lily was carried along with the crowd, her makeup of blues and reds and glitter, one eye bearing a fresh fist mark. There was two boys with them, dressed in their shorts and shoes, pit boys like Alfred, Chuck, me, and Erik. Each had a studded collar, a chain leash. They said nothing but glared at us in our cages. We glared back.

Ricky stood in the middle of the floor and waved his hand.

Everybody got quiet. He said, "We got some good fightin' sched-
uled tonight! My Chuck 'gainst Robert Williams's Ben. My Alfred 'gainst Suddie Miller's Joe."

There where whistles, shouts of appreciation and challenge,
cussing as the guests took their places behind the thigh-high plyboard under the window. Cigars and joints were lit; beer cans
and whiskey bottles were popped open. The two pit boys sat on
the floor by Afred's cage, their leashes tethered to steel rings in
the concrete floor.

"But first," said Ricky, moving to my cage and opening the
heavy padlock. "I got something special." I stepped out of the
way as Ricky reached under my bed and drew out the tray with
my accessories. I stood without speaking, without moving, as he
snapped a chain leash onto my own collar.

"I got me a deadweight here in my pit," Ricky continued.
"Haven't had him long, tried to teach him, but no luck. Tried to
sell him, but nobody wants his sorry ass." I held out my hands as
Ricky slipped the gloves on me—leather gloves, each finger fixed
with sharp, shiny blades. I thought, *Oh, shit, Erik, you're in big
trouble, boy.* Ricky adjusted the glove buckles so they were tight
around my wrists, nearly cutting off the circulation. I said nothing, and stared ahead.

"We gonna have our regular rounds," said Ricky. I put one foot
at a time on the bed as Ricky snapped the hooked spurs to the
backs of my shoes. A belt set with razor wire was buckled around
my waist. "But it's time for a shutdown. . . ."

Fuck it, no, he's a pussy but he don't deserve this. . . .

"And if you want to watch, it's gonna be good, but it's gonna
cost you fifty dollars each. You want your pit boys to watch, it'll
be another fifty dollars each. Otherwise, stick a bag over your
boys' heads and you go upstairs."

Everybody wanted to watch. They handed their bills over to

Ricky as he led me out of my cage. Ricky tucked the money in his front shirt pocket, then went for Erik. The boy whined and whimpered as Ricky put his accessories on him. He struggled as Ricky led him out to the floor. Behind the plyboard barrier, partyers grinned and rubbed their hands together. Their boys sat cross-legged on the floor, eyes cold, stares steady.

Ricky unhooked my leash, then Erik's. He went over to the steps and held on to the banister. "On count'a three . . ."

Erik looked at me, his eyes drawn up, red-rimmed. "Man, don't kill me. I swear I'll do better. I'll work harder. . . ."

"One . . ."

I said nothing.

"I'm sorry I whined and spit on you. . . ."

"Two . . ."

"Goddamn it, this is wrong, we ain't fucking roosters, we ain't fucking dogs!"

"Three!"

I lunged at Erik, spun him around so my forearm was tight around his neck. I heard him squabble, felt him jab at me with his own bladed gloves. I thought, *Erik, you little shit, I ain't got no choice.* I lifted him up over my head, dropped down on one knee, and drove his back down across my leg. His spine cracked in two with a loud pop. Erik screamed, and I dropped him. He lay on the floor, his head wiggling back and forth, drooling, mewling, the rest of his body paralyzed. The partyers roared with pleasure, and even the two pit boys by Alfred's cage smiled. The owners would be glad they got to watch. Seeing a kill sometimes made the boys tougher, more savage.

Ricky said, "All right, Hogie, shut him down."

I pulled Erik's head up by his hair and cut his throat with the swipe of a glove. Blood spurted over me, the floor, the cages. Ricky laughed. So did the others. Ricky put me back in my cage, and then hosed the floor down for the first real match, which I won. I won the second one, too, then got to have a go with Lily. At four in the morning, when everybody was gone, Ricky stitched us up, put salve on our wounds, and gave me a cooler filled with beer for a "fucking fine performance."

Of course, I shared with the other boys.

Melanie Tem has published ten solo and three collaborative novels, dozens of short stories, poetry, and nonfiction. Recently her first play was produced in Denver and Chicago. Her first novel, *Prodigal*, won the Bram Stoker Award. The chapbook *The Man on the Ceiling*, written with her husband, Steve Rasnic Tem, won the 2001 Bram Stoker, International Horror Guild, and World Fantasy awards. She is also a social worker and lives in Denver with her husband.

THE COUNTRY OF THE BLIND

by Melanie Tem

"Well, hello, there!"

Out of habit he hadn't bothered to break, Clement looked up. Goddamn. Somebody was here, catching Seph's attention. Loozy Anna growled, and under his breath, just between them, he said to her, "Good dog."

Seph was cutting across the garden. This time of year more vacant lot than garden, no yuppies tending their plots on lunch hours, no tomatoes to steal, no zucchini to make somebody feel like a hero giving it to the homeless when really what else would you do with all those zucchini, no good sweet corn, no early lettuce you could find by smell and touch in the middle of the night. Just dead vines and cornstalks now, rustling, no odor underfoot, no rows to guide a cane. But Seph knew where she was going, and he heard how fast she moved toward the stranger.

He went back to getting his shit together for work. Cardboard sign with enough letters still stuck on; he pressed down the edge of the P in *please* but it curled right up again. Soft rag for Loozy Anna to sleep on. Hat that would stay upturned if the downtown wind picked up whether there was a lot of money in it or only the starter.

For a minute he stood still to judge the weather, then dug another sweater out of the box. Buttoning it up, he felt some kind of embroidery around the collar, so it was a lady's sweater, but it fit okay, and it was warm but not too warm. Maybe it was pink. Seph claimed she could feel colors, so maybe if he asked her what color the sweater was, he could get her attention for a few seconds.

Or maybe not. "Welcome!" she was calling as she moved away from him toward whoever had stumbled into or come searching for their place. "Welcome to the Country of the Blind!"

Clement swore. This was how Seph had greeted him that first cold night when, kicked out of another shelter, he'd staggered into the community garden he hadn't known was here, thinking hazily he might be able to sleep or die in the shed with the compost bins and tools. He hadn't seen her yet, hadn't touched or tasted her, but the sound of her singing out that bizarre welcome and then her smell had hit him hard. A lot of people on the street smelled like that, maybe not so strong, and practically everybody had some crazy thing to say. Until Seph, Clement had kept to himself. Now, thanks to her, there were all these people in his life. No more. Too many already.

Quincy had already been with her, still with blue eyes flashing, and she hadn't yet christened him "Grandpa." Just a few days later, Martina showed up, and, since she'd heard about them on the street and had actually been looking for them, she went faster, calling herself "Auntie" even before Seph did, walking around with her eyes shut almost right away. Then Pia came, left and came back the same day with Pierre. They took their vows together, each of them holding the other down and then following Seph's instructions for treating the wounds, and then they took it farther by harnessing themselves together face-to-face, and down here who was to say they weren't conjoined twins? "Don't call us Siamese. We're French."

Clement did not like crowds. This was starting to feel like a crowd.

"Stay away from me, bitch! Fuck, what happened to your eyes?"

"Oh, you noticed!" Seph was flirting. Any minute she'd be inviting the kid to touch her sockets.

"Fuck," the girl said again, on the verge of tears, and it sounded to Clement almost like baby talk. Her voice and the noise of her movements came from farther away. The first sight of empty, scarred eye sockets made some people on the street want to fight. This one had backed off. Maybe she'd just go away.

They sure as hell didn't need no young girl, sounded about fourteen, white, stoned, scared, snotty, Northern accent like Wisconsin or Minnesota or maybe as far up as Canada. The kid Seph had been wanting. Didn't need no kids.

What they needed was all of them working, and if Seph took it into her head to try to turn some jailbait newcomer who'd stumbled into their place, you could damn well bet she wouldn't be singing on her corner anytime soon.

Clement punched the air. Loozy yipped and pulled at the rope, ready to go, and she was right. He couldn't hang around here all day. Had to get to work in time for the morning rush.

"I'm Seph," Seph said, and the purr in her voice just about made Clement puke. The jacket he'd found for her on the mall shuttle swished now as she gestured. "And that's Clement and his dog, Loozy Anna. She bites. Clement, say hi to our guest."

Like hell. The girl didn't say anything to him, either, just whispered another of her baby curses. Clement guessed she'd seen that he had empty eye sockets, too.

"Don't be scared, honey," Seph crooned. Clement thought of a python draping itself around its prey. "We're friendly. The dog bites, but the rest of us don't." Seph laughed.

"Ain't scared of you." She was, though. "Just get away from

me." The girl's voice broke, and she coughed, maybe to cover tears, maybe because she was sick.

Seph gushed. "What's your name, dear?" Clement was probably the only one of the three of them who heard the knife blade under her honeyed tone.

"Victoria."

Good as any, Clement allowed, maybe even her actual name. Seph murmured, "Pretty name."

"Not Vicky. Got it?" The girl was looking for a fight. People brought up the stupidest shit when they first met Seph. He himself had started blabbing about his baby boy, who'd be a grown man by now. Seph was a good listener, and she knew how to use what you told her. "Not Tory, either. Nicknames are stupid."

"Victoria." Seph practically sucked on the name. "What brings you here, Victoria?"

Clement announced, "Well, *I'm* going to work," crouched and patted the ground until he found the end of Loozy's rope again. The little dog started right off, pulling so hard Clement stumbled.

Seph intercepted them, her outstretched hands reaching him before the rest of her did. "My hero. Have a good day. Don't miss me too much." He loved her smell. She did know how to kiss, and the chapped roughness of her lips made it even better. Loozy snarled and jumped on him, clawing at his ankle. When Seph let him go, Clement had a hard-on, but he wasn't quite so pissed off or jealous or, for the moment, afraid.

The morning was gray and cool. He knew what gray felt like. The chill had gone through his clothes by the time Loozy led him across the tracks. Rather than stew about Seph and this Victoria, Clement set his mind to the daily decision about whether to wear shades while he worked. Seph kept saying people would give more if they saw the empty sockets. To Clement's way of thinking, it might work just the opposite, gross people out, scare them off. And the cold air hurt. No point in arguing with Seph, but once he was on his corner he could do what he wanted. Sometimes she did come by to check on him, stick her long fingers in his hat and stir up the money, pass her hands over his face and hiss something nasty if he was wearing the glasses. Today, if she had her way, she'd be busy with the girl, so it was up to him.

He could never be sure that Loozy took him to the right corner. Chihuahuas didn't exactly make the best guide dogs. But he felt safer going through crowds and crossing streets and light-rail tracks with her in the lead, and she always got him somewhere downtown. This morning when she stopped, the echo of traffic off buildings seemed right, and somebody passing by talking on a cell phone mentioned Curtis Street, and the wall was where it should be, bricks and glass behind his back. He squatted, folded the towel for Loozy, made sure she was settled on it, and sat himself down cross-legged in his usual place, or close enough. Then he made the decision to leave the shades on.

He hadn't even put his hat out yet when somebody tossed a couple of quarters at him, like stones. One of them landed on his knee but the other one he had to crawl for, pat the concrete where he'd heard it roll. That made somebody else give him folding money: "Here ya go, sir," and, still on hands and knees, he held out one hand, which was risky, you never knew what they'd put in it, spit or worse. This time it was a bill, probably a single but once, when he'd first been with Seph, a twenty. After the folks at two different missions had told them what it was, she'd loved him hard for that.

Except for thoughts about Seph and the new girl that wouldn't leave him alone, the morning turned out pretty good. No trouble, no weirdoes to speak of; Loozy let a couple of people pet her. By lunchtime, when Loozy started whining and he was hungry and even more thirsty, the hat was maybe two-thirds full, mostly of change but quarters added up, a half dozen bills which he stuffed into his pockets until he could get somebody he more or less trusted to tell him what they were.

At the hot-dog stand across the mall, he bought a Polish with kraut for himself, a plain dog for his dog, and a bag of barbecue chips for them to share. He found a bench, Loozy gave him to understand that nobody was sitting on one end of it, and the guy on the other end left when Clement sat down. Loozy gobbled her lunch and then jumped up beside him to demand his, so he shook the kraut off and gave her half the sausage.

Seph called what she was doing building a family. To her that was a wonderful thing. But Clement's experiences with "family" had never been what you'd call good, and the idea of her trying to build one around herself with him in it gave him the creeps. Loozy Anna was enough family for him. Loozy and Seph.

Pretty soon he heard Auntie Martina's top-of-her-lungs preaching, another voice or two hollering back. When she got close enough he called out to her through the lunchtime crowd, and after a lot of near misses and loud cursing she made it to his bench. Loozy growled and Martina growled back. They didn't get along.

"How're you doing today?" he greeted her.

She didn't have to lean close in order for the cloud of sweet-sour wine smell to fill his head, and she didn't have to whisper, but as usual Auntie Martina leaned close and whispered anyway. "I don't have eyes!"

"Yeah, yeah, join the club."

"There's worms in my eye sockets!"

"There are not." Every time she said that, Clement felt a niggle of uneasiness, because worms weren't totally impossible. He always thought maybe he ought to touch her sockets to find out, but he never did. "You know what I mean. I mean how're you doing money-wise?"

"Six hundred fifty-nine dollars and twenty-three cents," she said right away. "No, twenty-four."

For just a second he believed her. But then he punched her leg. "Knock it off, Martina. How much?"

"Pennies." She dropped four into his hand.

"Martina."

"Honest to God, Clement, that's all. People don't wanna pay for the gospel this morning."

He tried not to begrudge her the four or five dollars she'd be keeping back for wine. Everybody had necessities. And it was probably true that in her particular line of work there were a lot of bust days.

Martina leaned close again. "She ain't a Christian!"

"Who ain't?"

"Vicky."

"You mean that girl? Victoria?"

"She ain't a Christian!"

"Seph likes her," Clement said, and threw the ball he'd made of his food wrapper as hard as he could. He heard it bounce off the trash can.

"Fuck Seph," Martina said, and Clement couldn't tell if it was a curse or a statement of fact about Victoria. Either way, it made him sick.

Auntie Martina grabbed his beard, pulled off his sunglasses, wrenched his face toward hers, screeched, *"Repent!"* and stuck her tongue into his left eye socket. Clement howled and fought her off, not caring to think about the stirring in his balls. Loozy Anna went nuts, bouncing up and down and yipping and snapping. Her teeth caught his thumb. He growled and fought her off, too, knocking her off the bench. She was silent for a minute and he thought she was dead, but then she threw herself at his ankle.

Cackling and thumping her cane, Martina left them to their bickering and set up shop right there, just out of his reach, where she hollered at everybody, *"Repent! Repent!"* After Clement got

Loozy off his pant leg and held her in his lap until they both calmed down and made up, it took him a while to find his sunglasses, and Loozy was no help at all.

He should have gone back to work then. Instead, exhausted and nervous, he went to check on Seph. He should have stopped at the bank to have somebody tell him how much money he'd made this morning, or risked going to the store anyway. They needed milk and apples. Seph liked Granny Smiths, and they were easy to find by the way they smelled.

Instead he stuffed the coins and bills into all his pockets, spreading out his take so it would be harder for some street punk to grab. Then he put his head down and took the shortcut through alleys. Loozy balked and he ended up having to carry her under his arm, afraid he'd drop her, she was squirming so much.

Wind picked up, and he had to hold his hat on his head. That left him no hands for feeling his way. He stumbled, ran into things, probably walked out in front of cars. He definitely did walk out in front of the light-rail train, jumped and almost fell on the tracks when it blew its whistle at him. Somebody yelled, warning or mocking or curse, which got him more confused and flustered, so that he barely made it off the tracks in time. Loozy Anna challenged the monster, standing out stiff-legged from his chest and barking wildly, never mind that everything she did was lost in the rush of the train.

Navigating by sound and memory alone was hard. The city swelled up around him, and he found himself wondering if Seph was really anywhere in it. His eyes burned—his eyes, not his sockets, phantom eyes. It had been a long time since he'd lost his eyes, given up his eyes, and the pain always took him by surprise. By now he should have expected it. Crying was messed up now, too; he wasn't sure there could be any tears, but he *was* crying.

The tearless crying made him think about what else in his life was worth tears. It wasn't like items on a list, but all of a piece and pretty much endless: father school brothers yellow mother sunsets home flowers wife reading art sons sky purple Seph—

Not Seph.

He wasn't going to lose Seph.

Loozy Anna licked his chin. Clement stopped wherever he was and buried his face in her matted fur. She smelled of sauerkraut and autumn wind. She wriggled and whined with happiness, and he was happy, too.

"Yo. Dude." A young male voice to his left, quiet, smoky. "Lookin' to score?"

Clement hesitated. Weed would ease him, though it wouldn't give him tears when he had need of them. He had money.

"Nah," he said. The guy hadn't said enough for Clement to zero in on him, so he turned his head from side to side, scanning. "Gotta get home."

"Suit yourself." He was a lot closer than Clement had thought he was, and more behind than in front. Clement wheeled, almost lost his balance, almost lost his hold on Loozy, got ready to defend himself and his dog.

Either gone or lying in wait, the guy didn't make any more sound. Loozy had snuggled into Clement's arms, and from the way she was breathing and twitching he guessed she was asleep, even dreaming. Which would mean her eyes were shut.

Cautiously, he walked away, what he thought was away. Sirens tangled around him. At least one of them wasn't a siren but a cry, like a cat or a baby. He smelled vomit, coffee, flowers. Loozy sighed in his arms as if she thought she was safe. At this very moment Seph and that girl Victoria might be making love, or worse.

Clement was lost. There were familiar sounds—the clock in the tower, skateboarders in the concrete park—but he couldn't get himself oriented. Every time he made a turn, it got worse. Pretty soon he couldn't even tell for sure when he was making a turn. People kept yelling at him. Cars kept honking. Crossing one-way streets, he kept expecting the traffic to come from the wrong way.

This had happened to him a lot the first year or two after his eyes were gone. When the sockets were mostly healed—though the pain still flamed and he was still reeling from the shock of having nothing to close when he slept, nothing to open when he woke up, nothing to touch when he put his fingers there—Seph had held his hand and guided him, forced him out. Holding her hand had been nice. Holding her hand had made it possible. Loozy had come along, staying close.

They'd gone out of the garden, early spring, some plots newly planted, some not even turned yet. Down by the river, Seph had pointed out the smells and sounds, how things felt, how things tasted that he'd never have thought to taste if she hadn't insisted on putting them on his tongue. She'd taught him how to shop and how to shoplift, assigned him his corner and stayed with him while he learned his trade. Then she'd led him home again, home, and she'd taken him inside her where having no eyes was a gift and a pledge, the heart of the act of love.

The next morning she'd taken him and Loozy Anna out into the city and left them to find their own way home. Clement hadn't even realized she'd left until she was gone, until he reached for her hand, called for her. Loozy hadn't been of much help then, either. His sockets had been pulsing, struggling to see. It had taken him all day to find his way back to the garden. He must have walked a thousand miles.

For a long time after that he'd gotten lost every time he went out. Not as bad as the first time, but always a wrong turn, a sudden sickening realization that he wasn't where he meant to be. Loozy got to know some things and Clement got to know some things, and little by little they learned how to get back to what only Seph called the Country of the Blind.

Today he wasn't lost for more than a few minutes, but by the time he got himself back on track he was shaking and weak-kneed. He'd just figured out that they were on the other side of the bridge at the edge of the garden, and relief was flooding through him like wine, when Loozy Anna squirmed out of his arms. He heard her hit the ground, regain her footing, and scamper off.

"Loozy!" There was no point in yelling "come" or "stay" because she wouldn't.

He hurried after her as best he could. Under the bridge with the swish of traffic overhead, his footsteps and panting echoed. When he came out at the other end, he smelled compost and mulch.

"Loozy Anna!"

Pia and Pierre were dancing along the fence. They did that a lot. They sang in cracked harmony and couldn't help moving together, having conjoined themselves by straps and ropes.

"Hey, Clement!" Pia worked into the song.

Pierre chimed in, a melody Clement didn't think would fit with Pia's if they sang together, but what did he know? "Come dance with us, Clem!"

The twins always invited you to dance with them, and only Seph ever did. He kept going, yelling back over his shoulder, "Where's Seph?"

"In the zucchinis!" warbled Pia.

"Waiting for you!" trilled Pierre.

"Where's Victoria?"

"Who?" Pierre boomed, and Pia echoed but real high, about as far as you could get from his deep bass note, "Who?" and then they were off into some kind of musical game Clement wanted no part of, "Who? Who? Who? Who?" all over the place like hail.

Vines tripped him, and a zucchini they'd all missed at harvest, past rotten now to dried up and hollow, squashed under his heel. Not very far ahead, Loozy yipped excitedly, which Clement took to mean she'd found Seph. Loozy liked Seph, when she wasn't staying out of her way. As close as he could get to a run, he headed toward the hubbub. For a little dog, Loozy Anna sure could make a fuss.

All of a sudden the barking got higher and faster, mad now and scared. Clement hollered, "Loozy! Loozy Anna! Seph?"

Somebody got in his way. Auntie Martina, big, smelling like chilies, trying to stop him. "Stay clear of her if you know what's good for you. She's in one of her moods."

Martina was heavy and solid, but he shoved past her. "My dog—"

"She's got the knife out. That girl wouldn't stay. You know she's gonna use it on *somebody*."

"My dog." He kept going, toward the sounds of Loozy snarling, snapping, yelping.

Cornstalks snapped as he forged through them, and the faint smell of old tomato plants shot up as if there'd been some life left in them until just now when he'd crushed them underfoot. Loozy Anna's barking suddenly got muffled, and, knowing her muzzle was being held shut, Clement tried to go faster. Then she must have broken free because she was barking ferociously again.

He tripped, fell to his knees, swore at the pain and the delay, held on to a cornstalk to get himself back up, but it broke and he had to do it without any support or marker. Loozy Anna screamed, a high, prolonged sound he'd never known a dog could make.

"Seph! Don't!" Clement meant to scream, but it rasped in his throat.

Over the yipping of the little dog and his own coughing fit, Seph's voice came loud and clear. "She's not one of us." Loozy Anna and Seph were still out of his reach, but he didn't think by much.

Knowing full well it was beside the point, Clement pleaded, "She's a dog. My dog."

He heard Seph stand up, and the terrible sounds of his dog being hurt rose up off the ground, too. Loozy Anna had seen him, and was yelping frantically. He lunged, reached for her, missed.

Seph practically threw the wild little thing at him. He almost couldn't hold on, but Loozy pressed herself against him, tried to climb up his shirt like a cat. Passing his fingertips over her face, he found the wound, Seph's first cut, and a lot of blood, but both Loozy Anna's eyes were still there.

"You do it." The point of the knife poked Clement's arm.

"No way!"

"Then get out."

"Seph—"

"You and your *seeing* dog." She spat the word. "Just get the hell out."

"Seph—"

"You're either one of us or you're not."

"I am. You know I am."

"Prove it."

Clement's first thought when she said that was, *That means I've still got a chance.* Horrified at himself, he tried to wrap both arms around Loozy, but she wouldn't stay still, and he was sure she was going to jump down and run away and then, one way or another, he wouldn't have anything. "I did already," he begged Seph. "I did prove it. I gave my eyes. Just like you said."

Something came into Seph's voice now, sort of an excited watchfulness. If she'd had eyes he'd have thought she was watching him to see how far she could go. "Martina did that," she told him disparagingly. "The twins did that. But you're special, Clement. You and I have something . . . special. Don't we? I expect more from you."

To keep Loozy from throwing herself away from him he

stuffed her inside his shirt and buttoned it up. Her stubby tail poked out the gap where the button was missing, but being next to his skin like that and mostly covered seemed to settle her down. He felt her shaking. He was shaking, too.

All his life, he'd had the shakes. When he'd first run into Seph, eyeless and regal, he could hardly stand up. When she'd first loved him, he could hardly lie still. When he'd first understood that Seph, blind since birth and proud of it, demanded the eyes of those who would stay with her, as a vow and a brand, the shakes had made him throw up, back off, leave for four days, finally come back. When the needle had gone in at the corner of the first eye and then the point of the knife, the shakes had stopped.

Now he had to sit down on the ground because he and Loozy Anna were shaking so bad. Seph said, "Your choice," threw the knife down, and left him.

Clement sat there for a long time. There was nothing to lean against, and his back hurt, but Loozy Anna had quieted and he didn't want to bother her. Every once in a while he would call out, "Yo!" or "Hello?" or "Anybody there?" or "Help!" but out of the city noise all around him there was nothing that sounded like an answer.

His legs cramped. It had been kind of a warm day, but now it was getting cold, and by that and by the sound of traffic he guessed it was evening rush.

When Loozy Anna stirred, he realized he'd thought she might be dead and he wouldn't have to make a decision; he could just be sad the way he'd always been sad. She scrabbled at his chest and when he jerked at the shirt buttons to get to her, another one of them popped off. She wiggled and whined excitedly: dinnertime. He felt for the wound Seph had made and found that the bleeding had stopped. The knife was right there by his knee. He didn't even have to hunt for it. The blade nicked his thumb.

Clement laid the little dog on his thigh as if it were a cutting board. She squirmed playfully, believing he'd never hurt her. Holding her down under his elbow, with the thumb and forefinger of that hand he guided the blade wielded in the other, positioning the point the way Seph did at the outside corner of the first eye. He was shaking.

In the distance he heard the twins dancing along the fence, Auntie Martina preaching, Grandpa Quincy blowing on his horn. Farther in the distance, he heard Seph singing. He lowered the tip of the blade into the soft spot under the curly, grimy fur. Loozy Anna winced. Clement was shaking.

Clement dropped the knife and let Loozy Anna go. She bounced in front of him, wanting to take him somewhere, and then took off. He couldn't follow her that fast.

With nothing to hold on to, he struggled to his feet. Not finding any objects to orient himself, he took a while to get out of the garden. But, finally, he was out, kind of lost, alone, eye sockets burning. But the shakes had stopped.

Kathe Koja was born in Detroit, and grew up in an east-side suburb. In 1984 she attended the Clarion Writing Workshop at Michigan State University, with the generous aid of the Susan C. Petrey scholarship. A few years later she sold her first novel. Four more novels and a short story collection were published in the nineties. *Straydog* was her first novel for young people, followed by *Buddha Boy* and *The Blue Mirror*. *Talk* is forthcoming in 2005, all from Farrar, Straus & Giroux. She lives in the Detroit area with her husband, artist Rick Lieder, and her son.

RUBY TUESDAY

by Kathe Koja

Every Tuesday I go to the movies, Ruby Tuesdays at the Film Theater, the same movie every week: *Ruby Tuesday*. Also the main actress's name is Ruby, in the movie *and* in real life. It's a little confusing, I know.

Actually it's more than just a movie. It's like a party, a get-together, an *event*. Every week the same people go, and they dress up like nurses, or cowboys carrying gym bags; they throw confetti, and sing, and chant, *Just give me the medicine, big guy!* One man brings his violin and plays it in the nightclub scene where Ruby and Charles dance, and everyone hums along. Most people can't really hum on tune; have you ever noticed that? Maybe you've never been in a place where a hundred people are all trying at once. They start out okay but then everyone kind of warbles off their own way, like a machine slowly breaking down. It's funny, kind of, but people take it seriously; I mean, they'll be really offended if you laugh. I've never laughed, but sometimes other people do, the people who only come once or twice, the tourists, everyone calls them. Like, *I saw some tourists in the lobby just now*. Or, *I can't stand sitting next to tourists*.

Personally I don't care who I sit next to. I don't know any of them, not even the regulars, the ones who come every week and wear the costumes. I'm not really there to be with people; I just want to watch the movie. I'm planning to go to film school next year, when I get out of high school. If I get out of high school. I got into it with my father again yesterday; he was making coffee and I was passing through the kitchen, trying to keep my head down, but, "What do you do all day, Rikki?" he said, in that way that isn't a real question. "You certainly don't spend any time studying."

"I study," I said. We both knew I was lying.

"Not according to your teachers. They say you're pretty much failing everything but English." He rubbed his eyes, squeezed them shut, then opened them wide. The brewing coffee smelled so strong it made me feel sick. "Why aren't you doing your home-work? Is something wrong?"

I admit it, I laughed. *Is something wrong?* "No, Dad, nothing's wrong. Except that Mom's dying, and—"

You cannot believe how mad he can get. Nuclear mad or stone silent, those are his two modes now. . . . Why did he ask me anyway? What does he want me to say? That I don't give a shit about school? I don't. All I want to do is make movies, movies that really matter to people. Which is why I go to *Ruby Tuesday,* why I *study Ruby Tuesday,* the way the story arcs up then down then up again, the way people root for Ruby and Charles and Dean, what it makes them feel, *how* it makes them feel: that what's really just flickering light in a dark room can make someone watching laugh and cry. Which is a lot more important than geology papers or American civics, okay, Dad?

Plus I can sit in the dark for two hours. Two hours and eight-een minutes. And I don't have to talk to anyone.

*   *   *

The thing is, my mother *is* dying: of cancer. First they cut her, then they poured poison in her, then they cut her again. I don't know which is worse, the cancer or the "cure."

Now it's metastasized. I know what that means. But still, people keep telling me, *She's not going to die, Rikki*—oh really? Then why is she in the ICU now? Why does she look like . . . like bleached bones on a beach, yellowish bones as brittle as a bird's?—and her eyes, huge bright startled staring eyes, like she just can't believe this is happening to her. . . . When I squeeze her hand it's slippery and it's cold. And she never squeezes back.

You can't see anything from her window. Not even the parking lot. And you can't hear any birds.

At first the hospital seemed . . . not "glamorous," but kind of exciting, in a cinema verité way (you know cinema verité? it means movie truth, like realism, real life). That constant feeling of hurry and hustle, the exotic names for everything, the way it's in its own enclosed world, you step into it and you're swept away. But that's when things are going good, or at least it seems like they might. When it stops being good, it stops being exciting. And then it's another kind of enclosed world. Like hell.

In *Ruby Tuesday* the nurse is the hero. (That's pretty much true in the ICU, too. The one I like best is Gideon. He works weekends, he has cinnamon-colored dreads and he always smiles at me.) Ruby's a nurse in a slummy kind of hospital, where they don't have enough money for rubber gloves and medicine and stuff like that. One of the running jokes is that the character Dean, who's an ex-junkie, has to keep buying drugs off the street to give to Ruby's patients: Lortab, Vicodin, Codenol. Dean wears a blue denim cowboy hat, so the Dean people in the audience all wear cowboy hats. The Rubies wear nurse's uniforms and white running shoes. And everyone throws confetti in the wedding scene, when Ruby and Charles get married in the

ER parking lot, and everyone yells along with the fat man who sits up on the stretcher and says to Dean, *Just give me the medicine, big guy!* And then everyone laughs.

Then while the credits roll all the Rubies and Deans stand up, and everybody sings the last song, "Love is the Cure" by Alison Whyte—*I'll be the doctor/For your broken heart/Love is the cure*— and I put away my notebook (yes, I can write in the dark; they make red-light pens for that very purpose) and head out to my car, the white Toyota Victa that used to be my mom's. Technically it still is my mom's; all her stuff's there in the backseat: old newspapers and sticky travel mugs, her raincoat, some folders from her work. . . . I changed the radio stations, though.

And I drive home and heat up a Reddy Rice Bowl for dinner, and read through my movie notes. And then I go to bed and stare at the ceiling, at the taped-up pictures of clouds. And I hear my dad walking up and down the hallway, pacing the hallway, like an animal in a too-small cage, a criminal on death row. Back and forth, back and forth.

Love is the cure; yeah, right. But it is a pretty song.

In swim class, the green tile shiny under the lights, the smell of chlorine and warm water, like a giant washing machine. Mrs. Baum blows her whistle: *ladies, line up to change.* Jenna Masterton pokes me, fingernail in my back: "Hey, Rikki. Do you, like, go to that weird movie?"

"What?"

"That weird nurse movie, you know, where all the freaks go?" Smirking, pretending that she's pretending not to smile. She's laughing in my face is what she's doing. If only she knew how much I don't care. "Kayla said she saw you there."

"So what was Kayla doing there?"

She's stuck for an answer, but only for a second. "She went with Kyle; they were high. . . . So were you there?"

Yes, Jenna, I was there. I even saw them; the tourists always stick out like sore thumbs, especially when they're groping their brains out in the sixth row. People were laughing at them. Even the one really fat lady who sits and eats nachos through the whole thing was laughing at them. I was probably the only one who wasn't, but then I've seen Kayla and Kyle before.

"Yeah, I was there."

"So you go every week?" Her eyes are all crinkled up; she thinks this is hilarious. "And, and *sing* and all that? And some weird guy plays a violin? Don't you feel like a total freak?"

"Not really," I say, and knock her face-first into the pool.

Everyone stares; some people laugh. Mrs. Baum gives her whistle a workout. It's one of those things I really wish I could tell someone: *You should have seen Jenna's face. Most of it washed off.* If I had any friends, I would.

I used to have friends, people to hang around with, do stuff with. But when things happen, like cancer and the ICU, all of a sudden you're living in a different world from everyone else and no one can understand, even if they say they do, even if they really try. The way Jonah tried at first, and Cristal: They asked questions, they cried—Cristal did—they offered to go visit with me. But either you're in that world or you're not: There is no in-between. Not like *Ruby Tuesday,* where for two hours and eighteen minutes you can be at Harper Hospital and Health Care Center ("Be Patient with Us!") and then go back to your regular life. In the world of the ICU, it *is* your regular life. And there's nowhere else to go.

Finally they stopped, first Cristal, then Jonah, stopped crying, calling, asking. But they were the people I first saw *Ruby Tuesday* with—just as tourists, you know, we just went there for something to do. Cristal kind of liked it, but Jonah thought it was silly: *A bunch of adults playing dress-up,* he said. *Pretending.*

But it's not "pretending"; it's *acting,* acting out the movie.

Daily life—school dinner bed—that's what's pretending. If I had any friends, I would tell them that, too.

The actress who plays Ruby really is named Ruby: Ruby Chavez. She's been in a bunch of other movies (*April Flowers, The Red Line, Booty and the Beast*) (*Booty* is actually much better than it sounds) but no other real phenomenons like *Ruby Tuesday*. There's this long interview with her on Movienet, where she talks about how there's something in the movie, *intrinsic* to the movie, that makes people love it so much that they want to live in its world, and how very few films can claim to offer that kind of overpowering reality. *Because it is real*, she says in the interview. *The folks in the audience, they're right there, acting, singing, saying the lines; you can't get any realer than that.*

The interviewer tries to get her to make fun of it, very subtle, like *Gosh, you must be very honored when two hundred-pound guys dress up like nurses,* but Ruby Chavez won't buy into that: *I am honored,* she says. *To be a part of something that's bigger than I am, that will go on no matter what else I do, what other movies I make, you bet I'm honored.* She sounds like a pretty nice person, actually. When I make my movie I'm going to try to get her to be in it, just a cameo, you know, but enough so I can put her name in the credits: Helpful Woman . . . Ruby Chavez. That would just be so cool.

> [RUBY crosses the exam room, fiddles with the stacked boxes of latex gloves. She turns to DEAN and smiles.]
>
> RUBY: Thanks, Dean. You always come through for me.
>
> DEAN [tips his cowboy hat. In a cowboy drawl]: My pleasure, ma'am.

RUBY [diffidently]: Have you, um, seen Dr. Fisher today?

DEAN: You mean Charles? Your Charles?

RUBY: He's not "my" Charles.

DEAN: Well, he's sure not mine. . . . Listen, I gotta go; I have a noon appointment at the detox clinic. You need any Codenol?

RUBY [smiling]: Lots.

DEAN: You got it. [Turns to leave, then stops at the door.] He *is* your Charles, you know. Whenever you're ready.

All the things you see, when you watch something a million times—by now I've seen *Ruby Tuesday* thirty-six times—you move past what's on the surface, you notice all the tiny details. Like a scientist, watching through a microscope . . . Like in that scene, how Ruby raises her eyebrows when she says "um," like she's trying to keep her face blank but she can't help showing that she hopes. And when Dean pauses at the door, the way his voice softens and drops when he says "He is your Charles," like a big brother, so you know how much he's rooting for Ruby to get over her fear of falling in love and just go for it.

And it's not only the lines; it's the way the actors say them, the way the light hits their faces, the way the exam room turns into their own special private place while they're talking. . . . It's all in there, even though what you see is just the surface, the screen and the people in costumes and the sparkle confetti in the air. But under the surface, it's all doing what it's all there to do, what a movie is supposed to do: make a world for you to live in. Someday my movie will be a world, too, a place where anyone can go anytime they need to, say the lines, act it out, escape for as long as they can.

*　　*　　*

My father refuses to eat Reddy Rice Bowls, but he's not much of a cook, so when he's home we have a lot of takeout. Like today he stopped at Siam Spicer and got vegetarian pad thai, which I fork up even though I'm not hungry. He doesn't even pretend to eat, just drinks his coffee and watches me until, "Rikki," he says, then clears his throat. The bird clock on the wall hits the half hour: the finch's *tck-tck*. My mother bought that clock last spring, at a tag sale; my father and I both think it's silly. Or we did. "Tonight I need you to come to the hospital with me."

I don't say anything. My heart instantly starts to pound.

"There are . . . there are some . . . issues we need to talk about with Dr. DeAngelis. We both need to—" He stops, clears his throat again. I look at the clock, my plate, the clock. Finch, mockingbird, cardinal, robin. She said she bought it so she would always hear the birds sing. "I have a couple of things to take care of here. Then we can . . . we can go."

He isn't looking at me; he isn't looking at anything. I scrape my plate, take my water glass to the sink; now my head is pounding along with my heart, a thudding pain, a thin taste in my mouth. Up to my room—one step, two steps, just keep going, grab my bag and keys, and when I hear him in the hallway, I hop in the car and I go.

Head down and crossing through the lobby, I don't see anyone, I don't want to see anyone, the headache is knocking like a fist behind my eyes but, "Hey," someone says, a voice I know: who? Gideon. *Gideon?* The ICU nurse; why's he here? And for a second I panic, as if the hospital's chasing me, come to drag me back from *Ruby* world—but then I see he's wearing a T-shirt, not a uniform; he's with a Dean, cowboy hat and caramel skin and "Hi, Rikki," he says. "You a *Ruby* fan too? So's Daniel," as the Dean smiles and nods. "Daniel's really into this, but I never came before. Some show, huh?"

"Yeah."

"You come a lot?" Daniel asks me. His T-shirt says *RubyCon 4*.

The lobby's loud, too loud; my head hurts so bad, but "Yeah," I say, because I had to come here tonight, especially tonight, even though my dad will be alone with the doctor, even though *there are issues we need to talk about,* but I don't want to talk about them; I can't. I can't. "Every week."

Gideon smiles, the way he always does, and says, "You enjoy it, huh?" But not the way a tourist would, as if he can see why a person might come here, a person who wants another world, as if he understands—

—and just like that I'm crying, the pain in my head and the pain in my heart, the white blur of nurses and nurses, the two worlds dissolving together, all of it the real world, the only one, *some show, huh?*

—as Gideon says something to Daniel—*Her mother, ICU*—his hand on my shoulder, big and warm, and then Daniel's nudging me with napkins; they smell like nachos and popcorn and for a shuddery second I think I'm going to throw up but I don't. I blow my nose, I wipe my eyes and "Thanks," I say.

And Daniel tips his cowboy hat like Dean. More world-dissolve. He even looks a little like Dean.

"My pleasure, ma'am."

"Rikki," Gideon says. He looks so sad, sad but calm, like he sees this all the time. "Do you want a ride home, or anything?"

"No," I say. My voice is raw and wet. "I want to see the movie."

I'm still awake, staring up at the taped-on sky, the magazine ceiling-clouds. My dad's not home yet even though it's way after midnight, Wednesday morning, not Tuesday anymore. In the kitchen the bird clock gives the half hour, the finch. *Tck-tck.*

When he does come back I won't try to explain; I'll let him yell if he needs to; I won't say anything at all. Because what is there to say? *Love is the cure,* except when it isn't, which is always. *You can't get any realer than that.*

All I want in the world is to make my movie, and have my mom see it. That's all I want. That's all.

Brett Alexander Savory is a Bram Stoker Award–winning editor. His day job is also as an editor at Harcourt Canada in Toronto. He is editor in chief of *The Chiaroscuro/ChiZine*, has had nearly forty stories published in numerous print and online publications, and has written two novels, *In and Down* and *The Distance Travelled*—both of which are currently with his agent. In the works are a third novel, *The Falcon's Necktie*, and a dark comic-book series with artist Homeros Gilani. A benefit anthology called *The Last Pentacle of the Sun: Writings in Support of the West Memphis Three* surfaced in October 2004 through Arsenal Pulp Press. He can be reached through his Web site: http://brettsavory.com.

RUNNING BENEATH THE SKIN

by Brett Alexander Savory

The bullet tore a thin strip of flesh from his cheekbone and drove into the brick wall behind him.

He turned a corner, cut swaths through steaming sewer grates—smoky ghosts wrapping around his skinny legs. Dissipating.

Gone.

More bullets flew past his ears as he ducked around another corner, legs pumping hard, breath coming in thick rasps from his lungs. He didn't know this section of town, so it was just a matter of time.

Always just a matter of time.

Voices. Loud, harsh. Guttural bursts exploding from thin lips, wide mouths. Find him, fuck him up. The words didn't matter; their speakers did. The men who spoke these words could run hard and for a very long time. The man they were chasing could not match their endurance.

Gas lamps swam by on his left, shining, flickering, watching the man run. Lighting his way. Chasing away the shadows he wanted to hide in.

The man heard more shots behind him, wished for a dumpster, a garbage can, another brick wall, anything to hide behind. Make the game more challenging for all players involved. Then one of the bullets slammed into the back of his right knee. He gritted his teeth, but continued running.

Another bullet caught him in the left shoulder. He plunged ahead, driven forward by the momentum, lilting to one side, nearly losing his balance. But his left knee held him, and he kept running.

More shouting. Now coming from two directions.

He turned another corner, saw four of the men who were chasing him standing there, weapons raised, aimed in his direction. He stopped, stumbled backward, teeth clenched tight against the pain in his leg and shoulder. Three more men stood the way he had just come, grinning, their mouths black holes in their faces.

The shouting stopped.

Nowhere to go.

Seven distinct cocking sounds, as bullets entered chambers.

The man took one deep breath, held it. Closed his eyes.

The night burst open with sound and muzzled fire. The man crumpled. Red seeped out from under him, glistening in dim gaslight.

Hospital green.

Walls rippled when he opened his eyes. Fluorescent ceiling lights swam. He looked to his right. The woman in the bed beside him wavered, floated on crisp white sheets.

The man rubbed his eyes, heard a door open, whisper closed. Heard a voice, looked up, saw a young woman at the foot of the bed. A nurse. Her mouth moved, but the man heard no words.

She held a clipboard, her mouth moving again. Her brow crinkled she was frustrated that she was getting no answers to her questions.

The nurse was beautiful and the man would have answered her questions, had he heard them, had he been capable of hearing anything but his own blood pumping in his ears.

She turned the clipboard around to face the man; she pointed to it, held it closer to his face. Her arm stretching toward him undulated, the clipboard bobbing slowly in her hand. The man blinked twice, rubbed his eyes again, and tried to focus. He was tired, and wanted only more rest, but he also wanted to help the nurse, wanted to help this lovely woman with whatever information she needed.

Seeing the man squint, obviously making an effort, the nurse moved around to his right to give him a better look at the chart. The place where her finger pointed showed a scrawled name—the product of some rushed doctor's nearly illegible scribbling. He blinked a couple more times and was finally able to make out the name: Henry Kyllo.

Faraway sounds filtered into the man's ears. Mumblings in a tin can. He shook his head, clearing the cobwebs. The sounds swirled around in his head, formed words to match the nurse's red, red lips. She was asking if he was Henry Kyllo, was this his name on the chart.

The man put a hand to his head, glanced at the woman in the bed next to him. She had almost stopped floating on her sheets, was now staring at him hard, frowning. The man looked up at the nurse, smiled as best he could, and said, his voice a jumble of cracked rocks, "Yes, that's me."

The nurse mouthed more words to him, lost again to the pounding in his ears. Henry shook his head to let her know he couldn't hear her. She smiled in understanding, reached down and patted his hand. She was warm. Very warm. Henry wanted to move his other hand on top of hers, to feel the smooth skin there. He tried, but nothing happened. He looked down and saw the sling they'd put his arm in. His leg, too, was bandaged.

He wanted to tell the nurse that they'd made a mistake: He didn't need to be here. The sling and bandages were unnecessary. Some kind pedestrian had probably brought him in, or at least called an ambulance to take him away. But they were wasting good hospital supplies on him when they could be used for people who really needed them—perhaps like the woman next to him.

Henry looked again at this woman, and her frown had softened. The lines in her forehead smoothed out to show that she approved of the nurse's job, approved of compassion shown to another human being.

But she didn't know Henry. Didn't know what Henry was. If she did, the frown lines would most certainly reappear.

The doctors usually discharged Henry pretty quickly once they realized what he was, but the doctor who'd scribbled Henry's name on his chart so illegibly might have been in too big a rush to figure it out, or maybe too new to his job to notice the signs. At any rate, the nurse would figure it out soon enough and then, once he was able to walk again, he'd be released.

Quietly.

The way the hospital staff looked at him—and others like him—was always with disgust. When they removed the casts, the bandages, the IVs, or whatever other pointless machines they had him hooked up to, they'd ask two security guards to walk him down the hall of this hospital—or one of the other three in the city—the automatic doors would slide open, and they'd stand there silently, waiting for him to leave. Just staring. Afraid to touch him.

Henry was used to it, and knew that this time would be no different. . . .

The nurse patted his hand again, then released it, smiled once more, and walked out the door. The woman beside him looked away, focused on the mounted TV across the room, high up on the wall.

Henry tried to move his injured leg, but, as with his arm, no dice. He'd have to wait probably another hour, maybe two before he could walk with any degree of comfort again.

Just once he wanted to walk out of a hospital without being escorted; just once he wanted to leave of his own accord, even if the outside he was walking back to was the same cold place it always had been for him.

With his good hand, Henry touched the bandage on his face where the first bullet had grazed his cheekbone. He knew by now it would be nearly healed. By the time the program currently on TV had ended, the wound in his shoulder would be closed up, scar tissue already evident. Then, maybe another hour or so after that, his knee would operate as it always had— smoothly, and without a hint of pain.

When Henry was finally discharged from the hospital several hours later—amidst the requisite complement of security guards, and exactly the amount of disgust he had anticipated from the attending doctor—he walked straight home to his one-bedroom apartment, where the phone was ringing.

"Hello?"

"Henry. Milo."

Milo figured that the flesh beneath his skin was now about 90 percent lead, give or take. Milo had been at this game a long, long time. The game was Milo and Henry's connection. Their only real connection to anyone else.

"Caught another few slugs tonight, brother," Milo said. "What about you? Examined yourself yet?"

"Not yet, just got home."

"No way you'll ever catch up to me, you know that, right?" Milo chuckled.

"I don't want to catch up to you, Milo."

"Sure you don't. So why not just stay home, play it safe?"

Henry stayed quiet.

"That's what I thought." Milo chuckled again—this time with less heart.

Another few seconds passed before Milo broke the silence: "How long's it been?"

"Since I examined myself?" Henry said. "Couple of weeks."

"What's the matter—afraid to check?"

Fucking Milo. Always on Henry's ass about the same god-damned thing.

"Listen, why don't you lay off me for a while, all right, Milo? Today wasn't the greatest day I've ever had, and I don't need your shit making it worse. Don't you have anything better to do? Christ."

"You know I don't. Neither of us do."

Henry sighed, looked out his living room window. Snow had begun to fall—big, fat flakes that stuck to the window, melted, vanished. No lights on in his apartment yet, so the lone gas lamp outside his apartment building shone in, illuminating his sparse furnishings with a sickly yellow glow.

As if somehow sensing Henry's line of thought, Milo said, "You know what you need? You need a woman's touch over there, my friend. Someone to bring some fucking *life* to that shitty lit-tle hole you call home."

"I'm hanging up now, Milo."

"All right, all right, but check yourself out, chickenshit!" Milo blurted, knowing Henry meant his threat. "And let me know what—"

Henry hung up.

He crossed his living room, touched the base of a lamp.

Slightly less sickly yellow light flooded out of it, suffused the room. Henry touched the lamp's base twice more, until the light was closer to white than yellow.

More than just sparse: Stark. Empty. Hollow. Gutted. A home to match his personality. But that was Milo talking. Henry knew better. Tried to convince himself of better, anyway.

Shower. Maybe some TV, then bed. Fuck the examination. It could wait.

Henry hung his leather on the coatrack near the front door, made his way to the bathroom. Past piles of mystery novels stacked halfway to the ceiling; past a computer that he never used on a desk at which he never sat; past two loaded Magnums on the computer desk that he rarely took out with him on the Run; past pizza boxes empty but for the crusts of each slice, turned rock-hard, forgotten.

Henry flicked a switch on the inside of the bathroom doorway; a fluorescent light above the sink flickered to life.

He pulled his shirt over his head as he walked in, dropped his pants around his ankles, stepped out of them. He took his underwear off, then stood up straight, turned to his left, saw himself in the mirror. Nearly every inch of his torso held scar tissue; his legs more of the same. There seemed to be only small patches of skin left unmarked.

No way I'm even close, Henry thought. *Not a chance I'm anywhere near Milo's percentage.*

Fingers trembling, heart thudding in his chest, Henry brought his hands up from his sides, placed them gently on his chest . . . and moved them around there in slow circles. He rubbed around his nipples, pushed in near his armpits, squeezed the flesh around what remained of his ribs, sank his fingers deep into the soft meat of his stomach. Both arms, pressing, concentrating, trying to feel as deeply within his body as possible. It was a crude manner of examination for the information he was trying to obtain, but it was all he and others like him had.

Down to his legs, pushing, kneading, prodding around the knees. To his calves, the tops of his feet. Standing back up, checking his groin, buttocks, up to his neck, his hands roaming over his scalp as if washing his hair in the shower. But feeling gently, listening to the song of his skin.

Steel-jacketed lead.

Not pulsing through his veins, but replacing them, replacing flesh, tissue, organs—everything but bone. And even a good portion of that had been shattered, replaced by rows of bullets or clumps of shot.

Everything but skin. The skin remained, though forever changed.

Scarred.

The bullets in his body pushed flush to one another inside him. When he pressed on his abdomen, he felt them clinking together. They rippled under the skin of his forearms, writhed in his thighs.

Henry *had* caught up to Milo—had likely surpassed him. He estimated about 95 percent, maybe more. His head was the least affected part of him, as most of the bullets were aimed at his body, and because the natural instinct to duck away from higher shots was hard to resist. If he'd been able to control that reaction, he'd probably be near 100 percent.

And then . . .

But no one knew what happened then, because no one in living memory had reached 100 percent. Maybe no one had *ever* done it.

Henry showered, dressed quickly, flicked on the TV, and stared out the window again at the steadily falling snow. He gathered his thoughts, then dialed Milo's number.

Milo picked up almost immediately. "Well?"

"Ninety-five," Henry said, sweat on his brow, his hands slick. His voice was edged with a nervous tremor that Milo caught.

"Ninety-fucking-five," Milo whispered, and whistled low. "Holy shit, man."

"Yeah. I know."

"Another good Run, bro, and you might be there. You might just do it. . . . And before me, too, you cocksucker." ·

Henry grinned.

"So . . . belief?" Milo asked. "Which crackpot theory you subscribe to these days, my man? Spiritual transcendence? Transformation into a god of steel? Eternity in some kind of bullet-time Valhalla? Or maybe you finally show up on God's radar and he strikes you down for the freak of nature that you are. Any or all of the above?"

Henry thought for a moment, chewed his lip. "I don't know, Milo. I have no clue."

The snow blew hard against Henry's window, whipping up a white storm of flakes that mesmerized him as he stared outside, lost in thought.

"Still there, dipshit?"

"Yeah . . . yeah, still here, Milo. Gotta go. See you at tomorrow's Run."

On TV, the news had just started. The weatherman called for four inches of snow tonight, another two tomorrow afternoon. Harsh, blowing winds. Windchill creating a deep freeze to smash all previous records.

Henry, a frozen metal statue, running. Just for the sake of running.

And Milo running to be noticed.

Running to get on God's radar.

There were rules, just like in any other game:

You couldn't just pump shots into yourself—that was seen as

suicide. And like many other religions, kept you from the divine. The hunters wouldn't shoot if you stood there and waited for their shotguns to blossom, their handguns to light the night; you had to run, you had to be sport, or they wouldn't play the game. And this was the only arena in which the game was played. No time for common murderers; no time for cops: Jail time held you up, kept you from the Run. Kept you from the goal.

As for shooting each other, that was nearly as bad as shooting yourself. This was and always had been about ceremony. Tradition. The hunters hunt; the runners run. The path to enlightenment—to further evolution, some thought—was paved with bullets.

For as far back as anyone could remember, this had been the way of things.

Tonight, shadows moving quickly against a backdrop of random white, like the snow on a TV screen. Same running crew as always. Same hunters, too, save for a few new faces on both sides. Young faces—fathers teaching their sons.

Different parts of town attracted different kinds of runners and hunters. But with one thing in common the world over: All operated below the collective conscience. For most intents and purposes, invisible.

Everyone in this Run thought the gas lamps in this part of town—north of the railway tracks that cut through the town's middle—made for the best ambience; the electric streetlights to the south side of the tracks were too garish. Too modern. The game was old, had history; it deserved respect.

Henry and Milo sprinted side by side, two swaths of black cut out of the fabric of the storm. Henry had brought his Magnums this time—to present a danger. To keep interest up. Prevent boredom: hunters' flesh was not nearly as bullet-friendly as runners'.

A shotgun cracked nearby. Three hunters spread out, settled in behind Dumpsters in the alleyway Milo and Henry had entered, coming in off a main street. The wind cut to a minimum here. Henry recognized the area—it was the same part of town he'd fallen in last night. He and Milo hunkered down behind some trash bins, caught their breath, listened for movement from the Dumpsters.

"Fuckers hemmed me in last night," Henry whispered, pointing behind them to the corner where he'd gone down in a quick-flash spray of red.

"Tired of the chase?" Milo said.

"Must have been, yeah. Though I like to think I provide a reasonable challenge, you know?"

Another shotgun blast crisped the night, lit up the graffiti-strewn brick walls around them.

"That's why tonight," Henry said, cocking his Magnum, "we piss them off a little." He stood up fully, in plain sight, popped off a round in the direction of the closest Dumpster, where one of the hunters' feet was visible through the blowing snow. Henry's shot pulped it.

The hunter fell to the side, propped against the wall. Screamed his lungs out. Henry ducked behind the trash bin again, leaned to his right, just enough to see his target's head through the heavy snow.

Fired.

A clump of bone and gristle slapped against the brick wall, silencing the screams.

Words of anger filtered out from behind the other two Dumpsters. It wasn't often that the runners fought back.

"That did it," Milo said.

A shotgun exploded from behind one of the Dumpsters; machine gun fire opened up from the other. Anguished wails and screams of hate filled the thin spaces of silence between metallic staccato.

Hearing the bullets whistling above his head from where he

crouched behind the trash bins, Henry realized his opportunity, took a quick breath, closed his eyes . . . and popped his head up.

Three bullets in quick succession whistled into his cranium. The first two slammed out the back, but the third stuck hard. Two more sliced through his neck, butted up against several others already lodged there. Henry fell backward, exposed to the gunfire, unconscious. One more found its home in his chest as he lay there; then the firing stopped.

Milo, grinning, moved to pick Henry up.

The two hunters ignored Milo—he was too easy a target now—and shuffled to the Dumpster where their friend had fallen. Low, muffled curses whipped by wind found Milo's ears.

The hunters picked up their dead friend—each to an arm— and dragged him backward out of the alley, his booted feet leaving trails through the snow.

"Good haul, man," Milo said, hoisting Henry up and over his shoulder in a fireman's carry. "With any luck, I'll take a few in the back on the way outta here."

Milo trudged through the deep snow of the alley, past the three Dumpsters where the hunters had been, walking in the grooves left by the dead hunter's boots. He squinted against the wind, was nearly blinded by the street lamp's glaring reflection off the crisp, fresh snow. At the mouth of the alleyway, down and to his right, Milo spotted a dark shape, a man, lying on the ground, most of his head pulverized, a misshapen, bleeding lump in the darkness.

Oh, fuck, he thought. He looked up from the hunter Henry had shot, saw the man's two friends coming toward him. Scowls under hoods.

The closest one stopped in front of Milo, blocking his way; the other one stood behind the first, at his shoulder, glaring, stone-faced. The first one spoke: "This ain't how the game is played, friend." Then he pointed to Henry, a deadweight sack slung over

Milo's shoulder, still out cold and leaving a trail of blood in the snow behind them: "He killed my friend; now I'll kill his."

"Whoa, now, hang on a minute, fellas," Milo said. "Henry was just trying to liven things up a little, you know? Keep you interested. I'm sure he didn't mean to—"

Something metal glinted in the whitewashed gaslight, catching Milo's eye. He looked down. The hunter had pulled a machete from a sheath.

Milo backed up a step, shook his head once.

The machete swung, slicing through snowflakes, through air, through Milo's windpipe, his vertebrae.

Three crumpled heaps now, lying still in the dark. Bleeding.

Three hours later, when the sun tinged the sky dark red, a passerby noticed the three bodies in the street. Only one was still breathing. The passerby called 911; an ambulance picked Henry up, took him to the closest hospital. Upon examination, the paramedics quickly figured out what he was, had seen a few of his kind during the course of their job, but since there was no clear directive about how to handle them, they just treated them like they were normal people in need of assistance. Let someone else worry about them once they got to the hospital.

Henry started waking up a little during the bumpy ride. And even though he was barely conscious, he could still feel the paramedics' stares, their hatred, their fear, flowing from them in waves.

He wondered briefly what his percentage was like now—was it enough? He guessed not, because, if it had been, shouldn't . . . *something* have already happened? He wondered, too, if maybe Milo had been taken in another ambulance. Maybe Henry would see him at the hospital.

Henry closed his eyes, wished he were outside again, feeling the night's fat snowflakes falling gently on his lips.

* * *

Again—hospital green.

And again, the same nurse. Only this time warmer, due to familiarity.

"You here again?" she said, smiled a little, leaning over Henry, fluffing his pillow.

Henry's mouth felt stuffed with cotton, his head packed with burnt chestnuts. "Sure looks that way. Not for long, though, I suspect, once the doctors get wind of it. I'll be trotted out again, just like last time, security guards and all."

The nurse said nothing, just kept smiling.

Looking up at her pretty face, Henry suddenly remembered something Milo had said on the phone last night: *You need a woman's touch over there, my friend. Someone to bring some fucking life to that shitty little hole you call home.*

And he decided to give it a shot . . . before his head cleared some more and he was capable of talking himself out of it.

"What's your name?" Henry said, blushing, feeling like a complete fool. "Mine's Henry."

"I know what your name is," the nurse said. "The chart, remember?"

"Oh . . . oh, yeah. Forgot," Henry said, shuffling his hands and feet uncomfortably under his sheets.

A few seconds passed; then Henry asked where Milo was; he couldn't stand the unanswered question hanging in the air—like it always did whenever he actually worked up the nerve to talk to a woman.

"Who?" The nurse's brow furrowing.

"Milo . . . There wasn't another guy with me when I was found on the street? Tall guy. Skinny as fuck. Long black hair."

"No one else came in. I can double-check, but as far as I know, they just found you out there—the two others they found near you were . . . dead."

The nurse waited a beat, swallowed, averted her eyes from Henry's. "I'm sorry, Henry."

Inside Henry, metal shifted. Bullets and shot moved slowly, piecing themselves together. Like a puzzle.

"I, uh . . . I have to go now," he said. Some base instinct taking over. A need to be home. To be warm.

Henry swung the sheets back from his legs, got to his feet. Staggered, nearly fell. The nurse caught him, steadied him.

"Henry, your head. Jesus. You can't just walk out of here with—"

"Goddamnit, you *know* I'll be fine!" he shouted in the nurse's face. "You *know* what I am. I'll heal in a handful of hours, and be back out on the street, running through back alleys, eating bullets, chewing shot, lucky if they take off my head and end it for good, hoping that it all actually fucking *means* something!"

Henry took a breath, put a hand to his head—the walls swam and rippled. "Only now I'll be running alone," he said quietly, pushing the nurse away from him.

Walked out the door.

The nurse followed him, trying to convince him to go back to bed, stay and talk for a while. Just until he calmed down. But he kept walking. Wouldn't even look at her.

She gave up at the front door, where it was clear she wasn't going to stop him, no matter what she said. She watched Henry from the hospital's window. Watched him stumble slowly out into the blowing snow. Trip. Fall. Collapse on his side.

She cursed under her breath, threw her coat on, ran through the double doors, across the parking lot. She knelt down, tried pulling him to his feet, but he was too heavy.

"What's your address, Henry?" she shouted over the noise of the wind. "Come on, Henry! What's your home address?"

He mumbled it between ragged breaths.

The nurse stood up, left him lying in the snow, ran out to the sidewalk, flagged down a cab. The cabby pulled over; she approached the driver's side and explained the situation. The cabby put on his hazard lights, jumped out of the car, moved to help the nurse.

Together, they lifted Henry to his feet, shuffled him through the snow and ice to the back door of the cab. The nurse ran inside the hospital, fished around for some bills in her purse, came back out, paid the cabby, told him Henry's address.

The car pulled away from the curb, soon lost in a white sheet of snow.

It snowed for another three days straight, then cleared up suddenly to usher in sunny, blue skies. But colder now. Much colder.

Henry shivered in his apartment. Not only had the temperature dropped, but his bedroom radiator had given up. He was too tired to move out into the marginally warmer living room, so he wound the blankets around him as tightly as he could to keep in the heat. But no matter how many blankets he curled around himself, or how snugly he wrapped them around his frame, the cold still got in.

The cold of ice on steel.

His teeth chattered. He swam in and out of consciousness. Several times he had hallucinated the nurse from the hospital coming to see him, stroking his brow, telling him it would be all right. He just needed to rest to get through this. Just needed to sleep awhile longer.

Sometimes in the night, he dreamed of Milo: Milo standing at the foot of his bed, smiling. Just smiling. Snow in his hair. Then he'd walk out of the room, disappear, and Henry would wake up. Cold and alone. With pieces of the metal puzzle inside him still shifting around. Faster than at the hospital, steadily picking up speed.

In the chill of dawn, when the apartment seemed at its coldest, Henry felt he knew what the pieces of the puzzle were doing. They were moving within him to touch each other, form something. But what—and for what purpose—he had no clue.

He believed in nothing. Expected nothing. God was something that Milo had been after, not Henry.

The only thing Henry wanted now was to close his curtains. Since the storm had subsided, the sun streamed through his bedroom window. Too bright for Henry's eyes, which now glinted in the light. He didn't know it, couldn't see it, but they'd turned from deep brown to metallic silver.

The day after the storm had passed, Henry felt the puzzle inside him slowing, calming.

Milo came to visit him one last time, late that night. He stood at the foot of the bed, as he always did. Only this time, before he left, he walked over to Henry's bedroom window and closed the curtains.

The nurse knocked on the door.

No answer.

She knocked harder. Still nothing.

She fretted about whether or not to keep trying, questioned why she was even here at all. Decided to forget about knocking again and just try the knob.

It turned, clicked. The door swung open gently.

The apartment air was frigid. The nurse shivered and pulled the gray scarf around her neck tighter.

She walked in slowly, called out, "Henry? Henry, you home?"

Silence.

"I knocked, but—" She poked her head around a corner, looked in the kitchen, which branched off from the living room. Nothing. "—there was no answer, and the door was unlocked, so I came in. Hope that's okay. . . ."

The bathroom light shone bright in the relative gloom of the apartment.

"Henry?"

No one in the bathroom. Only one more room in the place.

The bedroom door stood slightly ajar. The nurse pushed on it softly, peeking inside. The curtains were closed. It was hard to make out anything but shadows layered on shadows. The nurse whispered Henry's name once more as she walked through the door, but her stomach had already begun to sink. It was so quiet. No hiss from the radiator. The sound of the refrigerator running didn't make it to this side of the apartment.

No breathing sounds came from the bed.

"Oh, God," the nurse said, putting a hand to her mouth. "Henry . . ."

He lay still on the bed. Bundled in blankets. Only his head uncovered. His medium-length dark hair, threaded with gray, hung in strings to the sides of his face. Unwashed for days.

For a brief moment, the nurse thought maybe he wasn't dead. His cheeks seemed rosy in the dim light. She moved forward, tentatively put a hand on his forehead. He was warm. Not only warm—burning up. But somehow there was no life in him. No breath. Just this wall of heat, emanating from his body.

The nurse's heart sank.

And that's when she noticed his eyes: steel gray. Wide open, staring at the ceiling. His face expressionless.

A tear slipped from one of her eyes. Dropped to Henry's bed, sank into the fabric.

She stood like that for a long while, looking down at him, feeling the warmth still coming from his body in waves, as if something inside were generating it. Gears spinning. Clockwork winding itself up.

Then she told him her name, and quietly left his apartment.

The following morning, a dark, heavy shape, unlike anything

this world has seen before, rose from Henry's bed, moved around the room as if waking from a deep sleep.

Outside Henry's bedroom window, a single snowflake drifted down, stuck against the pane, melted.

Vanished.

The first of a new storm.

Katherine Ramsland has published over three hundred articles, fifteen short stories, and twenty-two books, including *The Criminal Mind* and *The Forensic Science of C.S.I.* She has been a therapist and currently teaches forensic psychology at DeSales University in Pennsylvania. Her latest novel, combining vampires and forensics, is *The Blood Hunters*, and with the A&E network, she published *The Science of Cold Case Files*.

GRIM PEEPER

by Katherine Ramsland

I paid sharp attention to the psychiatric testimony, certain this perp would get off with some lame proposal for therapy, and just as certain that the stated reasons for it would fly as wide of the mark as an arrow shot backward.

"Scopophilia," I heard the slender, dressed-for-success psychiatrist pronounce. She then explained this "psychological injury" as a compulsive desire to look at sexually stimulating scenes.

". . . clinically important distress . . ." she was saying.

As with most professionals trying to diagnose this disconcerting behavior, she erroneously took it at face value: people getting off on watching others undressing or screwing. But she did not quite know how to address the added dimension: watching the dead. There was no diagnosis for that.

". . . an addiction . . ." she went on, pulling at the skirt of her navy suit. ". . . in this case, what stimulates . . ."

I moved uncomfortably on the wooden courtroom bench as she explained to the judge what impaired the defendant's ability to make appropriate decisions and to inhibit his antisocial impulses. ". . . it substitutes for genuine sexual participation . . ."

Inwardly, I snorted. She didn't have to tell me about these

necrophilous voyeurs and their flat denial that anything was wrong. I'd made them my life study. No matter what kind of security was kept in morgues, I'd heard of one useful trick after another for getting inside to watch the dead being undressed, handled, cut open, and poked with every manner of sharp and dull instrument. Some of them even became coroners or pathologists. And that gave them a way to layer their misbehavior with a professional veneer.

Few psychologists would even look at such a subject, but I'd done a few experiments—what some might call unethical—and the fieldwork for me had been a wealth of surprises.

". . . deficiencies in social relationships . . ."

Some people called them necrophiles, but they weren't seeking sex with a corpse. They just wanted to watch it being handled. A whole different category.

". . . satisfied only by covert observation . . ."

They had codes, too, for their ghost-encounters-of-the-third-kind. Ways to alert one another to a "good peep." One man who'd actually come for therapy had jokingly referred to himself as a "stiff," amused at his double entendre over what a stiff inspired in him. He didn't last long. After two sessions, he said he didn't want to be cured and off he went. But he'd taught me a great deal.

"There's a whole network of us," he had told me. "We clue each other in to primary viewing locations." For *his* freakish fraternity, the codes for the hierarchy of viewing experiences were based on colors. Orange was "okay viewing with low risk." Yellow was "better and also low risk." Chartreuse was "high risk but a reasonably erotic potential," while red was both "very hot and high risk—but worth it."

"How do you know each other?" I'd asked, wondering how one walks up to someone to inquire whether he or she likes to look at the dead.

He'd just smiled, as if he believed I already knew.

The most important thing he told me during those sessions was how it made him feel. It was not *offensive* behavior, he'd pointed out. It was *defensive*. There was no harm intended, just a sense of inner peace.

"It makes me feel better," he'd said. "It brings everything together for me."

I had sensed as he talked that having command over an unsuspecting person reconstituted his fragmented sense of self into an integrated whole. Looking at the dead empowered him and gave him some brief moment of mastery in his life. He didn't consider it a violation. To him it was a way to form meaning from an empty life—and that was arousing. He lived not only for the viewings but also for the community support that came with reporting his success to others.

In other words, it was not, as my colleagues liked to say, some deviant issue with impulse control or a symptom of a poor relationship with one's mother. There's nothing like an insider's view to throw light on the defects of psychiatric theory. That's why I left my armchair behind and went out looking for these people.

I hadn't thought of the courtroom before, but it was turning out to be a good idea. The man on trial had been caught peeping. But not in the usual sense of peering through some nonconsenting coed's bedroom window as she undressed for bed or sat in lacy underwear to brush her hair. No, he'd been caught pleasuring himself in a closet at the morgue. A small peephole was discovered, and God only knows how it got there or how long it had been in use. But he'd made a slight noise and was caught, quite literally, with his pants down.

". . . a victim of increasing media exposure . . . these television shows . . ."

Even with this psychiatrist's inept packaging of the defendant's case in fancy professional prose, she still managed to expose his history of incidents in a way that the prosecutor could not have done. She had to do that to show a pattern of mental illness, and that just made me smile. Like it or not, she was psychologically undressing him for anyone who cared to look. In a way, she was no different than he was, though I knew she'd deny it. I listened intently as she unclothed him.

He'd first been inspired as a boy on a class visit to a morgue, and from there had found volunteer work in such places, and then became a custodian. Once he had even tried his hand as a diener—an autopsy assistant—but the close contact had proved overwhelmingly erotic and he'd been fired. After that, he'd found stimulation from cleverly chosen hiding places.

This was a bench trial today, no jury, but oddly enough, it had attracted a number of onlookers. Surreptitiously, I shifted my gaze around the room, trying not to linger too long on any one of them.

This one was Joe College. That one, perhaps a hospital administrator. Another, a professor—I mentally tagged him "Doc." And one roguish man with dark-framed glasses looked like a writer. God only knew, if he was attending this proceeding for the reasons I believed he was, what he was writing. And there was a female, too. Perhaps the defendant's girlfriend? Or one of *them*.

She glanced toward me and I shifted my gaze to the window just beyond her. I wanted to see her without her noticing me.

". . . sublimated component instinct . . ."

I shook my head. Sublimated, deficient, antisocial—the psychiatric community had invented these words to get insurance money for a stipulated diagnosis. The words allowed them to pretend to know something while also erecting a professional barrier. They really didn't want to know.

But I did. That's why I'd gone out and found a few spots myself for this sick surveillance. Armed with a "yellow" and some "oranges," I used them on the next grim peeper who came my way. I let him think I was in the network and I gave him the addresses. In turn, I managed to interview a few other gore gazers. I got a real thrill out of letting them believe I was sympathetic, when all the while I was just watching them remove their own clothes, so to speak. They had no idea. And I learned just how truly depraved some of them could be.

The more I heard, the more interesting this world became and I started looking for places where I could watch them "in the wild" and see what they really do. I even started a code of my own: Therapy was orange, because it gave me a good view but no real risk. Better were the bars in which the stiff stalkers hung out. I made that a yellow, because they thought I was one of them, so it worked without being strained through the therapeutic screen. But there was also mild risk in those places that they'd spot my agenda.

What I was really seeking was "hot" exposure with controllable risk factors. I called that a purple. I so wanted just the right conditions. And I was getting close.

Even as I thought about that, I had to sit up and open a button on my shirt. I had to be careful. This work got quite intense, but if I gave signals to what I was doing, they'd guard themselves. I took a deep breath to ground myself.

When the court took a midmorning recess, I wandered to the front area where security scanners caught weapons, recorders, cell phones, and the like. I stretched my back to make it forget the uncomfortable benches and suddenly noticed a furtive look pass from Joe College to the writer. They did not greet each other or otherwise communicate, but I sensed a clandestine camaraderie of some sort, like followers of Robin Hood preparing to spring him from the noose.

One of them briefly raised his hand, curled into the semblance of a gun, with his index finger out. His lips puckered into a blowing pattern as he flashed the gun up to his mouth and then back down.

That got my attention. I had to interpret it, but I believed it meant he thought the defendant was going down: He was going to lose and serve some time. Now *that* was hot. I could get in as a psychologist to see him, perhaps. Then I'd have a whole new venue in which to study him. It wasn't full exposure, I knew, but it certainly had the feeling of some extensive disrobing.

I began to pay more attention to the others wandering around, and it wasn't long before I saw a similar gesture pass from the female to Doc Strange.

One of them glanced at me, so I averted my eyes.

I had the feeling I was in the presence of the defendant's network, standing right in the middle of all these unnatural eyeballers. This was too good. My heart started to pound.

But it was time to return to the courtroom to listen to more droning from the defense psychiatrist about the defendant's inability to get a life.

As she responded to questions from the attorney, I watched what I could of the expression on the face of Joe College, seated in front of me and to the right. His mouth formed an ambiguous line, somewhere between a grin and a frown. He raised an eyebrow.

Then I saw the projector all set up and knew we were in for a show. So that's what they were here for. They wanted to see the photographs of the body in question. I smiled to myself and made a mental note. This truly was a delicious arena. I'd added quite a lot to my stock of facts. While I was certain they preferred a live viewing, so to speak, they would take whatever they could get.

Wishing I had a better view of them all, like from the jury box, I settled back and watched the prosecutor present slides of the body in various stages of autopsy at the morgue as he forced the psychiatrist to address the voyeuristic violation. He was leading her away from the idea that the defendant could not help what he'd done and toward the offense as a truly sick kind of crime. Which it was.

But around the courtroom, something else was stirring. I held my breath as I let the subtle sensations of furtive movements shift the air around me. Some people sat forward, even as I did, to try to attune myself to them. I thought I saw an arm moving slightly, as if in some restrained stimulation. They had no idea how disgusting they were in the way they exploited others for their own pleasure. They actually believed this kind of thing was acceptable behavior. Setting such stuff within the framework of a like-minded network always makes the abnormal seem normal. They even had a special language for what they did to neutralize the acts: "examination," "observational encounter," or "fantasy enactment."

But who were they kidding?

The rest of the morning session was spent on the morgue photos, and finally we broke for lunch. I was so transfixed by my professional discoveries I could barely move from my seat. I wondered about the others—could they even get up without being exposed for why they were there?

I was amused by how long it seemed to take them to get to their feet and walk toward the exit as if everything were normal. The "writer" gave himself a cover by scribbling notes on his lap, and the female had the advantage of more hidden mechanisms for her excitement. I could only imagine what secrets they were struggling with in those moments of hasty withdrawal.

I finally rose to my feet to go find a quiet place close to here where I could write down my impressions. But first I had something to do. I retrieved my cell phone and looked up a number, then placed it in my pocket until I could speak in private.

As I walked down the outside courthouse steps, Joe College

brushed past me, bumping me slightly. I wanted to say something to him but didn't. I could catch him later.

It was not until I reached again for my phone that I realized what he'd done. He'd slipped a note into my pocket on which he'd written an address. I found a phone book to look it up. A morgue. He thought I was one of them. Whatever gave him that idea? I felt vaguely nauseous at the idea of a stranger mistaking me for one of these grizzly gawkers, but no matter. It meant that he did not realize what I was really doing there.

In fact, my morning had been quite a success in several ways. Not only had I gotten the defendant's entire voyeuristic history for my professional files, but I'd also seen others flock to the event to drink their fill. And no one had suspected my agenda.

I tapped the number on my phone, and when my colleague picked up, I said, "It's a purple. Really quite the spectacle."

Then I ended the call and looked for a private place to relieve the pressure from my morning's exertion. I needed to be ready for the afternoon session.

Yvonne Navarro lives in southern Arizona, where by day she is an operations officer on Fort Huachuca. By night she chops her time into little pieces, giving some to her huge adopted Great Dane, Lily; her husband, author Weston Ochse; her dad; and her little online bookstore, Dusty Stacks. Writing? Who has time for writing? Oh . . . somehow she finds it. Most recently she's written *Mirror Me, Hellboy* and the *Buffy the Vampire Slayer: Wicked Willow Trilogy* books. So far, she's managed to squeeze out nearly twenty novels and almost a hundred short stories. Visit her at www.yvonnenavarro.com.

CRAVING

by Yvonne Navarro

1965.

The girl is very . . . still.

The knot of kids gathered around her is growing, and Andre lets them prod him forward on the sidewalk, until his foot is almost touching hers. Everything about the girl is small, like him—small hands, small feet, a small, upturned button nose that's leaking a bright, shocking double line of blood down each flushed pink cheek until it disappears into her fine, blond hair. On her forehead is a blue-black lump the size of a robin's egg, the kiss of the monkey bar's metal when she slipped and fell.

"Move aside—you kids get out of the way right now!"

One of the teachers is finally pushing through the crowd. Andre doesn't know the teacher's name, just like he doesn't know the little girl's name. He moves back with the others and watches as the man touches a spot on her neck. Another teacher, a woman, has followed into the center of things and he tells her to call an ambulance, then turns back to the gawking kids and gestures at them angrily. "Go on, now—there's nothing to see here! Take off!"

Most of them obey, but not all.

Not Andre.

He hangs off to the side with one or two other kids, as close as he dares, enduring the aggravated glances of the teachers and the medics. As long as he stays back far enough, they let him alone—what are they going to do, chase after him? They are far too concerned with the girl, whose face has gone from a fragile, china white to gray, the color of a concrete sidewalk beneath the hot sun. Andre can feel the surface of his eyes drying out because he's not blinking; he's too afraid he'll miss something. Eventually they lift the girl onto a gurney and put her in the ambulance, and she disappears into the distance amid a circling of flashing red and white lights and lingering exhaust fumes.

Andre never finds out what happens to her, but he thinks a lot about the little girl over the next couple of days, wondering if she died, if maybe she was dead before they put her into the ambulance. He doesn't think so because on television *they*—that ambiguous, omnipotent group of people who seem to control such things—always put a sheet over dead bodies. Still, that doesn't mean she wasn't dead now; she could have died on the way to the hospital, or afterward when the doctors' treatment of her injuries failed. It doesn't matter. He will never find out, since the girl doesn't go to his school.

Andre is twenty-four when he meets Rebecca while standing a few feet away from a horrible accident. There aren't many people at the scene—apparently this one is a bit too much for most of the usual gawkers. Andre has been living in this neighborhood for almost three years, since he graduated from college, and there has been a steady stream of accidents at this corner. They usually happen at the intersection where the commuter train crosses the four-lane street and drivers, those who are willing to gamble with their lives in the hopes of getting to work a little faster, lose the game. It is Rebecca who approaches him—Andre is far too engrossed in his study of the man lying on the side of the road a few feet away to pay attention to any of the surrounding crowd.

"Do you think he felt any pain?"

Andre glances to his left and sees the woman who stage-whispered the question, then takes a second look. Like him, she is pale and small-boned, but where he has dirty-blond hair, hers is cut short and so dark it can only be described as gothic. Her dark eyes are wide with curiosity, like pools filled with glistening, black light. A layer of lip gloss makes her lips glitter as much as her eyes.

It is rare that something can divert his attention from the scene of an accident or its victim, but this woman does—he has to force his attention to go back to the man lying on the ground only a few feet away. Considering what happened, it's surprising that the police haven't demanded he move back, but they're still too busy talking to the bus driver. The driver is a pudgy, middle-aged black woman whose face has gone gray with shock and guilt as she tries to explain what she doesn't understand. Andre hears her. . . .

"I don't know. I was just driving past. He was standing on the curb and I glanced at the side mirror and saw him jerking all around, and then he just fell over. There was a bump under the back tires, and then . . . and then . . . "

She can't continue, but the rest of the story is on the ground at their feet. One of the young man's shoes pokes out from the bottom of a snow-colored sheet; at the other end, the top, the sheet is soaked with scarlet blood and disturbingly flat. It is the best accident scene that Andre has ever been to.

"No," he says to the woman at his side. "He had the seizure, fell in the street in front of the back wheel, and then it was lights-out."

"That's what I think, too." She nods, then looks sideways at him. "My name is Rebecca. I think I've . . . seen you before."

Andre considers this. He doesn't go out much, so if she *has* seen him, it's either on his way to his job or at another time like this one, when he's worked his way closer to the front lines to catch the details of some traffic accident or other incident. It's a long shot, but . . . is she like him? Secretly studying the damage that can be done to the fragile shell of the human body by so many things? No, of course not—that's impossible.

When she speaks again, her voice is quieter and a little breathless. "I saw you a couple of weeks ago. When that kid on the bicycle . . ."

She doesn't have to finish—Andre knows what she's talking about and, now that his mind fills with mental photos and revisits that afternoon, he remembers her, too. Her and . . . yes. That guy over there, about ten feet away. An average man with thick brown hair, glasses, average build; nothing special about him . . . except for the hunger in his eyes as he stares down at the red Rorschach pattern at the top of the sheet. As Andre looks at him, the guy suddenly lifts his gaze and meets Andre's eyes. Something knowing passes between them, a *kinship*, before the man smiles faintly and returns to his study of the dead man in the street. Andre's forehead creases as his gaze scans the crowd and finds more than a few familiar faces, the same people who, like him, come out when destiny does its worst.

Rebecca moves closer, and Andre jerks a little when she slides her hand against his. Without knowing why, he twines his fingers around hers. Actually, that isn't true. He knows *precisely* why he hangs on to this strange, wraithlike woman—because she *is* like him, and like the man a few yards away, and like the others he has recognized here and there throughout the years. Fascinated by pain, by death, by that rarely seen interval between violence and eternity. It is a captivation that disgusts most people . . . at least on the surface. Inside, where no one else knows the truth and beneath where so-called normalcy and decorum bind the senses and monitor the behavior, Andre thinks that the majority of mankind is *exactly* like him. But in the meantime . . .

Where in his life there was once only him, there is now him and Rebecca.

Theirs is an existence that most do not understand. The apartment in which they live is a monument to disasters and accidents, filled with framed prints showing wrenching scenes from September 11—the collapsing towers, an unidentified woman falling through the air in an almost absurdly graceful position as she exercises her only escape from the killing black smoke and agonizing flames. Another wall bears photographs from the Oklahoma City bombing, the rubble, the heartbreaking shot of the hopeful fireman carrying the toddler from the ruins; below that are what they call their "fire range": shots of the fireball devouring the compound at Waco, Texas, aerial views of the burned-out homes from a dozen forest fires in Colorado and California.

They have friends, more, perhaps, than most people would expect, a handful of people met in much the same way as Andre met Rebecca but who, like them, would never admit to having a secret, morbid side. Outwardly it all seems so normal, so *acceptable,* and likely it would be . . . if not for the way that Andre and Rebecca spend all their available free time: visiting one disaster scene after another, collecting touristy little souvenirs and postcards, picking up the rarer items through online auctions and, occasionally, via word-of-mouth black-market buys. Andre believes they have a great life: he and Rebecca are a joining of two souls whom he would have never thought could find each other in a world so concerned with things constantly politically correct and a Miss Manners who dictates everything from whether a person may cross his legs after dinner to how to sign off instant messaging. It's all so completely, utterly perfect. . . .

Except for that one, tiny problem.

Rebecca is getting bored.

Andre can feel it—her *blandness*—as surely as he can hear his own heart beat with excitement when they stop at the scene of the latest traffic accident, or get in the car to rush to the most recent in a series of lethal house fires that has beset the neighborhood adjoining theirs. It is so unthinkable to him, this sudden disinterest she has toward the things around which their relationship has so thoroughly revolved. Disaster and death have always been the crux of everything for them—when they make love, every time, it is to the flickering backdrop of the television's light as one of their disaster DVDs plays itself out. If her boredom becomes too great, if she actually *leaves* him, where will he find another woman with whom he can truly share the strangeness of his life and himself?

Losing her is incomprehensible.

He will do anything to keep her affection.

He will stop at nothing to regain her attention.

For a while, a very *short* while, the fires work. There are so many, and they are so close and easy to get to while they still burn. The flames reflect in Rebecca's dark eyes, and Andre can see her exhilaration in the orange lights that dance across her pupils, can feel it in the quickness of her breath as they whisper to each other about the firemen who rush in and out of the building, the ever-increasing number of ambulances and frantic paramedics and burn victims as the elusive arsonist targets larger and larger apartment buildings.

But as to everything, there is an end.

For Andre, it is the danger of being caught that forces him to discontinue his arson spree. Secretly he prides himself on the fact that Rebecca never knew—at least, he doesn't think she did—that it was he who set the fires, he who arranged for innocents to be sacrificed so that her love for him might continue to be fed by her addiction to the sight, sounds and smells of death. He is still a free man, he knows, only because he is not setting the fires because of a love for the flames themselves. He is not a pyromaniac, or someone hired to do a hasty job for insurance money. Because of this, he was always able to step back from his actions and plan them much more clinically, much more critically. There is no one breathing down his neck with threats or offered payment, and no logic-destroying physical or mental rush to be gained from watching the fire itself. Andre's thrill, his "drug," is watching Rebecca as she watches, so he is meticulous in his methods, infallible in where he procures his materials, untraceable by any evidence. Old high school chemistry books, household materials, planning and prep, utterly random targets and an extreme amount of caution. Detailed, but absurdly easy.

He is never caught, but he also cannot continue.

And Rebecca grows bored again.

She tries to hide it, but Andre can feel it in the way her gaze fails to linger on the victims, the way she shuffles from foot to foot if they stay more than five minutes at any one scene, and most of all, in the way she searches for new ones. Oddly, she begins to spend more time at places where tragedies have already occurred rather than seeking out fresh situations. She starts by bringing flowers to place in the pile in front of a house on the south side where a man went berserk and murdered his girlfriend and her four children before turning the gun on himself; then, incredibly, she flies to the Southwest to join the parade of mourners leaving teddy bears and baby toys in front of a storage locker in a nearly nameless dusty town where the mummified remains of three infants were discovered. Andre goes with her, of course, studying Rebecca and the others who stand around these places like silent ghosts and peer through windows and the cracks in locked doors. He tries desperately to understand her sudden desire to revel in the grief that happens *after* some cataclysmic event, to accept the change that has overtaken her. For him there is no joy in this, no excitement, no *need*, yet Rebecca's eyes shine with tears and sorrow, and if wallowing in grief could make a woman more beautiful, then she becomes exquisite. He loves her more than ever.

Back home they go through the motions of cohabitation, but he can see that she finds even less of a thrill in his touch than in the accident scenes that she no longer cares about. Through her, he loses his enthusiasm for the way his life has always been and he, too, stops seeking out the little tragedies that formerly kept him going. His life is as flavorless as dry white toast, and it is all Andre can do not to cry each morning as the sun crests the building and starts another day. He goes to work, he comes home, they grocery shop. He cannot do it himself, but he doesn't understand why, if he has become such a nothing part of her life, Rebecca doesn't simply leave him.

Until that final Saturday-morning trip to the store, when it all becomes clear.

Painfully so.

They are crossing Kimble Avenue a little south of Lawrence, jaywalking, and he is mulling, as he so often does these days, on how or what he can do to salvage his relationship with Rebecca. Her hand, the rounded fingernails coated by pale polish, is nestled in the crook of his elbow—despite their emotional distance, she has never stopped holding on to him in public. They pause in the center of the street to let a large delivery truck pass; it has vegetables painted on the side of it in bright, lifelike colors—a vibrant red tomato, a startlingly green pepper, sun-yellow corn. There's more, an entire assortment of others that Andre does not have time to notice before Rebecca's hand slips from his elbow, settles into the small of his back—

—and pushes him.

From where he is wedged beneath the truck, Andre's view is limited to a narrow slice of daylight, the distance between the filthy undercarriage of this Ford truck and the surprisingly chilly concrete beneath his cheek. He can't feel anything else, and he supposes that for this he should consider himself lucky; if he strains his eyes downward in the direction of his torso, he can just glimpse a pool of scarlet, his blood, as it rushes away from the confines of his flesh. There are several dozen pairs of feet crisscrossing the horizontal bar of his eyesight, so he must have been unconscious for a bit, long enough to gather a crowd. As he stares, he recognizes a familiar set of sandals; brown leather in a basket pattern with beads woven across the top—he bought them for Rebecca only a week ago.

Andre's vision is going a disturbing gray around the edges, images bleeding into the roadway until everything seems to have melted at the edges like the cheap special effects he's seen in a dozen different science fiction movies, the ones where the camera looks at the trappings of planet Earth from the attacking aliens' point of view. The circle in the middle where things are still in focus is growing smaller, but not so much that he doesn't recognize his beloved Rebecca as she kneels next to the truck and peers underneath; crouching with her is a face he also recognizes, even though it has been at least a year. The hair is still thick and dark brown, and the hungry eyes peering from behind stylish glasses haven't changed either since May 9, 2004—this is the man who was at the bus accident on the same day that Rebecca introduced herself to him. Even his faint, knowing smile is the same, and somehow Andre isn't surprised when he sees Rebecca slip her hand into the stranger's and hears her ask him, "Do you think he's feeling any pain?"

If he could only speak, this time Andre would tell Rebecca that yes, he certainly is.

Thomas S. Roche's hundreds of published articles and short stories in the horror, crime, fantasy, and erotica genres have appeared in a wide variety of magazines, anthologies, and Web sites. His books include three volumes of the erotic crime-noir series *Noirotica* and four volumes of fantasy and horror fiction, two of them, *In the Shadow of the Gargoyle* and *Graven Images*, coedited with Nancy Kilpatrick. For more information, visit his Web site at www.skidroche.com.

VIOLENT ANGEL

by Thomas S. Roche

I never should have let Satan talk me into killing the Chupacabra at the Decomposing Corpse show. I mean, that was just asking for trouble.

But it was all about the girl, which is never a good idea. Ever since Wendy did that clown in Reno (he really was a clown), Satan treated her like a full-on member of the gang. She got too big for her britches, which wasn't surprising, since those leather pants she wears all the time were about three sizes too small anyway.

"You gotta do it my way, okay?" Satan was growling, looking more than a little like his namesake. "You do this right, Winston, you'll be set up. The Family won't forget you."

"Don't call me Winston," I said. "My name's Rat."

We were all in the back room of Big Daddy's bar, where he does all his business 'cause he has it swept twice a week for bugs.

"Trust me, Winston, it's the perfect spot to kill the guy. Music so loud no one'll hear a thing, and if anyone sees anything, those underage punks will be so shit-scared you can push 'em over with a dirty look. I know the guy who runs the place, and I got him to leave the back door open. I got it all mapped out; I'll show you where to park your bike and where to go. Head up the alley onto Folsom and you'll be on I-5 before anyone even calls the pigs. I got a safe house, a trailer over in the valley; I'll keep you there for a few weeks, a month. Set you up with broads and everything. Finally get you laid."

"Fuck you, man, I've been laid," I snapped. Everyone started laughing, Cody and Killer and all the guys crowded around in the back room of Big Daddy's smoking cigs. "Look, Satan, it just doesn't make sense, doing this guy at the club, with all those people. Why can't I do it somewhere I won't get seen? I mean, everyone's going to see me! What if I get IDed in a lineup?"

"It's gotta be in public so everyone sees it, okay? I want everyone to get the warning. He's been watching his ass, lying low, because he knows I'm out to get him. But he never ever misses a *Corpse* show, okay? The Salvages love it when the guy eats sheep's brains onstage."

"I hate that part," I said, remembering a particularly stoned viewing of *Decomposing Corpse Live* on the shitty TV in Satan's basement.

"You would," growled Satan. "You do this my way, Winston. I promise you you'll walk out of that safe house having had more pussy than you ever dreamed of." And then, as if to slam it home, he looked at Wendy.

Which stopped it all right there, because I was not going to argue with that. Even the barest chance of getting into Wendy's pants was enough to bury any doubts I had. I gave Wendy a look, too, and she licked her lips again, ran her fingers through her trashy bleached-blond hair, and she knew, as I knew, that I was going to do whatever Satan told me to do. I mad-dogged him as if I knew what I was doing, which I didn't, but I was too scared to back down.

"Don't call me Winston," I said. "You gonna make me kill him with that crappy forty-five you taught me to shoot with?"

He chuckled. "No, Rat, we got a special gun for you on this one." I smiled, expecting like some smooth-ass black Glock or a silver .44 Automag like Dirty Harry, or a .357 at the very least. "It's a Beretta," he told me, and dug in the pocket of his leather pants.

It was a .25, ugly as sin and all scuffed up, about a thousand years old, with the serial number filed off and the grip and trigger wrapped in what looked like surgical tape.

Oh, never fear, it was a Beretta, all right, one of those old ones from the sixties that little old ladies with poodles put in their rhinestone purses, or like the gun the evil chick always pulls on James Bond and he takes it away from her, puts her in a headlock and fucks her brains out.

"What the fuck is that? I thought I was supposed to kill the guy, not give him a nipple piercing."

Wendy just gave me one of those withering glances of hers, and I shut up.

"This is the perfect piece for the job," Satan growled. "A twenty-five is plenty of firepower to kill a guy. It's got hollow-points, when they go in they just split open and tear this huge hole in the guy. The grip and the trigger are wrapped in this special cotton tape that doesn't take fingerprints. You just carry the one clip. They'll be frisking everyone who goes into the club, which is why the Chupacabra and his guys won't be armed. Just put it in your jockeys and no tough-guy doorman is ever going to feel you up there. Once you shoot the guy, you drop the gun right there. That way you can't be found with it later. With the tape on the trigger and butt, it'll be clean."

"What if the Chupacabra and his guys think of the same thing, smuggle guns into the club that same way, and when I pull out my piece I'm facing like ten little tiny guns?"

"They're not expecting trouble. Real gangsters don't carry guns all the time. There's too much risk of running into a real cop. Real cops will grab your crotch without even thinking about it. The Chup's guys won't risk that. They'll leave their guns with someone who waits outside. That's what they always do."

"You're sure about this?"

Wendy looked at me funny and stood up. "Jesus, Winston," she said. "I'm beginning to think you don't want to do the hit. Maybe we should get somebody else. Somebody with some balls."

"Don't call me Winston." I snatched the gun from Satan. "I'll do it."

I was scared shitless by the time the day of the show rolled around. The only way I could feel even remotely safe was by telling myself once I made some money with Satan I was gonna move up to Humboldt and live with my brother Frasier. He's this kind of Free Tibet hippie-survivalist gun-nut Earth-lover type with all these hot raver-X-head get-high-and-save-the-whales chicks who live with him, and I hear most of those hippie chicks put out. I was gonna be Humboldt County's only pot-smoking incense-burning hippie motherfucker with a complete collection of *Murderous Urge* bootlegs. But first I had to kill a man, one of the most feared sons of bitches in the state. Piece of cake, right?

I parked my bike, the crappy old Harley Shovelhead Satan had sold me for cheap, by the back exit to the Torture Chamber at the alley that opened up onto Folsom Street. There was a big gate there with a padlock hanging open. Seems that gate, and the back exit to the club, were normally locked, but Satan told me he arranged it so the door would be open, so I could just get the fuck out of there once the Chup was dead.

So anyway, I got the bike parked and checked out the scene

outside the club, making sure I knew what's up, what the layout's like. There were all these skanky greasy-haired metalheads hanging around, smoking generic cigs and waiting to get into the club. I joined them and mingled around, lighting up a Marlboro, trying hard not to look like the only eighteen-year-old there. The front sight of the Beretta dug into my cock and was making me walk funny. It was starting to hurt like hell.

I heard them coming before I saw them. The roar of Harleys filled up Folsom Street like a flock of helicopters just over the horizon. They were all wearing those little half helmets, so I recognized the Chup right off. Satan showed me a couple of pictures of the guy, but he'd changed a lot—fatter by maybe fifty pounds and he had a bunch of new tattoos all up and down his arms. A cigarette dangled from the corner of his downturned mouth. His face looked all craggy and etched, like he'd been squinting into the sun for a while.

None of the *vatos* were wearing jackets, just leather vests and black T-shirts or tank tops. That's one thing about badass bikers; they never wear leather jackets like you see in the movies. It's considered pussy to wear leather jackets. You gotta wear blue-jean vests with your arm muscles bulging, which is why I wear a leather jacket. But these guys, I could see each muscle standing out like they'd been working out every day for twenty years. There were six guys on Harleys besides the Chupacabra, and the Chup had a chick on the back. Kind of a scary-looking white chick, too, or maybe she was a *chica bonita* with her hair bleached out. I couldn't tell. She dressed like a Nine Inch Nails freak except for the bleached-blond hair and this strange tan that looked kind of orange. The Chupacabra grabbed her ass as she got off the bike. They kissed, and the Chupacabra turkey-fucked his next smoke off the chick's cigarillo. True love.

Anyway, it was pretty obvious what was going on from the way there was this one guy who stayed outside leaning on his bike, and it's the bike with these big saddlebags. Okay, that made sense; they were all loaded up but they had to keep the guns outside because they'd get frisked going into the club. No problem. The guy standing watch over their guns would be front, and I'll go out back to make my getaway. No problem. Everything seemed cool. Cool. Cool. Cool. Cool.

The Chupacabra and his crew went into the club—they didn't wait in line with all the other punks; they just pushed their way on through and nobody fucked with them until they got to the door. I could see them getting frisked inside. Everything was okay so far. I crushed out my cig and got in line with the rest of the lames, trying hard to stand there and just look cool and not itch my crotch, where the oil from the Beretta was irritating my skin.

This is what I heard about the Chupacabra: The name means "goat sucker," and it comes from this legend in Puerto Rico about a guy who goes around sucking the blood out of goats and sometimes people. Like a vampire, in those cheesy old movies that used to be on channel forty on Saturday morning. And I figured I was Grand Moff Tarkin's Dr. Van Helsing, come to drive a .25-caliber stake through this motherfucker's heart. We'll see how many goats you suck then, pal!

The long-haired security fucks let me in the club with no problem. Nobody grabbed my crotch.

Devil's Bitch, the opening act, was louder-than-fuck death metal from Iceland with a girl lead singer who set a giant stuffed bunny on fire and then screwed it in the ass with a butcher knife strapped to her body. Been there, done that. I guess they never got tired of the performance-art thing in Iceland.

I just stood there nursing a Bud Light and trying to look like your average antisocial loner metalhead without a gun in his crotch. My dick felt like it was going to come off, the metal of the Beretta rubbing against it every time I tried to move. So I just tried to stand real still. But it wasn't only the gun down there, which is why it was so uncomfortable. My jock was a fuckin' army warehouse.

I hadn't followed the plan all the way. I was just supposed to carry the one clip. But I got a buddy who works at a sporting goods store, and he lifted me a couple of extra clips and a box of .25 bullets. I loaded up the two extra clips and stuffed them in my jock alongside the gun. So now, in addition to the Beretta, I had two clips crammed into my Jockeys. It's kind of a wonder those guys at the door didn't find them, but I guess they really didn't want to grope my crotch.

Decomposing Corpse came on. Time to dance, motherfucker.

The Chupacabra's *hombres* pushed their way around their man so there was this three-foot area around him and his chick, who it turned out wasn't Mexican at all; she was just a white chick with a seriously bad tan. The lead guitarist laid down feedback in shuddering waves while a second held this chain-saw rhythm and the lead singer screamed into the microphone half in German or something and half in English, and it was all faster than the engine on a Harley opened full-out on a hill, and everyone was bouncing up and down in time with the jackhammer pulse of the music and I reached down my pants like I was going to jack myself off and out came the Beretta and I lifted it up and pointed it at the Chup and the music got louder and louder until it was so loud I didn't even hear a thing as I pulled the trigger and I guess I was so fucking pumped up on fear that I couldn't notice the little kick of the .25, and so I lowered the gun and stared at it, thinking the fucking gun misfired until I suddenly noticed the splash of red over the chick's orange face, her tan smearing and bubbling, and she didn't even notice for a half a second, except that the Chupacabra was falling forward against the stage with his arm around his chick and dragging her down with him, and it's only then that I realized that the gun really did go off. It was just a split second later that I noticed the *vatos* around the Chupacabra turn to look at him, then look around, and I knew in a second they were going to make me, so I leveled the gun again and pointed it at the Chup and pulled the trigger again, again, again, again, again, again, and the last time there was nothing, and the Chup's cigarette went flying up through the air like a trapeze artist and landed on a *vato*'s arm and made him jump and the girl was screaming, and the singer onstage was still screaming and the band thundered on through their crap-ass song, not even noticing what was happening down in the pit, even as the slam-dancing metalheads screamed and started to back away from me, from the Chup, from the other *vatos*, and now all six bikers were looking at me like they didn't realize what was going on and the Chup was on the ground and his chick's face was splattered with blood and smeared and white, and I thought, *God damn it, I hit her instead of him,* and then all six *vato* biker badass *hombre* motherfuckers reached for their dicks and unzipped their pants like they were going to take a leak on my shoes—so I knew in an instant that Satan was wrong and Winston "Rat" Morelli's short career in organized crime was over, faster than Sonny Corleone's, because I, my friends, was *fucked*.

That's when it was march or die, just like the Motorhead song.

I ran, screamed, waved the empty, useless gun, yelling at all the acne-faced long-hairs to get out of the way. They did, too, except for a few I had to shove. I had my bike's ignition key in my left hand. One of the clips for the Beretta had fallen out of my jockeys and was worming its way down my pant leg. I made it down the stairs, down the corridor, and I got to the back door, and in that second it felt like I was not just fucked in an "I'm fucked" sort of way, but that I was actually, without any competition, the *most* fucked individual on this fucking fucked planet.

The back door was closed and chained and padlocked.

I turned and saw the first set of booted feet coming down the stairs. Without knowing what I was doing, I shoved my hands down my pants.

Holding the ignition key in my mouth to make sure I didn't drop it, I got the second clip of .25 shells out of my underpants, rammed it into the pistol, and raised the gun. I didn't even aim, just chambered a round and pulled the trigger four times.

The stone stairs exploded next to the first *vato*'s foot and he fell forward, and then three of them bounced headfirst down the stairs, cursing and fighting to get up. All three were these huge motherfuckers with tattoos and muscles, and they all had these little tiny guns, which looked ridiculous in their big hands, but I didn't have time to laugh, and as more guys stumbled down the stairs on top of the first ones, I turned and pointed the gun at the padlock and pulled the trigger. There was a flash and the padlock jumped, but held. I tried to pull it open. No good, and the lock was so hot it burned my fingers. I put the barrel of the Beretta right up against the padlock as bullets hit the walls around me. I ignored everything and pulled the trigger.

The padlock blew apart into a dozen pieces.

I felt something smack into my arm, and my shoulder exploded in pain. I pulled the chain out of the way and kicked the door open and then I was out, jumping onto the bike, kicking up the stand, ramming the key into the ignition.

The *vatos* appeared in the door as the engine roared to life, and I heard pops and cracks through the ringing in my ears and then, you better believe it, I popped a wheelie for the very first time in my life, and as I hurtled on one wheel at the gate guarding the alley I saw that it, too, was padlocked. They suddenly got a fucking burglary problem around here or something? I didn't have time to think; I just aimed the bike at the gate and kept the throttle at full, and then I hit the gate and everything was stars and light everywhere as bullets hit the ground all around me and I hit the ground, too, hard, right on my injured shoulder. The bike went skidding off into the side of a building, sparks jumping up around it. I looked up and saw four bikers running at me raising those little toy pistols. I got up and got my hands on the bike and yanked it upright, and I jumped, sparks flying everywhere as .22 slugs hit the buildings on either side of me, and I made it on the bike, opening the accelerator all the way as I put my leg down to keep the bike from falling over, and then I shot faster than a fucking speeding bullet, or at least I hoped so, as the *vatos* behind me emptied the rest of their clips. I hit Folsom doing sixty.

Ten miles down the freeway I remembered I was supposed to drop the gun. I still had it in my hand, tucked between my palm and the brake lever. I couldn't drop it now—if the cops found it that'd tell them exactly what direction I was going.

So I pulled over, tucked the Beretta into the pocket of my jeans, and tried to reach down to get the extra clip of .25 shells out of my pant leg. But it was wedged under my knee something good, and that was the leg I hurt when I fell. I couldn't get the clip, so I just let it sit there, feeling like my knee was going to explode. My shoulder was hurt, too, but I couldn't believe I took a bullet back there—people don't just take .22 bullets in their shoulders and walk away like it's nothing, do they? Then again, I didn't exactly walk away like it was nothing.

I pulled back onto the freeway. The night air whizzed past me, freezing me, chilling me, and I said the "Our Father" a couple of times just in case somebody up there was listening. "I swear, God," I said out loud, into the roar of the wind, catching bugs in my teeth, "if you get me out of this I will never kill anyone ever again."

*   *   *

The trailer park was an hour south into the valley. I drove the speed limit the whole way. My shoulder hurt so bad I thought I might pass out. By the time I got there I had to piss real bad, and I'd had to piss for what must have been a long, long time.

Fourth trailer from the left. There was a pink flamingo stuck into the dry, skanky grass out front. I parked the bike outside, bent over and worked the .25 clip out of my right pant leg. I thought about how I oughta throw the gun into the creek, but then I figured no, the cops would find it and then they'd know exactly where I was. The gun was supposed to be cold, totally untraceable, but I was just too freaked out to dump it that close to where I'd be hiding. So I stashed the clip next to the gun in the right pocket of my jeans and then I thought, *Hell, it's too much of a pain to carry both the gun and the full clip down there.* So I loaded the clip into the gun. And put the gun, with the empty clip, back into my jeans pocket.

Limping, I went over to the trailer. The door was open but the screen door across it was latched. Wearing nothing but a pair of underpants with skulls on them and an *I Kill for Thrills* T-shirt cut off just below her tits, Wendy appeared in the doorway and unlatched the screen.

Five minutes later I was stretched out on the couch, a Pabst Blue Ribbon in my left hand, my jacket across my lap to keep me warm, since I was starting to get chilled. My Violent Angel T-shirt was ripped open wide and soaked with blood, and Wendy told me she had to cut it off me, since I couldn't really raise my left arm. *Fuck,* I thought, *I'll never get another Angel shirt now that they broke up.* But I just gritted my teeth and nodded.

"You want to get your pants off?" she asked, with this sultry, sort of suggestive look, like she was offering to screw me right there. But I knew if she helped me off with my pants, she'd notice the gun in there, and then I'd be in big trouble. So I acted like I was more bothered by the pain than I really was.

"Later. Just do my shoulder," I groaned. "Get it over with."

Wendy went into the little kitchen area and came back holding this huge butcher knife and climbed on top of me. I looked up at her in those panties and that tight cutoff T-shirt, holding that big knife. She slipped the blade against my skin and started cutting my shirt off. I winced.

"Did you drop the gun like we told you?" she asked.

"Sure," I said quickly, nervous, knowing Satan would kick my ass if he knew I didn't follow his instructions. I hoped I wasn't saying it like I was lying. Wendy seemed to believe me.

"Any of the Chup's people get a good look at you?"

I shrugged. "I don't think so," I lied. I know that all those biker guys with guns in their jocks got a great look at my face, scared like a rabbit in the fucking headlights of their little toy guns. But I wasn't about to tell Wendy that.

"You were limping," she said. "What happened to your leg?"

"Just bruised it," I said. "Fell off my bike. Nothing big. Don't worry about it."

Wendy got a cold look on her face.

"What happened at the club, Winston?"

"Don't call me Winston."

"What the fuck happened?"

"There was some shooting. The Chup's guys had guns. Little ones. I made it out back and they were shooting at me as I tried to get away. I fell on my leg. I don't know when I hurt my shoulder— I think I clipped it getting through the gate."

"They didn't hit you?"

"Nah, I was lucky."

"You better fuckin' believe you were lucky, Winston. Did you shoot back?"

"Only at the Chup," I lied.

"Anyone other than the Chup get hurt?"

"Yeah," I said, rubbing my sore leg. "I did."

Wendy didn't smile. "Anybody other than the Chup and you?"

"Don't think so."

"Good," said Wendy, and sat down next to me on the couch, her legs tucked up under her ass. "You know what they say about wounded animals."

She cut away the sleeve around my wounded shoulder. I gritted my teeth and looked away as she poked at it.

"Not too bad," she said. "Doesn't look like you got hit. Maybe you scraped yourself falling down. No big deal. But you're going to need something more than that beer."

So she got off of me and went into the kitchen for a bottle of Jack. I drank from it as she cleaned and bandaged my shoulder. Every once in a while I sputtered, and by the time she was done, a lot of the Jack was gone, but most of it sloshed down my face and onto the couch and I hadn't even caught a buzz. I hoped Wendy hadn't noticed I was wasting her booze.

I kept staring at her breasts under that tight top, couldn't take my eyes off of them. That's when Wendy smiled.

She set the butcher knife on the back of the couch.

"Ready for your reward, Winston?"

Now that the moment had finally arrived, I felt like I couldn't do it. My heart was pounding. I couldn't believe I was finally going to get laid, and by Wendy. I was scared—shit-scared.

But I just nodded and said, "Yes," in this hoarse, wimpy little voice.

Then Wendy smiled and reached for my belt. She unfastened my jeans, smooth and easy. Then she crouched over me, head in my lap, and I wondered if it tasted like gun oil down there. If it did, Wendy didn't seem to mind. Neither did I.

When she came up for air after a while, she started pulling my jeans over my hips.

"Let me get them," I said quickly. "My leg still sorta hurts."

"All right," said Wendy. "I'll put on some tunes."

She got up and walked across the little trailer, and as I pulled off my pants, still feeling the lump in the pocket, I saw blood on the front of my jeans. Whether it was my blood, or the Chup's, or someone else's, I didn't know. And I thought, *What if Wendy wants to wash my jeans or something, even burn them in case the cops come asking questions? She'll find the gun in them and then I'm screwed. Satan will be so pissed if he finds out.*

Wendy leaned forward over the stereo. I had to fight to keep my mind on what I was doing; I kept watching Wendy's ass to make sure she didn't turn around as I reached in and got the Beretta out of my pants pocket. I shoved the little gun under the cushions of the couch. It was still cocked and loaded with the last full clip. I'd have to get rid of it later.

"Violent Death Is Its Own Reward," Wendy purred at me, and she comes back to the couch as Violent Angel starts exploding through the speakers. "I know this is your favorite," she shouted over the screeching guitars.

It was the first song on the first Violent Angel album. My favorite song of all time at top volume, earsplitting, but I couldn't even hear it, I was so busy staring at Wendy.

Wendy smiled at me, reached down and took off her T-shirt. She took off her underwear and just stood there naked, looking down at me.

She got on top of me, sliding up and down my body. The music blasted all around the trailer. I should have been in the moment, digging what Wendy was doing to me with her hands and her tongue and her thighs. I shouldn't have been thinking about how I could scream at the top of my lungs and no one outside would hear anything.

Wendy straddled me. Her body worked up and down, the skin of her tits brushing back and forth against my face. Sweat dribbled onto my face and ran into my mouth as she slipped her pierced nipples between my lips. Her hair streamed down, brushing my face. Her tight body moved against me. Was I inside her yet? I couldn't even tell, I was so freaked out.

"Close your eyes, Winston," said Wendy, her voice a hungry lioness growl. "Open your mouth and close your eyes and you will get a big surprise." And then she laughed, her mischievous little laugh that sounded about 10 percent funny and 90 percent evil.

"Don't call me Winston," I said.

"Sorry." Wendy smiled. "I mean *Rat*."

That was what did it. That was what told me something was seriously fucked up. Because she called me "Rat," yeah, but also because I had never heard Wendy apologize for anything, not even to Satan.

She ground her hips against me, her legs spreading until she straddled me, creamy thighs wrapped like a wishbone around my crotch. Me poised at the entrance to Wendy's body. Me just waiting for her to sink down on top of me, take it inside her. "I said close your eyes, baby, close your eyes." Her rubbing her lips back and forth on me. Me groaning, arching my back, lifting my hips to meet her. Her lifting her body a little further so I can't quite get inside her . . . wicked, wicked look on her face that I see through slitted eyelids.

I could scream at the top of my lungs and no one outside would hear anything.

It all came together for me in an instant, every fucking thing about the hit made sense, in a way it didn't make sense before. Because as Wendy reared up on me, moaning and laughing, with this crazy look on her face, with the silver-shining butcher knife held high and about to plunge down into my throat, as she reared like a horse trying to throw its rider, as she got ready to punch my clock with that ten-inch butcher knife, my right hand, to my surprise and Wendy's, came up holding the Beretta.

The look on her face wasn't shock, exactly. More like confusion.

My face must have been a mask of fear, even as I pointed the Beretta at her chest, closed my eyes and pulled the trigger.

Violent Angel was on so fucking loud that I didn't hear the gun go off, but this time I didn't look at it in confusion. This time I knew what I was doing. Wendy dropped the knife and clutched her throat, slumped forward onto my body, blood pulsing out and soaking my face and hair even as my hips pumped upward . . . and I guess it was after I shot her the second time, in the belly, that I realized she was still moving and so was I. But it wasn't until after she'd stopped moving that I realized I had come.

I left Wendy there twitching and naked on the floor of her trailer. I siphoned gas off her bike and took the Shovelhead onto the freeway with the hot valley wind blowing a trail of death behind me.

It never should have happened that way, but it had to. Because I am one poor-ass James fuckin' Bond, and pricks like Satan and fuckin' femme fatales like Wendy are the scourge of all poseurs like me.

But this ain't no epic battle fought on the plains of Troy; it's a squalid one fought in a trailer park in fucking Fresno. What matters is that I am alive, and it's march or die, all right, march or fucking die. I'll start by heading out to Humboldt on the Shovelhead. Maybe Frasier can get me in touch with some of his hippie-survivalist friends and I can hide out in a fucking commune somewhere smoking weed—sure, it's all peace and love and that kind of shit (except for the guns), but I understand those hippie chicks put out. So maybe I can learn to like it.

I don't know if the cops or Satan will find me first. Could go either way. I figure someday I'll get found, by either Satan's guys or the pigs, and I better be ready for the day that happens, gun hidden in my crotch, murder in my soul. But until it does, until the day that violent angel comes for me, there's one thing I can be fucking sure about.

Nobody better call me Winston.

Michael Marano is a horror writer and media critic who divides his time between Boston, Massachusetts, and Charleston, South Carolina. His novel *Dawn Song* was awarded the Bram Stoker and International Horror Guild awards. His popular film column, "MediaDrome," appears regularly in *Cemetery Dance*. He has covered horror movies for the Public Radio Satellite Network program *Magazine International* for fourteen years. His short fiction has appeared in *Peter S. Beagle's Immortal Unicorn*, *The Mammoth Book of Best New Horror 11*, *Queer Fear*, *Queer Fear II* and *Gothic.Net*. Web site: www.mindspring.com/~profmike.

. . . AND THE DAMAGE DONE

by Michael Marano

I see them, and they know I see them. That is why they want to break me: because I see. The theater of stealth they enact is just that—theater . . . designed to exhaust me, so that I forfeit my vision. I should get up from the cigarette-scarred table, walk away from their performance. But my friend is dying, and I'd sooner die than leave her.

Marie smiles at me with lips turning the color of lead. She sips coffee with a mouth that should soon go into rictus, and I ache to kiss her mouth and say a true good-bye.

"So, I'm doing better," she says. The fact that she means it twists a flat blade in my heart. She runs her thumb along her cup while her eyes film, as if skins peeled from eggshells are pressed upon her irises. She has always met my eyes with her stone-deep gaze, and that is one reason I've always loved her. I should take the hand that has left her cup and now rests on the table beside a profession of love knife-etched into the wood years ago. But I'm afraid of what I'd feel under her skin, that the feeling would brim my vision, that I would flinch at the touch of loose skin sliding over bone. *They* who press their sight on me like sweat-slick fingertips would know that such vulnerability would clench my spine and make themselves yet more visible to me. My hand is bound to where it rests, as I am bound to this city of my hijacked birth.

Instead of taking her hand, I meet Marie's eyes, now gone the white-blue of watered milk. I smile back. The skin of her shoulders, of which she has always been vain, is as-yet unblemished, still snow-smooth and firm. Her tattoos seem transparent as stained glass. Both her hands, which have cupped my face while I grieved, now rest on the table. I hate that I have pinched out, even partly, the light that had come from her smile. Once, while awaiting a bus across from her apartment, I saw Marie's sister walk to the building's front door with the grace that only one who has studied dance as a child has and press the ringer. Marie leaned out her window and waved before buzzing in her sister. From above, Marie's smile had banished the gloom that clung to that shitty place more surely than did the dying paint on the chipped brick buildings. Her light challenged the sky, and, as if in shame, the sky rallied and for a few heartbeats seemed able to house choirs of seraphim, to become a sky like that over Sinai in a Bible painting.

I take her hands and redeem what I can of her light. *They* lean out of the faceless banks of the innocent, forcing themselves into my vision the way that stones in spring press themselves out of thawing soil; a remembered pain runs under my jaw from ear to ear and over my brow, and I feel the parting of skin that is not mine being cut like kid leather.

I should leave this city. But I am tied here by the only relation I have on this Earth, who despite the womb we shared is not, nor will ever be, a relation of blood.

One of *them* filths the space I share with my friend, setting down his newspaper and grinning as if Marie and I are lovers through whom he lives vicariously. In a more civilized time, one who lived in a port city such as I would never have encountered those with whom he is joined, for they would have been far-flung sailors afraid to drown. They who watch, and who do nothing else, are not sailors who dread scalding brine in their lungs; they bear the corruption unique to those whose hands will never know a callus.

I *see*. I do not *hear*. Such deafness can be a mercy. For the creak of the brittle leather that Marie's hands feel like would be more than I can bear. "Do you remember . . ." I say. "Do you remember how cold it was, the last time we held hands?"

"It was freezing," she says, and I reach as would a drowning man for the sensations of that fog-chilled San Francisco night. Her death-gloved hands grip mine tighter. "Why?"

"It was kind of nice," I say. "I liked holding your hands, then. Staying warm, the way we did, even though your granny brought down on us the wrath of the PC police."

"It was nice." She smiles a bit wider, showing the capped tooth that crystal meth had cracked, and turns her filmed eyes, now flecked with dust, upward an instant as she touches the January night that we, in the corner of a bar near the bay, had huddled in as if it were a quilt beneath the heirloom that was her grandmother's fur coat. The bar had no heat, and in back, near the old rotary pay phone, you could see your breath in air touched with sea smoke; less well than my breath, I could see the beautiful array of ha'penny nails, less solid than sun-blindness, that would one day protrude from the bar's blackened timbers. Under the fur coat, against the rich, silk lining, Marie and I held hands as we pressed our temples together. I could smell the sandalwood-like conditioner she used, and the ugly ghost of rubbing alcohol in the left sleeve of the coat.

The mercy of that memory, of blood flowing to our fingers, of silk and the warmth of that unethical yet wonderfully thick coat, dispels the feeling of her unliving skin against mine. Her hands dawn with smoothness. I feel the flecks of paint beaded on her nails. She never scrubs off the flecks or dissolves them with thinner, always wanting to leave a reminder on her person of the palettes she uses. Marie senses an echo of what I sense. Gooseflesh dews her skin, giving new texture to the indigo fan of peacock feathers painted into the milk of her right shoulder and to the cloud-whiskered face of Old Man East Wind tattooed on her left shoulder.

Despite the chill that writes itself upon her skin and the tomb color of her lips, her inner light that I had partly snuffed is rekindled, and it feels again as if angels might grace the sky. And sitting behind Marie, one of *them*, tauntingly removes a pair of shades from his jacket and puts them on. He then raises the ever-present newspaper to his face, and, as always, it is turned to tight columns of stock listings in print so fine as to make the paper seem a field of gray.

Later, in the sun, I kiss Marie and say only half my good-bye. "Farewell" is a word that bleeds from two wounds. She can't know what I see. I bleed alone. I can't change what will come. I have tried to help others less dear to me, but the lessons of inevitability that most learn from a play about a Scottish king, I have learned through sifting the ash of failure.

"You'll come to the showing?" she asks, running her hand from my shoulder to my wrist. "I'd really like you to be there. I'll be pretty scared."

"I'll be there," I say, and deny myself the luxury of letting my knees fall from under me, the luxury of screaming my grief at the mockingly bright sky, knowing that she will not be at the showing. Her bus charges around the corner a few blocks distant. She must meet it at the stop. I embrace her. We are in a neighborhood in which Spanish mingles with English. I whisper as a prayer by her ear what in Spanish is most often a mere phrase: "Go with God."

She walks away, the circle of her twenty-nine years closing, her white skin graced by the sunlight that cloaks itself upon her shoulders, that makes the peacock feathers and the face of the East Wind translucent in her flesh, that dances radiance off of the fog-dense glass syringe embedded in her arm below tightly knotted rubber tubing. Whimpers rise behind my throat as I watch her meet her bus, as I know with the certainty of each breath I draw that I will miss her each moment of each day for the rest of my life . . . as I know that in death, she will never be far from me, that she will loiter and brush against me in the way half-remembered dreams do upon my waking. One of *them* stands at the bus stop that Marie has marked with her absence, and pantomimes the pressing of a syringe into the crook of his left arm.

It took me days to remember there are such things as barbers. Drunk with grief, I walk into the shop and into the past that pools there like blood under a bruise.

I sit in the cracked leather chair as the old man sets a hot towel upon my face. I will not go to Marie's showing, that has since its announcement become her wake, looking like the drunkard she saved me from becoming.

"Ever since the AIDS came," the barber says, as he had the first time I had come here and the day after that, "the Health Department makes us wear doctors' gloves." He scrapes my face with a latex-sheathed hand that, in the corner of my sight, is free of the glove and of liver spots. I breathe slowly as the razor touches my skin where a blade less fine and wielded by a drug-addled grip had made its enduring mark on me. The past displaces the present in my awareness as a stone displaces water in a dish. Behind me, in the mirror, men the color of twilight sit in suits with broad lapels and await turns in the chair that had come and gone decades ago. They are like the men who had courted my mother, who told her they could give her "a better life" and lift her to respectability. I smell colognes no longer man-ufactured, and the ghost-scent of saddle soap; the cracked leather at my back feels whole and smooth.

As the barber finishes the task I cannot do myself, he pulls away the bib and fully leans me forward in the chair. "How's it look?" he asks, as I see what I can of myself in the mirror and the glimpses and scents of the past wink out.

"Great," I say . . . though the truth would be, *I don't know*. I'm thankful that I do not breathe, in the way that I just breathed the air of the past, the smooth suffocation reflected back at me.

On the street where the barbershop rots, a wind comes off the bay, cold. It touches the rawness of my freshly shaved face, and all of me feels the need to tremble.

"You're greedy. And selfish. Because you're not whole."

Imagine the beast that hid under your bed, the branch-clawed thing that cast moon shadows upon your window stepping from childhood fear and walking beside you on a street littered with the wrappers of take-out meals.

I look to the man walking beside me, to one of *them* who have hounded me since childhood; he draws my attention with the same revulsion and fascination a hornet does when it lands on my arm. I see *both* of him; the man's younger self walks like a gray shadow within the man's present self. Like all of *them,* the one who accosts me is a pale, slovenly old shit, paunchy from knowing the world from what he can grasp and consume. The man reeks of his own past.

"And you're cruel," he adds. I see past his worn denim jacket, his dashiki straining to cover his gut, and his kinte headwear, and glimpse the young man he had been when this city and what he understood to be the world had been indisputably his. I taste his hatred of me mingled with his stink.

The man's shadowy younger self wears a fringed jacket of suede and a wide-brimmed hat. It looks as if the man's older self has eaten his younger self, as if his own youth were yet another thing to be taken in to nourish him. A rose-colored newspaper is tucked under his arm; his younger self carries the *Berkeley Barb* the same way.

In the late afternoon, I step into twilight, into the dusk that made up the flesh of the men I glimpsed from the past. It is the dusk in which I am deaf—the wordless nonpresent in which past and future blur and bleed. I find safety there, as the old bastard spews forth his prattle. I walk miles to where I will take the bus that will bring me to the waterfront, where Marie's showing and remembrance will be. In my chosen deafness, the words of the man's present self, designed to erode my will, are as dim as words heard through a thick stone wall; the words of his past self are purely silent. I don't know why he . . . why *they* . . . now forsake their program of stealth and city-hidden harassment.

In a twilight I have made, I walk, with a monster from my childhood shuffling beside me, until the Civic Center, the rotten heart of this city to which I am shackled, looms ahead. The twisted trees before City Hall take afternoon shadows, and the row of portable toilets for the city's human detritus are packed close like a seawall containing the destitute who pool in the park nearby. The man beside me, who has spoken to me, his quarry, is too winded from walking to say anything. I step from my twilight. I see his goal ahead, the bus stop that is my destination, and the collision of fury and dread that has no name in any language I know cracks frost along my spine. At the bus stop is what looks like the mass of gray necrotic tissue I once pressed out of my wrist into a basin of scalding salt water when, uninsured, I had been bitten by a brown recluse spider. The mass waves as did the tendrils of dead flesh that had been part of me.

The mass is many of *them*, expectant and hungry as they await me at the stop. Their ghost-fleshed, younger selves that had first hunted me when I was a child mill within their softer, older bodies. In their translucency, their younger selves overlap. It is as if the film that infection coats on the lenses of my eyes has been given the form of living people.

They await me. Knowing this is the way I have chosen to go to the waterfront. Knowing that this is the way I have chosen to honor my friend whom they knew, from the diluted sight they have stolen from me, would die. They wish to ambush me in a group, the way they used to while I still drank to the excess to which they drove me.

I turn and cross against the light, ducking SUVs and minivans. The faces of children in one vehicle look away from the DVD they watch in the backseat to gaze at the man inches from their careening window.

Once across, I look back to the crowd of stalkers. Their ghost-bodies seem agitated, like river grass whipped in a current.

I walk quickly along alleys, ways impassable to cars and cabs should they try to follow. I take steep hills, knowing that they would not follow or keep up.

Alone, at the top of a hill, I let out my rage that they would so trespass on my pilgrimage to Marie's wake. She stirs again within me; the part of her that loiters in my heart and brushes against my thoughts has been soiled by *their* proximity. I lean against a wall of cinder block and, swearing, strike it with my palm as would one frenzied by angel dust.

The space had been many things. All it had been over the years puts pressure on my forehead; the weight of its past packs around me like the underneath of snow. The buzzing energy of the shouts of children, though not the sounds, echoes from when the place had been an unlicensed playschool. I bow my head from the pressure as I enter and lift my gaze slowly. . . .

And I drink what had been Marie. The taste is like the scent of a stem of rosemary drying. The feel is as soft on my skin as lake water in the summer. Few of those here mourn Marie, and I'm thankful for their hypocrisy; I could not have withstood a room of people wounded by the loss of Marie while I was touched by her art, and while they were so touched. I said I lifted my gaze to her art; that is only partly true. For to lift your gaze to her art is to be lifted by your gaze; it is for your vision to be drawn in the same way her deep brown eyes trapped your gaze, welcomely, whenever she spoke to you. The angels summoned to the sky above Marie's light seemed to grace what she had crafted with her gaze and her hands. To walk into the space where her art is hung is like walking into her arms, the very arms into which she pressed the numbness and death she had first melted in a spoon, the very arms which, holding you, would let you know the grief and love she wore as a raiment upon her soul.

A few patrons look my way, as if they know me. None is one of *them*. It is as if I am expected, though why, I cannot guess. Yet a few among the few who look at me do so the way that *they* do—as if I am their property that has rudely not acknowledged their ownership of me. I look away from them, and suddenly feel as if the earth rises to meet me. As if I have been taken by a swoon and fall to the floor of a red-sanded desert.

"I'm glad you came," says a soft voice as a hand places itself on my shoulder, as I remember such a touch from all the times Marie had so greeted me. I turn and see a mask of Marie, fleeting, as if I have stared at a black-and-white photo of her and suddenly looked to an expanse of pure white. The mask fades and a face like Marie's lingers in flesh where the mask had been.

Nell looks much like her sister, and what is more wounding to me, she smells like Marie, if such a family likeness is possible. She is the ground—the earth that supports—beneath the radiant sky that had been Marie. Nell's eyes are blue, the near opposite of the warm brown of Marie's eyes, yet just as deep and arresting. I place the hand I abraded on cinder block over the hand she has placed on my shoulder, and see under the sleeve of her blouse the raised, worm-colored scars along her forearm that are there, or that will be there one day. Where Marie has used a needle, Nell has, or will use, the teeth of a broken bottle.

"Marie said she wanted you here. For this." She swallows after speaking the last two words, as if to take them back.

"I had to come, and I wanted to."

"Could you . . . could I ask you to come with me?" She takes my chafed hand and leads me past the deep forests Marie had painted half from the banks of brush and trees in Golden Gate Park and half from her imagination, past the seascapes Marie had done of an ocean she had never seen but had only read about, past the small cottage in Berkeley she had painted that she had transplanted to a hillock like one in a work by Cézanne. Nell walks ahead of me with near-unreal gracefulness that shames me in a way that I cannot name. There is a memory that twitches warmly inside me, and I realize that Nell leads me the way Marie led me to the corner of that freezing bar in January.

Nell stops us before the far wall of the space, near windows that look upon the bay.

"Can you tell me who they are?" she asks, gesturing to Marie's portraits.

Empathy is what scholars say is the investment of oneself into a painting. It is an incomplete notion, for a painting can intrude upon *you* and your perceptions. Looking at the canvas that Marie painted, looking at how Marie had forced her own compassionate and loving sight to *stay* within the textures and strokes she crafted, I *felt* as all that is, that was, that had been, Janet intrude upon me. Marie had painted Janet reading a book in the park. The curling flames of Janet's rich, thick hair were draped over one hand; so perfect were the textures, one could see the motion of Janet's fingers twisting a lock as she read.

"Do you know her?" asks Nell.

"It's . . . she's . . . Janet. Marie and I knew her years ago. She disappeared." I stumble for the words. "Could you ask the curator, or whoever is handling the sales, not to put this one in the catalog. Or online? And maybe leave the work untitled?"

"Marie made those stipulations weeks ago," says Nell. Her words are clipped, not out of anger at my request, but out of discomfort for speaking of Marie in the so recent past.

Of course she did; of course she would, I say. Or think I say.

So frightened, so sleep-deprived had Janet been before she fled town and her stalking ex-husband, Marie and I had heard her scream when a lock of her hair, flowing around her like red-brown smoke, had been caught in a low-hanging branch one windy day.

"Marie said that she . . . *Janet,* you said? That she probably wanted to stay disappeared."

Nell next walks me to a portrait of Tom, whom Marie had painted in warm earth tones. In his portrait, Tom smokes while hunched over his coffee. Marie had caught the happy semigrin that Tom wore whenever he lit up, knowing that he had successfully displaced his need for coke to the less lethal need for cigarettes and caffeine. Tom had disappeared as well, either to leave the city and its temptations or to be consumed by those temptations elsewhere, with no witnesses to his defeat by that which steady smoking and coffee had held at bay.

" 'Tom,' " says Nell after I have named him. "I met him, I think. I just couldn't recall his name."

We next stand before a portrait of Paul, whom Marie and I had met while he wore a cast, as he was recovering from the vicious spite of a girlfriend who had smashed a jar of pennies onto his hand. Marie had painted Paul with his guitar on his lap—his face set as he worked the hand exerciser that might one day give him back his music. The play of light on Paul's face is like that of a Hopper; the look in his eyes is one of pain and hope. I tell Nell Paul's name and his story, though I do not know if he has ever learned to play again.

I feel my pulse throb in my neck as I speak to Nell, as I realize that Marie's art has become more beautiful with her death. While she lived, it was timid of her light, even though what makes it beautiful is the investment of her light.

Nell thanks me by offering me a plastic cup of jug wine from the crumb-ridden caterer's table. I decline, and she seems to nod, as if remembering. By the table, on a small podium, is a photo album of Marie's unfinished works. The cityscape view out of Marie's living room window floats like some half-realized dream in the album behind a clear plastic sheet protector. The album feels as if something close to me might sleep among Marie's other half-finished dreams and visions. If it is the face of another dead or lost friend, I can't bear to look at it.

Nell's glance falls to the album, to the cityscape that had filled the window beneath which Marie had died.

"Do you still have a key to Marie's place?" she asks.

"No," I say, giving Nell insight into my relationship with Marie of which she may not have been aware.

Nell looks down to the scavenged table, as if embarrassed by the question and my answer. She reaches for her purse and opens it.

They are coming. I feel them. Their approach is like the spread of wasp venom under newly stung skin. They have known my destination. They approach en masse, to reattempt the ambush they had intended for the bus stop. Because of their numbers, they feel close. Closer even than does Nell standing before me. I should flee to the anonymity of my apartment, to the safety of its smallness and the invisibility of its single window that faces a brick wall.

Yet there is a safety in this moment I feel as Nell reaches into her purse and pulls forth a key ring. *They* will not come, I know, until this safe moment is over. Nell removes a key from where it dangles next to a shiny, newly cut one just like it and hands it to me. I can feel the residue on it of the grief and the anger she felt when the clerk at the coroner's office handed it to her. The key scalds my hand, and I feel as if my palm might blister where she has placed it.

"I don't know how long I'll be here," says Nell. "Can you meet me at Marie's sometime after ten? There are things . . ." Her throat constricts, as does mine while I meet her eyes. "There are things Marie said she wanted you to have if anything happened to her."

Nell is furious; there is terrible beauty to rage on the face of one as graceful as she, even when such rage is hidden. Loss masks itself beneath her skin. She wishes to make her rage known, rage born of the sight of Marie's face, haloed by the glow of a metal slab, the face I had seen moving with the simulacra of life when Marie and I had spoken our maimed farewell.

"I can meet you there. After ten," I say, putting the key in my pocket.

"I have to play hostess. Please excuse me."

She gives me her hand, now slick with cold sweat. I have upset her, or she has upset herself. This moment and its safety dissolve around us. "Thank you for coming," she says.

I leave the showing. I walk past the colors and the palettes I recognize from the flecks on Marie's nails, from the smears on the horrid overalls she wore while working, from the reeking dropcloths that she piled in the corner of her kitchen. I take the back stairwell where the caterers loiter, feeling *them* come closer. At street level, I see *them* coming—a few cluster near rusted cars and vans parked in the waterfront lot.

They will position themselves throughout the neighborhood.

They will hunt me in bars and coffee shops, and coordinate themselves through their cell phones and voice mails and text messages. I do not fathom this breaking of the theater of stealth, and though I know going to Marie's home will savage my heart, I am thankful to have a place to go besides my home, which will be watched closely tonight.

Nell waits in the hallway outside Marie's apartment, tapping cigarette ash into a beer can. The sleeves of her blouse are rolled up, revealing smooth skin etched with as-yet-unbroken blue veins.

She smiles as I walk up the hallway, as I smile politely and smother down my horror at what she will do.

She drops her cigarette hissing into the can. She stands and again fixes me with her blue eyes. I hide what I see of her future, what I see of her choices and how they will write themselves deeply in her flesh. For the second time tonight, she says, "I'm glad you came."

There is no graceful reply to what she has said, so I say next to nothing: "Have you been here long?"

"About an hour. I couldn't stand being at the showing after a while. A lot of the so-called patrons were just vultures."

I smell *them* on her as she says *vultures*. They have been close to her, soiling the space of Marie's art, her empathy, and her mourning.

"Is there anything I can do? To help settle . . . things?"

"No. Not now. I just want you have what Marie wanted you to have. I need to see something *done*. I want to have a little bit of closure tonight."

She opens the door and the residual smells of Marie—the lingering scent of the expensive lotion she always used out of vanity for her skin, and also the scent of the sandalwood conditioner she said always made her feel calm—choke me with memory.

We enter. On the couch before us is an amorphous mass, the color and texture of which is immediate in the tactile memory of my hands.

"I couldn't figure out why she wanted you to have this ratty thing," Nell says, picking up her grandmother's fur coat. Trying a feeble joke, she says, "You're not going to wear it, are you?"

"No," I say, and the word is more coughed out of me than spoken. I can't bear the thought of touching the coat, even as Nell holds it to me. Nell, with her otherworldly grace, steps toward me and I nearly step back, as if out of fear. She hands it to me and I feel I could tear it as if it were paper. The sensation, the remembered feeling of holding Marie's hand under the silk lining, trembles in my blood.

"We . . . had . . . with the coat . . ." Nell eyes never leave mine. I see in her the frailty behind her strength that will lead her to run broken glass along her wrist. I want to reach through the time separating us from that moment and snatch away the bottle before it can rip her.

"You don't have to tell me," she says, and takes back the coat. She rests it on the chair that Marie and I had salvaged when the college kids down the street had moved and had dumped it on the curbside. Nell walks to the battered desk where sits Marie's paint-smeared laptop. Nell picks up a stack of disks and hands them to me. Some bear multicolored thumb- and fingerprints in oil-based paint.

"Marie didn't want you to know how she worked. She was almost kind of . . . superstitious about it. She said you always figured things out with just a few hints. She called you 'Sherlock,' sometimes. As a joke. Behind your back. She didn't want you to know that she took digital snaps of people when they weren't looking. She hated doing portraits from sittings. She didn't want you to know, because then you'd be self-conscious around her and her portrait of you would come out wrong."

I hold the disks as if fanning cards. Nell says, "These are the shots she took of everyone she did portraits of. I think they're all your friends and hers. She told me you had a real big heart. That you're sentimental. I think she wanted to print them out for you, but she never got around to it." Nell shrugs. "I'd do it, but I don't know how to work her printer, and I can't find the manual to save my life."

"I don't own a computer," I blurt, looking at the disks. More in control, I say, "But I can take them to a print shop, I think." I run my thumb along the oil-based mark of Marie's thumb on a disk of bright orange, remembering the feel of the flecks she preserved on her nails.

"Marie said you were a real technophobe," she says with a half smile. "There's another thing. I don't know if you'll want it. She never really said that she wanted you to have it, but I think you should at least see it." Nell leads me to the gutted walk-in closet that is—that *had been*—Marie's studio. We tip to one side the electric fans in the doorway that had been her ventilation system. A *person* awaits me in there. I feel his presence, almost in the way I feel the presence in this city of the one relation in this world that is *of me*, yet not truly of my blood, despite the blood we shared.

On the easel Marie's uncle had made from scrap wood is an unfinished canvas, a photo of which must have called to me from the album of incomplete works at the showing. The face of the man in the half-done portrait is the face I have not seen for days in the mirror. I recognize myself in the way that I had recognized Janet and Tom and Paul, refracted through Marie's eyes, illuminated by her light.

"She couldn't finish it," says Nell. "She kept trying to catch you in just the right moment, to take a digital snap that'd be just right. She took a lot of snaps of you while you weren't looking. She said it was easy, because you were always distracted. But she could never find a way to complete you. Do you want it? The art dealer wasn't sure he could sell it, because it's the only unfinished portrait. Do you want to take it?"

"I don't know."

I lean out the closet doorway, almost knocking over one of the fans. I grip the glass doorknob; it creaks. I let go of it, and am next aware that Nell's hands are strong. They are like the hands of a nurse used to heaving the sick and the dying from bed to gurney. Her strong hands lift me to my feet and guide me to the sofa. Discreetly, she leaves me to sob there, laid out as I sense that she has repeatedly sobbed in the same spot while she deals with her sister's unfinished affairs.

After a period of time I can't measure, after I have sat up, she walks to the sofa and says, "It's okay." She gestures to her own dry eyes. "I have nothing left. If you can still cry, I kind of envy it. If you still have grief to let go, let it go." She pulls matches from her purse set on the floor by the sofa and lights a candle that rests in a holder by Marie's laptop. "It's okay," she says, then shuts off the lights, leaving me in dim comfort. After a moment, I hear the refrigerator door opening and the cracking of a beer can in the kitchen. Nell returns, holding the can in one hand and a bottle of nonalcoholic beer in the other. "You don't drink, right?" she asks.

"No," I say, as I sit up a little straighter.

With her strong hands, she twists off the bottle cap, which seems to fly off. There's hardly any sound as the cap is released, so fast does she remove it. I take the beer and sip. It's flat, but very cold. I only realize it is flat as I take a second sip. I look to the amber glow of the candle. I drink again, and I *know*. I know that this is the candle Marie used to melt the smack that killed her. In the flame, in the flow of wax, I see who sold her the smack and why, and I realize I am partly culpable in her murder, that I led her killers to her. I realize, without the use of my sight, that *they* who have tampered with what Marie pushed into her veins have tampered with what I have taken past my lips. I look to Nell and stand. I won't make it to the door. Dumbly, moving like the drunk I once was, I turn to the window, the very window that Marie looked out to greet her sister below, the very window from which I had seen Marie's light shine forth. I see in reality the unfinished cityscape Marie had painted, thinking I might open the window and cry out to someone who might care.

In the dim-lit glass, my reflection changes. The smooth expanse that has covered my face fades and my features return to my sight for the first time in days. In my sight, *I* have disfigured myself in the mirror before, knowing of ugliness in my future I could not bear to see. Yet the new, smooth and featureless face, that I realize was not new at all, was no mere self-disfigurement, but *portent* . . . inevitability. A future I no longer see, because it is a future that is now arriving.

I turn back to Nell and speak meaningless syllables as the doped beer she has been given to offer me falls to the floor on which Marie died. My sight fades and returns. Nell stands in the doorway, cradling the phone in her hand. As I black out, I see that *they,* in their past and present split selves, will soon come through the door to claim their prize.

The fur coat is on me, draped like a quilt. Nell does not know that the people she helps, the people who have hunted me, have killed her sister with uncut dope . . . much stronger than anything Marie, or any user in this city, could withstand.

The place I've been taken to, the place I have been returned to across the gulf of my life, reeks of stale curry and incense. My life away from this spot, to *them,* has been mere caesura. The caesura now ends. I am on the floor. Nell holds my cinder block–skinned hand under the coat and through the reek of the place, I smell that she has anointed herself with the lotion and the conditioner her sister had used. Against my will, the sensation of the coat and the scents that Nell wears summon the memory of Marie that is more than memory, that I realize has been haunting me with greater force than any mere memory possibly could. *They* mill about, their grotesque treads making the floorboards creak as they light candles around the room.

What Nell had been given to slip me in the beer still addles my brain, though not nearly as much as does the sudden full and terrible restoration of my sight. So blind I have been, I did not know that I was blinded. I could not see my own future. I could not see this trap, because the mere envisioning of it in a future relative to the present I have just quit had gutted my sight to the future I could have otherwise seen. Inevitability . . . the lesson of the Scottish king.

I am prone on the very spot where I was born. It is the very spot that has tied me to this city full of the desperate and the wounded—this city full of those incomplete souls whom I could not leave once I knew them and loved them as my kind. I could not leave this city, even after I had left *them* who have lived in this house as a commune for decades, who have been held together as a community by their quest to reclaim me . . . the lump of flesh that came stifled and silent into their world, and that now draws shallow breaths upon the very spot where it had nearly suffocated at birth, the very spot on which I had been born sheathed in skin that is not my own.

Nell sees me draw breath like a grounded fish, sees me trying to speak and to warn and to plead. There is pity in her eyes, and beyond her eyes, which in this candlelight seem as brown as those of her sister's, there is the terrible beauty of rage. The rage half expresses itself in the play of candle shadows on her face. The shadows are like a portrait of her splintered fury and sorrow. Her pitying face is silent. The amber glow makes this unspeaking face look like that of a north German Madonna. The anger-shadows scream, distorted as a face painted by Munch. They bellow and they wail. And dimly, as if from underwater, I hear the anger-shadows speak what the pitying face of Nell does not. Deafness and all its mercy partly fall away.

I try to squeeze Nell's hand, to let her feel just slightly what I feel, the way her sister always could. My grip is weak; my hand has less strength then does a dying kitten.

The man who had accosted me on the street looms between Nell and me. He grunts as he leans his saggy bulk forward and runs his acrid, food-greased hand over my face. Up close, I see that he has the ugly ogre's teeth of one who has sucked his thumb into late childhood.

"It's good you got a shave this afternoon," he says, smiling, as his younger self smiles with teeth less yellow, that are lit by the sunlight that had once streamed through the window behind Nell that is now painted black. "We don't want to damage anything important," he says.

"They said you knew what Marie would do. . . ." It is Nell's fury that speaks. The words are nearly muffled, but are so loud to the faculty through which I have never truly heard before, it tears at my mind. I long for the sweet deafness I am losing.

"You brought this on yourself," says the man, happy now that I must hear his prattle. "Not sharing has made you incomplete. It made you cling to incomplete people that you used to feel complete. You're wounded. That's why you use the wounded. It's time to heal. Time to grow." Two layers of ogre's teeth speak at once, out of sync, looking as if they will crack against each other.

"And you didn't stop her, you shit!" Nell screams at me without breath, with the airlessness I will soon know.

The man's two faces are joined by a third. The space where his two faces now squat takes a face from the past, spectral—that of the untrained, self-appointed midwife who cut the bloody tether between my mother and me, when the commune this place had been had taken in my mother during the ninth month of her carrying me. And after the self-appointed midwife had cut the tether, she had raised the steak knife to my throat and face and peeled away my bloodless relation, the amniotic skin that through the ages has been a blessing to others.

"They told me," bellows the shadow of Nell as her nails cut my already skinned palm. *"They told me you could see her ghost if you wanted to. You could let me say good-bye to her, but that you wouldn't!"*

The silence of Nell's pitying face gives greater volume to the part of her that so wordlessly shouts. Marie's voice inside me stirs. It hears its sister's voice. It cries out in my mind; I wish to comfort it.

More of *them* stand around me, looking down. *They* from whom my mother fled. *They* who have harassed me from the moment *they* were aware of my still living in this city and of my inability to leave. *They* who have harassed me from the moment they were able to partly steal my sight, just enough to know what I saw while they hunted me. *They* who could partly steal that sight through that which they have owned over these many years, through that which had once belonged to me before I had owned anything on this Earth.

"You owe me. You owe Marie. You owe us our good-bye."

Against my will, the memory of holding Marie's hand, the scents of her hair and skin as worn by her sister, pulls Marie close. I call her as would a medium, as would a spiritualist. She is caught here in this place. What of Marie that has haunted me has been caught here, *trapped* in the home of those who murdered her, bound by the needle that killed her, that hangs from the ceiling above me like a reliquary on black thread spun from strands of hair stolen from her brush. The dangling syringe glints as it did in the sun, when I saw it as a phantom buried in Marie's arm. It is now not lit by the sun, but by an imprisoned light that should no longer be in this shitty world.

I speak the words, "*They* killed her," yet make a sound no more understandable than a death rattle.

The *Jar* is brought forth . . . the vessel I have always been aware of, because of its housing part of my awareness. That of me that *they* have owned is passed from hand to hand in a circle around me. I do not know with which sight I see the caul I was born with floating in its preserving brine. I do not know if it in true physicality swims in the brine, languidly flapping as would a manta ray.

"It told us of its loss," says the man who followed me. "What it lost was *you*."

And I know what *they* have always believed to be true is now true enough for *them* to make real: that I was not born with the caul that gave me sight—the caul was born with me. They have prayed and hungered this into reality.

Free of the Jar, it lives in *their* hands as *they* pass it wetly to one another, as *they* invest themselves with that which *they* once thought could grant them cosmic insight of what will come, but which *they* desire now only in order to accrue material wealth. It is returned to my face, dropped like a shroud after it has been pulled to the shape of one. The last breath my lungs draw becomes a still pocket in my chest.

The mercy of deafness, the mercy of muted hearing, is fully stripped away. I hear the cacophonic indifference of the universe. Marie's trapped ghost speaks through my smothered mouth. The taut skin makes sounds as would the buzzing of fly wings. Nell pulls away her hand and slashes my palm with her nails. She is screaming as I fall into Marie's sky, full of cruel seraphim and their awful songs.

Bentley Little is the author of numerous novels and hundreds of short stories. He does not write dark fantasy or suspense novels or thrillers. He writes horror. Hideous to look upon, Bentley lives alone in a one-room desert shack. He has no pets, no friends, no family.

POP STAR IN THE UGLY BAR
by Bentley Little

She walks in, the pop star. Arrives with her retinue, wearing a black leather outfit that shows part of one tit and is supposed to be revealing but just doesn't cut it here in the Bar. I can tell she's slumming, looking for action. The second she walks through the door she's acting as if she owns the place, and she tried to appear nonplussed when she finally figures out that no one's paying attention to her. She's wearing a wig, pretending she wants to travel incognito, but now that no one notices her she stands in her most recognizable poses, desperately willing people to recognize who she is.

Nobody does.

I do, but I don't say anything, just watch. I've seen her videos, read about her in *Playboy* and *Rolling Stone* and *TV Guide*, read how she's outrageous and into kinky sex, how she likes to pick up young black hitchhikers and have her way with them, and I see her now, this pampered bitch, and I have to laugh. Wild and outrageous? I'll show you wild. I'll show you outrageous.

Welcome to the Ugly Bar.

She said in an interview that she likes to be spanked, something pretentious about there being a fine line between pleasure and pain and that for her the two sometimes overlapped. Old news. Shocking maybe for Grandpa in Kansas but babytalk here in the Bar. I look at her smoothly unblemished, carefully moisturized skin and I know it's never experienced true funpain. I think of Desdemona, the time I carefully flayed her left buttock and rubbed vinegar and lemon juice on it while Deke pissed in her mouth, and I can't see the pop star going for that.

Well, I can, but I can't see her liking it.

Control freak. That's what we have here, folks. Walks on the wild side carefully modulated, well planned. Little fantasy trips with safe, padded boundaries, escape routes if things get too real, if the monsters get too hairy.

> *Pleasure and pain*
> *Are almost the same*
> *To me*

Isn't that a line from one of her songs? One of her videos? I look at her, at her Hollywood costume. Almost the same? I suddenly want to make her prove it. No matter that it's an act, that she's just entertaining people, trying to titillate them. The fact that she's here in the Ugly Bar means that it's no longer just an act, that she's starting to believe her own press, that she really thinks she's daring and provocative and out there.

I glance around the Bar, catch the nods, catch the looks, and I know they all want to be in on it.

I walk up to her, ask if I can buy her a drink. Her eyes take in my mask, my codpiece, and I see, for a second, fear. She's afraid. Not of me, not specifically, but of losing control. She might say in her interviews that she likes big men, hung men, that she's looking for a man who has enough between his legs to really satisfy her, but I can tell that now that she's seen one, she's scared. She doesn't like it at all.

I push aside her bodyguards, and two of the Others come out of the shadows and drag them quietly off, taking them away. She says with all the confidence she can muster, all of the confidence her money and power have bought, that, yes, she'd like a drink. The bartender pours it, holds it between his legs, stirs it with his cock, lets a couple drops of bloody jizz fall visibly into it and hands it to me.

I grin, give it to her. "Here, bottoms up."

She grimaces, puts it down an arm's length away on the bar, pulls away. "God."

The Others laugh derisively, and I think she realizes for the first time that she's just an amateur here.

She looks around for her bodyguards, notices that they are gone, and I see the fear on her face again, but she pretends she's not afraid, and she walks away from me, to the other end of the bar. She walks now with the grace and confidence of a dancer, the athlete she has to be in order to perform her stage show, and when I am through with her she will not walk that way. She will be hobbled and crippled, cleaned out with the razorcock perhaps, or violated to hemorrhage by the first three feet of Mr. Pole, and she will never be able to dance again. Each step she takes will be filled with pain and will remind her of her former pretenses and her forced knowledge of reality.

What if I cut her off at the kneecaps, cauterize the wounds with lighter fluid and fire, use the leftover blood to lubricate her bottom two holes?

Could she handle living on stumps?

She looks at me from the safety of the other side of the bar, faces me. "How big are you?" she asks, feigning boldness.

"Cock or arm?" I say.

She blinks.

"Two feet cock, four arm. More reach with the arm, too. I can maneuver around in there, feel out the womb, stroke those baby-growing sides with my fingers. Ain't nothing like it, babe."

She looks sick, looks like she wants to say something, looks like she wants to bolt, but her bodyguards are gone, she's a long way from the door, and she's been left here and hanging and knows she'd better make the best of it.

A crowd is gathering. The Mother and Deke and Mr. Pole and the Roothog. Ginjer and Liz. There's an animal smell in the air. Lust. Sexual lust. The lust of victors for more victims.

The Bar is never satisfied, is it?

I drink her drink with the drops of bloody jizz, walk over.

The Roothog approaches. "A question," he says. "Do you have to be in love to have sex?" It's clear he still doesn't know who she is.

She stares in open horror at his whiplike pizzle, and she nods slightly, tentatively. Her voice is a little girl's voice, frightened. "Yes," she lies.

"Love is spending time together," he says to her. "Sex is just sex." He grins, cackles and pulls on his pizzle, and I realize that he does know Who she is. He's just thrown a quote from her book at her.

And she's scared.

Sometimes the Ugly Bar surprises me.

She starts for the door. The Mother blocks her way.

I nod casually toward the Roothog's pizzle. "He's good with that," I say.

"Let me out of here!" She tries to maneuver around the Mother, who moves to the side, blocks her again.

"You want another drink?" I'm trying not to laugh.

"I want out of here!"

"Then why did you come in?"

She looks at me, doesn't answer. I'm the only one she's really spoken to, and she thinks that's established some sort of relationship between us, she thinks I'll feel sorry for her and take pity on her because I've looked into her eyes, but she doesn't know shit about the way things really work.

I stroke my codpiece. "I'll take you," I say. "I'll even hurt you if you want."

"Let me out of here!"

"No."

The flatness of my refusal throws her. Did she have lipstick on when she came in the Bar? It's gone now. Her lips are thin and dry. There's a tic starting in her left eye.

"You don't know who you're fucking with," she says. "There'll be a lot of people looking for me. A lot of people. You don't know who I am—"

"I know who you are," I say.

She stops, stares at me, and what little color she has left drains from her face, leaving it a beautiful porcelain white.

"Come on," I say.

I take her hand. It's soft, thin. I can feel the bones. I start to pull her toward the door to the Back Room.

"I-I'm having my period," she lies.

I grin at her. "The more blood the better."

"Oh, God . . . Oh, God . . . Oh, God . . ." she's crying. Scared and frightened. Runny mascara tears. Clear snot. She doesn't look much like a pop star now.

"Please . . ." she begs, sobbing.

And I lead her into the Back Room.

The water bed is filled with sperm and blood, piss and placenta, but I don't take her to the bed; I take her to the table and strap her into the stirrups. She is pliant and pliable at this point and I can do anything I want with her. She looks around, takes in the bones and the babies, the devices and the animals. Dazed, she tentatively touches the sticky wall next to the table with a finger, slowly puts the finger to her tongue as I strap her in; then she's gagging, spitting so she won't puke, and Liz comes and licks the spit off her face, off her mouth.

She struggles, squirms, and Liz slaps her face. Five times. Quickly.

The games have begun.

The pop star looks at me, mouth open, nose bleeding, eyes teary.

"Make a fist," I order.

She does, and holds it up, and Ginjer jumps on top of it, sliding slowly down, already slippery wet. The pop star reacts instinctively, cries out in disgust, tries to shake Ginjer off, but Ginjer's cunt is like a steel trap and she's clamped on tight and not letting go and she starts spinning, round and round on the pop star's arm, squealing wildly with each successive climax.

"Get it off!" the pop star screams. "Get it off!"

But Ginjer's still spinning, and the juice dripping down the pop star's arm is starting to mix with blood.

I'm not sure if it's Ginjer's blood or the pop star's.

The Roothog steps up, pizzle in hand, starts whipping her with it.

She's screaming. More fear now than pain although that will change.

Ginjer's already ground off the fist, and blood is streaming down the pop star's arm. Her chest is bruised purple by the pizzle.

They all want in on it, all the patrons of the Bar. I'm not greedy, I'm willing to share, but her mouth is mine. I've earned it. I stake my claim, pointing, and there are no objections. Deke holds down her forehead, while I bust out her teeth. She stops screaming, fainting, I think, but that makes no difference to what I want to do. There are shards of teeth left, and I clean them out with a piece of bone. Her mouth is filling with blood, just the way I like it, and she comes to, gagging, and I open my codpiece and take out my cock and start feeding it to her.

Her bladder lets go, but Liz is there to bathe in the spray.

It's gone too far, I realize. She's not going to make it. I wanted to leave her changed, marked, not dead, but there's no turning back now, and if that's the way it's gotta be, that's the way it's gotta be. Fame or no fame. There are no exceptions.

Everyone's the same in the Back Room of the Bar.

We take our time, and she's alive for much more of it than I would have thought, but eventually we finish her off, and by the time it's all over and done with, there's not even much of her body left.

What remains is thrown in the slush pile.

We celebrate with drinks.

They come in later, official representatives of the Law outside, looking for the pop star, but no, Officers, we haven't seen anyone matching that description. Lemme look at the picture. Nope. Haven't seen her. Any of you seen someone like that in here?

There is a slit-eyed older lieutenant in on the hunt, a Harvey Hardass, a faded jaded seen-it-all, and I catch the eyes of the Others, see the nods and the smiles, and I look again at the cop who thinks he's seen everything.

His friends are already moving away, out the door.

I nod to the Others, letting them know that they're to snag him if he tries to leave.

I look at him, catch his eye.

Confused, maybe a little frightened, he looks around the darkened room, then back at me.

I grin.

Welcome to the Ugly Bar.

John Shirley's newest novels are *Demons* and *Crawlers*, both from Del Rey books. His other books include the Bram Stoker Award–winning *Black Butterflies*, now out from Leisure, and the rather notorious collection *Really Really Really Really Weird Stories* from Nightshade. He has been the guest of honor at World Horror Convention and a special guest at Dragoncon. He was coscreenwriter of *The Crow*, and has written scripts for television series and cable movies. A singer/songwriter, he also wrote most of the lyrics on the most recent two albums by the Blue Oyster Cult. Visit his fan-created Web site: www.darkecho.com/JohnShirley.

MISS SINGULARITY

by John Shirley

She'd mentioned suicide to the therapist, but not in any real serious kind of way. The only time Lani told anyone she was seriously thinking of killing herself was at school, in detention, in a text message to her friend Bron.

Outside, the spring was prissily insistent. The northern California sunlight, Lani thought, was adamant about its detestable cheeriness. Through the classroom window she could see yellow flowers on the hill above San Jose Hills. Butter-colored daffodils, green-green grass, spotless blue sky, sunlight like a little kid who'd just thought of being sunlight: Lani found it all quite sinister and deceptive.

Thnk gonna kill mself soon 4 real, she messaged to Bron, on the little coffin-shaped cell phone. (Why do you think she'd picked this phone?)

Detent ovr n 14 min then freedom, Bron replied, thumbing away on his own.

Mr. Gornblatt, supervising after-school detention, didn't seem to notice or care about the cell phones, though theoretically they could be confiscated. He wasn't one of those teachers who got off on confiscating things—it was too much trouble. A chunky math teacher with a slightly crooked toupee, Gornblatt was sitting at his desk leafing through a *National Geographic*. He stopped on a photo page and stared, swallowing. It was hard to be sure at this angle but Lani suspected Gornblatt was looking at the topless aborigine women like some breathless sixth grader—and it was truly gross.

No serious not kddng maybe Fri day 2 die, she messaged. She had to send and go to a new screen pretty often. *Maybe not see u . . . yer dad pick u up rt after schl.*

She glanced at Bron. Felt some satisfaction seeing he was staring at her; she'd managed to shock him. Then she felt kind of bad about making him worry.

He scratched at the soul patch under his lip, giving her that owlish look that meant, *What the fuck?* He was proud of that tenuous black soul patch against his doughy skin; he'd had to fight to convince the school to let him have that and the shaved head. His thick lips—not too thick, really, kind of cute—were pierced on the right side by two studs, top and bottom. They clacked, very softly, when his lips came together: He liked that. Like her, he wore all black; hers was fringed with bloodred lace. They were two of four Unapologetic Goths at the school, as Bron called them. UGs—he relished pronouncing it *ughs*. The school had nurtured various pseudogoths and semigoths but only four UGs.

U cant, he messaged.

Y?

Tell U after schl my dad can just wait.

But it was her dad who came after school, which was a surprise; Bron's dad didn't show, which was not a surprise. Bron's dad, a sometime Harley salesman, was maybe on a drinking binge again, in which case his family's weekend camping trip to

Lake Tahoe would be put off because his dad was "feeling under the weather." Bron wouldn't mind, or wouldn't admit minding; he professed to hate the idea of vacationing with his family. Probably both did hate it and didn't. She knew that feeling.

So they were blinking in the sunlight in front of the school and Bron only got as far as, "Lani, you're so full of shit, and you're not going to do that. Abjectly true: You will not do it." *Abjectly true* was a phrase he'd coined, and frequently traded in. "Your friends are, like, going to be fucked without you, and there's a Death Club concert in three weeks and I have a ticket for you, a *free* fucking ticket, hello?"

She looked at him with studied pity. "Concerts . . ." She shook her head. She was beginning to be sorry she'd told him. But then again, maybe she wanted him to talk her out of it? She wasn't sure.

That's when her dad showed up. He was a tall, tanned man, with a small, sharp nose contrasting a firm jaw, amused blue eyes. He was quite fit, dressed in a golf shirt and jeans and tasseled loafers with no socks. He was not the usual picture of a physicist; he didn't need glasses, and his graying brown hair was only a little tousled. He played golf, pretty badly, and he jogged, and he liked to swim in the sun. But he was a physicist, all right: Sometimes, at the pool, he talked about Einstein's insight on the sailboat watching light in the water.

"Hiya, kid," he said, as he always did.

"What're you doing here? I don't need a ride, Dad."

"That's so touching, the way you greet your old man." But he didn't say it like he was really hurt. She'd never seen him show he was really hurt. She'd never seen him show much but a kind of surface joviality, and mild irritation. Sometimes he'd show her a little affection, sort of like the affection her older brother had given his gerbil. Her brother, Albert, hadn't wanted the gerbil, but his therapist said he should have a pet. Albert was in college now and they pretty much never heard from him.

Her dad looked at Bron. "Hey, Bron, what's up?"

"Not a whole lot, Mr. Burnside."

He smiled thinly. "Just chillin' at the skizzy?"

Lani winced. Bron said, "Yeah. The skizzy. Chillin' at."

Her dad considered the two of them. She cringed at what he might say next. She wasn't wrong. "You're kind of the odd couple, you two—except for the matching clothes. Lani, tall and skinny . . ." He looked at Bron, who was short and chunky.

"We're not 'a couple,' Dad," she said. "You're hurting Bron's reputation."

"We're a couple of *somethings*," Bron said. He looked like he was a long ways away, in his mind; she was afraid he was trying to think of a way to talk to her dad about what she'd text messaged. Maybe he'd just blurt out, *Your daughter's threatening suicide, dude*. That wouldn't be like Bron—but he might think it was an emergency.

"So are we going somewhere?" she asked her dad, to get away from Bron before he could say anything.

Dad nodded, taking his car keys out of his pants pocket. "Yeah. Let's go. You're coming to the lab with me. Your . . . We'll talk about it on the way."

She waggled her fingers in an ironic good-bye at Bron; he stuck his thumb and little finger out from his fist by his ear in a "call me" hand sign, and she nodded as she followed her dad to the BMW.

Her dad looked at a butcher-paper sign under the school windows that the pep squad had made up. It said: VOTE FOR MISTER AND MISS POPULARITY MAY 1!!!

Dad looked at her. She knew he was thinking about making a joke, and she knew pretty much what it was. Something about how she should run for Miss Popularity. She saw it in his face when he thought better of it.

*   *   *

"It's such bullshit to do it just because 'oh, the therapist recommends it,' " Lani said.

"But if we don't try it and you, I don't know, run off with the circus or something because you're depressed," Dad said, driving up the hill to the lab, "then we'll say 'Hell, we shoulda tried something, anything, and now she's marrying Boffo the clown.' "

"That's funny."

"You used to think my sense of humor was funny. But now you're a teenager. When I was a teenager I thought my dad was, I don't know, Hitler's long-lost son. We got to be pretty good friends later, after I realized that Republicans aren't actually fascists."

She remembered the way Grandpa had looked at her dad when he made excuses about not going to see Grandma in the hospice, and she didn't think they'd ever gotten to be "pretty good friends."

"I miss Granddad," she said.

You never knew, Granddad might be listening, if that afterlife stuff was true. She'd seen a show about near-death experiences. She doubted if it was real. It was probably all oxygen starvation. But maybe.

"I miss him too," he said. She could tell it was work for him to say that.

The road wound up, around the highest hill of the San Jose Hills district, on one of the ragged outer fringes of Silicon Valley.

Lani and her mom and dad lived in the two-year-old Hillview Hideaway gated tract-home complex, which was just now below and behind the car. She didn't turn to look at it when they spiraled around the hill again, the tract laid out under them. When she was a little girl, if she'd seen her neighborhood from above she'd have wanted to pick out her own house from the others: hard to do in a housing tract. Now she was reluctant to look at the development at all, especially from up here: Depression had levels of discomfort, and some things made it an ache. But she could see the walled tract in her mind anyway: a rat's maze of identical houses; now and then a tiny stunted little tree planted in bark dust. No wonder Mom was into that shiatsu massage guy—you'd have to have an affair just so you knew you were alive, down there. She wondered, for about the fiftieth time, if Dad knew.

She felt the pit open up in her—it was just like a trapdoor opening—and felt the suction from it, the vacuum drawing her downward. She'd been teetering on the edge of it all day. She felt the inner plunge, and her stomach recoiled in nausea when they took a hairpin turn. Staring at the snaky road seemed to make it worse, so she looked out over the valley, beyond the Hideaway tracts.

Blue-gray smog blurred the vineyards to the west, and the sun flared from the tangled Silicon Valley freeways to the south— freeways ribboning between endless Wal-Marts and Costcos and malls; patches of green residential areas.

It was like a great stovetop. It wasn't a very hot day, but somehow every place she looked at was something being cooked, and people were the main ingredient. Something, somewhere, was cooking up their souls for consumption. The something used time as its heating element, and when people finally gave up and became a kind of suburban zombie, they were finished being cooked, and the something consumed their souls. Sometimes the something aged them first before it ate them; sometimes it heated them up too fast and burned them. She thought of her friend Justin, who was drooling on himself in a long-term-care place.

Justin had been on the downside of manic depression for a long, long time, before the pill salad, and his dad kicking him out for hitting his sister—half an hour later his dad, regretting it, had gone out driving to find him but Justin had gone to San Francisco and somebody had given him some methedrine and the

needle. He'd gotten HIV from that one shot and when it was di-
agnosed ten months later he took that double handful of random
stuff from the bathroom cabinet . . . and it fried his brain.

She wasn't going to *try* to kill herself, like Justin; she was going
to do it right. She was going to be smart about it like the Romans.
Like the Hemlock Society. Justin panicked. That was stupid. You
had to ease your way out. . . .

But sometimes she just wanted it all to stop—quick. Trying to
tell people how she felt seemed so hopeless—like now, her dad
was rattling away next to her. She could try—she could break in,
yell at him, *You're so all up in your own self, you're all about playing the game really well and you only get excited by science and I
remember when you said that when people like Justin die it's just
"natural selection in action," well, fuck you, he was my friend and
no matter if you say you love me I never believe it, you're always so
distant about it and why do you think my brother never comes
around and why do you think Mom is like making moo-cow eyes at
that shiatsu guy because you abandoned her emotionally and—*

But if she did say that out loud everything would just get even
worse: He'd get all chilly and analytical and defensive and he'd
double her trips to the therapist—that nodding, smiling, pup-
petlike therapist Mary who made Lani's blood run cold—and
make her go on medication or something, like it was all in her
imagination. And she'd tried Prozac; it made her feel like she was
in a bottle, in no pain but all distant from things. Maybe it'd
turned her into what her dad was.

If she tried to really honestly talk to the therapist, the woman
just tried to convince her that she was wrong, that her view of
the world was unfair—but that was so *irrelevant*. It didn't *matter*
if she was mistaken, if it was all she could see.

And if she tried to talk to her mom, if she told her how she
really felt, Mom'd get mad, like Lani was blaming her parents,
like she was saying they'd fucked up the world. But she didn't

blame them—not really. They were clueless, is all. Everybody got to a point where they realized their parents were clueless and so were they. But you couldn't make them understand that—"Mom, it's like we're all so clueless, it's all meaningless. People pretend they know what they're alive for and what the point is but they don't. They're just trying to keep from screaming." And Mom would say that was "just drama," she'd refuse to get that—refuse to even try to understand it.

Lani wanted to say: *You don't have to agree but if you could* just feel it *too*, feel what she felt . . . *even for a moment . . .*

That was the point: you couldn't make anyone understand, really, except a few friends like Bron and Lucinda. They'd kept her going this far. But even they would say there were reasons to live. The world had adventure, it had friends, it had art. . . .

She shook her head. The world? Look closer. It was like the world was this vain sickly old woman who didn't realize she was about to die, insisted she was still twenty-five, and you just wanted to hold up a mirror and say, *Look at what you are, accept it and let go! Just die!*

Only the world wouldn't die. So the people in it had to die to get away from it.

She wanted to show her mom and dad and that educated idiot Mary the therapist what it really looked like, in Lani's world. Somehow that was the only way to communicate: Get them into your world. And that was impossible. You can't put two worlds in one space. That was the whole point: Everyone was isolated. They had some indirect contact with other people, but really they lived and died alone.

She looked at the traffic down below her on the freeway under the hill and saw hundreds, thousands of vehicles, each with a driver in his own personal daydream, her own impenetrable personal world, not thinking about being just another little metal box moving on an asphalt ribbon. They were all looking for some kind of comfortable equilibrium, which was the best you could hope for in the long run. And it was so . . . meaningless. It just went on and on and then you dribbled your life away like Grandma in the hospice, some sullen stranger cleaning the poop off you every day as you tried to remember your husband's name. Maybe that's when this feeling had started—when she'd gone to visit Grandma toward the end. How could you look Alzheimer's in the eye and think that life was meaningful?

She looked at the sky and its blue seemed to part for her, revealing itself as but a thin veil over the black aching emptiness between the planets; the remote stars. Matter spinning out there, burning, cooling, seeking its own state of dull equilibrium, as her dad had told her. Just a lot of empty process in the midst of infinitely empty space, headed for the fulfillment of the steady state theory or the heat-death theory, or . . . What difference did it make how the universe ended? What was one human life in all this—or even on the Earth? One human life was a single bubble in a cauldron on that stovetop. The bubble rose from the bottom of the heated pot, made a brief journey to the surface; there was a moment of seething and then it popped, was sucked away by the something, and was gone to be replaced by another bubble. No two exactly alike—yet they were all alike. Meaningless. Like Ernest Hemingway had said in that story she'd done the report on for English: *Nada, nada . . . and nada.*

And what'd Hemingway done, in the end? Blown his brains out. Had the good sense to be efficient about it. No time to think, just a clicking sound and then . . .

"We're here," Dad said, driving into the parking lot of Silicon Quanta Labs, at the very top of the hill. "Anyway, your therapist, that Mary what's-her-name, says you need to spend more time with me, says maybe if you understand my work more you'll relate to me, maybe even stop with the suicidal imagery. . . . And I have to work late today, so . . ."

She looked at him. What was he talking about? How did he know? "Stop with what . . . imagery?"

"From your poetry," he said, as they got out of the car. The sun was so bright up here, on top of the hill; heat thudding in waves from the asphalt. "On that Web site." Looking at his watch. "Your mom showed me—well, actually, Justin's mom sent it to your mom. Justin's sister saw it. I told your mom you're too smart for . . . to try what Justin did. You're just letting off some steam, but you know Mom—she's pretty dramatic."

"You guys read my *poetry?*"

"What are you being so outraged for? You put it up online! That never seemed like a public space to you? And you put your name to it!" He smiled crookedly at her and recited, " 'Death come, death numb, numb me like the bite of an arachnid so I cannot feel being eaten alive . . .' Vivid stuff! Imaginative! Melo-dramatic, yes—but hey, I was a teenager too. I remember when I was taken with *Stranger in a Strange Land* and your granddad thought Heinlein was a cult leader or something. . . ."

"My poem was at a site that only a few people are supposed to know about and it's . . . not *really* public, I mean . . ."

God, he could make her feel stupid sometimes. . . .

The little Filipino security guard, steeped in boredom, waved them through the double glass doors and then they were in the coolness of the building. Too hot outside, but too chilly indoors, in these air-conditioned, immaculate spaces; this lobby where the abstract art was selected to color-coordinate with the fur-nishings. The elderly secretary at the big horseshoe-shaped desk looked up from a laptop—which she snapped shut as they came in, probably watching a movie on it—and beamed at them. "Oh, Lani . . . hi! How are ya?" Her smile, as she gave Lani a visitor's pass, seemed completely unreal, disconnected with the bleak-ness in her eyes. And Lani saw the old woman in her coffin. It wasn't precognition, it wasn't hallucination—it just happened to

Lani a lot that she imagined people she met in their coffins. The old woman in her coffin at the funeral home with one or two mourners. An impatient son looking at his watch. Later the coffin slammed shut. Darkness inside . . .

"Hi . . ." Lani managed.

Dad just waved at the receptionist and led the way across the lobby; swiped his card through the scanner, and the door to Research opened for them. She followed him past offices and cubicles, past locked doors reeking of obscure chemicals used in experimental computer chips, to a special elevator where Dad needed to scan the card again before it would take them down to the primary Quanta labs: the ones the stockholders were supposed to get excited about, though the techs hadn't yet produced anything practical in quantum computing.

Dad's lab—she'd been there only once before—reminded her of a big industrial laundry room because it was dominated by a bulky circular machine with a round window in its center. Ranged clunkily around the circular centerpiece were angular solid-state machines, completely arcane to Lani, bright with chrome surfaces, restless with digital readouts ticking over.

Her dad went muttering to one of the computer workstations set up in the cramped space near the door. "Where the hell is Dinwiddy? He's supposed to be here. If he's smoking pot at work again I'll kick his ass. He fu . . . he screws up and wanders off every time he does that stuff. I hope you don't get into pot; you won't get a goddamn thing done."

"Stoners are retards." She said it automatically, but she believed it.

"He's left a program running, too . . ." her dad muttered, bending over a keyboard.

She approached the wire-clustered machine dominating the room, feeling like Dorothy walking toward the Wizard of Oz: like she was being watched from behind a curtain. The device was some kind of experimental new particle accelerator, for Dad's quantum physics project—a new kind of collider, supposed to be able to do within its tightly wound coils what the big ones did over miles of tunnels.

Light glittered, multicolored sparks fountaining and sinking back on the other side of the round window. The collider clicked and muttered to itself in a language without words or grammar.

"What the hell's he been up to?" her dad said, squinting at Dinwiddy's notes on a monitor. "He's not supposed to be running the damn thing when I'm not here. . . . Says he thinks there might be a singularity. Right. He *has* been smoking something."

"What's a singularity?" she asked. Almost interested.

"Uh . . . well, usually it's something in astrophysics." He was barely audible over the chirring, the hissing from the accelerator. "Theoretical point where physical laws break down . . . supposed to exist in a black hole . . . Anything you can think can be real there. . . ."

"That's tight. Break down the laws of physics. Like to do that myself."

"That's my girl," he muttered, poking through a sheaf of papers on Dinwiddy's desk. "Never mind Miss Popularity—she's Miss Singularity. . . ."

"You can't, like, make your own singularity?" She was trying to work out the glimmering shapes forming in the oval metal and glass spaces within the accelerator. As soon as she thought they were this or that shape, they were some other. "I mean, in a lab?"

"Maybe for a few seconds . . . Where'd he put that equation? Uh, some people say a singularity could be created with an ac-celerator if you could get the right balance of matter and anti-matter and . . ."

His voice trailed off as he tapped at a keyboard. She wasn't really listening to him anyway. She was staring into the circular window. Putting her hand on the glass. Something inside seemed to be looking back. . . .

She saw a baby inside. A familiar baby: She'd seen it in old color Kodaks in Mom's photo album. Then she glimpsed herself as a toddler, on the other side of the glass. Then a two-headed child; one head was herself as a melancholy ten-year-old; the other was herself too, only it was a different ten-year-old Lani—smiling. The two Lanis vanished one into the other and . . .

"Dad?" she heard herself say.

And there was her dad, inside: a teen in the sixties, with long hair, a headband; her dad as a U.S. Marine in Vietnam, later on. Only he'd never been a U.S. Marine, never been to Vietnam. He'd gotten some kind of college research exemption. But there he was in uniform, carrying an M16, looking scared and alone—and then he was gone and instead of toddlers and dads, there was an eye, just a black eye looking back at her. But it wasn't an eye, exactly—that was just the description that came to mind because it looked at you, you knew it was aware of you, and it was elliptical, but in fact it was a kind of squeezed tornado of space itself, spinning this way and that: whatever way she wanted. She felt sure of it, at that moment: It was responsive to her.

Oh, she told it, answering a question she never quite heard asked, *if only people could see the world I live in. If only two people really could share the same world . . . then maybe we could find some meaning.*

The eye seemed to blink. . . .

"Lani!" Her dad began dragging her back from the accelerator. "Get the hell away from that thing. . . . It's not shielded for whatever it's putting out. . . . Dim-witty is what he oughta be called. . . . Come on."

He took her by the wrist, drew her out of the lab. She glanced at him. He looked pale, shaken. "There was an eye looking at me from in there," she said. "Thought I saw pictures, too . . . of me, and you and—"

"Yeah, you get a lot of Rorschach inkblot effect with all those third-level energetic responses."

"No, it—never mind." He wouldn't believe her. And she was, she had to admit, pretty prone to imagining things. She saw faces in tree trunks, imagined Sasquatches in the brush.

"Come on, I'm gonna have to shut down the lab." Suddenly he stopped at the intersection of two hallways and looked at her. "You feel okay, kid?" She thought she saw real concern in his face. But no—probably not. How likely was that?

"Yeah. I'm fine."

"No nausea, or, uh . . . dizziness?"

"No."

"Uh—okay. Well, let's get something to eat. Screw the lab. I missed my lunch. I need a beer and a burger." He dug out his cell phone and speed-dialed Dinwiddy, but couldn't get him on the line.

And Dad never did get his assistant on the line. Nor did Dinwiddy ever return to his apartment. No one found Dinwiddy, anywhere. Not ever.

Lani picked at a shrimp salad, trying to decide if she'd imagined what she thought she'd seen in the collider. Dad ate a cheeseburger, every third bite or so speed-dialing to try to reach Dinwiddy on his cell phone. Finally he shook his head, tucked the cell phone away and looked at her as if trying to remember why they were in a restaurant together at this time of day. He seemed to realize he was supposed to talk to her, dad to daughter here, so he brought up exactly what she wasn't interested in talking about: how she was doing in school; told her that her sinking grades might not matter to her now but they would later. After that oh-so-surprising comment they had nothing much to say and they got home early . . . and when they were just getting out of the car, Dad saw Bergman, that long-haired, muscular shiatsu-massage guy, rushing out the side garage door, clutching his Birkenstocks in his hand, giving them a white-faced glance as he got onto his Zapbike. Rode off pretty fast.

Dad went into the house and found Mom half-undressed, her hair mussed, and she was saying it was just massage and he said then why's he *running* out of here and goddamn it, this is a con-dom, a *used* condom, the dumbshit's too damn stupid to take his condom with him, and Mom was bursting into tears, saying Dad hadn't touched her in so long, and—

An hour later they were talking soberly, quietly, in the kitchen, of divorce. There was no glimmer of reconciliation in their talk. It was all excuses, bitterness, and dismissive finality.

They usually made Lani eat dinner with them, but Mom just nodded when Lani asked if she could eat a sandwich in her room—Mom with her frosted golden-brown, spiky-top hair, thatch-hut straight at the sides: a look she'd seen in *Cosmo* that the movie stars had given up a year or two before; her eyes looked pouchy, her makeup runny. Mom tried to look young, tried too hard, even getting a little nose stud in one nostril—but now for the first time, looking at her, Lani noticed that faint cheek fuzz that women get after menopause.

Shrugging, Lani went to her room, ate only a couple of bites of the peanut-butter sandwich as she booted up her computer. Bron was online too, got a prompt that she was online and in-stant messaged her.

U OK? Concert?

Still here, she responded. *No concert. Dad caught Mom boff-ing shiatsu. Divorce now. Not joking.*

That's fucked up, he typed back. *Want me 2 come over?*

No. Feel like being alone.

Maybe not a good time 2 B alone. Go to concert w/me. Death Club & Desktop Junkies.

Can't stand 2 B around people. Fucking depressed.

I don't know if I should tell U this now but somebody will. Justin finally died. 4 real.

Shit. Really?

Really. Today.

But—and she decided it as she typed it—*that's a good thing, that's what he wanted, it's finally over 4 him.*

Not a good thing 4 his mom. She doted on that dude. U going 2 B OK? Serious! Answer serious. You have friends. Stuff 2 do. You were talking about—

Not going 2 commit—

—suicide. You're not?

She wanted to scare him by saying maybe, maybe not. But she knew that was just to get a reaction, it was selfish, so she typed. *No.*

K. Going 2 concert. You promise? No suicide 2nite?

I promise.

Concert? Concert concert concert! Yeah: Concert. Come.

No. G2G. Bye.

The depression ran like crude oil over everything she did, everything she saw and heard and said the rest of the evening—making her think of the old Sisters of Mercy song "Black Planet." Looking at the news window on the Comcast site—nothing but morbid curiosity, to take in the news—she read about a group of children blown to pieces by American land mines; read about birth defects caused by mercury in fish and about a woman who'd punished her child by making him kill his beloved dog; read about the lives of refugees in Chad. The journalist quoted a young woman as saying, "Why do we live, if we live like this?"

She went to the bathroom and heard her mom in the bedroom

next door shout at her dad that he had discouraged her from being an actress, from doing all she ever really wanted to do, and that dream was dead now . . . *dead.*

Lani thinking: *All she ever really wanted to do? Like raising Albert and me hadn't meant anything to her . . .*

And Dad shouted back that Mom was just a selfish, stupid woman, and, "That sums it up and I'm not going to say anything more to you except through a goddamn lawyer."

The divorce, her parents' argument, it was all just part of the same evaluation typing out in Lani's mind like the printout from an imaginary computer program: *You come from a family of hopelessly selfish people. Projected probability: You're going to be just like them. Unless you die.*

Tucked away in her bedroom, she went to that goth poetry Web site and read her poetry and now it seemed so lame, childish, as her dad had implied. She went to the forms, highlighted her stuff, hit *delete,* thinking: If only deleting myself were that simple and painless. And then she looked over at the mirror on her dresser; saw herself hunched like a question mark over the keyboard, a dreary, wearily angry expression on her face. Her hair looking stringy, hands long and thin and ugly. And she'd thought: Look at me. God I'm just a fucking human worm.

She looked out the window. The moon was almost full and she could see the face on it—a face so well etched, to her, so definite. But its usual arch expression was shifting now because there were black clouds blowing by, like twisted thin black-silk cloth drawn over the moon so that its expression shifted in the murk: angry, bitter, sadly amused. Nice of the moon to keep her company. When she turned off the desk lamp she saw the moonlight was falling across her bed; the moon would go to bed with her, too.

So she went to bed, lay in moonlight listening on earphones to Monster Magnet's song "There's No Way Out of Here," downloaded from the Internet, and then an album by Nick Cave. The music seemed to create a space that she could bear to be in, a dimension where tragedy was given meaning and perspective and form by art, and it eased her a little. But then she thought about the news, and her parents, and the look Grandma had given her, the last time she'd seen her in the hospice, like she wanted to say, *Save me!*, but she didn't know, anymore, how to ask for help; a look from the far side of a void.

And Lani made up her mind. It was not Nick Cave's doing—this was a decision that had been growing in her for a long time: She would kill herself on the following day, without fail. Then maybe her parents would feel something, experience something besides their own stupid worlds; and she wouldn't have to see people pretend day after day that living was meaningful, and she wouldn't have to end like Grandma after a life like her mother's.

Why do we live, if we live like this?

Yes. Tomorrow.

Her eyes snapped open a little after dawn on Saturday morning—which was something that *never* happened. On weekends she usually managed to nestle deep into sleep, to hoard it and mete it out like a miser with pennies, making it last till at least eleven in the morning, or noon.

But she was wide-awake not long after dawn, convinced that she'd given birth during the night. That's what the dream had been, anyway, a confused dream of missing periods and sudden pregnancies and babies erupting from her, half a dozen of them, wet runny blue-skinned babies crawling about the bed, all tangled up in their umbilici. . . .Though she had never had that kind of sex, just a little oral sex and some fingering, from that guy Corey with the skateboard he didn't know how to use and breath that smelled like cigarettes and tacos and beer. He'd told everyone, and she hadn't felt like finding a boyfriend after that.

Now she actually sat up and looked at the sheets between her legs for evidence of babies, little bloody footprints or something. She sneered at herself, and lay back down, curled up on her side. Go back to sleep, dumbshit.

Nope. Going back to sleep wasn't going to happen. She was lying there on her side with her knees vibrating together like she had drunk three cups of espresso. She got up and felt a trickle down her thigh; her period had started. She reflected on how death came to a woman's womb regularly, twelve times a year unless she was pregnant: the eggs breaking down in crumbling disappointment.

She had bathed the day before; she didn't feel up to showering now. She wiped her thigh, put in a tampon, put on black jeans, her red high-top tennis shoes, a *Lou Reed: The Raven* T-shirt, and went out back to feed the big koi in the concrete goldfish pond . . . and stared. Stared. Then she shook her foot, briskly—one of the fish had crawled onto it, using its new, copper-colored legs.

Mrs. Weirbacht, a widow of sixty-two who lived a block from Lani, had to get up early to be at the synagogue; the rabbi needed her there at seven because they had the kids coming for Hebrew school at nine; and as she went to the refrigerator, and opened it, took out a carton of milk, she thought about all she had to do at the temple. . . .

The bottom fell out of the carton and milk splashed onto the floor. She had to laugh at that. Have a word with the grocer. But her hands shook as she cleaned up the milk with a great many paper towels, on her hands and knees—as she finished and straightened up she hit her head on a cabinet door that had somehow come open while she was down there. As she looked at it, one hand to her ringing head, the shelves holding the pots up collapsed, and all the pots clattered out. She straightened up, carefully, breathing hard. So, don't panic, a minor earthquake, maybe?

But she closed her eyes, thinking about when Hillel had his nervous breakdown, the bad week when his father and sister were killed in the bombing in Jerusalem and his son had been arrested for a hit-and-run; Hillel shouting about everything falling apart, you could put it together but everything would just fall apart, and he'd started smashing the kitchen of their house, then, hammering things with a skillet. Everything would fall apart, no matter what you did. . . .

She felt dizzy, her mouth dry. Decided to get some orange juice. She reached into the fridge, took out a glass quart of orange juice—the bottom fell out of the glass bottle and orange juice splashed all over the floor. Four more containers chose that moment to open in the refrigerator, gushing over the shelves. At exactly the same instant, last night's garbage disposal grindings erupted from the drain of the kitchen sink, spewing onto the window looking out over the back garden. Where all her plants seemed to have turned black . . . and the ornate fountain in the garden that Hillel had built was crumbling, falling into a pile of disconnected, nondescript bones.

Darren J. Kenneck, gay bachelor of forty-seven, resident of Hillview Hideaway, was sitting on his front porch weeping. His roses had all gotten some kind of strange mold or smut on them and they had turned jet-black, from blossoms to leaves to stem: uniformly black. They stood up just as before, but they were jet-black. But he was weeping for his mother. She had died a month before and he could hear her voice coming from the moist black earth between the black roses, though she was buried way up the freeway at Colma. It was as if she'd crawled from her coffin, through the soil, never coming to the surface, digging like a mole mile after mile from Colma to here, to come up just under the surface of his rose garden. He could see the outline of her body there in the dirt, just faintly, lying there faceup; he could hear her voice distinctly.

"It's . . . lonely, Darrie," his mom said. "It's lonely. It's . . . lonely. It's . . . lonely . . . Darrie. . . ."

Mr. Raji Jhuran, a Sikh, postman for Lani's neighborhood, adjusted his turban and stepped out of the boxy blue-and-white U.S. Mail truck, with his satchel over his shoulder—and came to a dead stop, staring up the walk to 1209 Elm Grove. The two front windows of the house were the gigantic eyes of a pretty girl; the door was gone, replaced by the girl's nose; her lips were where the steps should be; the roof had curved to become her glossy black hair. The woman's head was as big as the house had been; was sunken past the chin into the earth; a giant living head that seemed to have been built the way you build a house.

Raji turned and looked down the street. The other houses were not what they should be, either; they'd all changed somehow. And a blizzard of black snow began swirling down through the air.

Raji called out to Guru Nanak, in Hindi, and retreated into the truck. The mail in the sacks behind him shifted and shuffled, as everything written up on it was spoken aloud, but softly, just audibly. *Dear Mom, I'm not sure when I can come out but if you could send some money, I might be able to pay . . . Dear Mr. Hingeman, we regret to inform you . . . A new Visa card is preapproved for Mrs. Elmer Chasburton. . . .*

Raji said, in Hindi: "I dream. Lord Nanak, raise me from this dream." He drove the truck in a careening panic back to the exit at the gates of Hillview Hideaway and the gates were closed, and locked in chains that hadn't been there before: chains of hair, glossy black hair. But trying to force the gates open—with his hands and then with the truck—he soon discovered that the long swatches of shiny black hair were hard as steel. He looked for another way out, thinking to climb the cinder-block walls, but he was afraid to go near them: The wall blocks shifted one on another like teeth grinding when he approached them. His cell phone did not work—or more specifically, it would only call people who did not know him, though they seemed to have his last name: they spoke no Hindi, and one of them said "Raji Jhuran? That's my grandfather, dude, guy's dead, stone-dead, like, what, many years now. . . ."

And he crawled under his truck, covering his head, thinking that he was being punished for coming to live in this bloodless place, this place with no understanding of the sacred: He had come from Punjab to California because this was where the world's money was kept, but since coming here he'd lain with a woman other than his wife, and now he saw that he must have died—died a mere *patit,* far short of *Khālsā*—and he'd been cast into one of the worlds to which you were consigned before you reincarnated, where demons mocked you with your karma, your karma falling like black snow from the heavens. . . . He wept and called to Gobind Singh, begging for forgiveness. . . .

The koi were crawling out of the pond on their scaly silver-orange legs, like those ancient fish that walked onto the land, the tetrapods; they were creeping about the edges of the lawn, susurrating and tittering softly, seeming to grin at Lani. Then she noticed the grass itself—jet-black. She reached down and plucked at it, thinking it had burned, was ashen and would crumble. But no, it was leathery hard, and it jerked back from her touch.

"Oh, shit," she said. Had someone dosed her with something? She decided that wasn't the case. It was harder to decide she wasn't dreaming, especially when she saw that it was snowing flakes of black that vanished on hitting the ground; that the clouds hanging low, nearly low as a ceiling over the neighbor-hood, were forming very distinctive faces, a crowd of teenage faces looking down at her; she knew only one of them: Justin, who was dead now. She knew somehow that all these other faces were dead kids, too. The cloud faces seemed to be singing some-thing, though she couldn't hear any words. Their misty heads moved back and forth, like people all singing along to the same song at a concert. The black snow plumed from their mouths in-stead of music.

But eventually Lani decided she wasn't dreaming. Especially when Bron showed up, about three minutes later, rushing in her back gate, his eyes feverish, mouth open in an oval like the shape of the collider in Dad's lab. "My mom was, like, screaming," he said, rushing up, getting it out between gasps, points of red on his cheeks. "She woke me up screaming and she said there was faces in the clouds and the grass was . . . And the phones aren't working, none of them, and you can't get out of the gates, you can't leave the complex. . . . I thought somebody'd dosed us but we're all seeing the same fucking stuff!"

They had some discussion about whether or not they could be dreaming the same dream somehow. But finally she said, "No. It's real. I've been sort of expecting something. The singularity didn't blink—it was winking at me."

"The what?"

She told him about the lab, and what her dad had said, and she thought that somehow she'd made a connection with the sin-gularity, and it was making her world real for everyone, external-izing her inner world, and as she said it they were both grinning, because now there was music rising on the air too—a dark, dirgelike rock music but somehow triumphant, emitting from the new, startlingly large lilies growing along the mossy fences of her backyard, as if their blossoms were those amplifying trum-pets on antique crank-up record players. The music sounded sort of like Switchblade Symphony, but then again it was sort of like early Nine Inch Nails or maybe Joy Division, but then again it was like Christian Death or Ministry, but on the other hand it was more like London After Midnight . . . or the early Cure . . . or . . .

"Can you make out the words?" Bron asked her, breathless.

"I . . . no. Well, yes . . ." She listened, repeated: " 'Have you seen my soul . . . I left it on the subway station . . . someone has taken it and . . .' Uh, I think: 'left it with freebox clutter in their closet . . . some semihuman evasion . . . planning someday to sell it . . . no one will ever get what it's worth. . . .' "

"I didn't hear any of that at all!" Bron protested. "I heard 'has the bell finally tolled, has my life measured out its ration. . . .' "

She shrugged. Thinking that in a way they were the same lyrics.

She and Bron both put out their hands to catch the black snow; and for .3333 of a second each flake was a distinct geo-metrical shape on their palms, like snowflakes under a micro-scope, but in onyx black and made out of an intricacy of interlocking death's-heads and skeletal bones—yet no two alike. When you looked close enough you could see the hard, inter-connected shapes in the black crystals replicating infinitely, a continuum of the resolutely bleak: infinite cancellation. And then they'd vanish—each going with its own soft sigh. Lani and Bron looked at each other and laughed. All the while the music played, changing from one sonic shape to the next the way col-ors shifted and overlapped when you turned a prism around and around: there was no one definite song—yet it was all one song.

She and Bron should have been scared, she supposed. But they both felt weightless, as if they'd dropped burdens they hadn't known they'd carried. They teetered near panic, too, es-pecially when shiny anacondas made of volcano glass oozed—slithering in ripples to the music that played—along the fence tops, jewellike eyes flashing as they snapped at the great swoop-ing bats: flying foxes. She felt a spasm of fear at two brief flur-ries of hail when she saw the hailstones were .22 bullets, still in their casings: ready for a gun.

"Those bats are fucking huge," Bron said, blinking up at them.

"That's how big they are in, like, Indonesia," she muttered vaguely, looking up at the flop-flapping leather wings. "I did a re-port for biology. They're flying foxes, actually, biggest kinda bat. . . ."

She was fighting off a wave of panic, as the volcano-glass ana-condas all turned to look at her, at once, as if awaiting orders; as a beam of black light struck down from the clouds and illumi-nated a coffin shape forming in the ground nearby; taking shape . . . opening invitingly. . . .

But the panic and fear were overwhelmed by a rising sense of triumphant belonging. Taking a deep breath, she reflected that this was her creation, and choosing to revel in her new world was a way to survive it; even to thrive in it. Lani only knew that the more she just accepted it, the more it felt increasingly right.

"Yeah—fuck it, it's *mine!*" She danced in place, kicking bullets and creeping crickets made of chrome.

Then she had a sudden thought, and ran to check her folks in the house—careful not to open the chattering closets, deciding not to see what was cooing hugely in the bathroom—and found her parents were still asleep, Mom in the bedroom and Dad on the sofa. They'd probably both taken meds to sleep, and their slumber seemed a good thing, in view of the feverishly growing bird-of-paradise plants outside the windows: snapping their or-ange beaks at the symmetrical filigrees of gray-black mold which spread, in seconds, to cover the window glass. . . .

Lani told the snapping flowers outside the window: *Stay out there; don't bother Mom and Dad.* They seemed to draw back a little at this.

Something took wing in Lani like a joyously hungry flying fox as she returned to the backyard, where the music seemed to boom even louder to greet her return, and the faces in the sky swiveled to gaze with somber affection at her.

"Come on, let's check out the street!" Bron yelled. Laughing—and afraid as he laughed.

They ran to the street out front. Stopped there on the sidewalk, cursing and marveling, gazing at Lani's own, her very own hot-house world. They noticed the cars first—or what they'd become.

"The cars are all changed," Bron said with approval. He'd done an essay for English on how he disliked cars. In their places were black mariahs and hearses, only they all seemed full of water, and swimming things.

Through the windows of the funereal vehicles they could see dark green and red fish, thin and transparent like scarves woven with eyes and gills, and octopi whose upper parts were human skulls, and detached but delicate human hands with black fingernails that pumped along like jellyfish. "You made them into aquariums! And the whole street . . ."

"It's like that painting I tried to do," she said at last, her voice almost lost in the pounding of her heart, "when I took art from Mr. Yee, and he said it was so, like, muddled, you couldn't make out a composition."

"I remember," Bron said, looking at the intricate vista of eagerly shifting darkness that the street, the whole neighborhood had become. Bron adding in an undertone: "You could tell Mr. Yee wanted to say it was depressing but he didn't want to be that personal. . . ." He looked at her. "So—even, like, right now—you're doing this somehow?"

She nodded. "I think . . . yeah. I am."

The composition had been poorly formed in her mind, even muddier on her canvas; but here it was as composed as a Goya, dark yet clearly etched.

The sun was a dead white disk through the heavy, low clouds draped only a few hundred feet above the houses—the pallid teen faces overhead still sulkily blowing out the black blizzard. The lampposts, the telephone poles, the eaves of houses, the little trees, the fences, the cars: Everything was fringed, edged with living pennants, thousands of them blowing toward Bron and Lani in the black blizzard wind. It was like the street was deep underwater, and the streamers were seaweed clinging thickly to sunken ships. But there: Instead of the black crepe was a woman's hair blowing thickly from a round roof; no, Lani saw, not a roof; it was a woman's head—some idealization of Lani herself—growing up out of the ground instead of a house, but then again it was a house too, the nose could open, swing back like a door. It did open, showing a red triangle, damp filling like the interior of a gourd. The eyes that were windows turned to look right at them.

"Fuck! Those giant eyes are looking at us!" Bron blurted, sounding scared for the first time.

And all the time the music played, its rhythms interlaced with the living motion of the street: the movement of black streamers, colored-ink fish, translucent anacondas, flitting bats, dimly seen forms chasing one another, tittering, in the quivering shrubs along the mold-laced housefronts.

She was looking at the house across the street from her parents; an owl big as a Bron perched in the Boltons' living room, looked out the picture window, turning its head to regard them gravely with big golden eyes; on the television set to one side of the owl was an image that looked like a home movie Dad had taken of Lani at the beach as a child, playing in the sand; she knew somehow it was playing on all the television sets in the neighborhood.

"You see that fucking owl?" Bron said, swaying to the music. He was looking even paler than usual; she could see him vacillating between being scared and exultant. "And Justin in the sky . . ."

She was past being scared—she had been stoned only a couple of times, and it was like that: You were in the grip of something in your bloodstream just sweeping you along with it.

She saw in her mind's eye a hillside opening up to show a great cavern with a stream emerging from it, a red stream of her own blood, and she saw herself carried on the stream in a white, carven boat, completely naked, hands uplifted like a priestess— just a picture in her imagination. . . .

Bron pointed the other way down the street, behind her, bursting out: "You're over there . . . naked, in a fucking boat!"

She turned and there was the hill that loomed over the housing complex, but now the hillside was literally riven by the cavern; now it spilled rusty fluid on which she rode naked in a boat made of intricately carved ivory . . . hands lifted in hieratic gesticulation. . . .

She turned to see Bron gaping at the naked Lani priestess in the boat. "Stop looking at that!" Glaring at Bron. He looked hastily away. She turned back in time to see the figure on the boat disappear behind one of the houses—going where? she wondered. What would that version of herself say to her?

She found she was clinging to Bron's arm as they moved a little farther out into the street, peering down the street toward the woman's head; taking in the pallid, evil-eyed imps wrestling and burrowing in a garden of black irises, daffodils oozing blood, tulips turned to brass; seeing a middle-aged man she didn't know, weeping on his porch beside a rose garden gone jet. Across the street from the weeping man a few huddled figures, a family she knew vaguely, peered from behind curtains that opened and closed, opened and closed in slow modulation as if the house were respiring. The faces in the clouds were boiling in and out of clarity, the volcano-glass anacondas snapping up fox-bats, only to sprout their wings and take flight like dragons, anacondas with big bat wings . . . And somehow it all continued to fit together into one deliberately articulated picture. . . .

It seemed to her then that the street's transmutation was moving in a kind of direction, as leaves and debris were caught up in hurricane wind and blown one way, one way only; it was going somewhere in time, too. It was going to come to a decision of some kind . . . even as the stunted little trees the contractors had planted began to grow up higher, higher, thicker, extruding Spanish moss, the trees groaning like women in labor as their damp limbs spontaneously populated with screeching, improbable tropical birds, the long ribbons of moss streaming out to follow the crepe fringe. The crepe, the black snow, the purling mist rising from the black lawns, all of it winding together into a kind of tunnel, an oval whirlpool in the air; the shapes on the street twisted one into the next, an owl becoming a raven becoming a burst of black butterflies, swirling into the vortex rotating around the eye in the distance: the eye of the singularity, winking at Lani. And she felt she was going to enter into it with a kind of glorious immolation, a joyfulness like the crash of a dark storm-driven wave bursting into pearls before falling away into the fatal anonymity of the sea . . .

"Lani—" Bron looked down the street toward his family's house. "What's gonna happen to the people here?"

"Oh . . ." She felt like she was falling asleep, into a dream of glory, some ancient palace, Nefertiti riding a flying sphinx through the night sky. Smoke rising from the temple below— they were greeting her with a sacrifice, which was only right and proper. . . .

"Lani?" Bron's voice was squeakily urgent now.

She twitched, shivering, coming partway back to herself. "Oh, what'll happen? The people here—they'll probably end up in another world, have to adjust. New rules. Gone from this place.

Some will die. . . . Couldn't be worse than this place was before, Bron."

"You kids!" Her dad's voice, shouting over the music. "Lani, please, oh, Christ—come here! You too, Bron! Get over here!"

Lani turned to see her dad, in his bathrobe and T-shirt, gesturing distraughtly from the front door of the house. Lani shook her head. She didn't want to go to her dad—she wanted him to come to her.

Wobbly and hugging herself, Mom came out on the porch in her nightgown, face stricken—frozen in a silent moan. A translucent anaconda dripped from the roof of the porch, wound itself around her mom, and Mom just stared at it, trembling, as hypnotized as a lamb about to be swallowed. Her dad tugged at the snake, cursing to himself, trying to pull it away from her. . . .

Lani glared at the anaconda. "Let her go!" Obedient to her, it slithered away from Mom, into the shrugging junipers.

Dad looked at Lani, then at the snake's receding tail, back at Lani, realizing. "It's Lani . . . Dinwiddy . . . she stood too close. . . ."

"Our Lani did this?" Lani's mother asked, chewing a knuckle, her face squeezed tight in fear, struggling to comprehend.

"I think so," Dad told her. "She was at my lab—I told you about the way the mind can shape things, if . . ." He shook his head. Too much to explain when he only barely understood himself.

Lani looked at the vortex—a black-hearted celebration calling for its guest of honor. . . .

"What we gonna do now, Lani?" Bron asked, his voice hoarse, almost lost in the growing roar of the increasingly discordant music, the seething of the wind, the cries of frightened people huddled in their houses.

"Lani!" her mom called, with surprising firmness. "Please, baby . . . stop this thing . . . stop it . . . come back to us."

But Lani took a step toward the vortex . . . swaying with the music, though its rhythm was almost lost in its increasing thunder.

"Hey, kid . . ." She turned to see her dad walking up to her. His trembling hands going to her face. "Baby . . ." His voice breaking. His eyes wet.

Lani looked at him and her mom in amazement—and really saw them for the first time in years. Her father and mother both, disclosed, paradoxically, by the darkness of Lani's world. Somehow it made their inner lives shine out against its backdrop. Its darkness opened theirs to her: She saw their fears, their dilemmas, for a moment laid bare. They were trapped too. . . .

She saw that her father felt things as much as anybody. She could see it in his eyes now, as if those shutters had been thrown open: worry, loneliness, fear . . . longing. Love.

He just didn't know how to show it. He was like a man whose limbs had gone numb, called to dance. But he heard the music.

And her mother, at the porch—her arms open now to Lani. Wanting her daughter in her arms, her husband beside her. Really wanting Lani alive and with them. Behind the shutters of her mom's eyes there was a light that was more than selfish disappointment—normally nearly impossible to see, but quite real.

Lani let her dad's touch guide her over to Mom. Bron came too—as if scared to be too far from Lani, the only locus of control over this world.

The music seemed to get quieter; some of the restless motion of the street slowed, as if the trees, the streams of black thoughts, the flying anacondas, all waited for Lani; Justin and the other faces in the clouds looking right down at Lani's house, right at this porch. Waiting for her decision.

"Is this how it is for you, Lani?" her mom asked, voice breaking, looking back at those faces; at the dark life on the street, as

Lani came to the porch. Hesitating on the flagstone walk. "It's really like a . . . dark storm—all the time?"

Lani nodded, and began to sob. "Like this—but worse. This is the way I make it okay. This way it's *a world I can live in.*"

Her dad nodded. His voice hoarse: "I see, kid."

She looked hard at him—and she could see that he really did see. He wasn't judging her anymore; he wasn't hiding from her—he was just there, *in her world,* with her. Lani's world surrounded him, and he could feel it like weather on his skin. She had captured them both, her mom and dad—captured them and carried them off into the hidden recesses of her life. And for once, they really did see; for long enough, they shared the same world with Lani.

Dad looked down the street. "Dinwiddy was right after all . . . and you . . ." He looked at her. "We're at the wrong end of the scale for this kind of control, sweetheart. Can you let it go?"

Lani closed her eyes. She saw the eye of the singularity behind her closed eyelids staring back at her. It spoke to her somehow, without words or grammar. Telling her that she would never again, in this life, have a chance like the one she was giving up. . . .

"Yes," she answered. "I know. Take it away from me."

The eye of the void winked at her once more.

Then the street sighed—and surrendered her living daydream. The flying anacondas burst into small flocks of black butterflies, which burst in turn into midges with tiny human faces, which burst into a black mist, which trailed away; the tropical trees shrank back, and melted, their birds taking flight and then becoming blossoms blown on the wind; the faces in the clouds lost definition, and the clouds blew into rags; the color leached back into the plants; the aquarium funeral cars burst open, water gushing out only to instantly evaporate, idiosyncratic fish unthreading, evaporating with it, SUVs and Saturns and Tauruses reasserting their glossy metal shapes; the crepe let go and melted into wisps of fog; the house that was Lani cried out once, a cry of bitter disappointment, then laughed, and crinkled, shriveled like an old gourd, till its rind fell away into dust and the ordinary house was revealed under it: Justin's house, Lani realized. The blizzard ceased, and the lilies fell silent. The music muted. Near silence . . .

Sunlight fell warm over the complex, glanced off car windows, glowed in green lawns. Daffodils perfumed the air. But Hillview Hideaway looked strangely cold for all the warmth of the sun; it looked like the maze of cookie-cutter sameness it was.

Lani's mom looked at their neighborhood, back to normal, shaking her head, still stricken by her daughter's point of view. "It really isn't that much better this way, is it?"

"I know what you mean," Dad said, looking around. He put his arm around his wife. She let him do it.

Bron walked away—staggering a little, as if coming out of a drunk—down the walk, toward his own house, his own family. Not even saying good-bye.

People came out of their houses and looked around. They looked at Lani. They bunched up, muttering, staring at them. They were joined by the Sikh postman, an old widow from down the street. Staring became glaring.

"Uh-oh," Lani said. They knew—maybe the video of her family at the beach, on the TVs. They guessed who was responsible. No one was hurt—she knew that, could feel it—but they'd all been terrified.

"Okay," Dad said, letting out a long, shuddering breath. "I need a lot of time to process this. Let's sell this place. These people are not going to like us being here. Let's all . . . let's go to the coast, hang at a motel. I'll call the real estate people tomorrow. . . . So Lani . . ."

He looked at Lani. She could see, now, that he really hoped

she wanted to go with them. To stay with them. And that they respected her choice.

And she felt . . . so much lighter now. She'd had a glimpse of possibilities, of the mystery at the heart of the ruthless but energized universe: and the perpetually unfolding heart of that mystery was the very fact of infinite possibilities. After seeing those possibilities, suicide seemed so small and narrow and crabbed a solution to Lani. Suicide was a pitiful little thing: a reeking, cramped broom closet of a choice. So many things could happen. . . .

Her dad looked at her. "You give us another chance? Me and Mom? All of us together? What do you say?"

"I say what the hell," Lani said. "Let's see what happens."

Poppy Z. Brite is the author of seven novels, three collections of short stories, and much miscellanea. Early in her career she was known for her horror fiction, but at present she is working on a series of novels and short stories set in the New Orleans restaurant world. Her most recent novels, *Liquor* and *Prime*, chronicle the further adventures of some of the characters from "The Working Slob's Prayer." She lives in New Orleans with her husband, Chris, a chef.

THE WORKING SLOB'S PRAYER
Being a night in the history of the Peychaud Grill

by Poppy Z. Brite

Leslie ducked through the swinging doors and approached the pass, setting her feet with care on the slippery tile floor. As always when she entered the kitchen, she could feel its steamy, pungent atmosphere settling onto her skin and permeating the long black braid that hung down her back. By the end of the night she would be filthy despite her best efforts, with food grimed into the sleeves of her shirt and greasing the quicks of her nails.

Beyond the pass, the heart of the kitchen was a cacophony of shouts, clattering pans, hissing water, and sudden jets of flame. "You got my entrées for table eighteen?" she called over the din. "They say it's been forty minutes."

The chef, Paco Valdeon, glared at her through the curdle of steam that rose off the sauté pan he was holding six inches above the flame. The ropy muscles of his forearm strained not at all as he supported the heavy pan, tattoos rippling and bulging. His slate-gray eyes were flat and hostile. A cigarette dangled from the corner of his mouth, something she'd always thought was just a cliché until she started waiting tables at the Peychaud Grill two weeks ago.

"Confucius say dumbshit who order porterhouse medium-well expect to wait forty minutes," he said. "*At least* forty minutes. I usually tack on fifteen more just as a kind of asshole tax."

"Goddamn it, Chef, I mean, please, Chef, I really need that food. Rickey, can I at least take the lady's fish? She's the one really giving me hell."

The young cook working the hot line next to Chef Paco scowled at her. He was a nice enough guy most of the time, but God forbid he should speak politely to a waitress in front of his chef. "Fish'll be ready when the porterhouse is," he said.

"Jeez, Leslie, just go back and lean over the table for five more minutes." This from Shake, the sous chef, presumably in reference to the extra button undone on Leslie's white Oxford shirt. The other waitresses called it the tip button. "Make the guy forget all about his nasty-ass burnt porterhouse."

Unlike the chef, Rickey and Shake were New Orleans natives, and their hoarse, full-throated accent grated on Leslie's nerves. She was from Brooklyn herself, and the people she'd grown up with sounded positively musical by comparison.

"Yeah, maybe let that black bra strap slide down a li'l bit—"

"Hell, just pop one right out—"

"Fuck you in the ass, you pig motherfuckers!" she yelled as loud as she could, which was considerably. No one in the kitchen stopped what he was doing—you couldn't stop when a kitchen was as busy as the Peychaud's was now, not without risking disaster—but there was the briefest suggestion of a shocked pause. "If I want any more shit from you, I'll scrape it off the end of my dick, OK? Now I'm gonna go out there and tell those people five minutes, and I'm gonna come back here in *four* minutes, and I want to see my food in the pass. I don't care if you have to throw the goddamn steak in the fryer. Got it?"

No one answered, but they glanced at her with sullen respect, a couple of them hiding grins.

"Good."

"Damn, Leslie," said G-man, the cook who was working the grill station, "we gonna have to elect you Freak of the Week."

"Dude, we can't make a *waitress* Freak of the Week," said Rickey.

"Not even if she has a dick?"

Ignoring all this, Leslie turned and left the kitchen. All cooks were pigs, and some of them thought waitresses existed to be shit upon, but they could forget about that garbage with a Brooklyn girl.

Paco Valdeon had learned to cook in Nancy, a little French town near the German border. In 1980 everything there was sausages and sauerkraut and fondue, but he'd scammed his way into staying with the remnants of a family, a forty-five-year-old woman and two teenagers who'd just been left high and dry by the man of the house. Well, maybe not precisely dry. Even at twenty Paco wasn't handsome, but he was young and already had the unclean virility of a born head chef. Among other things, Minette had been an excellent cook, and she taught him what was still the most important thing he knew about food: You could enhance ingredients by combining them, sometimes even to the point of culinary magic, but no dish could be better than its ingredients. This was a valuable lesson for a kid whose previous position had been in the pantry of a "gourmet" restaurant in Baltimore, trimming leathery green beans, slicing corky tomatoes, and picking the salvageable bits out of blackened heads of lettuce.

By the time he fetched up in New Orleans seven years later— long enough to break the curse of the hand mirror Minette had thrown at him the night before he left Nancy—he was sustaining himself on cocaine, tequila, and hate. He hated all restaurant diners, most because they couldn't appreciate his food, the rest because they could and thought it gave them some sort of claim on him. He hated all waitstaff because they made ridiculous amounts of money for working a tenth as hard as he did. He hated women on general principle, which did not prevent him from fucking them if he could.

At the Peychaud Grill he was as close to content as he'd ever been. Most restaurant owners were clueless assholes, and the Peychaud's was no exception, but at least the guy respected his food and generally stayed out of his way instead of trying to be involved. He'd worked for plenty of people who didn't know a goddamn thing about food, but wanted to tell him how to cook anyway, criticizing his food costs and making him vet every dish with them before it went on the menu. The owner of the Peychaud Grill seemed to spend most of his time betting on horses at the racetrack, and Paco thought that was just dandy. Even so, his contentment did not prevent him from being full of hate. He thrived on hate, would have felt bereft without it.

More than anything he hated prettyboy chefs. Paco had come up at the very beginning of the celebrity chef craze, and fervently believed he had been passed over for several jobs because of his receding hairline, his burgeoning gut, and a pair of ears that would have given Dumbo pinna envy. There were few things he enjoyed more than leafing through the latest trendy chef-driven cookbook, finding gorgeous color pictures of the chef in question and mocking his inevitable square jaw, broad shoulders, or carefully mussed hair. All other things being equal, he himself preferred a crew with obvious defects, such as excess weight, scars, missing teeth, and so forth.

That was the main reason he hadn't wanted to hire Rickey, a seriously good-looking kid with intense blue-green eyes and a grin that belonged in a toothpaste commercial. Rickey's friend and roommate, G-man, Paco's best sauté guy at the time, had had to plead Rickey's case with the skill of a trial lawyer: "Honest to God, Paco, he's the most hardcore cook I know. He never reads anything but cookbooks. He went to the CIA—"

"Fuck that. I'll have to make him unlearn all the bad habits they taught him."

"But he didn't graduate! He got kicked out for beating up a guy."

Embarrassingly, this account of Rickey's exit from cooking school was probably what had made Paco hire him. A few months later, when he finally figured out that Rickey and G-man were more than roommates, it softened the blow a little: anybody who'd gotten kicked out of school for fighting couldn't be all bad. Rickey and G-man were just regular guys, not faggy or PC or any of that shit, and after a while he stopped caring what they did when they weren't at work.

In the life of every serious cook, there is a chef who makes him (or her) understand that it is necessary to care so deeply about food that you are willing to make enemies over it. For Rickey, that chef was Paco Valdeon.

Rickey had come to the Peychaud Grill because it paid better than his last job and he wanted to work with G-man. Ever since high school, they'd always worked together when they could. Within a week, though, he understood that this job would shape him more profoundly than anything else he had done in his life. He was already a roller; he and G-man had both been rollers since they were sixteen or so. They could handle an unexpected rush without getting in the weeds or putting out inferior plates; they could generate tremendous volumes of food; they even had some experience designing specials. Most valuable of all to any-one smart enough to hire them both, they knew each other's kitchen habits and rhythms intimately, and they worked like two parts of a single organism. Paco Valdeon, though, was the first culinary genius Rickey had ever known. The fact that Paco was also something of a thug didn't bother him a bit; in fact, Rickey, who had grown up in a rough neighborhood, was still young enough to find his thuggishness part of the draw.

One of his favorite Paco stories was the one about the specialty condiments. Paco had spent some time in California wine country before coming to New Orleans, and at one point when his cook's job wasn't covering all the bills, he'd gone to a bulk grocery store and bought up dozens of gallons of cheap vinegar, mustard, and jelly. He had transferred them into fancy bottles and jars from a local thrift shop, gotten his then-girlfriend to label them in a nice round hand ("Strawberry-Zinfandel Confit"; "Rosemary-Infused Balsamic"), and peddled them to area gift shops at vastly inflated prices. Supposedly he'd cleared more than $500 on the scam, but what Rickey really admired was the way he'd demonstrated that most people had no taste; they would buy anything and call it good as long as somebody charged them enough money.

G-man hadn't liked the condiment story nearly as much as Rickey did.

"Sure, Paco's great," he'd said when Rickey related it, "but what's so cool about ripping off a bunch of people who just wanted to buy something nice? What if they were buying a present for their mom?"

G-man had grown up in a strict Catholic family and still had a touch of the altar boy in him. It infuriated Rickey, particularly when Rickey could kind of see his point.

"Their mom probably thought it was good too," he said sullenly. "If she ever opened it. You know most people just stick that kinda shit in their pantry and think *Oh, I'll have to try that one of these days.*"

"Uh huh."

There was a world of nuance in that *uh huh*, most of it disapproving. Anyway, Paco said he wouldn't repeat the stunt if he had it to do over again; there was enough bad food in the world with-out spreading it around. Rickey thought that was pretty cool too.

"It's not even sanitary," G-man said a few minutes later.

"Neither is most restaurant cooking. Jeez, drop it, will you?"

This conversation wasn't as hostile as it sounded, since they'd had it while lying in bed, legs entwined, immediately after hav-ing sex. This was how they spent much of their time when they weren't at work. They'd only been out of their parents' houses for a few years, and privacy was still a novelty, something they could wallow in. They hadn't yet learned to take each other for granted.

Sometimes, though, G-man worried that he was losing Rickey to the Peychaud Grill. During their previous term of employment at a stodgy old French Quarter hotel restaurant called Reilly's, they had come straight home most nights. Now they usually stayed and partook of whatever debauchery was going on after the dinner shift: prodigious drinking, pot-smoking, lines of co-caine laid out on the long copper bar, boxes of nitrous-oxide chargers that whipped cooks' brains instead of cream. G-man en-joyed all this as much as Rickey did, but sometimes he'd look at Rickey through the clouds of smoke and the haze of drunken-ness and think, *I wish we could just go home like we used to.*

He never said so, though, because ever since they started working at the Peychaud, Rickey had developed the alarming habit of talking about "fags." By this he did not simply mean men who slept with other men, against whom he obviously had no le-gitimate beef, but men who whined, bitched, ruined orders, or otherwise displayed some type of weakness. It was a habit he'd picked up from Paco, and one G-man disliked intensely, but he didn't dare say anything to Rickey for fear of being labeled a fag himself. He supposed his mother had been right years ago when she said he cared too much what Rickey thought of him.

"Sure, I'll drop it," he said. "I was just, like, registering as a condiment objector."

Rickey was still kind-hearted enough to laugh at his lame joke, and the little moment of tension passed. Even so, it was never exactly easy being gay in the culture of the kitchen, where your worth was measured by burn scars, where women and fags couldn't hang. At the Peychaud it was even less easy than usual.

When the couple walked in just after eight, the maître d' pegged them as serious eaters. It wasn't that they were fat or anything—the man was tall and lean, the woman small but rather muscular-looking. It was just an attitude they had, a mixture of anticipation and contempt. Serious eaters were disappointed so often that they kept their contempt just below the surface, ready to pull out at a moment's notice.

"How long have you been open?" the woman asked as the maître d' seated them.

"Three years."

"Really?" she said as if she doubted his word. "I don't know how we missed you before. We try to keep up with the various openings and closings."

"Well, we're glad you're here now." He pulled out her chair, handed them the menus, unfolded their napkins. "You folks have a good meal."

When the maître d' had gone, the woman scanned the menu with a practiced eye and said, "Look, Seymour, they have fresh sardines. That's always a good sign."

"Go for them, Doc."

"Well, of course I'm going to go for them. You know I order fresh sardines or anchovies anytime I see them on a menu, just on principle. Too many people are frightened of little oily fish. It's important to show the chef your support when he's taking risks."

"He's not taking *too* many risks," said Seymour. "There's that damn oyster and Pernod soup again. I'm getting really tired of seeing that everywhere. If you want to serve oysters Rockefeller, then *serve* oysters Rockefeller. Don't make it into a goddamn *soup*."

"I agree. But he's got to have a few sure-fire items, doesn't he?"

"The artichokes are a nice touch, anyway," said Seymour. "Practically everybody who attempts a facsimile of oysters Rockefeller feels compelled to load it up with spinach. I don't think Antoine's uses spinach in the original version. I think they use artichokes."

"I know, dear. Are you trying to talk yourself into ordering the soup?"

"Good God, no. I'm looking at the foie gras and the grouper. What are you ordering, Doc? Are you going for the osso buco?"

"No, it's served with cauliflower quenelles. You know I can't stand cauliflower."

"Sorry, I forgot. The pork shank, then?"

"I'm thinking about it. Are you having the Creole tomato salad?"

"Maybe. I'm interested in that shaved Vella Dry Jack. Why? Are you?"

"I'm not sure. I'm iffy on the pork shank—I may do three appetizer courses. Can you guess which ones?"

"The sardines, then the salad, then the terrine."

"Precisely."

"Do you think that'll be enough to eat?"

"I'm saving room for dessert," said Doc. "I hear the desserts here are very unusual."

Leslie came and took their drink orders. When she had gone, Doc glanced over the menu again, sighed deeply, and said, "But, you know, I think I really want that pork shank."

"Order in," said Leslie, hanging the ticket in the pass. "Hey, Chef, I think these people at table five might be food writers or something. From what I could hear, they went over every item on the menu."

"Great," said Paco. "Just what I needed tonight. I always like to have food writers in the house when I'm hungover."

"You're always hungover," said Shake.

Paco flipped him off without looking away from the row of tickets, then began to call out the new order. "Rickey, ordering one tomato salad, one terrine."

"One tomato and one terrine, Chef."

"G-man, ordering one sardines, one foie, one grouper."

"One sardines, one foie, one grouper, Chef."

"Shake, ordering one pork shank."

"One pork."

Paco improvised two amuses-bouche of prosciutto, asparagus tips, and Louisiana caviar. "Hey, Leslie," he said as the runner came back in, "take these to the food writers."

"Sure thing, Chef."

Seymour and Doc smiled rather smugly as the waitress placed the complimentary canapés before them. They were used to receiving amuses-bouche and other little perks in the restaurants they frequented, but it was especially nice getting one the first time they ate at a place.

"Lovely," they agreed as they used their salad forks to spear the little packets of air-dried ham and asparagus. They left the salad forks on the canapé plates, nonchalantly sure that new ones would be provided when their first course arrived.

The tomato salad and sardines came to the table a few minutes later. A runner had already cleared the canapé plates and salad forks. Doc raised her eyebrows as Leslie set the plates down and turned away. "Excuse me," she said, a hair louder than was strictly necessary, "may we have some fresh *forks*, please?"

"Of course. Excuse me." Leslie hurried to the wait station, grabbed two salad forks, and delivered them to the table.

"Thank you *very* much," said Doc, smiling up at the younger woman to signal that all was forgiven for now.

"You're welcome. Please let me know if you need anything else."

"I will," Doc said honestly. She cut a sardine in thirds with the side of her fork and put one section in her mouth. "Oh," she moaned as the mingled oiliness of the fish and buttery sour-sweetness of the sauce melted over her tongue. "Oh, that's so good."

"I don't suppose I can have a bite," said Seymour. Instead of answering, Doc just pulled her plate closer and snarled at him. "That's all right," he told her. "I know how you feel about those little oily fish. Anyway, my salad is very nice. I'm glad *someone* can still get tomatoes that taste like tomatoes."

Wanting to draw out the experience of eating the three tangy little fish, Doc put down her fork for a moment. "I *know*," she said. "That heirloom-tomato salad I had last week at Bayona tasted of absolutely nothing at *all*."

"Do you want to try this?"

"Yes, please, as long as we're not trading. Don't give me any pickled onions; I don't like them . . ."

As Shake broke down his station, scrubbing surfaces and covering what was left of his mise-en-place, he went over the conversation he'd had with his father this morning. He had already been over this conversation ten or twelve times, but he couldn't get it out of his head even though it caused a scary high-pressure sensation in his skull every time he thought of it.

"That restaurant is ruining you," Johnny Vojtaskovic said without preamble, coming into the kitchen as Shake downed his first cup of coffee.

It was hard to defend himself when he knew his eyes were red, his pits stank, and the mug in his hand was trembling slightly but visibly. That was Reason Number One why he really needed to move out of his parents' house: he was sick of making excuses for being a slob. Nonetheless, he said, "I'm fine."

Johnny snorted as he took eggs from the refrigerator, broke them into a skillet, stirred them and sprinkled Vegeta over the top. Shake's parents were native New Orleanians, born and raised in Gentilly Woods, but their Croatian-born parents had used Vegeta in everything; it was the taste of their childhoods. It was the taste of Shake's childhood too, but just now its familiar salty-green aroma made his stomach roll over.

"You know what you look like?" Johnny said, scraping the eggs onto a plate. They were barely cooked, still mucilaginous, the way his father had always liked them.

"I bet you're gonna tell me."

"A bum." Johnny forked eggs into his mouth. Shake wondered how he could stand to eat the snotty-looking things without toast or salt or anything but goddamn Vegeta. He forced himself to look away; he was going to make himself puke if he didn't watch it. When was he going to learn that he could do cocaine *or* tequila shots, but not cocaine *and* tequila shots? After all, he wasn't Paco.

"Well," he said carefully, "I guess I am kind of a bum. We all are. We're just working slobs."

He thought of a little refrain Paco had taught him, something Paco called the Working Slob's Prayer.

Please God, don't let me fuck anything up tonight.
If I do fuck up, don't let anybody notice.
If somebody notices, don't let them tell my boss.
If they tell my boss, let him be too drunk to give a shit.
Thank you, God, amen.

"That's what I been trying to tell you!" Johnny said excitedly. "You stay in that business, you gonna turn old before your time. Now look, you wanna come on with us, I can start you at ten an hour—"

"I'm *making* ten an hour."

"Ten twenty-five, then. Aw, son, it's breaking your mother's heart to see you throw away your life like this."

Johnny and Lydia Vojtaskovic ran a venerable and popular pest control business; they had been engaged in the Sisyphean task of killing New Orleans roaches since 1953. The hell of it was that Johnny's own parents, like most Croatians in Louisiana, were in the seafood business and had pressured Johnny to follow in their footsteps. Uninterested in oysters, Johnny had sold off the family beds as soon as his folks retired, moved from Plaquemines Parish to New Orleans, and started up his company with the profits. For years he had listened to his father's dire prophecies about how the chemicals would give him cancer, the blacks would shoot him dead in the street, his son would hang around the French Quarter and grow up a fruit. Perhaps because none of this had happened yet, Johnny felt free to nag his own son in exactly the same way.

"I'm not throwing away my life, Dad. I like cooking. I'm probably not ever gonna be a famous chef, but I work in a real good restaurant and I make a decent living."

"Real good restaurant. Ha!" The Vojtaskovics had eaten at the Peychaud Grill once, had pronounced the portions tiny and the prices absurd, and hadn't returned. Shake wondered what it would feel like to know your parents were proud of you.

"Yeah, I'm aware of how you feel, Dad," said Shake, but Johnny had dumped his plate in the sink and was leaving the room.

Thinking of his father's retreating back, he closed the door of the reach-in cooler a little too hard. "Something wrong, dude?" said G-man, who was breaking down his own station.

"Nah, just family shit."

"Tell me about it."

"Your folks a pain in your ass too?" He had wondered about Rickey and G-man's relationship, but had never asked. It was better not to go looking for information you didn't really want.

"Catholic," said G-man, and didn't elaborate. He didn't need to. On top of everything else, Shake's parents were Catholic too.

"So were those people really food writers or what?" said Paco. Service had been over for thirty minutes, and he was just settling in at the bar while the rest of the crew cleaned up the kitchen. Leslie was trying to sneak past him on her way out, hoping he wouldn't ask her this very question.

"Uh, no," she said sheepishly. "I finally asked them, because, you know, they kept talking about the *composition* of the dishes, and asking where you'd cooked before, and all kinds of shit. But no, they weren't food writers."

"What were they?"

"The guy was a poet. The lady said she was the coroner of Orleans Parish."

Leslie winced, expecting a torrent of abuse. But Paco only shrugged and said, "Well, did they like their meal?"

"Oh, absolutely. They wanted to meet you, but I told them you were swamped."

No matter how busy or slow the restaurant was, Paco Valdeon was invariably too "swamped" to make dining room rounds. Almost as much as prettyboy chefs, he hated chefs who thought half their job consisted of swanning around the dining room taking compliments on the food. He'd known chefs who kept separate, spotless white jackets for just that purpose, and would change into them when they left the line. Paco's own white jackets were stained, frayed at the cuffs, and unmonogrammed. He wasn't opposed to head chefs wearing a discreet monogram of their own name and the restaurant's, but lately it seemed as if a guy couldn't even get a sous chef job without running out and buying four or five brand-new jackets with fancy monograms, cloth-covered buttons, colored piping, and every other frill he could think of. It was like they thought the most important part of being a cook was getting to wear a cool costume.

Paco picked up the first of many tequila shots and tossed it down his throat. The smooth agave burn spread through him, familiar and comforting. Someday, he promised himself, he was going to write a book about all the bullshit he'd seen in his days of kitchen work. All the sordid sex, all the preening vanity, all the filth and corruption. People loved shit like that. He was sure it would be a bestseller.

Brian Hodge is the author of eight novels, most recently the crime tales *Wild Horses* and *Mad Dogs*. He's also written upward of one hundred short stories and novellas, many of which have been sucker punched and thrown into three acclaimed collections, the latest of which is *Lies & Ugliness* (Night Shade Books). A long-standing award nominee, in 2004 he broke an equally long-standing Susan Lucci–like losing streak with the International Horror Guild Award for best short fiction. He frequently wanders the hills around Boulder, Colorado, and sequesters himself in a home studio emitting dark electronic music and other ungodly noises. More of everything is in the works.

IF I SHOULD WAKE BEFORE I DIE

by Brian Hodge

My writing this can only be regarded as a tremendous act of faith. That I believe you will not only live to be born and see the world outside my belly, but that you'll reach an age when you can read this cumulative letter and understand what a miracle all of that will have been.

And I don't use the word *miracle* lightly. Used to, I was the type to roll my eyes whenever I heard prospective parents talk of their fertilized egg as being something miraculous. Cause for rejoicing, sure. But a miracle? It just didn't seem to qualify. It's the most natural thing in the world, something that happens somewhere every moment of the day. But then, that goes back to something said by Albert Einstein (and you'd better have studied him in school by now!): that we can live as if nothing is a miracle, or as if everything is. Okay, so you got me there. Still, I don't think I felt any different about pregnancy-as-miracle even after the doctor confirmed what the pharmacy test kit and I already knew.

But times change, my little one. In ways we can't possibly foresee.

We'll have to continue this later. It's morning, and I have to get things together for school, and don't take this personally, because I thought we were past all of this months ago, but you're making me sick.

Today was bad. But maybe now you'll better understand why I'm frightened enough to need this ongoing show of faith that soon I will see your beautiful squalling face.

Like most people, I've made a habit of not looking up. Sure, the sky could fall—but in my experience most of the things you really have to worry about live at ground level, so that's where you keep your eyes. Just by being watchful, I've thwarted two muggings in the past year alone, me and my trusty canister of pepper spray.

But this afternoon I looked up . . . had to, my attention drawn by the sight of deflated balloons high in some oaks, a splash of color against the slate sky and stark branches, their tiny buds struggling against the ice after a false spring. Helium-filled run-aways, let go by the careless hands of children during some function or other on the grounds of St. Mark's. I walk past the place twice each weekday, to and from school. It's the most peaceful route I can find, keeps me away from the busier streets and the incessant traffic noise that seem impossible to escape when you just want to think. So the balloons caught my eye, hanging before twin bell towers that, if you must know, preside over the crack dealers and prostitutes two streets over. They made me think of souls lost halfway to heaven.

And they were the only reason I saw the girl before she jumped.

She stood in one of the high, narrow openings near the top of the closer tower, portals through which the bells peal each Sunday to call whatever flock remains. All I saw was a pale face and an indistinct body framed by rough gray stone. When she nudged one foot into empty space, at first I thought she was only reckless.

Our eyes met then, I think—she did seem to look down in my direction. So was this her cue to jump? To do it before anyone could try talking her out of it? I took it that way, but then (not to speak ill of your grandparents) I was born and raised for guilt.

No scream, from either of us. It was a remarkably quiet death. I stared at her all the way down, past seventy-odd feet of stone. She didn't thrash, and even seemed to fall in slow motion. I barely heard the impact over the traffic two streets over.

Maybe she lived for a moment, or maybe not. Certainly there was no life left by the time I reached her. Kneeling beside her hip, I tried to ignore the blood seeping from the back of her skull onto the walkway. Her face, fragile and too young, looked oddly peaceful and resolved, her eyes half-open.

I put one hand on her belly—flat, definitely flatter than mine right now, but the skin felt slack and loose, as recently deflated as one of those balloons overhead. For me, it was as good as a signed suicide note. There was no baby in a crib somewhere. It lay like wax in a fresh little grave. Or worse, if she'd miscarried early enough, it became hospital waste, incinerated with wrappings and tumors.

"I'm so sorry for you," I told her. "I felt like doing this too, after I lost mine."

So few of you seem to make it out of the third trimester these days.

The hand I held must have been cold even before death, and didn't squeeze back.

And to be totally honest with you, I still can't say whether or not I would've given in to my despair had it not been for you. You and I may have lost your twin, but because you'd hung in there and survived, I knew there was something yet to live for.

I told about the jumper at group tonight, to a rapt and silent audience. At group, it goes without saying: We've *all* been up in that bell tower. If only for a few moments, we've all looked down and stuck a foot into empty space. All of the women, and maybe a few of the men, too, the guys who haven't been too stoic to admit they need the support of strangers after their hopes for fatherhood came unexpectedly slithering out in an ill-formed mass from between the thighs of their wives and girlfriends.

I'm very aware that I'm sometimes describing things in a way that no mom should describe them to her child, at any age . . . but why sugarcoat it? Along with love and care, I owe you truth: You're struggling for life in a perilous time, just as I'm struggling to maintain hope.

About the jumper, a woman named Danika said, "Ain't nobody should die alone that way. Did you get to her in time?" Danika's been coming to group for a month. "Did she say anything at the end?"

"Just barely," I told her, and in the silence of our borrowed classroom you could hear the slightest creak. "She asked me to forgive her. Because she knew it was wrong. I know I don't look anything like a nun, but maybe she thought I was from the church."

We'd all stood in the balance and wavered, then chosen life.

But for some, I suspect that the debate still isn't entirely settled.

Group—ah, yes. What seems so thoroughly a part of my life right now will, I hope, by the time you're reading this, be just a distant memory.

Citywide, these past months, support groups have become a

way of life, a spontaneous network arising to meet a growing need. They meet in church basements, in classrooms, in fraternal halls and civic centers. Their attendees drink lots of coffee and smoke lots of cigarettes, because now, for them, there's no reason not to. They find themselves in the heartbreaking position of suddenly having no unborn to think of.

Except for me. Even in groups bound together to survive losses that we don't understand, I don't entirely fit in. If any other woman out there is in my position, lucky enough to still be carrying a surviving twin, I haven't heard of her.

How else to describe what's going on but as a wave of spontaneous abortions? Pregnancies failing first by the handful, then by the dozens, an epidemic that cuts across all ethnic groups, all income levels, that reaches into urban and suburban wombs alike. It continues to stymie the Department of Public Health as much today as after that first spike in the miscarriage rate . . . which I was part of, dismally enough. The Centers for Disease Control is here, but has yet to find any evidence of one. Nothing in the water, nothing in the air, nothing in the tissues scraped for tests. No genetic abnormalities in a thousand sperm samples; no toxins contaminating the food supply. Or, should I say, nothing worse than usual, still within the "safe" levels allowed by law— but I *am* thinking of you, trying to eat organic whenever I can afford it.

I started attending group on the north side while staying with my parents after the miscarriage that robbed us of your brother. At the time, it was a way to get out of the house for a couple hours to escape my parents' habit of tiptoeing around me as if I were china poised to shatter.

Except that first group was just as bad, in its own way. Yes, they all knew how I felt. I knew how all of them felt. We understood one another . . . to a point. But I wasn't one of them, not anymore, if ever, and they knew it. Knew it in my clothes, my hair. I imagine they thought I'd just strayed into the wrong neighborhood, with no idea that I remembered what it was like to grow up among them.

You'd think that a thing like a plague of miscarriages would be enough to tear down the walls of pretense, to let us at least see eye-to-eye on our shared tragedies. You'd think our differences wouldn't matter, but they did. Oh, the others were polite enough. They're often polite. But as we traded tales of sorrow and struggle, I couldn't help but notice an undercurrent of judgment, so many of these inwardly sneering women seeming to believe that they had lost so much more. *My child would have had potential,* they might as well have said. *What would your child have been but an eventual burden on the rest of us?*

I hadn't told them about you, you see. I wasn't showing as much then as I am now. So I'm glad I hadn't said anything about you, because while they could pass judgment on me all they wanted, how dared they judge you. How dared they think they know you, your future, your dreams and your determination. By the time you're reading these pages, I hope I've told you this so often it's running out of your ears, but here it is for the very first time: *You can be anything you want to be.* Me, I'm working on it. I know there are plenty of people who'd say that if all I am at this stage in my life is an underpaid teacher and unwed mother, then I haven't exactly set the world on fire.

To that, I'd just say that it seems to burn quite well on its own.

So. While I didn't like this particular group, I found the idea of a support group in general to be very therapeutic, and found the fit much better much closer to home. Where we meet isn't nearly as nice—of course not; it's a classroom in a public school, one district over from where I teach. The paint may peel and the ceiling tiles may have huge brown water stains, but from the moment I walked in, I could tell that nobody was going to care if in my off-hours I still had a stubborn streak or two about totally outgrowing the aesthetics of my malcontented youth.

Please don't take that as a license to make my life miserable someday. I prefer to delude myself into thinking that with me as your mother, you won't have anything to rebel against.

You're giving me a terribly restless night, I hope you know. We should be asleep right now. I'm game. But you, at two A.M., are evidently competing in a swimming meet. Let's blame it on the neighbors, shall we? Somebody fired off a gunshot and you mistook it for a starter pistol.

But I don't begrudge you your recreational activities one bit, for reasons that should be obvious.

You know something . . . ? The strangest thing for me about this letter is that I'm writing to someone who doesn't have a name yet. For that matter, your gender is a mystery as well. I haven't wanted to know, and the few who do are under strict orders to not say a word. I want surprises, the kind of good old-fashioned surprises that went out of style after doctors gained the ability to peek inside and see what I've been growing all these months.

Odds are, you're a boy. But maybe not. If you and the brother we'll sadly never know were identical twins, of course you're a boy. But if you were fraternal twins, well, we're back to a toss-up again, aren't we?

So for now, I just think of you as the Tadpole.

What your nonamphibian name should be fills me with constant soul-searching. I half suspect that our destinies are intrinsically tied into our names, as if these are templates imposed for us to fill. If my parents hadn't named me Melody, would I still have gone into music? Who knows, and maybe I overstate the case— those who can't do, teach, right? Well, all I have to say to that is: *You* try making a living off talent alone when your repertoire rarely extends much past 1790.

So I'm sure there will come a point when you find it thoroughly humiliating that your mom's great sustaining passion, besides her brilliant and talented child, of course, is a batch of instruments with names like recorder and *schreierpfeif* and krummhorn.

Say, that reminds me of an Early Music joke: What's the difference between a krummhorn and a lawn mower? You can tune a lawn mower.

Someday you'll appreciate just how funny that really is.

Who knows if we'll still be doing it when you're old enough to humiliate, but for now, I'm with a group of like-minded women who specialize in the hits of the late-medieval era and beyond. The Hedgewaifs, we call ourselves, and our performances have begun to attract a devoted little following, although there's endless debate about whether that's because of the music or what we wear to perform in. Well, we do make quite a fetching quintet, in our lace and corsets and dark lipstick.

Whenever we play or practice, I'm sure that in each of us it scratches different itches. For my friend Heather (she plays the viola da gamba, and can't wait to meet you), it's the best way to shut out the rest of the world. She grew up in a factory town, where even her dreams were filled with the sounds of machinery, so taking up a horsehair bow was her way of driving them back.

For myself, our music recalls a different age, in which I can at least imagine there was more civility than today. That's important, civility. You wouldn't think I could miss it so badly, an age I never even knew. Oh, but I do. Especially on days like today, after encounters like the one this afternoon.

After school, I went to my favorite used-record/CD shop to see if I could find a few things I wanted for class. Buried treasures always seem to await there, which makes it worth straying into the block it's in. A few doors away, I walked past this guy who wasn't doing much of anything, just leaning against a grimy brick wall and smelling of whatever he'd been drinking during the day. He noticed me, I could tell. If you live here, you can't help but develop this radar; you *know* when somebody's just decided to include you in his day, in all the wrong ways. He looked at me—looked down at *you,* actually—and here's what he said:

"So. Haven't lost it yet, have you?"

I had no idea what to say to that. Not that it deserved a response.

He went on: "Maybe later. Looks like there's still time."

The thing that got me is that he didn't even say this with any particular scorn. It was so flat and without affect, as if all the losses going on around him were complete trivialities. What kind of deadness is at the heart of a person when he thinks that's an acceptable thing to say to someone?

He's far from alone, too. This may have been the most face-to-face it's been, but I've been encountering these kinds of sentiments for months. They're in homemade signs, in graffiti, even in new music from local artists . . . an undercurrent that seems to regard this death of innocents as some answer to a prayer for population control. I've seen the most terrible clinical pictures reproduced on flyers, with the most terrible slogans, actually celebrating what's going on.

We're getting it from both sides by now, too. Let one woman miscarry, and she's treated with sympathy. Let it happen to a thousand, and we're often shunned as defective, or contagious. Or those who claim to have a direct link to God's brain shout at the top of their lungs that we're undergoing the cleansing of His latest judgmental wrath, one final warning before He toasts the rest of us from the face of the earth.

Awfully considerate of Him, don't you think?

I've just now taken enough of a breather to realize what I'm saying and who I'm saying it to. Shame on me. I shouldn't be venting to you before you're even born. So if you're reading this someday and wonder what the black marker scratch-outs are all about, trust me, the letter has been censored to protect you from wondering what the hell was wrong with Mom back then.

Hi, Tadpole. My little miracle worker.

I've heard of people becoming addicted to support groups, and have been hoping that that isn't what impels me to go as often as I do, but I've finally realized the appeal. Out in the world, I'm just another one of the growing number of defectives. But at group, because I have you, I'm a beacon of hope. It doesn't matter what I've lost. I'm the glass that's still half-full, rather than half-empty.

I just thought you should know how deeply you've touched a couple dozen lives already, before you've even drawn your first breath.

And if there's anything that's needed now, it's hope. Group wasn't especially supportive tonight. It's nobody's fault. We were just preoccupied with the news that the miscarriages are spreading. At first it was local. Now we're the epicenter, the red dot on the map surrounded by concentric rings.

A thousand times a day I wrap my arms around the bulge you've made of my belly, trying to hold you inside me. There are even times I think I'd rather keep you there forever, where it's safe and warm and snug, away from what's waiting for you on this side. This machine out here that only wants you to be one more tooth in its grinding gears.

I wish I could play now, for both of us, to take our minds off what's going on, but it's too late at night. I know the reaction it would bring: hostile pounding on the ceiling over our heads from, yes, the very same upstairs neighbor who thinks nothing of blasting his TV six hours at a stretch, so loud I can sometimes tell what he's watching. He has a name, I'm sure, but I just like to refer to him by a word you're not allowed to speak until you're twenty-five.

Good night, Tadpole. Feel free to dog-paddle around tonight, a little. You and I are as close right now as two people can be, which makes it all the more difficult to explain how alone I feel sometimes.

It's my free period at school, so we don't have much time, but I'm wondering:

Just what do you *hear* inside there?

In one sense you're a world away, yet I also have to remember that there's only a few layers of me between you and the world that's waiting. All in all, that's much less insulation than what's protecting us from the neighbors.

I remember the doctor telling me that you—not just you, but all of your short, damp, wrinkly kind—hear a constant soft rush of the blood as it's pumped through my body. But you wouldn't just hear it, would you . . . you'd be enveloped by it.

So I wonder what else you hear. Everything, I imagine, as long as it's loud enough. Maybe it sounds muffled and watery, like hearing something going on beside a swimming pool while you were sunk a foot or two under. But you'd hear it.

This is really starting to concern me lately. Like, I'll walk by a construction site near my school, and the earthmovers will be scraping away, or some worker will have a jackhammer going, and I'll wonder, "Oh, what must Tadpole think of that?"

Because you have no context for these things. You've never seen them. You've never had them explained to you. You just know what they sound like, somewhere on the other side of the wall.

If it seems like I'm fixated on this, we can thank Danika for it. Remember her, one of the women at group? The other night she got to talking about the day before her loss, something I hadn't heard about before. She lives in the flight path near the airport, and on the day in question, a commuter plane crashed two blocks away. So for hours, her neighborhood was this ungodly riot of sirens and fire trucks and ambulances and wreckage equipment, and all the screaming and shouting that goes along with them.

Danika blamed her miscarriage on the stress of that day.

Sometimes, when I think of everything you must hear, I think that all of us out here have so much to apologize for.

Like I said, support group is a way of life these days.

But now you attend at your peril.

I told you how the miscarriages were spreading beyond? Well, they just keep going. The way they've spread, you'd suspect there was something viral about it, except nobody has managed to find a single thing to indicate that. Which hasn't stopped some people from jumping to the conclusion anyway. They come in from miles away and they look at us here, the first ones affected, as having caused it. They want someone to blame for their own losses, and we're the most convenient Typhoid Marys.

They firebombed the locations of two groups earlier tonight. Not mine, and nobody was hurt, but the ignorance and hatefulness in such an act is beyond my comprehension. I've been watching it on the news and wondering if this is the way of the future for us now . . . we've lost our babies so now we're pariahs, and the only response is to drive us away, into hiding or extinction.

I don't know what's worse: trying to get this all out of my system by telling you about it, or sitting here dwelling on it. Either way, it feels like I'm putting you at risk, that it will seep into you.

We can't have that. You keep me going, you know?

You're much too little to lean on, but you still keep me going.

* * *

Do you dream, Tadpole? Do you *dream* in there?

If we can watch cats and dogs while they're asleep, with their paws twitching and their mouths smacking, and accept that they must be dreaming, then why not unborn babies? You just wouldn't dream like the rest of us, would you? You couldn't dream about things you could see, because you haven't seen anything yet. You haven't smelled or tasted anything, either, so you couldn't dream about those. You can only feel and hear. That's all your developing mind has to work with.

Maybe now I know what it's like, a little, because last night I had a dream like that. I dreamed of what it must be like to be you, in the only place you've ever known, curled up all warm and wet, in the complete absence of light. I was *inside* myself, I guess . . . literally. And it felt wonderful, until the noise began and it all started to get oppressive, as if everything were shrinking around me . . . like I was in a duffel bag and someone had cinched the opening and was twisting it around and around, squeezing me into a smaller and smaller space. And the whole time there was no getting away from the noise, this huge screeching roar that revved and pulsated and just went on and on and on. . . .

Did *you* dream that, Tadpole? Was that *your* dream in there?

We share things all the time. Oxygen, nutrition, blood, going back and forth between us. With so intimate an exchange going on, why not a dream?

I woke up and you were kicking, but it wasn't quite like any kicking that I can remember. It wasn't . . . strong. More like you were flailing weakly about in there, or just trembling. In five seconds I went from being sound asleep to being absolutely terrified, so I did the only thing I could think to do: got my mellowest recorder, a tenor made of maple wood, and tried to serenade you, tell you somehow that everything was all right . . . and who cares if Mr. A**hole upstairs hears and thinks it's after-hours?

It seemed to work and you quieted down, so we could go back to sleep. Except by then the damage was done. Not to you, to *me*. Next it was my turn to come up with bad dreams. Should I tell you? You'll think I'm silly if I tell you. You'll be disappointed if I don't.

Very well . . .

I was in the classroom where we have group, okay, but it was obvious nobody had been in the room for a very long time. Nobody came here to learn; nobody came here to mourn. Nobody came here at all anymore. All that was left was a lot of dust and a couple empty chairs. I was sitting at a desk in the very center of the room, both feet on the floor and facing forward, the way we rigid teachers expect you to sit. And then *you* came in . . . crawled in, actually. You couldn't have been more than several months old. I watched you crawl across the front of the room, then turn the corner and crawl down the length of the room at my left side. The whole time, you were moving along the baseboard, stopping to eat the paint chips flaking from the walls. Do they even use lead-based paint anymore? I don't think so, but it didn't matter, because the place was so old. I kept trying to tell you not to put them in your mouth, but you never seemed to hear me. You just kept going until you moved out of sight, behind me, into the back half of the room. I could see the trail you'd left in the dust, and every now and then I'd hear you eat something else, so I waited for you to come around into view again, on the right side of the room. Except you never did. And I couldn't turn around to see where you were and what had become of you . . . because nobody had given me permission.

If we're sharing dreams, I hope it's a one-way connection, that *that* one didn't seep through to you, along with the soy milk I had before bedtime.

And you're probably wondering again, aren't you: What the hell *was* wrong with Mom back then?

Don't judge her too harshly. I think she was afraid she was poisoning you, just by being alive.

If anyone knew how many support groups I've attended lately, they'd think there was something wrong with me. That I'm developing an unhealthy obsession, unable to function without them. True, that's about all my life is lately—school and group.

But I call it something else: research.

I started out by asking the question at my own group. Then, night after night, I've been going to another, and another, and another. I'll walk up and be sure to thank the cop or security guard on duty, assigned to look after the place and protect it from attacks. They don't seem to have them covered 100 percent, except on the north side, but it's better than nothing.

It isn't just loss groups anymore, either. Now there are meetings for pregnant women who still have their babies, praying they won't have to change groups.

I can go to either one, and belong.

I'm quiet at first, the way newcomers are. Even within tiny, temporary societies founded on grief and fear, there are unwritten rules, taboos you don't break. I listen to their heartbreaking stories, their outpouring of anguish. The voices may be new, but I've heard their stories already. There can be only so many variations.

After a while, they make room for me, ready to accept me because I've been respectful, so I tell my own version . . . or part of it. Whether or not I say much about you depends on the group. Sometimes I get the feeling that they'd think I was gloating, so I say as little as possible. Other times I know how much hope you'll bring, so you're front and center in more ways than one. I've gotten good at judging the moods of these groups.

And finally, when I sense that I can, I'll ask the question: "Do you/did you ever get the feeling that your babies are/were dreaming?"

Some of them look at me like they think I'm crazy. Others . . . it's obviously the first time they've considered this, but they don't necessarily dismiss it. And others . . . I can tell just by looking into their eyes that they've felt it too. They know exactly what I'm talking about, each woman thinking it was something unique to her, or that it was her imagination, and that nobody has quite brought it up before.

So we talk about the experiences that everyone's had, and, in fewer instances, whatever impressions we felt were shared between our babies and ourselves. There are variations; I'd expect this. But compared to the dream of yours that I felt I tapped into, they're all much more alike than not.

My God, all of you, you tiny things, you're in there, and you've grown terrified at what you hear waiting for you, haven't you?

"So they've been letting go," a woman said tonight, the conclusion she'd drawn. This was the first I've heard it spoken aloud, but maybe it's something that many of us, deep down, have intuited. Because for all the tests, all the theories, nobody has come up with an explanation for this plague, much less a way to stop it.

And I think that's about as far as anyone was willing to go tonight. But what I want to know is: If it's true you're letting go by the dozens, by the hundreds, *who told you how?* Who told you all that you *could?* Who gave you *permission?*

So now I keep wondering what would've happened if I hadn't awakened the other night, if I'd remained asleep and so had you, without me to serenade and reassure you, knowing what you were dreaming in there: the noise and the compression, squeezed before your time . . . like garbage in a truck. In such a dark place, experiencing the first dreams you've ever had, how could you possibly distinguish between what's real and what isn't?

And from all the way out here, how can I possibly protect you every moment?

No school today. For me, that is. For everyone else it's education as usual.

I did get halfway there. Walking, like I normally do. I've always maintained it's good for us . . . me and my Tadpole, out for a stroll. Ever since the jumper, though, I've been detouring from the usual route. My mistake. Keep going by the bell towers, and all I would have had to contend with is a daily reminder of what that poor girl did in front of me.

The block I was in is kind of run-down, but then, close to home, they all are; it's just that this one wears its age in a more picturesque way. There's a deli that's been in the same family for four generations, and a flower shop run by a woman old enough to have diapered at least three of those generations from the deli. I wasn't even there yet, just crossing the street, when I started to hear someone crying. I wasn't quite sure where it was coming from, just that it was getting louder, and seeming to echo off the bricks.

Before I even saw her, I knew where she must've been, because by then a little crowd had gathered, so as I came up, I was thinking, "Well, surely somebody's with her, somebody must be taking care of this . . ."

Except nobody was.

She sat at the bottom of a stairwell leading up to some second-floor apartments, half-in and half-out of the doorway, one leg tucked underneath her as she sat beneath a row of mailboxes, one hand hanging on to the doorknob. And the other . . .

The main thing I remember is the bright red stain seeping through the yellow fabric bunched around her waist.

Somebody pointed and laughed; I recall that much. Everyone else, once they had the idea, they went on their way. Conversations resumed, footsteps quickened to be away from her. I wanted to help, I really did, and I know that I would have if she could've just *shut up* for a minute, but instead she kept crying, and crying, and . . .

I didn't want you exposed to it, I guess. So I did an about-face, turning around to go home. I looked over my shoulder once, at the end of the block, and could see her arm still reaching out of the doorway.

All in all, not one of my prouder moments.

So it's just you and me today. Maybe all the rest of this week. The way I feel right now, maybe until after you're born.

The thing that gets me, though, is that no matter how hard I try, when I think back to that final glance I had of the woman in the doorway, with just her arm visible, I can't quite remember if she was still beckoning for help . . . or pointing. At us.

Which probably wouldn't be a big deal at all, if it weren't for that stupid dream I had last night, about you whispering something in your brother's ear. Right before . . . well, you know.

That's just me being silly, right? First-time pregnancy jitters and everything?

All I want is to keep clinging to the same reassuring hopes that every woman has for her baby: That you can be anything you want to be. That instead of being forced to bend to the world's will, you can make it bend to yours. That you can plant your ideas like seeds, and they'll take root and spread like wildfire. That you'll discover your own way to make things better.

Except right now I can't help but wonder: Have you started that already?

Come on, Tadpole . . . tell me I'm just being neurotic. Because the more I think about this morning, the clearer it seems to me that the woman in the doorway really was pointing at us. In accusation. I mean, for a moment there, I saw her eyes. But why would she do that? What did we ever do to her?

So come on, Tadpole. Tell me I'm just stressed out. That you didn't talk your brother into letting go. Not with a whisper, but with a dream. Tell me that if I check with the doctors and demand to know, they won't tell me he wasn't merely *one* of the first to be lost . . . but *the* first. That you haven't dreamed a dream so dreadful it echoes on and on.

Tell me nothing went wrong in there. I only want you to be normal.

Okay, all this is destined for the black marker. But I feel so much better getting it off my chest.

Remember our Einstein: "There are only two ways to live your life: One is as though nothing is a miracle; the other is as though everything is a miracle."

To me, in this world, every day that you and I have together is a miracle. When you're born, I promise to celebrate you as one. No matter what.

Until then, I promise to keep serenading you, to tell you how much you're loved and that everything will be all right . . . or I'll try to, at least. Lately there seems to be something terribly wrong, either with my playing or with my instruments. I never knew they could make these kinds of ghastly noises.

But you seem to like it anyway.

It perks you right up, and you dance until I'm sick.

Elizabeth Engstrom is the author of nine books and over 250 short stories, articles, and essays. Her most recent books include *Suspicions*, a collection of short fiction, and *Black Leather*, a dark erotic thriller. Engstrom is a sought-after instructor and speaker at writers' conferences around the world, and currently serves as the director of the Maui Writers Retreat. She lives in the Pacific Northwest with her husband.

HONING SEBASTIAN

by Elizabeth Engstrom

Sebastian found the paper sack at 0217 hours on Monday, the sixteenth of Aout, the day of our Lord Hammersmith 12. He saw it in the corner of the doorway of an old apothecary, and made note of all the details in his journal before he approached it.

He expected it to be empty, something blown there from the other world, but when he touched it, he could tell it had weight. He made note of that in his journal, along with the words that were printed in green on its side. The words made no sense to him, but he copied them as exactly as he was able.

Then he looked inside the sack, and the terror seized him. He cringed, hunkered down over the sack, expecting to hear sirens. He expected the great hands to grab him, rough fingers bruising him, lifting his bony body off its feet and carried by burly, face-less, hairy creatures in blue to throw them into a caddy and land him on concrete with four walls.

But no sirens. No caddy, no blues. He gave a furtive look both ways down both sides of the street, then tucked the bag inside his trou.

Then he made a note of it, but he didn't note what he saw in-side it, and all the way home, the pencil stub and his journal glowed white-hot in his pocket with the omission. The rents would want to know what he didn't note. They could see into his mind. They'd see that he hadn't written everything down, as were his orders, and he would be punished.

But he didn't think the rent punishment would be worse than the blues, so he took his chances.

Now that, too, was a thought he ought to write down, but couldn't. Maybe he needed a different journal. One to write down the things he showed to the rents, and one he kept for himself. Because not only was the stub and the notebook glowing like a "Fuck Me!" sign in his pocket; so was the bag in his underwear. He could hear it, too, with every step. He crouched lower, and told it quietly to hush, but he didn't think it heard him. It didn't have to. It was too valuable. It could think whatever it wanted, be as loud as it wanted, and nobody would care. It could scream, shriek, be vulgar, and still everybody would want it. Especially the rents and the blues.

But Sebastian had found it, so it was his. He'd have to keep it secret from the rents (*A secret from the rents!*).

But then, he wondered, as he neared the D, what good was it if he couldn't let others know he had it? By itself, it wasn't valuable at all. It was only valuable when others knew he had it, and therefore he had the power.

He ought to write that down. Not for the rents, for himself. In the alternate notebook.

Why had someone left it in the bag in the doorway, anyway?

Maybe it wasn't real.

Sebastian scuttled past the D, all the way to the river. The fire wasn't so big today, but still there was enough smelch for him to hide inside it for a few minutes. This was where he came to do his secret things. He had secrets he'd never told the rents. Maybe that's why this was so easy. Sometimes he came to the river to talk to himself, and sometimes he put his hands in his pants, and sometimes he talked to the rents in a whisper, when he was certain nobody else could hear him. He was a sinner.

This time, enshrouded in the black acrid smoke, Sebastian pulled the bag from his underwear, opened it up and looked in again.

The sight of it scared him, and he had to keep himself from flinging it into the burning river, or shoving it back into his trou. He needed to look at it, to touch it, to handle it, to make certain it was what he thought it was.

It was. Riches far beyond his imagination. Oh, what he could do with this.

He ought to make a note.

But he didn't.

Instead he talked to himself, he talked to the rents, he put his hands in his pants, and when he went back to the D, he was a sinner for certain.

"Whereya been?" Slicer asked as soon as Sebastian ducked inside. "You stink."

"River." Sebastian was certain now that not only did his journal and stub glow, but so did the bag and so did his face. He was going to lie to Slicer, and someday she'd find out and hate him.

"Why?"

He pushed her out of his way and walked quickly past the tattooing, then slid down the pipe into the tube, then, not hearing her behind him, began to run along the tracks. He'd never run before that he could remember; nobody ran, especially down here in the dark. But Sebastian ran, and he liked the way it made his lungs and legs hurt.

His blanket was in a safe zone; the rents never went that far out, although Slicer and the rest of the hoons did. The young ones were thieving, vandalizing little shits, so Sebastian never left anything there but his blanket. They didn't want his blanket; they wanted valuable things. Sebastian never had anything of value; just his old journals, and they were valuable to him only because the rents would be mad at him if he didn't produce the current one on demand. And it better be up to date. Up to the minute, even.

Once back at his blanket, Sebastian sat with his back in the corner of his nook, his stomach rumbling. He'd forgotten to find grinds after he'd found the sack. Now he had to decide where to hide (*hide!*) the sack and its magic from the rents and the hoons. He had no idea how to even begin to go about it.

He wrapped up in his blanket, listening to the dark wind blow through the tunnel. The wires vibrated and sang with songs of long ago, and sometimes Sebastian hummed along, matching their tone.

But not today. Today Sebastian needed to search his soul. He had to decide if he was going to defy convention and embrace sin, or if he was going to confess, take his punishment, and slip back into anonymity.

He kind of wanted to search his soul, but he already knew what he was going to do. He just had to get his courage up. And figure out how to hide the bag.

The papers were real; he'd seen enough of them. Occasionally a hoon found one and one of the rents snatched it away. This was a whole bundle of them. Big, fat, heavy bundle. The rents would want it. The other hoons would want it. He wanted it. He wanted to go up with it, into the street, and become a civilian. He could wear real linen, he could grind real food, he could walk in the sunshine.

He'd seen sunshine; he'd seen the civilians wandering around in it as if it were free for the taking. Perhaps it was for them, but it could never be for Sebastian. He wore the black. He had the tattoos. He lived underground. "As it has been, so will it be." That's what the rents said, quoting the Hammersmith.

But now he had the means to pay his way.

"Hey." Slicer climbed up onto his ledge, startling him. "Whatcha doin'?"

Slicer had a way of sneaking up, her clothes black against the dark, hair black, face smudged, hands and forearms tattooed, rending her almost invisible, which worked to her advantage. The whites of her blue eyes shone bright in the dimness, and Sebastian could see her hair shining yellow where it had grown in at the part. Yellow, like sunshine.

"Thinking about sunshine," Sebastian said.

"We could go tomorrow," Slicer said.

"Into the sun?"

"I go every day."

"You lie," he said in disbelief. "How?"

"You think I tell the rents everything?"

Sebastian nodded. This idea of withholding things from the rents was a brand-new concept to him, but apparently not to everybody.

"Well, I don't." She picked at a ragged fingernail.

"What don't you tell them?"

"That I go up there and walk with the civvies."

"The civvies let you?"

"They don't stop me."

"What about the rents?" he asked.

"What about them?"

"They'll read your mind."

"They can't," Slicer said.

"They can. They took Suki and read her mind and then punished her for blasphemous thoughts. She told me."

"Suki's a tweeb," Slicer said. "She should die."

Sebastian knew there was more that Slicer wasn't telling him. He was amazed that she walked in the sunshine with the civvies. That was blasphemous. Punishable. "What else?"

Slicer put her hand in her lap and looked him square in the

eye. "I found my family again," she said. "And sometimes I visit them."

Sebastian was astounded at this news. "Then why do you live down here?"

"I don't think they want me," she said, and went back to torturing the fingernail.

"Do you grind with them?"

She shook her head.

"Talk?"

Again, she shook her head no.

"Do they see you?"

"No, but—"

"Then how do you know they're your family?"

"Because I want them to be."

Sebastian had such an overwhelming feeling of affection for Slicer that he almost revealed his secret to her. He had a moment of clear fantasy where they went upstairs together, lived like civilians, had a baby, played with it in the sunshine. On grass. The words were on the tip of his tongue. He was about to take her hand and tell her that they could do that, they could make a family just like the one she wanted to be hers, the two of them, but then she opened her mouth one more time, and the illusion, the dream, evaporated like a wisp of riverfire smelch.

"Dicks and I are running away together," she said. "We're going to Hollywood."

Sebastian pulled away from her and hugged his blanket. He hoped his hurt and disappointment didn't show. "When?"

"Now. I come to say good-bye."

"I'll miss you," he said, and meant it. A hot ball of emotion stuck in his throat and he couldn't say anything more.

She reached forward and wrapped her arms around his neck, then up on their knees, she pressed her body next to his.

The bag in his crotch crinkled. Sebastian hoped she hadn't heard it.

"What's that?" she asked, pulling back.

"What?"

"That noise. What's in your trou?"

"Nothing."

"Don't lie."

"Don't tell anybody."

"As if I would," she said.

He trusted her. She went to the sunshine. She and Dicks were leaving, breaking *all* the rules. He trusted her and he loved her. Maybe if she saw the swag, she'd stay with him. They could escape together into the sun. The fantasy was back.

He reached into his trou and brought out the bag.

"Hammers," she said. "Did you note it?"

"Yeah," Sebastian said, "but not what was in it."

"What?"

He opened the bag and let her look inside. Before he could stop her, she reached inside and pulled out the papers.

"Hammers, Sebastian, you're rich."

"Come with *me* to the sunshine, Slicer." He felt suddenly desperate. He'd shared his secret, and now he wanted to share its fruits. Being rich was no good alone. "Forget Dicks. We'll be our own family. We'll have a baby."

She looked at him with surprise in her eyes. "A baby," she whispered. Then with an anger he'd never known from her before, she ripped the bag out of his hands. "You stupid," she said, then jumped off the ledge and ran off down the tube. Sebastian listened to her footfalls echo as far as the D, and then he couldn't hear them anymore. He was alone with the black wind that blew down the tunnel and right through his heart.

Sebastian stayed curled up with his blanket for longer than he ever had before. His heart was broken—he could feel the sharp edges cutting haphazardly inside his chest; he could hear the pieces rattle around when he got up and went down the tunnel to make. He didn't grind. He didn't talk. He saw no sun. He had no dreams. He just lay with his blanket and let his eyes leak.

Now and then one of the hoons, or occasionally a small gang of them, came around and tried to roust him, but Sebastian had nothing to say to them. They could rob him of . . . of . . . of what, his pencil? . . . he didn't care. They could beat him and he didn't care. They could kill him and that would be good. But they didn't. They just poked at him and when he didn't respond, they wandered off.

Sebastian wanted Slicer back. He wanted the papers back. He wanted the power—no, he wanted the dream. There was a dream inside him that shone forth for a quick minute, and then it was gone, and he missed it.

But as he lay there, cold against the concrete, he began to think of Hammersmith, and why he would give Sebastian a dream and then deny him. That part didn't make any sense. Perhaps Sebastian had been too long without grinds, but he thought that maybe the rents were wrong.

More blasphemy, Sebastian, he told himself, but he didn't care anymore. He didn't care about the rents, he didn't care about himself, he didn't care about anything. Just when he decided that he'd go into the sun and ask a civilian his question about the dream and the rents and Hammersmith, a hoon raced by. "Rents!" he shouted, and Sebastian's heart began to pound. Rents? This far out? Why?

He pulled his legs up underneath him, wrapped his blanket around them, and tried to make himself invisible squenched into the corner of his nook. It wasn't long after the hoon came by that he heard footsteps coming down the tube, and even though it was dark, he could see the rent's face. It was as if he had his own light, he was so clean and white.

"Sebastian?" the rent said with a soft voice, and Sebastian thought he was going to faint at the sound of it. He scrambled for his journal, the most recent one—but he hadn't noted anything in it since that day he found the bag.

"Aye," Sebastian said.

"Are you sick?"

"No."

"We heard you were sick."

"No." Sebastian couldn't stop trembling.

"Stand up."

Sebastian stood, but his trou threatened to fall to his ankles, so he gripped them. His knees shook. The rent had a kind face. This was not like any of the rents he'd ever seen before, with their hooked noses, red hair, and hard, evil mouths.

"When was the last time you ate?"

"Ate?"

"Grinds."

"Don't know."

The rent held out a brown paper sack. "Here," he said. "Don't tell anybody I gave you this."

"Tell who?"

"Anybody. Hoons. Rents."

Sebastian cowered until the rent placed it on the ground at his feet. Then the rent smiled and turned away.

Sebastian could smell grinds in the bag. They made his stomach grumble. They made his mouth water. But this rent, this was not an ordinary rent. This was a civilian. He could ask his question.

"Dreams?" he said to the man's back. "What about dreams?"

"Dreams?" the man said, and turned back around. "What kind of dreams?"

Sebastian couldn't answer. His mouth was befuddled with the emotion in his throat. His eyes began to leak and he hicc'ed and couldn't catch his breath. "Dreams of sunshine," he finally choked out. "Babies on the grass."

"We are made of dreams, Sebastian," he said. "Is that yours?"

Sebastian began to sob. He stood, holding up his trou, water running down his face, and nodded. He felt more pitiful than ever.

"Anything else?"

"Slicer."

"Slicer?"

"She's a hoon."

"Ah," the man said. "Love. Good." He held out his hand. A soft, white hand with clean fingernails that seemed to glow of its own accord in the darkness. "Well, come on, then."

Sebastian was confused. "Am I dead?" he asked.

The civilian laughed, and his white teeth flashed like Slicer's. "Soon enough. C'mon."

"Trust?"

"That's part of your dream, isn't it?" the man said.

Sebastian put his skinny, dirty, tattooed hand into the man's, and jumped down off his ledge, leaving his blanket and his journals. "I had power one time," he said.

"I believe you, son."

Sebastian, his heart filled with a hope he'd never known, walked next to the big man down through the tube, but instead of ducking into the D, they kept walking, all the way to the light stairs. Sebastian had never been to the light stairs before. He knew about them, of course, but up those stairs was where the rents lived out their miserable lives, and none of the hoons wanted anything to do with them, much less enter their territory on purpose. It wasn't so much that nobody wanted anything to do with them, it was more that everybody was afraid of them. Sebastian was certainly afraid. The rents had mystical powers. The rents could pull information right out of your mind. Sebastian didn't want anything pulled out of his head.

Sebastian hung back. "Rents," he said, and nodded toward the stairs.

"It's okay, boy," the man said. "You're with me. Remember your dream."

Sebastian's heart beat so hard in his chest that he found it difficult to breathe. The man took his hand again, and pulled him along, pulled him almost against his will, to the stairs, and then up them, one at a time. Almost against Sebastian's will, but not quite. Sebastian was afraid, but intrigued. Could the dream be on the other side of the door at the top of the stairs?

Could a black-clad, tattooed hoon ever really go into the light? Or was he doomed to live like a rat in the tunnels, foraging for grinds and a pittance to hand over to the rents so they wouldn't hunt him down and beat him?

There were a few old hoons, but not many. There were lots of old civilians. Sebastian looked up at the man beside him, in the faint light cast by the magic stairs, and he saw the civilian's gray hair and lined face. This was no hoon. This was a champion.

Sebastian pulled his hand from the man's, took a deep breath, straightened his back, tossed his hair and took the stairs of his own free will. They'd take him to hell or they'd take him to freedom, and he was soon to find out which.

At the top, the man pulled out a key and opened a heavy door. They stepped into a stinky corridor with light emanating from an indeterminate source. Sebastian could hear someone crying.

"This way," the man said, and Sebastian, feeling small and weak again, uncomfortably out of his element, followed. They went through a series of light corridors, stairs and doors, and finally opened a glass door and stepped into a bright room with big windows on the street that let in all kinds of light. It hurt Sebastian's eyes.

"What's this, Leo," an older woman said, peering over half

glasses at Sebastian, "something the street vomited up?" She looked like a rent with her gold earlobes.

"This is Sebastian," the man said. "He has a dream."

The woman cackled, and Sebastian wanted to shrink, to turn back, to run back to the safety of his blanket. It seemed as though the man was making fun of him. He felt hot nose water run down on to his upper lip, and spread out through his thin mustache. He wiped at it with the back of one hand, while the other held on to his trou. He wanted to guard his head so she couldn't pull information out. He didn't want her to know about Slicer going to Hollywood with Dicks and the bag of papers.

The man shuttled him through the room full of furniture and papers and into another little room with a soft place to sit. He closed the door behind him and they both sat down.

"So far so good, Sebastian?" the man asked.

Sebastian nodded. He wondered if this man was a rent in disguise.

"I'm going to help you find your dream, Sebastian. Do you believe me?"

Sebastian nodded. The man hadn't locked the door. If he felt his mind being invaded, he could just run.

"Do you know what makes people sick, Sebastian?"

Sebastian shook his head.

"Doing the wrong thing."

Here it was. Sebastian felt the rents creeping inside his skull.

"Doing things that aren't right. Stealing. Lying. Not carrying your share of the load. Do you know what I'm talking about?"

Sebastian's muscles tensed. He nodded at the man, trying to understand how he could look so nice, yet be an enemy.

"Is there anything you'd like to tell me?"

Sebastian shook his head.

"Confession, Sebastian, is what the soul craves. Unburden yourself, because if you're ever going to find your dream—"

They knew he was hiding. It was too late. If he didn't say something, they were going to suck it out of his head. "Slicer stole my swag and went to Hollywood with Dicks," he blurted out.

The man nodded. "We know about them," he said. "They're not in Hollywood. They're right here. Safe. Like you."

Sebastian exhaled a sigh of relief. He felt better. The man was right. He felt lighter, unburdened. That was what they wanted from him, then. He could go. He stood up, felt like he stood a little taller, even though he'd ratted out his girl. "I'm going," he said.

"Know who the rents are, Sebastian?"

No, Sebastian did not know who the rents were. He sat back down. This might be valuable information.

"Tenants. They pay rent on this building we're in. Know who they pay rent to?"

Sebastian shook his head. He wasn't certain he understood all of this.

"Me. I have an enormous cash-eating machine that requires a lot of income. Wives. Airplanes. Swimming pools. Know where my income comes from?"

Sebastian suddenly knew where this was going, and he was afraid. He wanted to throw himself on the floor and kiss the man's shoes. Sebastian knew who he was talking with, but he didn't want anyone to utter the name. The holy name.

"My income comes from the tenants. They get their income from you folks, who work the streets for them. Know your place in the hierarchy? There are crows and vultures in the natural world, Sebastian, who clean up the roadkill. Carp keep the streams clean. Worms recycle earth nutrients. You and the hoons pick the streets clean every night. Sometimes things of value are passed to the rents, who pass them on to me. So see? Your place in the world is part of *my* dream. I need you, Sebastian. And

Slicer and Dicks and the rest. But I'd like my dream to be your dream, too."

Sebastian felt a little bit calmer. What the man was saying was making a strange sort of sense. He felt like maybe he had a defined place in the world after all. He relaxed.

"I need you to keep doing what you're doing. You make a tremendous contribution to the rents, to me, to the city, to the other hoons. You provide jobs and income. You and the others, Sebastian, you're the ones that make the whole system work. Do you see what I'm saying?"

Sebastian nodded.

The man put a soft white hand on Sebastian's shoulder. "When Slicer and Dicks decided to go to Hollywood with the bagful of money, they were disrupting the system, and the system can't be disrupted if it's to work right. We can't have crows killing raccoons, now, can we?"

Sebastian didn't understand that, exactly.

"So I need you to go back to work, keeping your journal, reporting everything you see and hear, for the betterment of society, Sebastian. All of society. We each have our place in it. And now do you know how to make your dream come true?"

Sebastian shook his head.

"When you make your reality your dream. Understand?"

Sebastian sort of did. He nodded.

"Good boy," the man said. "I'm sorry about your friends, but if you walk the straight and narrow, just as the rents ask of you, you'll be leading the good life. The life that was laid out for you to live. It's important what you do. Your actions have value to me and to the others. Okay?"

Sebastian nodded.

The man stood up and offered Sebastian his hand. Sebastian shook it. "If you have any more questions, son, come to the light stairs and ask for me. I'm Leo. Leo Hammersmith."

Tears choked Sebastian again, and he couldn't speak. He was in *the presence*.

Hammersmith showed him out, and gave him vague directions as to how to get back to the light stairs.

Sebastian stumbled his way along. When he got to the place in the corridor where he could hear the crying, he recognized the voice. Slicer.

But he couldn't help her. He had a job to do.

After working a variety of jobs, and writing in his spare time, **Joe R. Lansdale** became a full-time writer in 1981 and has practiced his craft ever since. He is the author of over 200 short stories, articles, and essays, as well as twenty novels and several short-story collections. He has edited or coedited (some with his wife Karen Lansdale) seven anthologies—five fiction, two nonfiction. He is well-known for his series of crime/suspense adventures, several of which have been optioned for film, including *Mucho Mojo*. Joe has also scripted teleplays for the Emmy–award winning animated *Batman* series. He has scripted comics, including the award winning DC Comics *Jonah Hex* series, and also *It Crawls*, the comic that revived the Lone Ranger. He even had his own comic series at Dark Horse. Joe is a member of the Texas Institute of Letters. He's won several awards for his work, including the Edgar Award for best novel, six Bram Stokers, the British Fantasy Award, the American Mystery Award, the Horror Critics Award, and many other awards and recognitions.

THE SHADOWS, KITH AND KIN

by Joe R. Lansdale

" . . . and the soul, resenting its lot, flies groaningly to the shades."
—THE AENEID, by Virgil

There are no leaves left on the trees, and the limbs are weighted with ice and bending low. Many of them have broken and fallen across the drive. Beyond the drive, down where it and the road meet, where the bar ditch is, there is a brown savage run of water.

It is early afternoon, but already it is growing dark, and the fifth week of the storm raves on. I have never seen such a storm of wind and ice and rain, not here in the South, and only once before have I been in a cold storm bad enough to force me to lock myself tight in my home.

So many things were different then, during that first storm.

No better. But different.

On this day while I sit by my window, looking out at what the great, white, wet storm has done to my world, I feel at first confused, and finally elated.

The storm. The ice. The rain. All of it. It's the sign I was waiting for.

I thought for a moment of my wife, her hair so blond it was almost white as the ice that hung in the trees, and I thought of her parents, white-headed too, but white with age, not dye, and of our little dog, Constance, not white at all, but all brown and black with traces of tan; a rat terrier mixed with all other blends of dog you might imagine.

I thought of all of them. I looked at my watch. There wasn't really any reason to. I had no place to go, and no way to go if I did. Besides, the battery in my watch had been dead for almost a month.

Once, when I was a boy, just before nightfall, I was out hunting with my father, out where the bayou water gets deep and runs between the twisted trunks and low-hanging limbs of water-loving trees; out there where the frogs bleat and jump and the sun don't hardly shine.

We were hunting for hogs. Then out of the brush came a man, running. He was dressed in striped clothes and he had on very thin shoes. He saw us and the dogs that were gathered about us, blueticks, long-eared and dripping spit from their jaws; he turned and broke and ran with a scream.

A few minutes later, the sheriff and three of his deputies came beating their way through the brush, their shirts stained with sweat, their faces red with heat.

My father watched all of this with a kind of hard-edged cool, and the sheriff, a man dad knew, said, "There's a man escaped off the chain gang, Hirem. He run through here. Did you see him?"

My father said that we had, and the sheriff said, "Will those dogs track him?"

"I want them to they will," my father said, and he called the dogs over to where the convict had been, where his footprints in the mud were filling slowly with water, and he pushed the dog's heads down toward these shoe prints one at a time, and said, "Sic him," and away the hounds went.

We ran after them then, me and my dad and all these fat cops who huffed and puffed out long before we did, and finally we came upon the man, tired, leaning against a tree with one hand, his other holding his business while he urinated on the bark. He had been defeated some time back, and now he was waiting for rescue, probably thinking it would have been best to have not run at all.

But the dogs, they had decided by private conference that this man was as good as any hog, and they came down on him like heat-seeking missiles. Hit him hard, knocked him down. I turned to my father, who could call them up and make them stop, no matter what the situation, but he did not call.

The dogs tore at the man, and I wanted to turn away, but did not. I looked at my father and his eyes were alight and his lips dripped spit; he reminded me of the hounds.

The dogs ripped and growled and savaged, and then the fat sheriff and his fat deputies stumbled into view, and when one of the deputies saw what had been done to the man, he doubled over and let go of whatever grease-fried goodness he had poked into his mouth earlier that day.

The sheriff and the other deputy stopped and stared, and the sheriff said, "My God," and turned away, and the deputy said, "Stop them, Hirem. Stop them. They done done it to him. Stop them."

My father called the dogs back, their muzzles dark and dripping. They sat in a row behind him, like sentries. The man, or what had been a man, the convict, he lay all about the base of the tree, as did the rags that had once been his clothes.

Later, we learned the convict had been on the chain gang for cashing hot checks.

Time keeps on slipping, slipping. . . . Wasn't that a song?

As day comes I sleep, then awake when night arrives. The sky has cleared and the moon has come out, and it is merely cold now. Pulling on my coat, I go out on the porch and sniff the air, and the air is like a meat slicer to the brain, so sharp it gives me a headache. I have never known cold like that.

I can see the yard close up. Ice has sheened all over my world, all across the ground, up in the trees, and the sky is like a black velvet backdrop, the stars like sharp shards of blue ice clinging to it.

I leave the porch light on, go inside, return to my chair by the window, burp. The air is filled with the aroma of my last meal, canned ravioli, eaten cold.

I take off my coat and hang it on the back of the chair.

Has it happened yet, or is it yet to happen.

Time, it just keep on slippin', slippin', yeah, it do.

I nod in the chair, and when I snap awake from a deep nod, there is snow blowing across the yard and the moon is gone and there is only the porch light to brighten it up.

But, in spite of the cold, I know they are out there.

The cold, the heat, nothing bothers them.

They are out there.

* . *   *

They came to me first on a dark night several months back, with no snow and no rain and no cold, but a dark night without clouds and plenty of heat in the air, a real humid night, sticky like dirty undershorts. I awoke and sat up in bed and the yard light was shining thinly through our window. I turned to look at my wife lying there beside me, her very blond hair silver in that light. I looked at her for a long time, then got up and went into the living room. Our little dog, who made her bed by the front door, came over and sniffed me, and I bent to pet her. She took to this for a minute, then found her spot by the door again, lay down.

Finally I turned out the yard light and went out on the porch. In my underwear. No one could see me, not with all our trees, and if they could see me, I didn't care.

I sat in a deck chair and looked at the night, and thought about the job I didn't have and how my wife had been talking of divorce, and how my in-laws resented our living with them, and I thought too of how every time I did a thing I failed, and dramatically at that. I felt strange and empty and lost.

While I watched the night, the darkness split apart and some of it came up on the porch, walking. Heavy steps full of all the world's shadow.

I was frightened, but I didn't move. Couldn't move. The shadow, which looked like a tar-covered human shape, trudged heavily across the porch until it stood over me, looking down. When I looked up, trembling, I saw there was no face, just darkness, thick as chocolate custard. It bent low and placed hand shapes on the sides of my chair and brought its faceless face close to mine, breathed on me, a hot languid breath that made me ill.

"You are almost one of us," it said, then turned, and slowly moved along the porch and down the steps and right back into the shadows. The darkness, thick as a wall, thinned and split, and absorbed my visitor; then the shadows rustled away in all directions like startled bats. I heard a dry crackling leaf sound amongst the trees.

My God, I thought. There had been a crowd of them.

Out there.

Waiting.

Watching.

Shadows.

And one of them had spoken to me.

Lying in bed later that night I held up my hand and found that what intrigued me most were not the fingers, but the darkness between them. It was a thin darkness, made weak by light, but it was darkness and it seemed more a part of me than the flesh.

I turned and looked at my sleeping wife.

I said, "I am one of them. Almost."

I remember all this as I sit in my chair and the storm rages outside, blowing snow and swirling little twirls of water that in turn become ice. I remember all this, holding up my hand again to look.

The shadows between my fingers are no longer thin.

They are dark.

They have connection to flesh.

They are me.

Four flashes. Four snaps.

The deed is done.

I wait in the chair by the window.

No one comes.

As I suspected.

The shadows were right.

They come to me nightly now. They never enter the house. Perhaps they cannot.

But out on the porch, there they gather. More than one now. And they flutter tight around me and I can smell them, and it is a smell like nothing I have smelled before. It is dark and empty and mildewed and old and dead and dry.

It smells like home.

Who are the shadows?

They are all of those who are like me.

They are the empty congregation. The faceless ones. The failures.

The sad, empty folk who wander through life and walk beside you and never get so much as a glance; nerds like me who live inside their heads and imagine winning the lottery and scoring the girls and walking tall. But instead, we stand short and bald and angry, our hands in our pockets, holding not money but our limp balls.

Real life is a drudge.

No one but another loser like myself can understand that.

Except for the shadows, for they are the ones like me. They are the losers and the lost, and they understand and they never do judge.

They are of my flesh, or, to be more precise, I am of their shadow.

They accept me for who I am.

They know what must be done, and gradually they reveal it to me.

The shadows.

I am one of them.

Well, almost.

My wife, my in-laws, every human being who walks this earth, underrates me.

There are things I can do.

I can play computer games, and I can win at them. I have created my own characters. They are unlike humans. They are better than humans. They are the potential that is inside me and will never be.

Oh, and I can do some other things as well. I didn't mention all the things I can do well. In spite of what my family thinks of me. I can do a number of things that they don't appreciate, but should.

I can make a very good chocolate milk shake. My wife knows this, but she won't admit it. She used to say so. Now she does not. She has closed up to me. Internally. Externally.

Battened down hatches, inwardly and outwardly.

Below. In her fine little galley, that hatch is tightly sealed.

But there is another thing I do well.

I can really shoot a gun.

My father, between beatings, he taught me that. It was the only time when we were happy together. When we held the guns.

Down in the basement I have a trunk.

Inside the trunk are guns.

Lots of them.

Rifles and shotguns and revolvers and automatics.

I have collected them over the years.

One of the rifles belongs to my father-in-law.

There is lots of ammunition.

Sometimes, during the day, if I can't sleep, while my wife is at work and my in-laws are about their retirement, which consists of golf and more golf, I sit down there and clean the guns and load them and repack them in the crate. I do it carefully, slowly, like foreplay. And when I finish my hands smell like gun oil. I rub my hands against my face and under my nose, the odor of the oil like some kind of musk.

But now, with the ice and the cold and the dark, with us

frozen in and with no place to go, I clean them at night. Not during the day while they are gone.

I clean them at night.

In the dark.

After I visit with the shadows.

My friends.

All the dark ones, gathered from all over the world, past and present.

Gathered out there in my yard—my wife's parents' yard—waiting on me.

Waiting for me to be one with them, waiting on me to join them.

The only club that has ever wanted me.

They are many of those shadows, and I know who they are now. I know it on the day I take the duct tape and use it to seal the doors to my wife's bedroom, to my parents-in-law's bedroom.

The dog is with my wife.

I can no longer sleep in our bed.

My wife, like the others, has begun to smell.

The tape keeps some of the stench out.

I pour cologne all over the carpet.

It helps.

Some.

How it happened:

One night I went out and sat and the shadows came up on the porch in such numbers there was only darkness around me and in me, and I was like something scared, but somehow happy, down deep in a big black sack held by hands that love me.

Yet, simultaneously, I was free.

I could feel them touching me, breathing on me. And I knew, then, that it was time.

*　　*　　*

Down in the basement, I opened the trunk, took out a well-oiled hunting rifle. I went upstairs and did it quick. My wife first. She never awoke. Beneath her head, on the pillow, in the moonlight, there was a spreading blossom the color of gun oil.

My father-in-law heard the shot, met me at their bedroom door, pulling on his robe. One shot. Then another for my mother-in-law who sat up in her bed, her face hidden in shadow—but a different shadow. Not one of my friends, one made purely by an absence of light, and not an absence of being.

The dog bit me.

I guess it was the noise.

I shot the dog too.

I didn't want her to be lonely.

Who would care for him?

I pulled my father-in-law into his bed with his wife and pulled the covers to their chins. My wife is tucked in too, the covers over her head. I put our little dog, Constance, beside her.

How long ago was the good deed done?

I can't tell.

I think, strangely, of my father-in-law. He always wore a hat. He thought it strange that men no longer wore hats. When he was growing up in the forties and fifties, men wore hats.

He told me that many times.

He wore hats. Men wore hats, and it was odd to him that they no longer did, and to him the men without hats were manless.

He looked at me then. Hatless. Looked me up and down. Not only was I hatless in his eyes, I was manless.

Manless?

Is that a word?

The wind howls and the night is bright and the shadows twist and the moon gives them light to dance by.

They are many and they are one, and I am almost one of them.

*   *   *

One day I could not sleep and sat up all day. I had taken to the couch at first, in the living room, but in time the stench from behind the taped doors seeped out and it was strong. I made a pallet in the kitchen and pulled all the curtains tight and slept the day away, rose at night and roamed and watched the shadows from the windows or out on the porch. The stench was less then, at night, and out on the porch I couldn't smell it at all.

The phone has rung many times and there are messages from relatives. Asking about the storm. If we are okay.

I consider calling to tell them we are.

But I have no voice for anyone anymore. My vocal cords are hollow and my body is full of dark.

The storm has blown away and in a small matter of time people will come to find out how we are doing. It is daybreak and no car could possibly get up our long drive, not way out here in the country like we are, but the ice is starting to melt.

Can't sleep.

Can't eat.

Thirsty all the time.

Have masturbated till I hurt.

Strange, but by nightfall the ice started to slip away and all the whiteness was gone and the air, though chill, was not as cold, and the shadows gathered on the welcome mat, and now they have slipped inside, like envelopes pushed beneath the bottom of the door.

They join me.

They comfort me.

I oil my guns.

*   *   *

Late night, early morning, depends on how you look at it. The guns are well oiled and there is no ice anywhere. The night is as clear as my mind is now.

I pull the trunk upstairs and drag it out on the porch toward the truck. It's heavy, but I manage it into the back of the pickup. Then I remember there's a dolly in the garage.

My father-in-law's dolly.

"This damn dolly will move anything," he used to say. "Anything."

I get the dolly, load it up, stick in a few tools from the garage, start the truck and roll on out.

I flunked out of college.

Couldn't pass the test.

I'm supposed to be smart.

My mother told me when I was young that I was a genius.

There had been tests.

But I couldn't seem to finish anything.

Dropped out of high school. Took the GED eventually. Didn't score high there either, but did pass. Barely.

What kind of genius is that?

Finally got into college, four years later than everyone else.

Couldn't cut it. Just couldn't hold anything in my head. Too stuffed up there, as if Kleenex had been packed inside.

My history teacher, he told me: "Son, perhaps you should consider a trade."

I drive along campus. My mind is clear, like the night. The campus clock tower is very sharp against the darkness, lit up at the top and all around. A giant phallus punching up at the moon.

It is easy to drive right up to the tower and unload the gun trunk onto the dolly.

My father-in-law was right.
This dolly is amazing.
And my head, so clear. No Kleenex.
And the shadows, thick and plenty, are with me.

Rolling the dolly, a crowbar from the collection of tools stuffed in my belt, I proceed to the front of the tower. I'm wearing a jumpsuit. Gray. Workman's uniform. For a while I worked for the janitorial department on campus. My attempt at a trade.

They fired me for reading in the janitor's closet.

But I still have the jumpsuit.

The foyer is open, but the elevators are locked.

I pull the dolly upstairs.

It is a chore, a bump at a time, but the dolly straps hold the trunk and I can hear the guns rattling inside, like they want to get out.

By the time I reach the top I'm sweating, feeling weak. I have no idea how long it has taken, but some time, I'm sure. The shadows have been with me, encouraging me.

Thank you, I tell them.

The door at the top of the clock tower is locked.

I take out my burglar's key. The crowbar. Go to work.

It's easy.

On the other side of the door I use the dolly itself to push up under the door handle, and it freezes the door. It'll take some work to shake that loose.

There's one more flight inside the tower.

I have to drag the trunk of guns.

Hard work. The rope handle on the crate snaps and the guns slide all the way back down.

I push them up.

I almost think I can't make it. The trunk is so heavy. So many guns. And all that sweet ammunition.

Finally, to the top, shoving with my shoulder, bending my legs all the way.

The door up there is not locked, the one that leads outside to the runway around the clock tower.

I walk out, leaving the trunk. I walk all around the tower and look down at all the small things there.

Soon the light will come, and so will the people.

Turning, I look up at the huge clock hands. Four o'clock.

I hope time does not slip. I do not want to find myself at home by the window, looking out.

The shadows.

They flutter.

They twist.

The runway is full of them, thick as all the world's lost ones. Thick as all the world's hopeless. Thick, thick, thick, and thicker yet to be. When I join them.

There is one fine spot at the corner tower. That is where I should begin.

I place a rifle there, the one I used to put my family and dog to sleep.

I place rifles all around the tower.

I will probably run from one station to the other.

The shadows make suggestions.

All good, of course.

I put a revolver in my belt.

I put a shotgun near the entrance to the runway, hidden behind the edge of the tower, in a little outcrop of artful bricks. It tucks in there nicely.

There are huge flowerpots stuffed with ferns all about the runway. I stick pistols in the pots.

When I finish, I look at the clock again.

An hour has passed.

Back home in my chair, looking out the window at the dying night. Back home in my chair, the smell of my family growing familiar, like a shirt worn too many days in a row.

Like the one I have on. Like the thick coat I wear.

I look out the window and it is not the window, but the little split in the runway barrier. There are splits all around the runway wall.

I turn to study the place I have chosen and find myself looking out the window at home, and as I stare, the window melts and so does the house.

The smell.

That does not go away with the window and the house.

The smell stays with me.

The shadows are way too close. I am nearly smothered. I can hardly breathe.

Light cracks along the top of the tower and falls through the campus trees and runs along the ground like spilt warm honey.

I clutch my coat together, pull it tight. It is very cold. I can hardly feel my legs.

I get up and walk about the runway twice, checking on all my guns.

Well oiled. Fully loaded.

Full of hot lead announcements.

Telegram: STOP You're dead STOP.

*   *   *

Back at my spot, the one from which I will begin, I can see movement. The day has started. I poke the rifle through the break in the barrier and bead down on a tall man walking across campus.

I could take him easy.

But I do not.

Wait, say the shadows. Wait until the little world below is full.

The hands on the clock are loud when they move, they sound like the machinery I can hear in my head. Creaking and clanking and moving along.

The air has turned surprisingly warm.

I feel so hot in my jacket.

I take it off.

I am sweating.

The day has come but the shadows stay with me.

True friends are like that. They don't desert you.

It's nice to have true friends.

It's nice to have with me the ones who love me.

It's nice to not be judged.

It's nice to know I know what to do and the shadows know too, and we are all the better for it.

The campus is alive.

People swim across the concrete walks like minnows in the narrows.

Minnows everywhere in their new sharp clothes, ready to take their tests and do their papers and meet each other so they might screw. All of them, with futures.

But I am the future-stealing machine.

I remember once, when I was a child, I went fishing with minnows. Stuck them on the hooks and dropped them in the wet.

When the day was done, I had caught nothing. I violated the fisherman's code. I did not pour the remaining minnows into the water to give them their freedom. I poured them on the ground.

And stomped them.

I was in control.

A young, beautiful girl, probably eighteen, tall like a model, walking like a dream across the campus. The light is on her hair and it looks very blond, like my wife's.

I draw a bead.

The shadows gather. They whisper. They touch. They show me their faces.

They have faces now.

Simple faces.

Like mine.

I trace my eye down the length of the barrel.

Without me really knowing it, the gun snaps sharp in the morning light.

The young woman falls amidst a burst of what looks like plum jelly.

The minnows flutter. The minnows flee.

But there are so many, and they are panicked. Like they have been poured on the ground to squirm and gasp in the dry.

I begin to fire. Shot after shot after shot.

Each snap of the rifle a stomp of my foot.

Down they go.

Squashed.

I have no hat, father-in-law, and I am full of manliness.

The day goes up hot.

Who would have thunk?

I have moved from one end of the tower to the other.

I have dropped many of them.

The cops have come.

I have dropped many of them.

I hear noise in the tower.

I think they shook the dolly loose.

The door to the runway bursts open.

A lady cop steps through. My first shot takes her in the throat. But she snaps one off at about the same time. A revolver shot. It hits next to me where I crouch low against the runway wall.

Another cop comes through the door. I fire and miss.

My first miss.

He fires. I feel something hot inside my shoulder.

I find that I am slipping down, my back against the runway wall. I can't hold the rifle. I try to drag the pistol from my belt, but can't. My arm is dead. The other one, well, it's no good either. The shot has cut something apart inside of me. The strings to my limbs. My puppet won't work.

Another cop appears. He has a shotgun. He leans over me. His teeth are gritted and his eyes are wet.

And just as he fires, the shadows say:

Now, you are one of us.

Nancy Holder is the author of more than sixty-eight novels and over two hundred short stories, essays, and articles. Many of her novels are tie-ins based on TV shows such as *Highlander: the Series, Buffy the Vampire Slayer, Angel,* and *Smallville.* She has received four Bram Stoker Awards from the Horror Writers Association, one for her novel, *Dead in the Water,* and three for short fiction. One of her *BTVS* novels was nominated for a fifth. Her work has appeared on the *USA Today, LA Times, Locus,* and other best-seller lists, and she received a special sales award from amazon.com for one of her *Buffy the Vampire Slayer* tie-in novels. Her work has been translated into over two dozen languages, and has been recognized by the American Library Association, the American Reading Association, and the New York Public Library System. Her novel, *Spirited,* is a retelling of "Beauty and the Beast" set during the French and Indian War. Her novel *1941: Pearl Harbor* was recently used in San Diego high schools for a section on World War II. She is the editor of an anthology entitled *MOTA 4: Integrity,* published by TripleTree Press. She also teaches writing at the University of California at San Diego. She lives in San Diego with her eight-year-old daughter, Belle. Her Web site address is www.nancyholder.com.

Award-winning author **Nancy Kilpatrick** has published fourteen novels, five collections, and over 150 short stories. This is the eighth anthology she has edited or coedited. Her most recent book is the nonfiction opus *The Goth Bible: A Compendium for the Darkly Inclined,* from St. Martin's Press. She lives in lovely Montréal with her *chat noire,* Bella, and travels the planet with her companion, photographer Hugues Leblanc, seeking out the macabre. You can check out her latest exploits at: www.nancykilpatrick.com.

EXTENSION OF COPYRIGHT ⌐